irresponsible adult

About the Author

Lucy Dillon was born in Cumbria. She won the Romantic Novelists' Association Novel of the Year Award in 2010 for *Lost Dogs and Lonely Hearts*, and is the bestselling author of four other novels: *The Ballroom Class*, *Walking Back to Happiness*, *The Secret of Happy Ever After* and *A Hundred Pieces of Me*. Lucy now divides her time between London and the Wye Valley where she enjoys walking in the Malvern Hills with her basset hounds, Violet and Bonham. You can follow her on Twitter @lucy_dillon or on Facebook www.facebook.com/pages/LucyDillonBooks.

irresponsible adult

Lucy Dillon

HODDER &
STOUGHTON

First published in Great Britain in 2024 by Hodder & Stoughton
An Hachette UK company

1

Copyright © Lucy Dillon 2024

The right of Lucy Dillon to be identified as the Author of the Work has been
asserted by her in accordance with the Copyright, Designs and Patents Act 1988.

A CIP catalogue record for this title is available from the British Library

Hardback ISBN 978 1 399 71969 8
Trade Paperback ISBN 978 1 399 71970 4
ebook ISBN 978 1 399 71971 1

Typeset in Plantin Std Light by Manipal Technologies Limited

Printed and bound in Great Britain by Clays Ltd, Elcograf S.p.A.

Hodder & Stoughton policy is to use papers that are natural, renewable
and recyclable products and made from wood grown in sustainable
forests. The logging and manufacturing processes are expected to
conform to the environmental regulations of the country of origin.

Hodder & Stoughton Ltd
Carmelite House
50 Victoria Embankment
London EC4Y 0DZ

www.hodder.co.uk

For my sister Alex, who is wonderful.

Prologue

According to my big sister Cleo, there are two types of cleaners. One is that person who can't bear to see a smeary work surface or a corner with a cobweb in it without reaching for their feather duster. The kind of habitually neat person who keeps a special cupboard in their house specifically for cleaning products, racks of different mops and squeegees, shelves of designated cleaners, racked up like weapons in the war on grime. That's Cleo. She actively enjoys rolling up her sleeves and obliterating mess, whether in her house, your house, or someone else's house. I've even seen her get out her travel wipes in John Lewis.

For Cleo, I suspect, it's all about control. Restoring the world to its perfect, unspoiled, untouched-by-careless-human-hand state is commendably hygienic but it also puts her firmly back in charge. She knows the contents of every drawer, the exact freshness of every pillowcase, the absence of anything untoward under the bed. When Cleo's house is spotless, she's calm. When it's not, well … You want to stay out of range of the bleach spray until it is.

I'm more the second kind of cleaner, someone who cleans to take their mind off something else. I am not a tidy person, literally or metaphorically. My life has always felt like an accidental patchwork of moments, rather than a smoothly unrolling carpet of interlocking patterns, and my brain is even more random: it jumps from one idea to the next, worrying, forgetting, second-guessing, panicking, third-guessing. However, give me a list and a repetitive task and something magical happens. The thoughts stay in line, the doubts fade into the background and I am On Top of Things, if only for a minute or two. But you can make a lot happen in a couple of minutes.

I wouldn't go as far as to say cleaning is better than therapy, and it's definitely *not* a way of life. However – and I never ever thought I'd be this person, because I am to cleaning what cats are to scuba-diving – this much is fact: mops and scourers slowly took me from chaos to, if not order, then smoothed-out chaos that smells of fresh linen for a couple of hours. It definitely wasn't easy. It definitely wasn't fun. But it's only now my house (and my head) is in order that I can see what a state it was, and how much easier it is to live in both of them now. I also have not one, not two, but *four* thriving rubber plants.

The story of how I tidied up my world – and learned to understand my big sister – isn't just about cleaning. It's about learning that once you've found a place for everything, including yourself, you don't need to worry about making a mess ever again. Because you can always put things back.

I

~ To remove fingerprints and smears from stainless steel surfaces, wipe with a little baby oil on a clean cloth.

The first text appeared while I was showing the Pedersen family around what the rest of the office had taken to calling the Doom Barn, and which I was currently calling 'a unique combination of rural tradition and ultramodern comfort'.

It was certainly unique. Blackberry Barn was a hulking conversion that looked unnervingly like Darth Vader in photographs, no matter what angle we tried to take them from. It was huge. It was clad in dark Siberian larch. And it was hard to make a positive of the original owners' decision to build the conservatory *around* a stone cider press the size of a small car instead of removing it. But if anyone could shift this unfortunately located, overpriced aircraft hangar of a home, it was me.

So far, the viewing had been going to plan. I'd started in the impressive kitchen-diner which ran almost the full length of the barn, and their reactions had been as I'd anticipated: Steve Pedersen had nodded thoughtfully at the concealed appliances, while his wife Katherine warmed to the clinical smoothness of everything, once I'd mentioned how easy it was to clean. I was reeling off the mod cons when I was interrupted by the message alert.

> Robyn. We need to talk.

No name, no recognisable number. I swallowed as my brain flipped hurriedly through several possibilities.

Had Diana the office manager opened my secret filing drawer, the one where my paperwork was concealed for urgent sorting?

Or was it Cleo, complaining about the state of a client's house? Some of the end-of-tenancy cleaning jobs I put her way were a bit hard-going. But she had her own ringtone alert on my phone, and she never texted me when she could call and yell directly into my ear.

Or was it Johnny from the office, trying to put me off my stride? That was more likely. Our manager, Dean, was offering a prize for the first person to get an offer on the table for the Doom Barn.

As the Pedersens inspected the soft-close triple oven, my guilty conscience slid sideways to a couple of longshots: Tyler, the conveyancer I'd had a few dinners with then ghosted several months ago? Or Doug, ditto (but antique dealer)? I wasn't great at break-ups.

Another text followed.

> How about tomorrow night? I have exciting news on the architect.

And then I knew exactly who it was and my heart corrected its anxious plunge and swooped upwards like a fairground swingboat. It was Mitch Maitland, calling about the Secret Project. I inadvertently let out a squeak of excitement, and Steve Pedersen asked me if everything was all right.

I shoved the phone in my pocket and adjusted my expression.

Don't think about Mitch right now, I reminded myself as I launched back into presentation mode, just *sell this house*. But hearing from Mitch gave my pitch an extra something. Hysterical excitement. I abandoned the explanation of the central hoovering system and went for the emotional approach instead.

'You know, I probably shouldn't have favourite proper-ties,' I confided, 'but what I really love about this place is that it's a real year-round home.' I gestured towards the garden. 'It's stunning now in the spring, with that cherry blossom by the front door, and the outdoor kitchen is fabulous in summer, but winters would be so cosy in here too! You've got the height for a full-size Christmas tree in here *and* one in the hall. With your own holly and ivy from the orchard!'

I knew there was holly, ivy and mistletoe in the orchard because we'd been trying to sell Blackberry Barn since last August. It was now April.

'And hopbines along the oak beams!' Katherine exclaimed, as if she could suddenly see them, and we nod-ded happily, me most of all.

I could tell that the Pedersens were almost convinced that they and this cavernous barn were an ideal match. Katherine seemed taken with the barn's 'aspirational entertaining area', her hand lingering on the black quartz work surface that the previous viewer had said, in feedback, made the kitchen look like 'a goth operating theatre'. Steve had agreed with me that the timber-framed garden room would make an impressive backdrop for his Zoom calls, and that the cellar was ideal for a hobby cave, say, for example, a massive train set. It was perfect for them. Perfect.

None of the above was a coincidence, of course. I'd done my homework, which was as simple as having a nice chat. I liked talking and I liked houses, so my job wasn't so hard, really. I'd spent ten minutes with Katherine while we booked in the viewing and in that short time I'd learned that she was a data analyst who dreamed of setting up her own gluten-free cake business; that Steve worked remotely for an American law firm; that they needed space because his train set took up their entire garage; that they both wanted a forever home – dogs, attics, 'space for full-height Christmas tree', the lot.

This was the forty-third house they'd viewed. The forty-third. I hadn't as yet managed to winkle out what exactly it was that they so far hadn't managed to find. A unicorn stable, maybe.

Katherine's phone rang, and as she answered it a pained expression crossed her face. 'I'm sorry, Robyn,' she said. 'Would you excuse me for a second?'

And as she hurried out, I observed Steve's shoulders sag, then brace against whatever was coming ... Was I about to find out the reason for their extreme fussiness?

'We thought it would save time to do the viewings on our own,' he explained. 'They're so ... *fussy* about random stuff but I suppose it's only fair – they'll be living here too ...'

I suddenly knew where this was going. His difficult mother? Her controlling father?

'I apologise in advance,' Steve blurted out, as the sound of indignant squabbling came into earshot.

The current owners of Blackberry Barn had spent a fortune and used two different builders to create a bathroom straight out of an interior design magazine. The focal point was a Victorian slipper bath with a wrought-iron bookrest, but it had to compete with the shimmery green tiles lining the walk-in shower, Jack and Jill basins, Jack and Jill lavatories (no, me neither), and a reclaimed chandelier from a stately home in Ireland. Even the grout was specially imported from ... somewhere that made expensive grout. I forget exactly where.

'Isn't this gorgeous?' I asked rhetorically, because it truly was. I loved a good bathroom.

'You had me at slipper bath,' breathed Katherine, touching the brass taps with a reverential fingertip.

Steve gave it an appreciative nod, then went back out onto the landing to do the pointless knuckle-rapping of plaster so beloved of the male property viewer.

'Baths are gross,' announced Eva, the elder Pedersen child. 'You're basically sitting in your own dead skin.'

She was ten. We'd established that as soon as she burst in with her sister, Millie, in tow. Millie was eight. Viewing houses was 'boring', but waiting in a car with no phone signal or Wi-Fi code was 'borderline child abuse'.

Katherine winced. '*Eva*. It's a lovely bath. And look at the shower. It's like a mermaid's shower, isn't it?'

Eva smirked and cast a sidelong glance from under her dark lashes at Millie, who covertly kicked the bath's ornate leg.

'Don't kick the bath, Millie,' said Katherine automatically.

I checked my phone, which was buzzing in my pocket. Another text, this time from the office.

> Are you going to tell them?

It was from Johnny. I texted back:

> It's OK, they've seen the cider press. They're going to convert it into a cocktail bar.

He texted back immediately:

> I'm not talking about the cider press!!! Dean says we have to be completely transparent with viewers about the issues.

I turned my phone off and followed Steve out to the landing, while Millie and Eva's bickering filtered through from the bathroom. I recognised the familiar spiralling whine of complaints (and *sotto voce* hiss of parental refereeing) from many arguments in which Cleo inevitably got the weary sigh from Mum while I got the narrowed eyes and occasionally a sharp tap. Although she denies this.

Steve was gazing at the solid beams and I gave him a few moments to spot the original features for himself. 'So much history! This wood must be centuries old!'

'Properties like this don't come along very often,' I said, truthfully.

'So what I don't get is why it's been on the market for nine months.'

'But she *started* it …' wailed someone in the bathroom, followed by a shrill and accusatory, 'Ow!'

'And I can see it's been sold three times in the last six years.' Steve raised his voice to be heard over the resulting outburst. 'Be honest with me, Robyn – is there a problem you're not telling us about?'

I wasn't daft: I had a selection of good reasons ready to go.

'Barn conversions aren't for everyone,' I explained. 'Some people find them too open-plan if they have family they want to get away – I mean, if they need quiet space. And while who wouldn't *love* a garden this size, the reality is that it requires a bit of upkeep which, again, some people don't want. Did I mention that the vendors are throwing in their ride-on mower, though? Have you ever been on one? Ride-on mowers are *great* fun – this one has a drinks holder!'

Steve was momentarily distracted by the thought of a ride-on mower, but he had the bit between his teeth. 'The big question for me, I guess is … they did a lot of work, so why not stay and enjoy it?'

'Well …'

'I'm unusually sensitive to atmospheres in houses,' he continued, 'and I did get a funny feeling in the kitchen. So please – you can tell me the truth …'

For a second, I wondered if he'd already spoken to Johnny in the office. I won't lie, I was surprised because personally I thought the stories were a lot of old pony, but Steve seemed genuinely spooked.

Then he looked me straight in the eye and said, 'Are they getting divorced?'

I breathed again.

'I know, I know, client confidentiality and all that, but we looked at a house in Hartley, absolutely ideal on paper …' Steve shook his head as if too discreet to reveal exactly what the problem had been. 'Bad vibes.'

Katherine appeared at his shoulder, and her irritated expression told me instantly that Steve's 'sensitivity' was the reason they'd seen forty-three houses without an offer. That and their need for train-set space.

'No,' I said, firmly. 'The vendors are *not* getting divorced. Mrs Brady has accepted a once-in-a-lifetime job opportunity in Glasgow and it's simply too far to commute. It's a reluctant sale.'

Eva and Millie materialised behind their parents. They were doing that sisterly glance-nudge-muttered-trigger-word sniggering routine that had driven my own mother so demented she locked herself in the car for three hours during one family holiday in Dorset. The earlier squabbles had vanished, replaced by shared-joke suppressed giggles.

I saw Eva mouth 'bad vibes' at Millie and, just like I had when my big sister shared a secret joke with me, Millie dissolved into silent laughter.

It gave me an unexpected burst of nostalgia. At their age, Cleo and I were the closest we'd ever been and the memory of that summer holiday in Dorset rushed back: the smell of Mum's spray sun cream, Cleo's Body Shop perfume oil (so sophisticated), scorched skin against car seats, that giddy feeling in my stomach I always got when Cleo made me laugh without even speaking, just by doing That Look.

As we'd grown up our relationship had waxed and waned – sometimes close, sometimes barely talking – but at heart we were those two telepathically conniving little girls, sharing crisps and secret code words. Or at least that's how I felt.

Millie nudged Eva, flashed a look at me and said something under her breath that made Eva widen her eyes theatrically. Then they both shook with mirth.

I turned back to the adults. As Dean would have reminded me, honesty at this point was the best tactic, as long as you were being honest about *something*. 'Between ourselves, a couple of offers have fallen through because of chains collapsing. No one's fault, but still, disappointing for everyone. Might that be what you're picking up, Steve? Disappointment?'

He nodded, pleased to be right. 'And I suppose this was a barn, with animals ...'

It was a cider barn. I wasn't sure apples left psychic traces of distress.

'And nothing problematic has emerged in surveys?' Katherine asked. 'Like … damp? Or flooding?'

'Anything that isn't original eighteenth-century is brand new,' I reassured her. 'They've even installed a heat pump and solar panels on the garden office.'

The Pedersens exchanged glances and I saw the glint in their eyes. They looked very much like a couple considering an offer.

Tell them about the slamming doors, protested the diligent voice of my inner estate agent. *You have to tell them about the Woman in Grey.*

I frowned. The Woman in Grey was, as far as I was concerned, utter nonsense that the owners previous to the Bradys had invented to make their common-or-garden barn sound more interesting. If the neighbours hadn't told the Bradys, then they'd never have been looking out for slamming doors and 'cold spots'.

I mean, show me a house in the country that doesn't have a cold spot. And a draughty spot. And a spot where flies mysteriously go to die. It's what country houses are *like*.

Still, I struggled with my conscience. They were about to spend a lot of money. They had two children. And it was my professional duty to give them all the facts.

But *what* facts? 'Funny feelings' weren't facts. It was hardly something you could tick on the declaration form: 'We took the neighbours to court over the wheelie bins, and there's a spectral nun.' Unexplained cold spots were a matter for the surveyors, not an estate agent.

Eva was staring at me, her head on one side. 'You've gone red,' she observed. 'Are you menopausal? My form teacher is menopausal and she has to carry a fan round with her, and when she thinks no one's looking, she puts it …'

'Eva!' said Steve and Katherine simultaneously.

I shoved the protesting voice in my head to one side. I needed to make this sale. I wanted the case of beer, and more importantly, I needed to impress Dean because I was already on a warning for what he called 'slack admin'.

(For the record, I was not menopausal. Not quite yet.)

'Shall I give you a moment to walk around on your own?' I asked the adults sweetly, then turned to Millie and Eva. 'Girls, do you want to see something amazing?'

'No,' said Eva, spinning on her heel and marching back to press buttons on the electric curtains.

'Yes, please,' said Millie.

So I showed Millie the secret stairs down to the wine cellar, and apparently that was what swung the deal. If Millie spotted the Woman in Grey while we were down there, she didn't let on.

It was nearly four o'clock by the time I waved the Pedersens off, and I contemplated going back to the office without much enthusiasm.

It was the right thing to do. The pile of paperwork in my desk was now so high I had to shove it down before locking the drawer; I fully intended to find a quiet time to blitz through it, but I didn't want an audience for the associated phone calls, most of which would have to begin with, 'Sorry for taking so long to get back you …' followed by an elaborate excuse. A big part of my job was chasing people who didn't always enjoy being chased – clients, solicitors, sometimes other estate agents – and I hated it. Johnny, on the desk opposite mine, had developed an annoying habit of snorting ostentatiously at my excuses, often so loudly I had to pretend it was traffic outside.

I gripped the wheel and tried to dredge up the motivation to go back. It wasn't the admin as much as the shame of how late it was. Plus, I wasn't quite sure exactly how bad the problem was because I could never look straight at it, just in small peeks.

You're a grown woman, Robyn, I told myself. *Every day you put it off, the worse it gets.*

Organisation, or lack of, was my Achilles heel. It always had been. When I'd started at Marsh & Frett, I'd made a monumental effort to create the best possible impression with my colleagues, as well as the clients. I hadn't just purchased the usual sackload of files and pens and notepads – although obviously, I went in hard on the stationery – but I'd found an actual routine planner on the Internet that I'd printed off to keep me on track.

Breakfast: power smoothie at 7.30 a.m.

Leave house by 7.50 a.m.

Fifteen minutes prep before the team meeting at 8.45 a.m.

Energy bar at 3 p.m.

Write up viewings and finalise task list for next day before leaving office.

That sort of thing.

Compulsive list-making as a chaos prevention strategy had worked for me throughout my education, when my ever-drifting attention was more or less controlled by forty-five minute lessons punctuated by loud bells – and a fear of failure – and I'd stuck to it for several months, long enough for some of it to have solidified into proper habits (the energy bar at 3 p.m. mostly). But the last few months had been manic, thanks to the extra work I'd had to do for Mitch Maitland's development, and I'd been so busy that I just couldn't stick to my routine. And so the paperwork had started to pile up, along with the excuses and the 'lost' emails.

I pulled out of the lane onto the main road and finished the half-eaten banana which had been my lunch. Being hungry never helped my decision-making. The traffic back into town was already building up, and I hoped the Pedersens weren't stuck in it.

I could call it a day and head home; it would take ten minutes and I could make some calls from the car. If I stayed in this traffic jam, it could take half an hour to get back to the high street, and the office might be closed. I'd have to come home anyway, plus I'd have wasted a whole hour.

My good intentions were already slipping when my phone rang, and the decision was removed from my hands.

'Where are you?' demanded Cleo. 'And why aren't you here?'

I had a good reason for my life being somewhat disorganised at the moment: in the space of a few weeks, I'd sold my own flat – completed in an agency record time, I might add – and moved into what I hoped would be temporary rental accommodation. I'd only been there a week, and hadn't yet learned the cut-throughs or neighbourly parking routines, hence it took me a while to find a parking space. I ended up leaving the car two streets away, and walking back to Duncannon Avenue as fast as I could in my work heels, my hobbling pace spurred by the thought of Cleo's mounting impatience and two text reminders from her of all the other places she had to be.

I rounded the corner and saw my sister leaning against the railing on my front doorstep from the end of the street. Cleo's hair always drew the eye. She had a bright white-blonde bob, which she wore either swirled round her head in a candyfloss Marilyn Monroe blow-dry (spotted headscarf optional) or, off duty, in a mini ponytail. It was glamorous, attention-grabbing, uncompromising and high maintenance. Cleo's mission statement, basically.

Standing next to her was our mum, Melanie. Petite, like Cleo; dark-haired, like me; strong eyebrows, like both of us.

Mum waved and Cleo stopped texting, or whatever she was doing on her phone, and shouted, 'What time do you call this?' so loud that a dog walker on the other side of the street jumped and looked around nervously.

'I couldn't find anywhere to park.' I hurried towards them before Cleo could shout any more of my business to the neighbours. If I'd learned one thing in my job it was to make sure you kept the neighbours on side, or at the very least, gave them nothing to hold against you later.

'We've brought your things,' said Mum, gesturing to the boxes and bags at her feet. 'Cleo's got the rest in the boot.'

Cleo was alternating between protective glances at her black Range Rover, and more suspicious ones up and down the street.

I paused in unlocking the door. 'Don't worry, Cleo. We haven't had any carjackings recently. My car hasn't even been leafleted.'

'Your car's filthy, Robyn. No one wants to sell a pizza that much,' she muttered, but followed me inside, not even sighing with effort as she heaved four large bags up two flights of stairs to my new accommodation.

Ideally I would have arrived home half an hour earlier to tidy up before Mum and Cleo saw my flat for the first time.

It's not that it was particularly messy – and I *had* just moved in – but Mum's house always looked like a show home, and Cleo had not only inherited Mum's tidiness but had created a business out of it. Taylor Maid offered domestic cleaning and end-of-tenancy blitzes, a service I frequently engaged on behalf of Marsh & Frett's tenants and landlords (and no, she did not do mates' rates). These days Cleo had an OU degree in Business Management but she'd started cleaning as a hard-up young mum who needed more housekeeping money than her boyfriend Elliot was earning as a mechanic. Cleo was a meticulous cleaner, and before long, had more clients than she could handle alone, so she roped in friends from her NCT class to help; within a year, she'd set up a cleaning business with her own perky blonde self as the cartoon logo. Mum had drawn it for her to save money. Think Tinkerbell with a squeegee and an attitude.

Cleo and Elliot were, it was commonly agreed, made for each other. Elliot was as determined and ambitious as Cleo, going from mechanic to head mechanic to manager, then onto bigger and better things, until he was the youngest divisional director in the country for a leading recovery network. They had it all – three lively boys, house in a good street, two holidays a year, his and hers 4×4s – until one morning Cleo turned up on our doorstep and announced that she'd kicked Elliot out.

'We've grown apart,' was the sum total of her explanation.

I won't lie: it was a messy split. Their break-up made everyone feel discombobulated and a year on, it still felt wrong. True to her tidying-up instincts, Cleo managed to put a sort of gloss on their 'conscious uncoupling' for my nephews, Orson, Alfie and Wesley, while saving her real feelings for me and Mum. She didn't spare *us* her thoughts about Elliot. You could have unblocked drains with them. His workaholicism. His selfishness. His lack of support for her as an individual. His inability to listen. His snoring. His breathing. His bucket of worms in the garage. (To be fair, Elliot was an angler.)

Although, as Dad said in an unguarded moment, 'There are three sides to every story. His side, her side and the truth.'

To which Mum said, 'Paul!' and I said nothing.

Privately, I also thought there was more to it than Cleo was letting on. She'd always had a take-no-prisoners approach to life, but there'd been a brittle edge to her for a while now, as if she was constantly alert for reasons to be pissed off. Since the split, I'd tried to coax her over for a night in, one with a Chinese takeaway over-order, a Baileys too many and a taxi home, but she was always too busy. Didn't I know she'd given up ultra-processed foods, or had to get up early to do a VAT return or wash the boys' PE kits?

It didn't help that Elliot had talked me into interceding with Cleo on his behalf, early on in the separation when she was refusing to talk to him. He'd looked so tearful and distraught that I couldn't refuse. He *had* been part of my family for over twenty years. A mistake, as it turned out.

'You need to decide whose side you're on!' Cleo yelled at me, and I'd backed off. There was no such thing as political neutrality with Cleo.

She dumped the bags on the sofa, and gazed round the 'cosy' sitting room.

I followed her gaze and flinched at the mess. It didn't help that most of the furniture was covered in boxes and random carrier bags; I'd had to move out of my own flat at short notice, shoving my worldly goods into whatever came to hand. A 'man with a van' and his mate had brought the essentials and the rest had been piled into Mum's garage. 'For a limited time,' she'd warned me, as I struggled to stack my plastic crates of shoes and hair masks on top of her spare chest freezer.

'It'll be better when I've unpacked,' I said, defensively. 'But I've been busy.'

Cleo raised a microbladed eyebrow. 'Surely it's worth spending a few hours to get your life in order?'

'Cleo, I've literally been coming home and falling asleep. It's stressful, moving.'

'Of course it is, love.' Mum hesitated, then placed the weeping fig she was carrying on a box just away from the window. She'd mercy-grabbed the struggling house plants from my flat and repotted them 'to save me a job' – a job I hadn't been aware should be on my list. The weeping fig wasn't my only plant. I had a weeping begonia, a weeping umbrella tree and two positively sobbing succulents. My record with plant life was woeful, but it didn't stop me buying them from Tesco. Thriving house plants were an index of successful domestic life, like a decent sofa and a mortar and pestle.

'Why don't I pop the kettle on? Make us a cup of tea while you two empty the car?' She paused and added, 'You … have got a kettle?'

'Yes, Mum,' I said. 'And there's milk in the fridge. It's fresh, before you sniff it.'

'I wasn't going to,' she protested, but her shifty expression said otherwise.

I could hear Cleo bouncing down the stairs in her white Stan Smith trainers, ready to punch any carjackers in the face; she spent an hour most days at the gym at one violent cardio class or another. Regular gym attendance. That was another sign of being a proper adult.

I trailed after her, already out of breath, trying to work out where I could put the rest of the boxes. It looked like I wasn't going to be making those calls to clients this evening. I also knew I'd be having anxiety dreams about being buried alive in cardboard.

I'll get up an hour early, I promised myself. I'll definitely get things sorted out in the morning.

From the piercing scent of citrussy chemicals drifting from the kitchen, Mum had made a discreet start on cleaning while we dragged the last of the boxes up. More troublingly, I didn't have any Cif in the flat, which meant she'd come equipped.

She slammed the dishwasher closed as I bustled into the kitchen and handed me a tray of mugs to take through to the sitting room. 'I brought you some provisions,' she said, brandishing some chocolate digestives, 'in case you hadn't had time to go shopping.'

'Thank you,' I said. 'And thank you for whatever cleaning you've just done.'

She flushed. 'If you'd let me know, we could have come over and given the place a proper scrubbing when you moved in.'

'No, we couldn't,' interjected Cleo from the sitting room. 'I'm rushed off my feet right now. Robyn's perfectly capable of cleaning her own flat.'

'I'm not,' I said. 'You know I'm not.'

'Stop saying that, as if being messy is some kind of protected characteristic ...' Cleo was talking but, as I moved down the hall with the tea, stepping over the bin bags, I could see her swiping dust off the windowsills with my gym T-shirt. She literally couldn't help herself.

I put the tray down on the coffee table and cleared the box of toiletries off a chair so Mum could sit down. Then I dumped my weighted blanket off the sofa, sat down and glared at Cleo. I couldn't work out whether I wanted her to stop cleaning, because it just felt so pointed, or whether I wanted her to carry on, because I was never going to get round to dusting the woodwork myself.

'I have to say, Robyn, I still don't understand why you rushed into this,' said Mum. 'I thought you liked that flat of yours.'

'I did,' I said, and had a sudden gulp of regret.

I *loved* my flat. It was the final link to a part of my life that felt further and further away with every month that passed.

When you hear the words 'child actor' you tend to think of precocious tap-dancing poppets screeching inappropriate show tunes and then careering into rehab, via Only Fans. That wasn't me: I became a child actor mainly because I had nothing to do in the holidays. When I was eight Mum enrolled me in a drama summer school (Cleo had friends so didn't need to go) the same week a London casting director happened to be scouting background kids for a very big, very famous film. I had two lines, but I was on set for most of the school holidays and a few weekends, and I earned a stack of cash, tax-free, salted away by Mum into an inaccessible bank account.

After that, I was in two seasons of a children's show called *The School for Detectives*, playing a know-it-all junior Miss Marple, and I was in the background (again) of a Christmas advert for Waitrose which was gleefully re-enacted by my classmates until roughly Easter. But it's surprising how quickly kids lose interest in you being on television; having met Ant and Dec did little for my popularity. Because I was diligent, and scared of falling behind, I fitted everything in, creating list after list, working late at weekends so as not to let anyone down, but Dad drew the line when my GCSEs started.

'You can always come back to acting,' he said, and to be honest, I was relieved. It was fun at first – I liked pretending to be someone other than myself, and my agent, Geraldine, shielded me from criticism, as well as negotiating Equity adult rates for me – but I found learning lines a struggle, and routinely vomited with nerves before auditions.

Of course, when I was ready to go back to acting after university, everything had changed. I wasn't cute anymore; I was self-conscious and self-critical. I failed to get into any of the drama schools I applied for. To pay the bills, I temped at an estate agency, and slowly that turned into a full-time job, helped by the fact that nearly every client thought they already knew me from somewhere. Geraldine sent me a kind letter, asking if she should stop sending me audition info, and I sent her some advice about buy-to-lets and didn't renew my Equity membership.

So that was my acting career, done and dusted before my braces came off. I made a decent living as an estate agent, but it was thanks to my parents' financial caution and an ability to cry on demand that I was eventually able to buy my own flat. A flat that someone had just offered to buy for two and a half times what I'd paid for it, in cash.

'It was an offer I couldn't refuse,' I explained. 'Dean was selling a house for a divorcing couple, the husband wanted to stay local so he could share childcare, and there was absolutely nothing on the market. Dean asked if I'd be prepared to sell mine and ...' I shrugged. 'He was offering crazy money.'

'How much?' asked Cleo.

'Crazy money,' I repeated.

'And you moved, just like that?' Mum asked, incredulously.

Mum and Dad hated change. Dad nearly went into a decline when they switched the five-pound notes to plastic.

'It's in the catchment area for St Bridget's.' Cleo snapped a digestive in two and ate the smaller half, leaving the bigger portion for me and Mum to eye up. 'I had a client who bribed her son's piano teacher to have her post delivered there, so they could claim eligibility.'

Mum looked at me, horrified, and I nodded in confirmation. I'd bought it on the 'worst flat in the best area' principle, but the chances of me having a child in the next ten years, let alone one academic enough to get into St Bridget's, were zero. It didn't seem worth turning down such a ridiculous offer on the off chance that some yummy mummy might bribe me to be a postbox.

'Anyway,' I said, 'it's worked out perfectly. I'm in a strong position now – I've got cash in the bank, I can move quickly …'

'Because you're still basically packed-up,' Cleo observed. I glared at her.

'It's such a lot of money to have sitting there in the bank, though.' Mum frowned anxiously. 'Are you getting proper advice? Your dad's concerned.'

To be honest, it *was* a significant chunk of money, especially for someone on my salary, but I dealt with much bigger mortgages and deposits day in, day out. I wasn't blasé about it, just not freaked out in the same way Mum was. 'It's fine,' I reassured her. 'I know what I'm doing. I know this place is a bit, um, basic, but I didn't want to eat into my capital while I'm waiting for the right property to come onto the market.'

'You should get on to whoever you're renting it from and find out who their end-of-tenancy cleaners are,' said Cleo. 'They could do with a kick up the arse. Have you seen the state of the bathroom?'

I hadn't realised she'd been in the bathroom. Cleo moved silently and discreetly, noticing everything – and not just the tidelines and fingerprints.

'I suppose it's fine for now,' Mum said, a bit too quickly, 'but it needs a proper scrub before you unpack. You know what it's like, you never get round to it once you're settled in.'

'A proper scrub,' Cleo repeated.

They both looked at me with expectant faces.

'I'm not going to spend the weekend up to my elbows in soapy water, if that's what you're thinking,' I said, robustly. 'For one thing I'm run off my feet at work, and for another, I'm happy to pay someone to do it properly.'

'But Robyn ...'

'I'm a terrible cleaner. I don't enjoy it like you two do. I get distracted. I get bored. Because it *is* boring.'

Cleo shook her head, sadly. 'You're scared of ruining your nails.'

'If you knew how much I spent on these nails, you'd be the same,' I retorted. 'I have to look groomed for work.'

'These nails are capable of a hard day's work.' She brandished her own flawless manicure.

'You don't do any actual *scrubbing*,' I pointed out. 'You're more likely to break a nail phoning a client to explain their cleaner's late.'

'Girls! Don't fight!' Mum hated us squabbling. It seemed to upset her in a disproportionate manner for something that came very naturally to me and Cleo.

Again, family disclaimer: Mum's own mum and younger sister Kirsty died in a road accident when she was a teenager.

It was something we *never* talked about. When I was about six, after a particularly petty spat over a Toblerone that ended with me telling Cleo I wished I didn't have a sister, her saying I wasn't her sister, I was a fat pig that had been rehomed by the farm for being too disgusting, and Mum fleeing the room in tears. Dad sat us both down and told us, in an urgent, serious voice that we'd never heard before, that the reason Mummy hated to see us fight was because her own sister was dead, and she would do anything to have Kirsty back.

That shocked us into silence, I can tell you. We wanted to apologise immediately, and ask a million questions but Dad made us promise not to. It would upset Mummy too much, he said. The best thing we could do was never to mention her again. So we didn't, to the point where Cleo and I sometimes forgot Mum had ever had a sister. As a self-centred teen, I did sometimes wonder what it would be like if Auntie Kirsty was still around (to provide us with cousins, and/or holiday spending money) but I didn't want to discuss it with Cleo, in case Mum somehow overheard and was sad. Better to say nothing.

There was just one photograph of Kirsty, which I'd found tucked into a battered student cookbook of Mum's. At first glance, I assumed it was a photo of me and Cleo: two little girls a year or two apart, one dark-haired, one blonde, both in sunglasses, sitting on a tree stump – we had so many photos like that at home. But on the back someone had written: Melanie and Kirsty, Keswick 1981. I'd wondered if it had hurt Mum to see her own daughters make such a similar matching pair, one dark, one blonde.

I showed Cleo, then hid the photograph in my diary, a secret.

'Don't be like that.' Mum patted my arm, always peace-making. 'Cleo was just suggesting that she and I might come round and help you. Settle you in.'

'Was I?' Cleo rolled her eyes. 'I don't think I was …'

'Well, that is very kind of you both,' I said. 'But not necessary. I won't be staying here long, it's just a stopgap.'

This was cutting off my nose to spite my face, big time, but there was something about the way Cleo and Mum seemed to confuse a degreased oven with higher moral authority that rubbed me up the wrong way. They both had a habit of making me feel about twelve, although to be fair, I think only Cleo enjoyed doing it.

'Anyway,' I said, changing the subject to something Cleo loved talking about even more than cleaning, 'what's the latest with Orson's football team?'

'I wondered when *someone* was going to ask,' said Cleo, and launched into a detailed account of Orson's county U15 trials while I ate three chocolate digestives in a row, and wondered if either of them would ever ask me how things were going for *me* at work.

They would, I thought, as the conversation moved on to Wes's eczema, when the Secret Project finally came good. If Mitch Maitland's message was anything to go by, before long Cleo wouldn't be the only entrepreneurial success story in the family.

2

~ To clean vases, swirl some uncooked rice around in the bottom with warm water to loosen any dried-on leaves, then pour hot water over a dishwasher tablet and leave overnight.

I'd met Mitchell Maitland when he chose Marsh & Frett to market his high-end development of an old boarding school on the outskirts of the town.

He'd 'interviewed' four agencies before deciding who would be entrusted with the sale and my boss, Dean, had gone all out to make sure Mitch (and his invisible business partners Nihal and Allen, whom we never saw but who apparently 'handled the financials') anointed us as the delivery partners. Glossy brochures, ambitious PowerPoint presentation, croissants and macaroons, and a designated 24/7 team – of which I was but one of four assigned agents. There were only ten of us in the office full-time, including the receptionist, so this was quite a statement.

'I want you to sit in the meeting, but say nothing,' Dean warned me, as we filed into the glass-walled conference room. He would be leading the meeting as the senior partner, flanked by Diana, his executive assistant/office manager, who'd be taking notes, and Johnny, the red-trousered, red-cheeked agent who handled any house that came with a paddock or a tennis court. Plus me. I wasn't exactly junior, but I'd only been working there eighteen months – although in this time I'd already made more sales than Johnny had in four years.

I'd opened my mouth to point out that maybe everyone should say something, just to show we weren't there for decoration, but Dean narrowed his eyes and added, 'And I mean *nothing*, Robyn. Let me do the talking, OK?'

It's not in my nature to let everyone else do the talking, but for once I did. To be honest, Mitch Maitland was so unnervingly good-looking that I clamped my mouth shut for the first ten minutes because I knew from experience that whatever came out of it would be embarrassing for at least one of us. As Mitch sat back and waited for us to commence jumping through hoops, I had to force myself to look at Dean, then Johnny, then Dean in turn, just to stop myself staring at him. Mitch had one of those Confident People smiles that make you smile back automatically, and I didn't want to look like the office bimbo who'd been brought in to smile at the client.

I'd distracted myself by mentally casting him in the biopic of my life, a satisfying daydream I'd honed over many years, one which had the advantage of giving my face an authentically 'engaged' expression while people droned on in meetings. Mid-period Tom Cruise, I decided. Or Ryan Reynolds with dark hair. Someone comfortable in his own skin. The real Mitch was about my age, mid-to-late-thirties (I liked to keep it vague), no wedding ring, suit jacket slung over the back of his chair so the label – from a tailor, not Next – was visible. He kept glancing over at me while Dean was being terribly earnest about client satisfaction and environmental auditing, raising an eyebrow as if to say, 'Don't I know you from somewhere?'

I'd got used to that. It inevitably prompted the soul-destroying exchange – 'Yes, from *The School for Detectives* ... ha, ha ... No, nothing since then ... Yes, I always wanted to be an estate agent ... No, I didn't meet [insert celebrity of choice] ...' Urgh. I had, though, recently taken steps to nip it in the bud by giving strangers a different reason to 'remember me from somewhere', and I crossed my fingers that Mitch was recognising me from my online viewings.

Diana noticed us exchanging glances and frowned at me to stop, but Mitch winked. And when Dean finally paused for breath, Mitch pointed at me and said, 'I've got to ask, you're the "Say Yes to the Address" girl, right? Our office manager *will not stop* showing me your TikToks!'

That was my cue. I improvised about my marketing vision for the development: how I could walk potential buyers around the apartments, tailoring my approach for different platforms and user profiles, creating the warm, unscripted, customer-led marketing that had boosted our viewing requests by over 200 per cent since I'd started our channel.

'If you want to be in them too, I don't mind working with extras!' I added, and he laughed, generously, and relaxed back in his chair, as if the meeting had suddenly taken a turn he approved of.

Afterwards, Dean had grudgingly admitted that I might have swung it for the agency. Diana asked me if I could forward her the social media analysis I'd mentioned; obviously I said I would, but didn't add, *just as soon as I've done it*. Johnny asked me what TikTok was, so I told him it was a dating app for clock enthusiasts (I literally heard him on the phone later, urging his dad to sign up).

When we got the call from Nihal to say we'd been selected as the launch agency for the development, Diana was instructed to go out and purchase the coldest, most reasonably priced champagne available on Longhampton High Street. And when Nihal's follow-up email requested that I was to take the marketing lead, working closely with Mitch, I got a reluctant pat on the head from Dean and, crucially, what amounted to a promotion – a desk further away from the front door.

We completed on all ten apartments ahead of the target date, every single one over the asking price. I negotiated four of them myself. I also got to spend at least five hours a week with Mitch Maitland and, exactly as I'd hoped, that initial click soon developed into the kind of flirty friendship that always felt – to me, anyway – just one after-work drink away from tipping into something more. Mitch was fantastic company, funny and well-connected, and the more he talked about the process of property developing, the more I wanted to know. Spotting opportunities, briefing architects, marketing the projects – it sounded fascinating.

'I think you'd be a natural,' he told me. 'You understand people, you understand property. The rest is just paperwork.'

Which wasn't exactly my strong point, but Mitch didn't need to know that.

'I really appreciate you making time to have a look at this place with me,' said Mitch as we swept up the drive to Lark Manor in his BMW. 'I know how busy you are right now.'

'Never too busy for you,' I said, casually. I *had* earmarked the evening for the aforementioned admin blitz, but as soon as Mitch had rung to ask if he could borrow me for an off-the-record second opinion on a property, I'd abandoned that good intention faster than you could say 'permitted development'. 'I've wanted to have a nose around inside Lark Manor for *so long*. I call it the Turret House – you know, you can see them over the treetops as you come down the hill? Can you imagine having a bedroom up in the turret? Waking up to that view ...' I sighed. 'There must be so many stories in a house like that. The parties, the weddings, the balls, the proposals.'

OK, so I'd been bingeing a lot of *Bridgerton*.

Mitch glanced across from the driver's side, amused. 'I love the way it's always about the people and the stories with you, not the square footage.'

'Isn't that what houses are? Places for people to live their own stories?'

I said it only half-seriously, in case I needed to pretend I was joking (I wasn't).

'I've never thought of it like that,' he said. 'But now you mention it ...'

'Dramatic people need a house that gives them drama,' I elaborated. 'Staircases to flounce down, lots of doors to appear in – or slam. Statement wallpaper, quirky features. Peaceful calm houses are for quiet people, open-plan, lots of white. When I'm conducting viewings, I sometimes try to imagine who'd suit the house and then kind of ... channel them while I'm going round. Clients see themselves in the house because I *show* them how easy it would be to live there.'

It was like acting, though I didn't tell Mitch that. As far as I knew, he wasn't aware of my previous life, and I didn't want to have that 'but I prefer property, honest!' conversation with someone as successful as him; my failure to transition to adult acting (not adult *film* acting, acting as an adult – you know what I mean) was a failure any way you tried to spin it.

Mitch grinned at me as if I'd said something brilliant. 'And *that's* why I wanted your professional insight on this place. I think it's going to require some vision.'

I smiled and discreetly stretched my new dress over my knees. It was nearly six o'clock and we were in that ambiguous no man's land between work hours and social hours. Mitch and I had often had lunch together when we'd been collaborating on the St Anselm's offer, but this was the first time we'd met outside the office. I wasn't sure if it was an actual *date* date, but I'd nipped out and bought something fresh to change into, just in case. Unfortunately I hadn't bothered to sit down in it in the changing room, and I really should have done.

I wriggled in my seat, feeling something sharp between my skin and my bra, and realised, too late, that I hadn't cut out the swing tag either.

Lark Manor wasn't on the books at Marsh & Frett. It was being marketed by a London chain with regional offices, which suggested that whoever was selling it had big ambitions. Mitch told me that he'd pulled a few strings to view it before the other local developers. Even Dean hadn't mentioned it, and Dean liked to be first with *all* the news.

I'd done some covert research in the office when I should have been filing my expenses: Lark Manor was a substantial Gothic Revival mansion with several acres of gardens, originally built for a Birmingham businessman and his family.

During the First World War it had been requisitioned as a hospital, then was turned into a school, then a hotel and, most recently, a meditation retreat. Thanks to the businessman's social aspirations, it had been a focus for much county set activity in its heyday, and I'd spent at least an hour browsing through newspaper archives, planning permissions and sepia photographs of Victorian housemaids, then nurses, lined up by the orangery in their starched uniforms. By five o'clock I was desperate to see inside the turreted old pile, no matter what state it was in.

I supplied Mitch with some of these picturesque details on our way over; I had a knack for doing quick deep dives into topics, even if the information didn't always stay in my brain for longer than twenty-four hours.

'You realise this place isn't exactly ballroom-ready, don't you?' he said, in one of my rare pauses. 'As in, no one's lived there for years? The last lot were hippies, and they weren't growing oranges in that orangery.'

'Yes, but imagine the staircases,' I reminded him. 'And the ice house!'

'And the damp and the compromised foundations ...' Mitch pretended to look serious. 'There will be mice, Robyn. They probably don't turn into coachmen at midnight.'

'Yeah, yeah.' I didn't tell him about the pet cemetery. I'd save that for later.

When we pulled up outside – I noted the satisfying crunch of gravel – the agent was already waiting by the front door with a leather document wallet under his arm, checking his phone and glancing warily at the stone griffin over the door, as if it might collapse on him.

Mitch turned to me in the half-shadow of the car's interior and gave me a conspiratorial look; excitement fluttered in response, deep in the pit of my stomach. 'Now, I've told Simon you'll be looking round with me, but I haven't mentioned in what capacity. Didn't want to make things awkward for you.'

I raised an eyebrow, not sure what he meant. Was this a roundabout way of enquiring if I had a boyfriend? 'Awkward with …?'

'With Dean,' Mitch clarified. 'We might not be involving Marsh & Frett.'

'Oh, right. Yes, of course. Dean.'

'But if you have any questions,' he went on, 'about the house, the location, whatever you want to know, go ahead and ask. I'm interested in your opinion.'

The seriousness with which he said that was flattering. 'As a conversion project?'

'Yes, a conversion project. It's a bit big for me on my own.' While I was still registering that Mitch had just confirmed he was single, *unprompted*, he added, 'Although if you carry on about the balls and the parties, I might be persuaded!'

Before I could come up with a suitably flirtatious answer, Mitch had slid out of the driver's side. I heard him say, 'Simon! Great to see you!' followed by some matey banter and arm-slapping.

I gave it a second, to make sure Mitch was out of the car and also so my face would go back to normal, then nearly dislocated my shoulder trying to pull off the swing tag without him seeing. It came off with an ominous rip. I exited the car as elegantly as I could in a dress that, in hindsight, wasn't really me at all and which I would now be unable to return.

Still. This was already the best day of my month so far, and I hadn't even got to the ballroom.

It took Simon several shoves to get the front door open, on account of the original Arts and Crafts hinges, but once we were inside Lark Manor did not disappoint. Well, it didn't disappoint me, anyway.

'It's not on the market yet, as you know,' said Simon, peevishly brushing rust flakes off his suit. 'But I have to tell you that we've had a substantial amount of interest already.'

I said that at least seven times a week, and it was rarely true. It was something you recited at the start of a viewing, like a mantra.

'We appreciate that,' said Mitch, and I nodded, already imagining starting my virtual tour with a close-up of the stone Great Danes a previous owner had left guarding the steps. No, further back, at the start of the sweeping stone steps. Or even further back, a speeded-up zoom along the tree-lined drive?

The front door swung open into a magnificent entrance hall dominated by an oak staircase soaring up the middle to a huge landing. I could smell dust and neglect, but I wasn't worried; the house had that grand calm bestowed by high ceilings and lots of wood. Simon guided us into the first reception room, which I could tell had once been a much bigger salon from the way the mouldings running around the ceiling like wedding cake icing abruptly stopped; mentally I knocked the partitions back down to reveal an elegant drawing room. And then had to remind myself I was supposed to be slicing the place up into units, not restoring it to former glories.

'As you can see there's a ton of potential,' Simon went on, gesturing at a luscious stained-glass window over a full-length window seat. 'They managed to leave most of the original features, just slapped a lot of MDF over most of them.'

Mitch was rapping on the walls with his knuckles, up and down along the chimney breast. He frowned, as if performing complex mental arithmetic. I tried to look knowledgeable but I was distracted by that staircase. It was almost impossible not to imagine sweeping down it, Martini in hand. Or winding pine garlands round the bannisters at Christmas, tiny lanterns on every other rise. Carol singers gathered in the hall. Mistletoe.

With some effort I dragged my attention back to Mitch and Simon, and made myself listen carefully to Mitch's questions, noting which of them Simon wasn't answering.

We passed through a series of rooms on the ground floor – a stone-flagged Downton-esque kitchen the size of my current flat, two reception rooms with views out to the wilderness that was once formal gardens, a strange bathroom where the loo was in one corner and the basin was in the other, a boot room that smelled strongly of damp coats even though the hooks were bare, and so on. Mitch glanced at me, raising his eyebrows in question; I wasn't sure how I should react, so I rapped a nearby wall the way he'd done. The second his back was turned, a chunk of plaster cracked off, so I hastily kicked it under a moth-ravaged chair and followed him out of the room.

By the time we were climbing the staircase to the first floor (six bedrooms, two bathrooms, billiard room, panoramic views of the park which made me want to stand by the window and murmur, 'My darling, we must talk,' in a low, urgent purr), I was itching to get my own deposit down on the first apartment; I placed imaginary rosebowls in a communal hall, where I'd exchange pleasantries with neighbours; I parked my car outside on the gravel; I threw balls for two bouncing Scottie dogs on the lawn, which was of course now restored to lush stripes. I'd viewed hundreds of flats in my time, and the 'small corner of a big pile' model had always appealed to me. All the architectural glamour of a big house but with a fraction of the bills. Obviously I had no idea how much it would cost to convert it, or how you'd do it, but I could definitely see myself selling it.

And more to the point, living in it. Although the reasonable voice in my head pointed out that apartments like these, particularly once spec'ed-up by Mitch's designers, were way outside my budget.

I had no idea what Mitch was thinking. He was playing it cool, merely nodding at the various rooms as we passed. Then we were outside on the moss-scabbed steps again, Simon was leaving and reaching for my hand to shake. It felt good to be treated as an equal, and I liked the way Mitch said, 'We'll be in touch!'

We.

He waited until Simon's car had disappeared down the drive then turned to look quizzically at me, holding the silence just long enough for my heart to start pounding. The early evening air was fresh with the smell of green leaves, excitement buzzed between us, as though we'd just discovered a hidden treasure, oh my god, I didn't want this to end.

'So,' said Mitch. 'Thoughts?'

'Lots,' I said.

'How about sharing them over a glass of wine?'

I made myself check my watch – *as if there was anything else I'd rather do* – and said, 'Maybe just a quick one.'

For want of a better option on the drinks front, I was forced to navigate us to Ferrari's on Longhampton High Street, which I swear isn't as bad as the name might suggest. It's the kind of place your parents go for a 'date night', but the food's good and it's the only place in town where they have more than one size of wine glass.

Gratifyingly, Mitch asked for the quiet corner table in the bar, and we were soon being settled in by the head waiter with a bottle of wine and some better than average snacks.

'What do you think?' He popped an olive in his mouth, revealing his perfect white teeth. 'Was Lark Manor as full of stories as you'd hoped?'

'Definitely. Although you were right when you said it wasn't ballroom-ready.' I chose my words carefully, not wanting to reveal my ignorance. 'How many apartments would you want to create?'

'OK, so this would be a boutique development. One-two beds, period detailing, bespoke interiors … Aimed at single people, professional couples, people downsizing. We don't just do big projects like St Anselm's. And smaller projects mean quicker turnarounds.'

'How quickly could you get it to market?' I asked, thinking of the general air of dilapidation. 'Apart from the legal side, it's impossible to get hold of builders round here, they're booked up for *months*.'

Even as I said it, I knew it was a stupid question to ask a property developer but Mitch, to his credit, answered without rolling his eyes. 'We've got teams working on different projects across the country, moving them around as they're needed. My project manager's a miracle worker. Never lets the plumbers stop working long enough to go AWOL.' He flicked another olive into his mouth with a cheeky glance at me. 'Anyway, now I've looked at it, I don't think it's actually that big a job.'

'Can you tell just from a walk-through?' I was curious about where you'd even start on a house as big as Lark Manor. 'Don't you need a structural survey? I mean, there's damp isn't there? Everywhere? And the roof – is it even safe?'

The dark cracks in the upstairs plaster looked like subsidence even to a non-builder like me, not to mention the prospect of bringing the house up to modern safety, environmental and insulation standards. The more I thought about it, the more daunting it seemed, pulling apart the whole house to fix the bodges of the past and then rebuilding it into neat shapes.

'Surveys always pick up something or other you weren't expecting.' He shrugged. 'Can't worry about that till then. But in terms of what we were talking about the other day, the sort of properties that you're selling …'

I nodded. 'There's definitely still a market for character apartments like that. I sold one last week the same day it went online. It's the combination of historic detail, but with modern amenities.'

'We'd have superfast broadband, underfloor heating, car charging points, alarms everywhere …'

I nodded. 'But with original tiles, stained glass, high ceilings. Plus, it's the ultimate in recycling, isn't it? Making an old house like this warm and safe and modern, capable of housing six families rather than just one. A green house, with an orangery.'

Mitch looked pleased with that. 'That's a great line – can I have it?'

'Feel free,' I said.

'The main thing is, can you imagine yourself living here?'

'Yes, I can.' I nodded. 'Very much so. And if there was anything like that on the market in my price bracket you wouldn't be talking to me right now, I'd be measuring it up for curtains.'

'Ah. Yes. I was going to ask how the flat-hunting was going.' Mitch hovered the wine bottle over my glass until I stopped making 'maybe not' faces and nodded. 'From the look on your face, I'd say not great?'

I sighed, but inside I was thrilled that he'd remembered. Mitch had been in the office when the final paperwork went through; he'd gone out and returned with a doughnut from the bakery opposite and a bottle of champagne, which he made me promise we'd share at the first opportunity.

'I've gone into rented.' Should I invite Mitch round to toast my new flat? I had a mortifying vision of the heaps of crumpled laundry, the stacks of unread books, the boxes of junk, and instantly discarded the idea. I rarely let anyone into my house, other than immediate family. It was too much like a glimpse inside my head.

'Rented, eh? So you can move quickly when the right flat comes up? Smart thinking.'

'It would be if there was anywhere to move to.' I took the refilled glass, and sank back in my seat.

'We need to get moving on Lark Manor, then.' He smiled. 'And which flat would madam prefer?'

'The garden apartment, please.'

'Oh? And why's that?'

'Warm summer nights, bifold doors opening onto the stone patio flags ...' My mind was back in the Doom Barn which had, for all its faults, a rather lovely kitchen garden with raised herb beds and thick lavender hedges. 'Walking barefoot on the grass under the night sky, listening to the owls, imagining the people who'd strolled on the lawn before me ...'

Mitch sipped his wine. 'And in the winter?'

'I'd put a big squashy armchair by the window so I could watch the snow falling onto the topiary. With a cup of hot chocolate and a dog curled up on my knee.'

I paused. Adding the dog really sent that into the realms of fantasy. The ideal, sorted-out me of the future had thriving house plants, a proper sofa, a marble mortar and pestle, and a dog. I just wasn't confident I'd ever get that far.

Mitch smiled. 'This is what I hoped you'd see in the place. Even I want to live there now, and I know what the service charge is going to be! You're really good at this, Robyn.'

I made a polite, embarrassed noise.

'Don't undersell yourself.' His expression turned serious. 'You're the most effective negotiator in the office. I've seen your sales figures. The client feedback. You could be running your own agency in a year or two. You *should* be. You just need to believe in yourself more.'

It wasn't the first time he'd told me that – and I wasn't quite daft enough to buy into his flattery – but the wine was going to my head. 'I'd rather be doing what you do.'

'And what's that?'

'Property developing. Making new homes out of old buildings.' It came out a bit slurred, and I wished I'd eaten a proper lunch instead of trying on dresses. 'Taking something neglected and fixing it, making it better. Creating homes.'

And meeting successful people, changing my car every two years, splashing fifty quid on a bottle of wine. Gaining the respect of people like Cleo, who judged you on things like cars and wine, even though she denied it. And Mum. It would be nice if she and Dad would stop covertly worrying about me.

Mitch didn't reply. He was looking at me as if debating whether to say what was on the tip of his tongue.

'What?' I said. I knew I was blushing because I could feel the outer edges of my own ears. They were hot.

He pushed his glass to one side and tapped his two fore-fingers on the table in front of me. 'Robyn, how would you like to get involved in this project?'

'What? Marketing it?' My mind spun. 'I probably could. Would I need to take time off?'

'No, I mean *personally* involved. As a co-investor.'

Mitch's dark eyes were locked on mine, twinkling as if we were about to hatch a brilliant plan. 'You're looking to buy somewhere for yourself, right? And you've got cap-ital sitting in the bank, doing nothing. Well, why don't you invest that money in this development? You can choose the apartment you want, spec it however you like, then we'll come to an arrangement about final sale price. *Or* you could have it back with a share of the profit if you found something better.' He grinned, delighted at the neatness of the idea. 'It's not going to be a long-term project, I reckon you could be measuring up for curtains before the end of the year.'

'That soon?'

He nodded. 'You say you want to get into property developing – well, this wouldn't be a bad place to start. It's a straightforward job. And if you wanted to be involved in the marketing? You'd be motivated to make it amazing.' He swung back in his chair, always a risky position to take at Ferrari's considering their furniture was so old it had gone out of fashion and come back in at least twice. 'I'd teach you everything I know.'

'Oh, really?' I said, with a hammy raised eyebrow.

'Oh, *really*.' He returned my gaze with a wicked expression that managed to be both camp and also unnervingly sexy.

The blushes had spread down from my ears and were now running across my whole body, making me hot and cold. Not just because Mitch was flirting with me, but something even more exciting than that: he was offering me a genuine opportunity, a chance to step into a different world.

He tipped his head, waiting for my answer, and I forced myself to say nothing.

I also made myself eat an olive to buy more time while my staggering brain considered the proposal.

There was no way I could afford to get into property developing on my salary, not unless I won the lottery. But I could work out for myself how much money Mitch's company had made from the St Anselm's development, and those were just the figures I'd seen.

I also needed somewhere to live. The windfall I'd scooped on my flat had been a fluke: I wasn't going to have a lump sum like that ever again. It wouldn't get me into a luxury flat like the ones I'd just sold for Mitch, but maybe this way it could – I'd get a first step on the property developing ladder *and* end up in an amazing home.

Dad had drilled financial caution into me and Cleo our whole lives – not always successfully. Normally, I'd say opportunities like this were too good to be true, but I couldn't see the downside. I genuinely couldn't.

Mitch waved at the waiter to get the wine list back, turning to me to check with a tilt of the head that I'd got time for another. The gesture was so easy and confident that I instantly felt more sophisticated.

I could walk home from here. Or get a taxi. I settled back into my chair and let Mitch refill my glass.

'So?' he asked, throwing an arm over the back of his chair. I could see a long, strong muscle under the fine cotton of his shirt. 'Is that a yes, so we can stop talking business and move onto more interesting topics of conversation?'

'I'll think about it,' I said. I made myself say that. In reality I'd already thought about it for the nanosecond it warranted, and was halfway through working out how to get the money out of the deposit account I'd put it in.

And by the time we left, I had Mitch's business bank details, as well as his personal phone number.

3

Exactly forty-eight hours after I'd shown the Pedersens around the Doom Barn, they made an offer.

Slightly under the asking price, but an offer nonetheless and one that the Bradys lost no time in accepting.

'And that,' I said, hanging up on the call, 'is the last we'll see of *that*!'

Johnny leaned back in his chair. 'Did you tell them about the Woman in Grey?'

'Nope.'

He pulled a face.

'One,' I said, counting on my fingers, 'it's a load of nonsense, and two, I don't want to give them cause to sue the vendor for falsifying the Fixtures and Fittings should a ghostly apparition *not* appear in the pantry.'

'Yeah, well, don't blame me if it comes back to bite you on the arse,' he muttered.

'It's a ghost, Johnny,' I said, 'not a vampire.'

I opened up the Memorandum of Sale document, as per the office timetable, filled in what I could, then while I was on a selling roll and the weather was nice, I went out and filmed another video walk-through, this time for a flat near the park that boasted no suspected hauntings but was decorated entirely in the colours of Longhampton United (red and black).

I might have spent a bit longer on that than I meant to, because when I came back after lunch, Diana accosted me. She was brandishing a sheaf of papers, bristling with Post-its; she had a colour-coded range of them to indicate priority, starting with a brisk yellow and culminating in an urgent cerise. There was only one stage above cerise and that was Diana herself standing by your desk while you completed the paperwork.

'I hope those aren't all for me!' I eyed the stack nervously.

'Not all,' she said, sectioning off the top two-thirds. The little flags were mainly cerise. 'Most of them, though. I have had two clients ask if you're still working for us, as it's so long since they've heard from you.'

'It's been mad busy, sorry.' I tried to keep my face neutral as I glanced at the top letter: a set of queries about a retirement flat that I thought I'd forwarded on to the buyer last week. Oops. Obviously I hadn't.

'We've spoken before about your paperwork, have we not?' Diana was keen on her rhetorical questions. 'Have you sent the Memorandum of Sale to the Pedersens?'

'I'm doing it! Just waiting for some additional information from the vendor.'

'Well, that needs to go off today.' Her beady look intensified. '*Today.*'

'Absolutely.' I was saved by the arrival of a middle-aged couple at the door, casting their gaze awkwardly around as if looking for someone before committing to entering the office. 'Would you excuse me, Diana? I think they're here to see me.'

I gestured at the couple, who waved with some relief.

'Buyers?' enquired Diana.

'Potentially.'

'Memorandum of Sale. By close of play,' she repeated, and stalked off to grill some other poor sod about their to-do list.

I went over to the potential buyers and escorted them to my desk.

OK, so they weren't potential buyers. As far as I knew, anyway.

'Hello, there,' said Dad, loudly. 'We're looking to buy a house. Do you have anything for about a million pounds, with its own helipad?'

'Paul!' hissed Mum, as if him saying that aloud might obligate him in some way.

'With two helipads,' Dad corrected himself. 'His and hers.'

'Do sit down while I check my current portfolio of properties,' I said. 'Ah, I see we have a couple of those, are you proceedable?'

'What does that mean?'

I leaned forward. 'Is your own house under offer?'

'No!' Mum looked horrified. 'We're not moving! Paul, stop it!'

'I must say, you're very busy,' said Dad, gazing around the office.

'That's because Marsh & Frett is the most popular agency in Longhampton,' I said, in my best voiceover voice.

There were two reasons the office was busy. Firstly, we actually were the most popular agency in Longhampton, not least because of our (my) innovative approach to social media marketing. But secondly, rumours had been circulating via Karina the receptionist that 'a structured rationalisation' was on the cards, so several people who hadn't been seen behind a desk on a Friday for months were now putting in some performative appearances, making the office seem unusually well staffed. I knew I'd been spending a lot of time out of the office lately, but it took me nearly an hour to place Tim Pollard, agricultural sales division. He was certainly a stranger to his suit. I wasn't sure I'd even been introduced to the bloke on the lettings desk.

All of which was even more reason to get on top of my admin. Although, I thought, with my habitual inward swerve away from paperwork, it was only polite to find out why my parents were visiting me in my workplace.

'Can I get you a coffee? Tea? Hot chocolate?' I gestured towards the state-of-the-art beverage station Dean had installed after we landed Mitch's last project, intended to 'set the scene' for the 'high-rolling clientele' we were now bound to attract. Its shiny features had starred in a couple of TikToks that had achieved record views for office-based content. I tried not to get any of the agents in the background; the sight of Johnny typing, frowning and eating a banana at the same time would have diluted the aspirational effect I was aiming for.

'That's a fine piece of equipment,' said Dad, approvingly. He loved a kitchen gadget. 'Do you want a hand?'

I let him accompany me to press the various buttons and as we returned, bearing microfoamed lattes, I spotted Mum hastily shoving her phone back in her bag. From her guilty expression you'd think she'd just shoved my laptop in there as well. And the free pens.

'So, if you're not buying a house …?' I prompted her when we'd made the appropriate noises about Dad's barista skills. 'Did you just come in for the free coffee?'

'No!' It wasn't a totally convincing denial. 'No, we were in town, so I thought we'd pop in and say hello.'

'Really?'

'It's a shopping trip,' said Dad, with all the enthusiasm of someone invited to a colonic irrigation workshop. 'For your mother. Clothes.'

'I've been asked on a very important date,' said Mum coyly.

'Wow,' I said. Mum's social life was her monthly book group, her twice-weekly Zumba, whatever grandson-related event Cleo had roped her into helping with, and us. *We* were her social life. 'Where are you taking her, Dad?'

'*He's* not.' Her enigmatic smile broadened, but she didn't elaborate. By the significant way she was raising her eyebrows I intuited that I was supposed to guess.

I looked to Dad for help. I didn't mind putting off my admin for a bit but even I had my limits.

'Your sister's invited your mother to be her plus one for the Women in Business Awards next week,' he explained. 'You wouldn't have any nice biscuits to go with this nice coffee, would you?'

'The mayor's hosting a champagne reception before the awards so you know, it's a very prestigious occasion!' Mum elaborated. 'The local press is going to be there, so Cleo's going to get a hair and make-up artist to come round and glam us up beforehand. It's black tie, apparently. Cleo's taken the afternoon off today to help me find something new to wear!'

I knew what that meant. It was Cleo's way of ensuring Mum didn't wear her 'old faithful' M&S Autograph suit, the one she wore to everything, with a revolving selection of scarves and brooches.

'Isn't that kind of her?' Mum prompted.

'That's very kind of her,' I said dutifully. She could have asked me. I was also a Woman in Business, whereas Mum was a school secretary. A brilliant one, but not even the secretary in charge of the PTA fundraising account.

'She was going to take one of her team from work,' Mum continued, 'but apparently there was a change of plan, so she's invited me instead.' She smiled broadly, her cheeks pink with excitement. 'I'm honoured.'

'As you should be,' I said. 'You taught Cleo everything she knows about her chosen profession. So you deserve that award as much as she does.'

'Oh, I don't know …' Mum flapped the compliment away. 'Cleo's made a tremendous success of her business. She's a dynamo.'

'We're very proud of both of you,' said Dad, unnecessarily. I wished he didn't feel obliged to say that.

The conversation froze, momentarily, as the three of us had the same simultaneous montage of thoughts: me appearing on the big screen at the local Odeon (parents proud, if stunned), me starring in the Waitrose advert (parents showing it on their phones to random strangers in the street), me not getting another acting job (parents having to explain to neighbours that no, I wasn't in Hollywood these days), me moving home to start working full-time as an estate agent (parents never mentioning the World of Acting ever again).

'I just sold that house, you know,' I said, pointing at the Doom Barn brochure next to my keyboard.

'Really? Which one was …? Oh. That one.' Mum flinched at the ominous black roof. 'Well done, Robyn.'

'Crikey,' said Dad.

I suddenly became aware of a pungent cologne filling my nose and realised Dean was striding across the office towards the door. Staff generally got a ten-second advance warning of Dean's movements, thanks to his heavy hand with the Hugo Boss. 'Hello!' he was saying in what I can only describe as a thrilled tone. 'How are *you*?'

'Hi, Dean!' The voice was familiar, and a lot less enthusiastic.

Cleo.

Was this now some kind of meeting/cafe venue for the whole family?

I pushed my chair back from my desk to get a better view of my boss lavishly air kissing Cleo, who was twisting her mouth to one side in order to avoid smudging her lipstick on his shoulder. Dean didn't air kiss anyone, particularly not contractors, but Cleo had something that compelled hardened leaders of commerce to act like ladies who lunch.

She also dressed like the sort of person you'd air kiss. Today her blonde hair was swept up under a black velvet beret which, along with her trench coat and pencil skirt, made her look like a very chic spy. It was hard to remember that this was the same Cleo who'd been given a one-day suspension at school for wearing 'a T-shirt with a slogan designed to offend' to non-uniform day.

Cleo disentangled herself from Dean, and indicated towards my desk. He happily escorted her over, even pulling a chair from Johnny's area for her to sit down, but she declined. Too much of a rush, apparently.

'Hi Dad. Hi Robyn. Listen, Mum, are you ready to go? I need to get back for four now, I've got a situation brewing with a deep clean in Southey Street,' she said, checking her phone as she spoke. 'Oh, for … Honestly.' She stared at the screen. 'What is *wrong* with people?'

'Staffing issues,' Mum mouthed at me.

'Shh!' Cleo looked up, frowning. 'Not in here, Mum.'

'I'll pretend I didn't hear that!' I said, jokingly. 'Although … I've got a big pre-sale deep clean for you,' I added, gesturing at the brochure.

Cleo looked down at it and flinched. 'Do you need it exorcised first?'

'Well, funny you should say that …'

Dean reappeared. He looked much less air-kissy than a moment ago.

'Sorry to interrupt,' he said, 'but could you come into my office for a moment, please, Robyn? Quick word.'

I turned back to my family. At least they were seeing how indispensable I was to the boss. 'Sorry, folks, duty calls. Hope you find something nice, Mum.'

'Is it OK if I wait here?' Dad asked. 'I won't get in the way.' He eyed the coffee machine.

'Fine, just flick through a few brochures or something,' I said. 'And if anyone comes up to you and starts talking about houses, tell them you're proceedable with a budget of one point three.'

Dad looked blank.

Cleo was texting and hustling Mum back into her jacket at the same time, but Mum spun round and raised a warning finger.

'Tell them nothing of the sort, Paul. I don't want to get home and find my house full of packing boxes.'

I left them to it and went into Dean's glass-walled office to see which bit of his computer he needed me to reboot.

He didn't waste any time.

'I've just had Kath Pederson on the phone,' he said, indicating for me to shut the door and sit down.

I beamed. 'Great news, isn't it? I thought we'd never shift the Doom B— I mean, find the right people for Blackberry Barn, but I think they're going to love it.'

'Let me stop you there, Robyn,' he said. 'They're not.'

'No, they are, they've agreed an offer. I'm just doing the Memorandum of Sale now.'

'Well, don't bother.' Dean ran a hand over his bald head. 'They've withdrawn it.'

'What?' My heart stopped. 'Why?'

'Because they popped back there this morning with Hannah ...'

'With *Hannah*?' Hannah was one of our new agents. She wasn't usually let out on her own, due to her habit of providing a running commentary on the vendors' decor choices. 'Why didn't you call me?'

He gave me a look. 'We *tried*. Diana called you repeatedly this morning, but you weren't picking up messages.' Dean narrowed his eyes. 'We've had the phone conversation so many times, Robyn. You've *got* to answer it. It's non-negotiable.'

I started to argue back, but it was true. My phone had been off while I edited the videos; I told myself that I needed to concentrate but the truth was that, at certain times, phone calls made me weirdly anxious and I couldn't make myself pick up. Not ideal for an estate agent, I admit, which was partly why I'd started doing the virtual viewings in the first place – it saved me from answering questions.

'Anyway, while Hannah was helping the Pedersens check whatever it was they wanted to check,' Dean continued, 'she asked them how they felt about moving into a house with a poltergeist.' He paused so the significance would sink in. 'And this was the first they'd heard about it.'

Duh. Of course Hannah would have asked them about that.

Dean seemed to be waiting for me to respond.

I hesitated. What did he want me to say? That wouldn't be why the Pedersens had withdrawn their offer, surely? It would be one of those lame excuses people invented when they woke up with buyers' remorse. You'd be amazed how many people don't want to hurt the feelings of vendors they'd never meet. 'We can't do the entertaining space justice.' 'We don't have a pony to put in the paddock.' 'Geoff's allergic to concrete.'

Dean sighed, and wiped his hand over his face. 'Do I need to spell this out, Robyn? Why didn't you tell them?'

'Tell them what ... About the *poltergeist*?'

This was bizarre. Dean, of all people, was not someone who'd let an imaginary friend get in the way of a sale. And it wasn't even a poltergeist, it was a grey lady.

'You know there's no such *thing* as ghosts, Dean?' I said, carefully.

He leaned over the desk to make his words very clear. 'That's not the point, Robyn. If the client thinks we've withheld information from them once, they're going to wonder what else we haven't told them.'

'But ...'

'But nothing. This was discussed. Even the Bradys wanted it out in the open, in case it caused problems later. You chose not to follow specific instructions, and what's happened?' He threw his hands up. 'It's caused problems. We've lost the sale.'

'Fine, well ...' I scrabbled for a fix and Cleo's words popped into my head. 'Why don't we offer to have the house exorcised before they move in? I'm sure I can find a vicar to, I don't know, wave some sage around while they're doing the deep clean? Cleo's probably got some detergent that can shift ghosts. That oven cleaner she uses needs a chemical licence.'

'Do I look like I'm laughing?'

'Oh, come on, Dean. It's not as if I tried to cover up a *murder*. Or planning permission for a chicken farm.' I remembered fleetingly that I had actually once covered up planning permission for a chicken farm, and moved swiftly on. 'Look, I'll ring them and apologise. I can explain.'

'It's too late. They're adamant it's not for them. The husband is very sensitive to things like that, he says he could never settle there now.'

'What if the vendors dropped the price? Might he settle then?'

Dean looked outraged. 'What? No! It's not up to *you* to tell the vendors to take a hit because of your cock-up! I'm sorry, Robyn, but this isn't the first time we've been here, is it? Offers withdrawn because of information not disclosed? There's a reason people don't trust estate agents. It's been a mission statement from day one: be honest.' He gestured at the wall where the agency slogan was painted in already slightly dated calligraphy: *Our business is home truths.*

'But if you look at my sales record …'

Dean ignored my protest. 'And then there's the issue of your admin. Diana says she's had some phone calls. Again, holding up the progress of sales, letting clients down.'

'Yes, well …' I squirmed. I hated being hauled over the coals for things I knew I should have done better.

'Shape up, Robyn. We live in interesting times,' he said, meaningfully.

I didn't know what he meant by that.

'And just so you know,' he added, as I was on my way out, 'that was another verbal warning.'

I was slouching back to my desk – where Dad was still happily flipping through magazines and sipping an elaborate hot chocolate – when the door was flung open by a woman in a full-length cashmere cardigan. She stormed in so aggressively that the cardigan seemed to fly out behind her like a beige cape. While I was still admiring her dramatic entrance (and also wondering how much the cardigan had cost) she spotted me, pointed a finger in a not very friendly manner, and started to make a beeline in my direction.

'Everyone's looking for you today, Robyn,' observed Diana, tartly.

I fixed my face into a smile while I racked my brain. This woman obviously knew me. I wasn't so sure I knew her.

Johnny stopped his clickety-clackety typing – *why* was everyone behaving as if they were in the background of *News at Ten?* – and stared. So did Karina the receptionist and Tim Pollard, agricultural sales. So did the clients sitting at Hannah's desk, and the two random people sitting in the reception area waiting for someone to get to them.

Dad remained engrossed in *Tractors Today.*

'Robyn? I want a word with you,' the woman began.

'Fantastic! Can I get you a coffee?' I played for time. Was she the vendor from this morning's virtual viewing? Had I left a gate open? Had her cat got out? Was it my new neighbour? Was it the ex-wife of the man I'd sold my flat to, enraged to find that her idiot ex was now living on her doorstep?

'You don't remember me, do you?' she went on.

'Yes, I do!'

She put a challenging hand on one hip.

I floundered. 'OK, I bet if you told me the name of your property I would!' It was a gamble. A big gamble. I'd sold quite a few properties since the start of the year.

'Twenty-three Rookery Road,' she said icily.

Oh dear. No, I didn't remember.

We stared at each other. My smile faltered. I could feel the eyes of everyone in the office on me, and sweat began to prickle under my armpits.

She waited, both hands now on her narrow hips. She looked absolutely furious. I realised she must have stormed out of the house in whatever she was wearing, which in this case was sheepskin boots and very loungey lounge pants.

'Um ...'

My heart was racing now. The whole office had gone silent. Even the phones had stopped ringing. And she wasn't going to let me off the hook: she was waiting for me to guess wrong, so she could explode properly.

I glanced at Johnny, my eyes begging for help, but he shrugged. I could see Dean through the window of his office; even he had stood up to see what was going on. Everyone was looking at me. I wanted to die.

And then suddenly – out of nowhere – my brain finally helped me out.

'Is it ... Mrs Rossiter?'

She looked momentarily disappointed – hurray, I'd guessed right – then snapped, 'Well, no, now it's Ms Wilson, because thanks to the total nightmare I've had with my house sale, my marriage has collapsed, along with the whole fucking onward chain!'

Johnny sank his head into his hands.

Now she snapped like that I *did* remember her. The Rossiters had been arguing even while I was measuring up their kitchen; he (Leon?) wanted to stay, she (Emma) wanted to sell, neither of them could agree on how much the house was worth. Nothing had worked with them, not charm, not diplomacy, nothing. They'd been seriously hard work from the first day, and maybe I hadn't been quite as diligent about progressing their sale as I might have been.

'I'm so sorry to hear that,' I said, trying to steer her towards the relative privacy of the conference room. 'I really am.'

'No!' Emma slapped my hands away. 'Don't touch me! I don't want to talk to you!'

'OK ...' But hadn't she just said she did want to talk to me?

'You are the worst estate agent I have ever had to deal with,' she spat. 'You promised so much! And you have. Done. Nothing. For. Us.'

I swallowed. This was humiliating. I couldn't blame her – collapsing chains were enough to make anyone emotional – but she seemed determined to have this out in a very public way.

'Maybe we could talk in here?' I suggested, to no avail.

'What makes it worse ...' She took a long, dragging breath, stared at the ceiling, then stared directly at me. Her eyes were glittering with frustration. 'Is that you seemed so *nice*! So *efficient*. You promised us that we'd have a buyer by the end of the month, no bother. And we did! But since then it's been nothing but delays after delays, and I found out this morning that our vendors have got sick of waiting and put our house – our dream house! – back on the market. And ...'

She took a step nearer, and I took an instinctive step back because I genuinely didn't know if she was planning to slap me.

'And *then* I had a phone call from a solicitor who said it was *highly unusual* for him to contact us directly but since he'd totally failed to raise any response from you, he thought we ought to know that our buyers were pulling out.'

'No!' I knew there were some emails I hadn't dealt with, but surely I'd have noticed that?

'So now,' Emma dropped her voice to a hiss, 'I'm trapped with that selfish, controlling, *smelly* bastard for the foreseeable and it's *your* fault.'

My heart was now thumping so hard I wasn't sure I might not be edging into heart-attack territory but I fought to keep an outward appearance of calm. I'd managed to manoeuvre us out of the centre of the office and behind a screen, which was something. But in doing so, I got a different view of the office and realised that Emma hadn't come alone. Her (ex?) husband Leon was standing a few metres away, smiling smugly.

Well, up until she called him a smelly bastard. That knocked the smile down a few notches.

He was filming everything on his phone. He pointed to it, just in case I hadn't got the message.

Oh god.

I started to panic. 'Tell me what I can do to—'

'I don't want you to do anything!' Emma cut me off. 'In fact, I'm going to tell *you* that as of this morning, I have started legal proceedings to—'

'Tell me what *we* can do,' said a man's voice behind me, as calm and fruitily English as a cricket tea.

I spun round. It was the new lettings manager. His voice didn't go with the Dad cool jeans and box-fresh hoodie. He looked as if he'd be more at home in ironed clothes.

Johnny stood up at his desk, pantomiming something about …

I squinted at his awful miming. The king? Something about his head?

'I'm Tony Marsh,' he said, holding out his hand for Emma to shake. He had a signet ring. 'I'm the group MD, and I'm sure we can put this right.'

Emma shook his hand distractedly, and he ushered her into Dean's office, pausing only to shoot me a truly poisonous look. Leon followed them, still filming.

He swung round to get a reaction shot of me and I was too stunned to react.

The group MD? Was that why everyone was working so ostentatiously? Because he was doing a sneaky undercover boss thing? Why had no one told me?

I glared around the office but of course now everyone was tapping away at their keyboards or pretending to make a phone call.

Above the coffee machine the words Marsh & Frett blurred and focused, then blurred again.

The tears were right up in my throat now. I couldn't remember the last time I'd been so humiliated.

'I tried to warn you,' said Johnny.

Four minutes later, the whole episode was on TikTok. I know that because Johnny, Karina, Diana, the Pedersens, and two clients helpfully tagged me in the comments. Which were not kind. Not kind at all.

4

~ *Hoover your mattress every so often. You will be amazed and repelled by how much dust comes out of it.*

The precise details of my subsequent meeting with Tony and Dean remained a blur, but the upshot was clear enough: they'd terminated my employment on the spot.

'You haven't left me with much choice,' Dean had whined, as if I'd massively inconvenienced him by forcing him to sack me, on top of everything else.

I stumbled out of Dean's office, unable to connect myself to the situation unfolding around me. There was a weird, nervous energy in the air. I could hear the phones ringing, and Johnny and Karina doing a forced laugh that told me that my recorded shame had spread beyond the walls of Marsh & Frett and was already making its way back. 'Ha ha … yes, a stunt,' I heard Johnny say. 'No, she's not … ha ha.'

He kept his eyes glued to his monitor as I walked past.

Incredibly, Dad was still engrossed in his coffee and magazines, and only looked up when I robotically began sweeping my belongings into the box Diana had placed on my desk. (He hadn't noticed that either. It must have been some tractor he was reading about.)

'What's—?' he began but stopped when he saw my face. Stunned, he helped me pack, then carried the box to the car and drove me home, while I alternated between silent sobbing and silent staring out of the window. None of it felt real yet.

'Please don't tell Mum,' I'd begged him. 'Promise me.'

'Robyn, you know I can't promise that.' Dad's gentle face twisted in discomfort. 'Your mum and I don't have secrets. You know what she's like.'

We stared at each other, remembering the handful of occasions when one of us had tried to have secrets from Mum. For someone who refused to talk about her own family, she was bracingly clear that it didn't work the other way around.

'I won't say anything tonight,' Dad conceded, unable to bear my misery. 'She'll be full of her shopping trip with Cleo, then she's off to book group. Why don't you give her a ring in the morning?'

And say what? I wondered. I didn't have to tell Mum at all. That wasn't the same as keeping a secret. She wasn't on TikTok. As far as I knew, anyway.

'Don't worry, love,' he said, comfortingly. 'It'll all work out for the best.'

I wasn't so sure about that, but I thanked him, dragged myself inside and lay down fully clothed on my bed. My mind was stuck in a loop, replaying the day's mortifications, but I must have dropped off at some point, because at 7.15 a.m. my alarm shrilled by my left ear, followed five minutes later by my second, backup alarm clock on the dressing table.

I was almost in the shower before I realised I didn't need to rush myself out of the flat by 7.45 a.m. because *I no longer had a job to go to.* So I went back to bed and resumed staring at the cracks in the ceiling.

Irresponsible Adult

It transpired that the man in the flat above mine – who I had yet to meet but knew from his misdirected post to be called Tomasz Wilk – did an online weights session at lunchtime, and the grunting and thumping directly above my head forced me to engage with the daylight. Grey flakes of plaster were floating down with every repetition, which explained what I'd assumed was mysterious body dandruff on my duvet, and as the grunts intensified I felt I was getting to know Tomasz on a slightly too intimate basis. Since I already knew there was no way I'd ever go up there and tell him to keep it down, I got up, turned off my phone – which was already covered in message notifications that I didn't want to read – and faced the future.

Well, I made a cafetiere of coffee first. And emptied the recycling bin. And watered the three plants that had apparently lost the will to live in the brief window between leaving Mum's and moving back in with me.

Then I faced the future.

Diana had handed me a formal letter as I was leaving. She always was prompt with her admin, but even in my stunned state it did make me wonder if she'd had a template ready to go and, if so, for how long. I took it out of my bag, fought back the temptation to shove it unopened into a drawer and made myself read it properly.

It wasn't great news. Just before embarking on her public performance review, Emma Rossiter had sent Marsh & Frett an email to announce she was taking the agency to the Small Claims Court on account of my 'negligence'. There was some legal waffle that my brain skated past, but it transpired that, with this dismissal, my notice period was not required and that Marsh & Frett would pay me a month's salary, plus any holiday outstanding. There was, of course, no holiday outstanding, because I took a day off every month to tackle my life laundry; a day which – hands up – I usually wasted wandering around the shops.

I took a deep breath, like someone halfway through ripping off a very long plaster. Then I gritted my teeth and reached for the carrier bag of bills I'd brought from my old flat, to try to work out how quickly I needed to find a new job.

It wasn't that I was scared of financial matters – I had recently conducted a major property transaction without any hiccups – I just never managed to get myself organised enough to deal with my day-to-day running costs. Somehow when it came to money my accounts got tangled up with strange emotional seaweed; I was terrible for impulse buys, usually after I'd guesstimated how much spare cash I had, and couldn't bring myself to look at how much I'd spent on interest when I'd missed credit-card payments by forgetting when they were due.

But now, I resolved, *now* I was going to turn over a new leaf! I'd been meaning to conduct a financial audit on my bills now I was in a new place. Most of the utilities were paid by direct debit so I hadn't thought properly about how much prices had risen until I saw the figures in front of me. The reality was sobering, and I spent an hour browsing various money-saving websites for budgeting tips, until I caught myself comparing air fryers and had to reel my attention back in.

In with my bills were two parking fines that I'd ignored for so long they'd basically quadrupled to 'next stop: bailiffs!'

levels. I paid them, trying not to think about how much less it could have been if I'd sorted it months ago, and then found a reminder about my road tax, which was overdue. I had a mild panic attack thinking of the number of police cars I could have driven past with no road tax (wait, did I have an MOT?) and paid everything in one go so it was done.

Next, bank statements. I got the highlighters out and started isolating essentials, like food and utilities, insurance, council tax, gym membership, petrol, and so on. I hesitated over my twice-monthly payments to Magnolia Nails and Lashes, then highlighted that too. Grooming was essential to finding another job. To be fair to my nails and lashes, I also highlighted my two-monthly haircut. And the waxing and eyebrows.

Then I added it up. Then I added it up again, because I'd clearly got it wrong the first time. After bills and essentials, I'd been operating on a monthly surplus of £3.23. No wonder I'd been at the edge of my overdraft.

And now I had nothing coming in after my next pay cheque.

The figures swam in and out of focus in front of me, and I forced myself to stand up, shaking off the 'run away!' impulse before it took hold. I *had* to sort this out. No naps, no quick cups of tea, no procrastination. My first thought was to call Cleo for advice, as I had done for guidance on everything from bad tans to bad break-ups, but as I reached for my phone, something stopped me.

What *would* Cleo say when I told her I'd got myself fired for negligence? The old Cleo would have laughed at my stupidity then helped me find a new, better job – and also offered me three different untraceable ways to revenge myself on Emma Rossiter. But the new Cleo,

Businesswoman of the Year Cleo, the post-Elliot single lady Cleo … I wasn't so sure she wouldn't side with Emma and Dean. She'd even given Dad honest advice when he asked her to sample his signature bake for the Cake Club.

'If you can't be honest with your own family, what's the point?' she'd demanded when a visibly deflated Dad had shuffled off to 'educate himself on buttercream'.

I'd said nothing. I'm not ashamed to say I prefer kindness to honesty.

'Facts,' I said, as if speaking my advice out loud might make me follow it. 'Let's get the facts.'

I opened my banking app to see exactly how much money I had. There was enough to cover my outgoings for a month, more or less. Then what? A wave of anxiety rolled over me like nausea. For the first time in my life I had no savings to fall back on; I'd used up my emergency buffer paying the parking fines and road tax and, even though as recently as last week I'd had a giant heap of cash, I'd transferred the whole lot into Mitch Maitland's company bank account two days ago in return for an investment in the Lark Manor project.

Maybe it hadn't cleared yet. Was there still time to grab some back? I checked my online banking again to find that … no. It had gone. I had £7.24 in my savings account.

Slowly, I leaned forward until my forehead rested on the cool kitchen table and yearned, not for the first time, to turn the clock back just ten minutes. Five minutes, even. Why hadn't I done the sums *before* I paid those fines? I could have paid them in instalments.

I was considering my options – none of them great – when the phone rang.

It was Mum.

'Do you fancy a coffee?' she asked. 'I was going to pop round to your office but I wasn't sure if you were working today.'

I stared at the cheap kitchen cabinets. Sunlight was illuminating the smeary fingerprints. Ugh. I had to tell her sometime. Why not now?

'I've been sacked,' I said, and hearing the words aloud – that I was not good enough – brought back a feeling I hadn't had in a while: that 'thanks for coming in' polite audition dismissal. Without warning, I felt small. And scared.

'What?' Mum's reaction was so shrill I could hear her outside the door of my flat.

I got up and went to the door to save her the bother of pretending she hadn't come round to do some covert hoovering while I was out. She was standing there, phone to her ear, mouth agape.

'Come in,' I said, still on the phone, so she did.

Mum put the kettle on while I recounted the whole story – more or less. She was so indignant on my behalf that she almost took a layer of metal off the sink she was scouring.

'It's outrageous!' she interrupted, before I'd even got halfway through. 'You should sue!'

I almost explained why this wouldn't be a good idea, then decided against it. Mum's outrage was comforting, like being wrapped in a blanket on the sofa. A second, metaphorical blanket; I was already wrapped in my most comforting fleece throw. So I nodded, let her rant on about my successes, and tried not to get cheese on toast crumbs on the newly wiped table. Mum always made cheese on toast when Cleo or I had some kind of childhood crisis (me = a bad test; Cleo = detention and, in yet another instance of something our family never spoke of, suspension).

Once or twice my conscience nearly pushed me to set her straight, but hearing her marvel at the houses I'd sold and tell me how proud she and Dad were of me for selling my flat for such a gigantic profit – well, I needed to hear some positivity about myself. I wasn't generating a lot right now.

Mum suddenly stopped scouring and put her hands on her hips. 'Your dad's friend, Philip – he's a solicitor. I think he works on employment issues. Do you want Dad to give him a call?'

'No! I mean, no, it's OK.' The last thing I wanted was to speak to anyone about Marsh & Frett. I'd braved a two-second glance at my phone and even the opening lines of the messages winded me like punches in the chest. Apparently I was a meme on the Our Longhampton Facebook group. A *meme*. (Thanks for that heads-up, three people from school.) The mere thought of walking into town, knowing total strangers were mocking me, gave me a physical urge to hide.

'Surely they should have given you more notice?' said Mum, peering at me closely. 'Is it legal, to just sack someone like that?'

'Mum, I don't want to go back there. I'm sure I'll find something else,' I said with more confidence than I felt.

'Of course you will.' She draped the wrung-out cloth over the sparkling taps, and looked around for something else to clean. There was a lot to choose from. 'And of course you've got that nest egg from your flat sale safe in the bank.' She paused and gave me a stern look. 'Although it would be silly to fritter that away, sitting around doing nothing for months.'

'No,' I mumbled. Probably not the time to tell her where that nest egg was.

She seemed pleased with the confirmation of my sensible financial attitude, and began attacking the hob. The more Mum cleaned, the more energy she generated. 'In the meantime, you could give your sister a hand – Cleo was telling me only last night that she was recruiting new team members. She's got more enquiries than she can handle!'

'I'm not working for Cleo,' I said, just in case she wasn't joking.

'She's expanding her business into housekeeping,' Mum went on, as if I hadn't spoken. 'She was telling me she's thinking about hiring a marketing expert, and I mean, that's more or less what you've been doing, isn't it? You're so good at social media. Why don't you pop round later? Have a chat about it?'

'Mum, I can't work for Cleo, it would be a disaster.'

'Why?' Mum seemed surprised. 'I know you two have your moments, but she's your sister, she'll want to help you out of a tight spot.'

'I think it would be a mistake,' I said, firmly.

Mum sighed and sat down at the kitchen table, pulling her chair nearer mine. I lifted my blanket like a wing, and she snuggled in with me, linking the fingers of her left hand with my right, the way she did when I was little, her other arm slipping around me. 'People come and go, Robyn,' she said. 'But your family … we're here forever. If you're having a tough time, Cleo will *want* to help you, I'm sure of that. Just like you used to help her.' She paused, hoping I'd smile.

I managed a feeble smile.

'Remember those Brownie badges?' she added.

Cleo stuck to the 'recollections may differ' defence, but when I was nine I read all the books she talked so enthusiastically about for her Book Lover badge, and even polished the brass candlestick for her House Orderly badge. I know, ironic. I had twenty-one Brownie badges, to Cleo's four. Brown Owl, a retired head teacher of the old school (literally and metaphorically), wouldn't let Cleo leave until she had eight badges. We'd blitzed the last four together as a joint enterprise one summer holiday.

I'd never been happier. It had made me feel grown-up – and valuable – to help Cleo break out of Brownie Jail as she put it. She'd given me her old DVD player and some Rimmel lipsticks. I still had the lipsticks in a box somewhere.

'Things have moved on a bit since then, Mum,' I said.

'Not really. You two, you're still my little girls.'

'Even if we're both bigger than you?'

'Even when you're pushing me to the M&S sale in a wheelchair.'

Mum gave me a nudge, and we shared one of those half-sad, half-happy smiles that covers a multitude of memories. It felt like another warm blanket thrown over us both.

'I don't mind giving Cleo some social media strategies,' I lied, to be nice. 'But honestly, I'll find a new job soon.'

'Maybe this could be the start of a new direction?' Mum persisted. 'It's such a great opportunity for you two to work together.'

'We do work together,' I pointed out. 'I've been putting thousands of pounds her way in cleaning contracts.'

'*Proper* working together, I mean. A family business. I've said to Cleo for a while that she needs a deputy manager, so she can spend more time with the boys. It's hard for her being a single mum, she never has a spare moment, working the hours she does and then coming home and looking after them by herself.'

This was a bit much. Setting aside the casual dismissal of my actually quite lucrative help for a moment, Cleo took outrageous advantage of Mum's on-tap grandma services, and had enough free time to attend networking dinners and personal training sessions, whereas Mum still hadn't used the massage voucher I'd given her for Christmas because her availability was 'limited'.

'She has more free time than you do,' I said. 'You're virtually on the payroll as it is, the amount of babysitting you're doing for her. She takes us for granted, assuming we're always free to do her bidding. I couldn't pick Orson up from football the other night and she more or less accused me of neglecting my responsibilities. *My* responsibilities?'

It came out more sharply than I meant it to.

'Oh, *Robyn* ...' Mum suddenly sank her head into her hands and didn't speak for several moments.

I waited, then said, 'Mum, are you all right?' I hadn't meant to upset her.

Besides, weren't we supposed to be worrying about me?

She stayed where she was then, to my relief, raised her head and said, slightly tearfully, 'I just want the best for you both. It's what you do when you're a mum. You'll get it one day. You just want to be able to fix everything, make everything better. Sometimes you can, and sometimes—'

'Sometimes you have to leave it to us to fix our problems,' I insisted. I didn't want to go down the 'when you're a mum' road. That was a whole other annoying kettle of fish. 'And I can. I've got a couple of things in the pipeline, as it happens. I will be fine. Honest. But there's no need to tell Cleo about any of this, OK? Not until I've got myself sorted out.'

'I won't, love,' said Mum.

But I knew she would. Cleo got everything out of everyone, eventually.

Once she'd left, I phoned Mitch. I hardly wanted to discuss my ritual humiliation, but I'd rather he heard it from me than the Internet.

'Robyn!' he said with such enthusiasm my mood lifted immediately, like the sun coming out from behind a cloud. 'I was just thinking about you.'

'Really?' Even better. I felt an unexpected tingle. Talking to Mitch outside work was different now. We were partners, working on our own project. Together.

'I've got the official documents here from Allen about your investment.'

My investment. My money hadn't gone, it had just moved. That made me feel a lot better. The metaphorical sun moved beyond the cloud and a rainbow came out.

'I can stick it in the post and you'll get it Monday, unless …' Mitch hesitated. 'Unless you're around this afternoon? I'm going to be driving through Longhampton, I can drop it round to you. If you give me your address, I could—'

'Why don't we meet for a coffee?' I asked quickly. I'd have suggested a drink, but maybe it was a bit early in the day to suggest toasting the deal. I didn't want to look like an alcoholic.

'Yes! Why not? Want to suggest somewhere?'

Double rainbow. Result.

Mitch was sympathetic about my job situation. I didn't tell him the complete story, obviously, but more than I'd told Mum. I anecdoted what I could anecdote (like Dad being engrossed in an article about combine harvesters while all hell was breaking loose) and skipped over the painful bits. He'd find those out for himself soon enough – although I tried not to think about that.

'So if you know of any jobs going …' I finished, hopefully.

'I will certainly keep my ear to the ground,' he said.

'Doesn't have to be local.' I chased the last bits of cake around my plate. 'In fact, ideally *not* local. But, you know … marketing, sales, whatever.'

I hoped Mitch would say, 'Come and start work on the Lark Manor project right now,' but he didn't.

'I'll have a think,' he said. 'I've got a mate who's setting up a commercial agency in Birmingham, he might have something. And we work with a few property search agencies who always need people with local knowledge. You'll be fine, though, Robyn. Everyone hits bumps in the road now and again. This time next year, you won't even think about this, I promise you. It'll be like it never happened.'

He swirled the last of his coffee around the cup, then looked up at me from under his lashes. 'Don't forget, you're a great negotiator. I'd have you on my team any day.'

Mitch's kindness made me feel a bit overwhelmed and I pretended to look in my bag for my phone to disguise the surge of tears. I'd managed to shake off my earlier gloom with a frantic hour of self-improvement before we met, but the adrenalin was wearing off and the reality of finding a new job was sinking in.

What would I do for a reference? I hadn't even thought about that. Could I ask Mitch to give me a reference for the work I'd done with St Anselms?

A shadow fell across the table and I breathed in some expensive cologne, close to me. I felt Mitch's finger slip under my chin then, with the gentlest pressure, lifted it up.

I raised my eyes to his. Mitch was gazing straight into my face, leaning in to check I was OK.

He really was gorgeous, I thought, distractedly. Gorgeous men weren't usually this kind and supportive, not in my experience anyway. If I was being honest, even I hadn't expected Mitch to be as sweet as this.

'Chin up,' he said, with an encouraging smile. 'You're going to be fine. Trust me.'

I took a deep breath and before I could even think, 'Is he going to kiss me?' he'd reached for his own phone and was scrolling through his contacts, firing off suggestions of people I could call.

Maybe it was going to be all right, I thought, writing down names and numbers as the pieces of my shattered self-confidence slowly began to regroup. Maybe this was actually the best thing that could have happened to me.

Although, obviously, it would take a lot of time for me to start feeling grateful for Emma Rossiter.

Unfortunately, on Friday, two things happened which stalled some of my positivity.

My car, which had gone for its overdue MOT, *failed* its MOT, and cost me the best part of my final pay cheque to fix.

The second thing was that, for the first time ever, I opened a brown envelope as soon as it arrived and discovered that rather than getting a council tax rebate for my flat, as I was blithely assuming, I actually owed *them* money. An amount almost exactly equal to what I had left.

I also got two 'thanks for applying but no thanks' emails for the other two jobs I'd applied for, and a TV licence reminder, but by that point I'd stopped counting. I had no money left, and the rent was due in twelve days. I no longer cared about television because my life now resembled the worst kind of made-for-TV drama.

Obviously, I spent a few hours staring at the ceiling, listening to Tomasz's workout and praying for divine intervention, but when Mum popped round to see if I wanted some frozen lasagne, her weakest excuse yet, it didn't take much for her to nudge me over the cliff edge.

Fine, I would go and work for Cleo. Just for a few days, only on her social media, in her office, and the *nanosecond* one of Mitch's contacts came good, I'd be off.

I saw the text Cleo sent Mum in response.

> Happy to help Robyn out but obviously on probationary terms. Cxx

A true vote of sisterly confidence.

5

~ *Hot water makes the ingredients in bleach inactive, so always use with cold water.*

I turned up at Cleo's office on Monday morning in the relaxed version of what I wore for viewings: grey skirt, white blouse under a sleeveless knit, mid-heeled shoes. I wanted to show her that I was taking this job seriously, even though she was family, but at the same time that I wasn't breaking out the designer labels, in case it looked like I thought I was too good to be working for a cleaning agency. That was quite a complex impression to achieve, purely through the medium of a skirt and blouse. But first appearances really matter, and I took a lot of trouble to make a good one.

Cleo's office was located above the garage of the Edwardian semi she used to share with Elliot. It was a traditional oak-framed structure, with what I would professionally term 'versatile potential', that is, it would have made an awesome gym, with its floor-to-ceiling window offering views over their back garden, or a therapy studio, or an au pair hutch. Cleo used it as her headquarters, and now Elliot's Range Rover had gone from the carport below, the space was filled with stacked boxes of cleaning solutions, branded with Cleo's cartoon logo.

I hadn't expected to feel so nervous, as I parked outside. Mum's wistful words about families working together had taken root in my brain, and I'd begun to imagine a rosier scenario in which Cleo and I bonded over my digital media insights, and she showed me how to deep clean my phone. Between work and motherhood and our different life choices, Cleo and I hadn't really had the chance to get to know each other as adults. Maybe this was it.

Cleo was already firefighting the day's problems on the phone when I knocked and let myself in; she waved at me, and pointed towards a pink loveseat opposite her desk. An upright man in chinos and a checked shirt was occupying the other pink sofa by the door in the reception area; he was pretending not to listen to the conversation.

I knew Cleo was struggling with her temper because she kept jabbing her pen on the desk, as if she were tapping out swear words in Morse code. She'd always done that. It used to drive her form teachers insane. If she started pulling on her earring, then I pitied the person on the other end of the phone.

'... yes, if you could just ... if you could ... if you could just let me ...' she was saying through gritted teeth, then put the phone on mute and snarled, 'Just shut up, you impossible- to-please *plank*!' then unmuted the phone and carried on. 'Absolutely, I understand ... no, of course ...'

I made eye contact with the man, and smiled. Bit surprising that Cleo was allowing a client to listen in on a conversation like that. *Not* the best first impression. Although somewhat reassuring to see Cleo still had some of her original features left, viz, her temper and occasional foul mouth.

'Can I get you a coffee?' I asked the upright man, over the sound of furious pen-Morse. My first job for Cleo could be shielding a client from her Monday morning mood.

'I'm waiting for …' He motioned towards Cleo.

'I'm sure she won't be long,' I said, louder. 'But a coffee? Go on. I'm making myself one.'

'Well, yes, that would be nice.' He fumbled a smile, and I beamed back to put him at his ease.

'Milk? Sugar?' Cleo had a fancy bean-to-cup machine on a table at the far end of the office; it was even flashier, I noted, than the one Dean had acquired for Marsh & Frett. Turning on the bean grinder usefully masked whatever Cleo was snarling over the mute button this time.

I glanced back to see her squeezing her forehead with her fingers.

'Sorry to keep you waiting, our housekeeping teams are in great demand at the moment,' I said, over the screeching of the steam wand.

He nodded again, now with a wan smile.

I handed him his coffee and racked my brains for cleaning chit-chat. I didn't have a lot in the cupboard, so to speak, but I knew if I got him talking I'd find a way in.

'My name's Robyn,' I said instead, offering him a hand to shake. 'With a Y!'

He swapped his cup to the other hand. 'Jim,' he said, shaking mine. 'With a J. The usual way.'

'Is there any other way? Gym, I suppose. With a G? Ha ha!'

I noticed Jim's fingernails were short but not bitten, and his handshake was firm. Old watch, on a leather strap. At work, I had a reputation for guessing what clients did before they told us, and Jim was …. maybe ex-Forces? A policeman? He had a robust, straightforward presence, and smelled clean, of freshly ironed clothes, fresh air.

A recent divorcee, I guessed, no ring. The pieces fell into place in my head: long hours at work, big house or maybe new flat. I'd heard Mum say that Cleo was adding other services onto her offering: ironing, house management, window cleaning. Maybe this was what he was here for, the divorcee package.

'So, are you already familiar with the different ways Taylor Maid can make your life easier?' I asked.

He regarded me over his coffee cup. He had clear grey eyes, with little creases at the edges, and straight brows. His hair was dark, cropped close to his head, but thick, not receding. Something about his stillness and his watchful expression reminded me of an eagle, restrained but taking in everything around him. The sort of man who listened before speaking, which always made me witter nervously. 'I think I'm pretty up to speed on that, yes.'

'Cleo's the best person to explain our various packages, to be honest, I'm more on the marketing side,' I went on, trying to read his face. 'Social media, Instagram, TikTok.'

'I'm not really one for that,' he said.

'No?'

A dry smile. 'Rather fake, isn't it?'

'Well, that depends.' Not ideal, but at least we were talking.

Cleo had finally finished her call and put a stop to our conversation by marching over and making herself a latte.

'Jim, this is Robyn,' she shouted over the coffee machine, pointing between us. 'Robyn, Jim.'

'I know, we've met!' I said brightly. 'We were just discussing the merits of social media.'

'Were you?'

79

'I didn't realise you'd hired a social media manager,' said Jim. 'Anything I should know?'

I looked between the two of them. The watchful eyes had started twinkling with amusement, and Cleo's bad mood had lifted as soon as she started talking to him. A definite smile was playing on her red lips. If he was a client then he was clearly a special one.

Or was he Cleo's accountant? Her solicitor? Her divorce solicitor?

Oh, wait. A realisation dawned. Had I read it wrong? Was Jim Cleo's *boyfriend*? If he was, she'd kept that quiet.

And she hadn't told me, I thought, outraged. Thanks.

'Well, this is awkward,' said Cleo. 'Robyn, you've got your wires crossed.'

Great. The day had got off to the exact start I'd hoped it wouldn't, with me on the back foot. 'In what way?'

'You two are going to be working together today.'

'What?' I said, at the same time as Jim said, 'I'm sorry, what?'

'Well, I say working together, you're going to a big job in Hartley but Jim will be showing you the ropes. Taylor Maid cleaners are always deployed in pairs.'

Cleaners?

Jim coughed, that self-important little 'I don't mean to correct you, but ...' cough some people do, just before correcting you. 'Not always ...' he started.

'Always,' Cleo insisted. 'It's for everyone's benefit. Safety, accountability, efficiency. Yes, I know,' she raised a hand to quash his protests, 'you've been working on your own for a few weeks but that was because of staffing problems. Fortunately Robyn is here now.'

I glanced at Jim just in time to see him giving Cleo a 'can we talk about this?' look so pained that I felt affronted. I wasn't that bad, surely?

'But that's just for today?' His tone made it clear that he would prefer that, please.

'We'll see how it goes,' said Cleo.

I sensed a battle of wills and was surprised to find myself rooting for Cleo. What on earth was his problem?

I thought there was going to be more from Jim, but after a moment's silence, he put his cup down on the side table. 'Well, if you'll excuse me,' he said, politely, 'I need to get the van ready.'

'Thank you, Jim,' said Cleo sweetly.

He gave me the briefest, flattest, driest smile ever – a real cream cracker of a smile – and left. When his feet clattered down the wooden steps outside, Cleo turned to me. 'OK. First off, have you got a court appearance today? You're dressed like a repentant shoplifter.'

'No! Presentation,' I said. 'Your brand image is neatness and tidiness, so I thought …'

Cleo was wearing white jeans, clogs and a polka-dot blouse. Hardly appropriate for a hard day's mopping.

'Mum said your website needed updating? I could do that, or refresh your social media? Not being rude, but I've had a look and it could be working harder for you – before and afters, top tips …' I'd made notes in preparation. Deep down, I wanted Cleo to be impressed with what I could do.

'I need a *cleaner*.' Cleo spoke very slowly. 'That's what I want you to do today. Clean.'

'Seriously?' I said, incredulously. 'You can't mean that.'

I was untidy to my very bones. When we were little, Father Christmas brought me and Cleo a vintage doll's house and, after a couple of weeks, Cleo stuck red tape across her half so her doll family wouldn't have to live in the chaos that reigned on my side of the house. We could play happily with our respective families, making up their family arguments and marrying off their children, until she instigated 'a spring clean' and then the fun would stop.

I won't even describe our shared bedroom. Cleo's red tape came out there again too.

'I'm so short-staffed that at this point, I have no choice,' said Cleo. 'I've got this urgent crash job in Hartley, two people have dropped out, and if you've got arms and legs, you can work a mop. Jim will look after you.'

'He doesn't seem very happy about that.'

'He's not happy about very much. But that's Jim.' Cleo was throwing back the scalding coffee in gulps, gasping between each, so she could get back to her desk. 'However, he's my best cleaner. He's going to show you the ropes. God help him.'

I stared at the door, as if Jim was waiting to come back in, this time in his suit with Cleo's annual return tucked under his arm. 'But … he's not a cleaner. Is he? Is this like… community service?'

'Cleaners come in all shapes and sizes, don't be such a snob.' Cleo was already slithering into her office chair. 'All you need to know is that he's exceptionally good at it, and you could learn a lot. Now can you get a move on and join him downstairs, please – we're already an hour behind on this.'

I gave it one last shot. 'But your website does need updating, let me do it instead,' I pleaded. 'Surely it would be better use of my skills, to bring in more business?'

She didn't even look up from her emails. 'I've got too *much* business right now, and not enough operatives. It's what happens when you're successful – you get great word of mouth.'

'But I can't clean dressed like this!' It was my final card.

'You're right.' Cleo finally looked up. 'Go downstairs into the garage and find yourself a pair of overalls.' She paused. 'I'd size up if I were you, there's no vanity sizing in workwear.'

I was speechless. With horror and also fury.

'Chop chop,' she said, like I was an annoying toddler, and went back to her emails.

I'd driven past the house many times on my way to work: Merrybank was the last in a row of pretty 1930s detached properties with whitewashed exteriors and steeply sloping rooflines; they reminded me of cuckoo clocks. Idling at the traffic lights outside, I'd admired the smooth lawn, with red tulips in cheerful lines along the borders, and pictured the interior to be equally pre-war smart – an enamel stove with printed tea towels over the spotless rail and bright Clarice Cliff china arranged on a sideboard. Spick and span, clean and tidy.

Which shows you how much even an estate agent knows.

The front door was wide open, and I could smell something bad before Jim and I were halfway down the garden path. It was as if the whole house had burped: a mixture of boiled cabbages and unmade beds, of damp and dust, papers left in piles for so long the layers of junk mail had started to compact like coal.

I stopped, revolted. How could it smell that appalling when the garden was so nice? I turned to say as much to Jim, but he was snapping on his rubber gloves in the manner of a crime scene investigator.

Inside, a whole team was hard at work. All the windows (original, Crittall, very nice, if not ideal for energy ratings) had been flung wide open, and a pair of hoovers was roaring away inside the house, upstairs and down. I spotted a yellow skip tucked down the side return, already one layer of bin bags full. A worker in Taylor Maid red overalls leaned out of a bedroom window as we approached and dropped a bag on top of the pile. It landed with a weighty thunk.

'So,' said Jim in a matter-of-fact tone as we stepped over buckets of cleaning products and another industrial hoover to get into the hallway, 'the way we normally work on a job like this is two cleaners to a room. We've been assigned the kitchen.'

He pushed the kitchen door wider, moving a trolley piled up with jam jars, margarine tubs and skeletal geraniums shrivelling in desiccated soil. The kitchen was like nothing I'd ever seen before, not even in my own worst nightmares.

And the *smell*.

'Oh my god.' I couldn't help it. It was terrible. But what was worse was the clutter. Every surface was piled with so many things that you couldn't actually *see* the surface. Nearest me was a stack of newspapers. I checked the top one: it was seventeen years old. My chest tightened with every breath until it felt like I was suffocating. 'Where do you even *start*?'

Jim ignored my shrill tone. 'You get your Marigolds on,' he said, 'and start in a corner, work outwards.'

'Who lives here?' I asked then, in the light of the age of the newspapers, amended it to, 'I mean, *does* someone live here? Have you just found it like this?'

The cogs in my brain had begun to turn. The gloves, the urgency, the smell … Had someone *died*? Was that why it smelled so bad?

'It belongs to a lady called Margaret Jennings.' Jim was scooping piles of junk mail from the counter top and dropping them into a green bag.

'Is she … still with us?' I asked as delicately as I could, given that I was barely breathing in.

'She's in hospital, recovering from a hip operation, and her family have booked us to get the house sorted out for when she's discharged tomorrow.'

Thank god for that. Margaret was alive! But …

'Tomorrow?' The initial relief swiftly drained out of me, as I looked around us at the chaos. 'There's no *way* this will be clean by tomorrow.'

'Yes, it will, if we get on with it.' Jim was being cordial, but I wouldn't call his tone friendly. While we'd been speaking he'd filled a recycling bag with the newspapers; now he tied it and dropped it outside the kitchen door, where another cleaner carrying four more bags bent with a neat dip, picked it up and carried on out of the door. I heard a distant thud as all five bags joined their mates in the skip.

When I looked back, Jim had made a marble counter top appear from nowhere. Well, a corner of a counter top. It looked vulnerable, a little island bravely holding out against the hungry tide of clutter, but it was a start. He picked up the roll of bags, ripped another off, and passed it to me. 'Start obvious. All junk mail, newspapers, parish magazines, everything in there.'

I hesitated, because … how were we meant to know Margaret Jennings wasn't saving the parish newsletter for some important phone number? I had loads of magazines and things lying around my house that I would be furious if Mum threw out before I'd had time to read them.

I picked up a flier for a steam train trip to Inverness and a specialist reading light and bagged them. 'Do you think she's keeping this?' I asked, waving a Stannah stairlift leaflet.

Jim didn't break his regular pick-chuck-pick-chuck rhythm. 'Bin it. It's all information available on the Internet.'

I was willing to bet Margaret thought differently but I binned it obediently. 'Oh, maybe this …' Flowers – with a special offer! Maybe save that. Funeral homes. Probably shouldn't leave that. Bit morbid.

'There's no need to inspect everything. Important post goes in that plastic box by the door – Mrs Jennings' daughter is coming round later and she'll go through it.'

'OK.' I dumped some food delivery leaflets without looking, then immediately worried I might have ditched a council tax bill within the pile. I jiggled the bag to check there was no brown envelope. This was going to take forever. But I had to admit it was easier than tackling my own junk.

'What about recycling?' I picked up two jam jars. Most of them were rinsed clean, some had labels from supermarkets I hadn't seen in years. When did Safeway stop trading?

'Skip it. The skip people have a sorting station.' Jim had finished the counter top and was opening the tall cupboards above it.

I stopped, unable to tear my eyes away, bracing myself for what might be inside – Jars of human teeth? A dead cat? – but to my great relief, there was almost nothing. A box of teabags, some powdered milk and a faded mug on the bottom shelf. On the very top shelf, a nested set of apricot china teacups and saucers, unused. Behind it, another nest of cups, and another.

After the tumbling mess everywhere else the sparse cupboards were surreal. They were the cupboards of someone who didn't expect visitors, I realised. Someone who didn't think it worth treating themselves to a nice biscuit or the best china cup for their Horlicks. It felt like an intrusion to know that about Mrs Jennings.

Jim didn't pause. He took out the coffee and the teacups and started spraying and wiping the shelves. Without looking round, he said, 'Would it help you focus if I set an alarm? We've only got two hours on this kitchen. Then we have to move onto the dining room.'

I didn't reply. A strange emotion was bulging and rumbling inside my chest like a thundercloud: it wasn't just revulsion at the reek of neglect, or fury at Cleo for tricking me into cleaning, or panic at the scale of the task, or even pity. It was something else. Something I hadn't been expecting and couldn't put my finger on, beyond the fact that I didn't like it at all. It felt personal, like a dream I'd forgotten but which still lingered at the edge of my consciousness.

I grabbed the jam jars and dumped them in the bag so hard Jim turned round.

He looked at me for a long moment, assessing me with his shrewd grey eyes.

Probably trying to work out where he knew me from. I'd seen that look before.

I lifted my chin, defiantly.

'Careful,' he said in his mild voice, and carried on bagging.

I dealt with the overwhelming kitchen by making a mental list – bin, bag, recycle – and applied it over and over until I could see clear shelves, countertop, floor. Then I sprayed and wiped that section, and moved on to the next. I refused to look further than the section in front of me, because if I did, the fizzing panic distracted me. Meanwhile, Jim cleaned the units, replaced the contents (minus the items that were out of date, which was nearly everything), scrubbed tiles with a giant toothbrush and de-gunked the hob. It was bright stainless steel underneath the black crust.

He worked with a relentlessness that made me feel slow in comparison but the satisfying emergence of order in the chaos motivated me to carry on. If this was sped-up on the Internet, I thought, I'd watch it for *hours*.

Jim must have been aware of me observing him because he stopped, wiped his forehead with the back of his hand and said, 'You look like you could do with a break. There's coffee outside if you want some.'

He said it as if he personally wouldn't be stopping but a lesser mortal like me might need to.

I glanced at my watch: we'd been at it for an hour. It felt like a lot longer.

'I'd love a coffee,' I said. 'White, no sugar. Mind if I check my messages?'

There was no phone reception in the kitchen, and I was waiting to hear back about another job. I couldn't remember when I'd last not checked my phone for this long.

'Sure,' said Jim. 'The refreshment table's outside. Help yourself to biscuits.' Then he went back to his systematic elimination of built-up grime.

A woman called Veronica informed me that 'crash teams' were provided with a refreshment table outside on jobs like these, 'so we don't use the client's facilities and get in the way of the kitchen squad'.

'I'm the kitchen squad today!' I said, cheerfully. 'Me and Jim.'

'Jim?' She looked vague.

'Tall bloke? Short hair.' I paused, not wanting to say, 'Looks like a headmaster', in case they were friends. 'Quite … stern?'

Her face cleared. 'Him? Wow. Good luck,' she added as she sailed off with four coffees clumped together.

I helped myself to a biscuit. I hadn't expected such a generous offering from Cleo: two boxes of mid-range M&S biscuits, tea, coffee, sugars, oat milk, soft drinks. No one took the mickey and lingered too long. In fact, I got a couple of side eyes for taking a second coffee, but in my defence I was knackered, I could feel three of my nails had broken inside my rubber gloves, and my right arm ached from scrubbing.

The atmosphere was friendly but focused. Some cleaners wore headphones, some chatted, everyone seemed to know each other, but beyond a few polite hellos, no one talked to me.

Which wasn't a problem, I reminded myself, because I wasn't doing this again.

Jim summoned me back into the kitchen for the final push, but before I could congratulate us on a job well done, he moved us on to the dining room. If anything, it smelled worse.

'Watch out for dead mice or birds behind those piles of boxes,' he warned me, and I blenched. How could you live like that? Not even knowing if there was a dead bird in your house?

Still, I set to and started bagging. The phone reception was better in this room, and I got a text from a recruiter about a job; Jim shrugged when I popped out to reply. Knowing I had options made me feel better about the back-breaking work, and maybe I spent a bit longer replying than I meant to.

Maybe I went outside more than I should have done. I had literally only nipped out for five minutes to text Mitch an idea I'd had about targeted marketing, when someone tapped me aggressively on the shoulder.

'What?' I spun round.

A woman with a long ponytail was standing with a mop in her hand. 'Stop slacking,' she said.

'What?'

'I've seen you. This is the fourth time you've snuck out here to text or do whatever it is you're doing.' She glared. 'This is a team, and we get paid as a team, and you are delaying completion.'

'Hey, that's not ...' I took a nervous step back.

'I miss my bonus, *you* owe me.' She jabbed a finger in my direction.

'OK, Sierra.' Jim had appeared behind me. 'You've made your point.'

'Jim, talk to her.' Sierra wagged the finger and stalked off.

'Did you hear that?' I demanded, shaken and also offended. 'She can't speak to me like that!'

'Listen, I appreciate this is your first day and this is a baptism of fire,' said Jim. 'But we've got nine hours to clean this house.'

'We're here for *nine* hours?'

'We're here until it's done. As a team. We get a team bonus if we finish on time.' He gave me a level look. 'And if we're late, or there are issues, none of us gets the bonus. A few extra quid might not make a difference to you, but it makes a difference to other people on the team.'

I bridled at the implication that I was some posh girl slumming it. 'I'm doing my best! Do they know this is literally my first job? And that some of us aren't natural-born scrubbers?'

That last comment came out before my brain could filter it. I'd meant it in the sense that Mum and Cleo liked cleaning, whereas I didn't, but too late I realised that wasn't what it sounded like to anyone who didn't know us. The split-second reaction I saw in Jim's eyes made me feel about five centimetres tall.

'Not many of us are,' he said, reproachfully.

'Sorry,' I mumbled at his retreating back.

Two hours till home time.

We were done by six. I couldn't remember the last time I'd felt so exhausted, but the dining room was spotless and I'd thrown thirty-five bin bags into the skip.

At ten past, on the dot, a minibus appeared, most of the crew piled in and announced they were off to the pub. There were cheers, hugs goodbye. Not for me, obviously. No one asked me if I wanted to come to the pub.

Jim was in charge of signing off the job. I was trying to salvage my nails when he appeared with a woman about my mum's age: Sarah, Mrs Jennings' daughter; smart look-ing in a navy suit, Bluetooth earpiece still tucked under her blonde bob. Her body language screamed: I am a very busy woman.

She shook hands with us both. 'Thank you so much for fitting this in at such short notice. The family ... we're so grateful for your help.' She spoke quickly, and though her voice was pleasant, the muscles in her neck were tense.

Too busy to clean her own mother's house, I noted silently. And she knows we're thinking that too.

'We've done a top-to-bottom clean as discussed with Cleo,' said Jim, steering her down the hall, drawing her attention to the now-glossy woodwork. 'The skip will be collected by lunchtime tomorrow and the stair carpets will be dry enough by the morning for the stairlift people to start fitting.'

Even I was impressed by the transformation. With light filtering through the windows, delicate rainbow prisms glinted off a collection of crystal glasses, washed, polished and lined up on the shelving units. The grey rug in the middle of the sitting room was pink, with a Persian pattern. I definitely wouldn't have guessed that first thing this morning.

But Sarah said nothing.

'We've filed any paperwork on the dining-room table,' Jim went on, as if her lack of response wasn't rude, given how hard everyone had worked, 'and the laundrette is going to deliver the bed linen in the morning. If you want one of us to be here to collect it and make up the beds, that's not a problem.'

There was a long silence, then eventually Sarah turned round. She was holding a porcelain cat that had been under the sofa, along with a bag's worth of used tissues, three remote controls and a dead bird. Obviously, we hadn't left those for her.

I realised she was struggling to hold back tears.

'I'm sorry. It's …' she said, then swallowed. 'I gave Mum this cat for Christmas, the first year I got a job. I haven't seen it in decades. Seeing it again reminded me how …' She squeezed her eyes shut.

Jim looked at me, and tipped his head towards the kitchen.

'Would you like a cup of tea?' he asked Sarah, gently. 'Sounds like you've had a long day. Did you say you'd driven from Newcastle?'

Sarah nodded, and he guided her towards a chair. I could hear him talking as I boiled the kettle. He'd barely said a word to me all day but now he was managing a soothing stream of barely audible conversation about the M1.

I gazed at the units, wishing I'd taken some before and after pictures so Sarah could see just what a miracle we'd worked. Since the house finally had company, I used the apricot teacups.

'We had no idea Mum had let the place get into such a state.' Sarah was shredding a tissue, trying not to cry. 'She's always been independent, refused to have anyone come in, not even a cleaner. We tried, honestly, we tried *so hard*, every time she came to stay with one of us we'd try to get help arranged but …'

'A fresh start,' said Jim. 'Much easier to keep on top of.'

I put the tray down on a coffee table that had until recently been hidden by *Women's Weeklies*.

'Here you go,' I said. 'Wasn't sure if you took milk and sugar. So I brought them both. We cleaned everything in the cupboards. And wiped them out. And the cutlery.'

Jim frowned at me, and I stopped. What? What had I said?

It wasn't as if Sarah was listening. 'I don't think I realised how bad it had got until I saw what you've done today,' she was saying. 'My sister took Mum into hospital after her last fall and said the paramedics struggled to get inside.'

'It was quite a job,' I said. I couldn't help myself.

Sarah bowed her head, tucking her chin into her neck. 'Please tell me it wasn't the worst you've ever done.'

'No,' said Jim quickly. 'Not remotely. Nothing a bit of elbow grease and some recycling bags couldn't sort out.'

I widened my eyes at him over the top of Sarah's chair. If the kitchen had looked like that, I couldn't even imagine what the bedrooms had been like. Or the bathroom! God, the bathroom …

But he glared back at me, giving me the full force of that eagle-like intensity, and I shrivelled.

'These are pretty cups,' said Sarah suddenly. 'Where did you find them?'

'In the cupboard.'

'I think they were wedding presents.' She smiled, and her face seemed younger. 'I'm glad Mum's using them.'

Wisely, this time I said nothing.

Jim took me back to Cleo's where I'd left my car that morning.

'Thanks for your help today,' he said.

'I don't think I was much help,' I said. The glow of Margaret Jennings' house transformation had dimmed, and I kept thinking about the unused cups and the dead bird. Sadness clung to me like the smell. Which also clung to me.

'It got done in the end,' said Jim, which wasn't the praise I was hoping for. 'Will we see you tomorrow?'

'I'm not sure,' I said. 'Maybe.'

He inclined his head slightly as if he'd been hoping for a more emphatic 'no'.

'Are they …?' I hesitated. 'The jobs, are they all like that?'

'Not really. That was quite extreme. Mostly it's just cleaning showers and hoovering. But to be honest, I find houses like that the most satisfying.'

Of course he did. 'Because you can see the difference?'

'Yes, but ...' Jim wiped a hand over his face. 'In my opinion, cleaning isn't always about cleaning. It's about restoring order. Houses don't get like that because someone's too lazy to run a cloth over a sink. There's more to it. That's what you're helping someone with.'

I didn't say anything. I often felt as if the mess in my flat was ganging up on me. It didn't feel like a fair fight. The more stressed I was, the worse my house got. The worse my house got, the more I loathed myself.

Just thinking about my flat made me feel weary. I remembered I'd have to drag all my unironed laundry out of the bath if I wanted a soak tonight, and the ache in my bones ramped up another notch.

'I will never let my bins get as bad as that though,' I said.

'That's probably what Mrs Jennings thought at one point.'

I turned. Seriously? 'Is that supposed to make me feel better?'

Jim's expression didn't change. 'No. But it's the truth.'

Something about the vicar-ish way he said that, as if he was the only beacon of order standing between these poor slatterns and an unexpected burial under a pile of local newspapers, riled me.

'Oh, for—'

There was a rap on the window and we both jumped.

It was Cleo.

'Good day?' she asked, and I gave her the special deadeye smile we'd perfected as kids. I couldn't see, but I imagined Jim was doing something similar.

6

~ *Microwave your kitchen sponges and cloths to blast bacteria. Remember to leave them for a minute, though, as they'll be scalding hot.*

I woke up the following morning to the sound of rhythmic grunting from upstairs. A female voice was cutting in between the grunts, and I realised Tomasz had company.

I should have guessed, I told myself, trying to make my ears seal over as motes of dust drifted down from the ceiling, dislodged by the impact of something slamming against the wall over my head. This would be *why* the flat was so cheap, and so readily available. How could I call myself an estate agent when I hadn't even bothered to check the neighbours?

Sad fact: it's impossible to check for the real neighbourly habits which will drive you insane. You can see a giant seven-dog kennel or a yard full of rusting Morris Minors. You can't see a fixation about recycling bins. Or a trombone.

Above my head, the woman started counting backwards from ten, which somehow made me feel even more horribly involved in whatever was going on up there, until she suddenly yelled, 'Let's go, Peloton!', Tomasz let out a roar and I swung my legs out of bed and headed for the cup of coffee that would hopefully drive those images out of my head.

I drank a lot of coffee. Partly on account of my erratic sleeping patterns, which I knew was not a coincidence.

The phone rang while I was scrolling through the photographs I'd taken of Lark Manor and trying to decide if a walk-in shower or a slipper bath would look better in my apartment. Or both?

'Robyn.'

'Cleo,' I replied, matching my sister's clipped office tones.

It was our traditional greeting. Well, our modern version. Cleo used to say, 'Hey, stinker,' when she rang me (and I'd say, 'Yo, hairy'), but since she'd started Taylor Maid, Cleo had adopted this formal work persona that had gradually spread into the rest of her life.

'How are you this morning?' she asked.

'Bit sore.' I rubbed my neck where I'd cricked it, trying to get at the detritus beneath Margaret Jennings' cupboards.

'Good,' she said. 'Hard work never hurt anyone.'

I waited optimistically for a crumb of praise.

'Did Mrs Jennings give good feedback?' I prompted, when none was forthcoming.

'What? Oh, yes, Jim said her daughter was thrilled, and she's booked a regular weekly clean to keep on top of it.'

I noticed, as the kettle chugged towards boiling point, a furry layer of dust on the edge of the splashback behind the hob. I ripped off a square of kitchen roll and removed it with a swipe. That only revealed how unpleasantly discoloured the grout was. I'd never noticed the colour of grout before. The kettle wasn't quite boiling, but I poured hot water on the coffee and turned away before I could think any more about grout.

'And …?' I prompted her again.

'And what?'

I rolled my eyes. Was Cleo really going to make me say it? I hated myself for asking, but I couldn't stop the neediness. It controlled me.

'Did I meet your high professional expectations?'

'Jim says you got stuck in and were quite helpful,' she conceded. 'Well done.'

Quite helpful? Thanks, Jim.

'Good. The thing is, Cleo,' I said, before she could give me a breakdown of what I could have done better, 'I'll be honest, I'm glad I could help out but cleaning isn't my strong suit. If you're still short-staffed, why don't I organise some recruitment for you?'

I reckoned I could do that. I needed the money, and one day's cleaning wasn't going to cover my rent.

'That's kind of you to offer, but it's not why I was calling,' said Cleo. 'Jim says you've got the spare keys to the van.'

'I don't think I have.'

'He said he gave them to you so you could get your phone, and you didn't give them back to him.'

I felt around in my jacket pocket. Oh yeah. There they were.

'Anyway, he's doing a job in Hildreth Street at ten o'clock, so why don't you pop down there and hand them over?' She paused. 'And if you wanted another day's work, I'm sure he could use a hand?'

'In the office?'

'No.' Cleo sighed. 'Not in the office.'

I was going to say thanks but I wasn't going to put myself through *that* again, when the post fell through the letter box, and I could see one of the letters had an EON logo and the word REMINDER on it.

So I went.

Terry Gilchrist was eighty-seven and he was the youngest of thirteen, two of whom were twins (Leslie and Leonard) and one of whom had been in prison in France (Kathleen). He was a retired postman, cider factory worker, former semi-professional darts player and he still had all his own teeth. He could also play the spoons.

This much I learned in the first ten minutes of cleaning Terry's kitchen. I also learned, all by myself, that he had an unhealthy relationship with Mr Kipling and didn't clean his cups properly.

When I pitched up outside Hildreth Street, which was just round the corner from my flat, Jim greeted me with polite enthusiasm. The sort of polite enthusiasm we used to show towards the students who'd appear in the office to do luke-warm work experience before their GCSEs. I didn't know what the cleaning equivalent of filling envelopes with fliers was, but I suspected that was the level Jim had put me at.

'New girl, is it?' Terry enquired, when he let us in. 'Thought you preferred to fly solo, eh, Jimbo?'

'I do,' said Jim, 'but two cleaners is the policy so here we are. Terry, this is Robyn.'

'With a Y,' I added, automatically.

'And this is Terry.' He extended a polite hand towards the elderly man in the wheelchair.

'With a T,' said Terry.

I frowned. 'A t?'

'Thanks, love, I will, if you're making one.' He roared with laughter at his own joke, and gestured towards the kitchen. 'Cups on the side, bags in the packet by the window.'

'Fair enough,' I said.

'Let me explain the hot-water system,' said Jim, and steered me into the utility room off the kitchenette.

'He's a one, isn't he?' I said, indulgently.

Jim made sure Terry couldn't hear us, then muttered, 'Terry is a *talker*,' under his breath. 'He will distract you with endless stories which is fine, he's the client, but do *not* let him stop you getting on with what you're here to do.'

'Which is?'

'Sixty minutes' general cleaning. You focus on the kitchen, I'll start on the bathroom and make my way across the flat.'

'The kitchen. Again?'

'You can put into practice what you learned yesterday.'

'So that's …?' I looked helpless until Jim cracked and counted off on his fingers: 'Clean the surfaces, bin anything that looks binnable, spray and clean the sink, clean the hob, wipe down any touch points, empty the bins, recycling goes in the green bin outside the front door, and then hoover and mop the floor.'

'OK,' I said, trying to remember all that. 'Then what?'

'That'll take you the best part of forty-five minutes. Don't underestimate how long it takes to clean a hob thoroughly.' He spoke at a brisk clip, as if he couldn't wait to get started on his own tasks. What a weirdo. 'You need to soak the metal frame in the sink, double clean the base, scrub the frame. Glass spray to remove any smears on the stainless steel.'

'Obviously.' I made a mental note of the order I was supposed to do that in. I'd never actually cleaned my own hob. I waited until the build-up solidified into chunks I could flick off with a fish slice.

'If you've done that with time to spare, move onto the sitting room – I'll start with the bathroom and meet you in the middle.'

'And what if it takes longer than sixty minutes?'

Jim fixed me with a firm gaze. 'It can't. We leave at eleven, no later, so we can get to Moffat Street at half past.'

'There's another job after this?'

His face said, Of course there is, but in his calmest tone he said, 'Didn't Cleo give you a time sheet?'

'No, she just told me to meet you here with the van keys. She didn't tell me I'd be working *all day*.' It came out more truculent than I'd intended but Jim didn't react.

'Well, my schedule for today is Moffat Street next for two hours, then a break for lunch. Then the Armstrongs on Coleridge Terrace. Then a check on a couple of dogs in Portland Place for half an hour, then that's it for the day.'

'Do we clean the dogs?' I asked, trying desperately to leaven Jim's intensity with a joke.

It fell on deaf ears. 'We walk them round the block,' he said. 'Their owner is on shifts.'

'So if I'm here working with you, we should finish early,' I suggested. 'Two people, half the time, right?'

He held my gaze. 'Probably not, if I have to keep explaining everything to you.'

Jim really was hard work. I had no idea why someone with such undeniable middle-management vibes was working as a cleaner but clearly it wasn't because a glittering career in comedy had fallen through.

We regarded each other with politely concealed but mutual impatience.

'So,' I asked, 'should I make a cup of tea for Terry or not?'

'Make it,' said Jim. 'But only make one for yourself if you're confident you can clean and drink at the same time.'

'You'd be amazed at what I can do simultaneously,' I quipped, but Jim was already heading out of the room.

I made Terry's tea – 'milk, three sugars' – in a well-worn World's Best Grandad mug and, at his insistence, one for myself in an equally faded Happy 70th Dad mug. I noticed he had quite a collection of mugs in his cupboard, but these two were the favourites.

He stationed himself in his wheelchair in the corner of the kitchen and started firing off anecdotes, while I chiselled coagulated jam off the counter tops.

'I like toast,' he explained, when I'd made him some to go with the tea. 'Not supposed to have it with jam, but you've got to have a few pleasures in life at my age.'

'Absolutely.' I sprayed and wiped, trying not to notice Jim tapping his watch at me every ten minutes from the hallway.

'Now my wife, my Gillian, bless her soul, she'd ruin a snack, always going on about the bleeding calories. You couldn't have a biscuit with your tea without Gill telling you it was ninety calories for a digestive but only seventy-two in a Rich Tea.'

'Is that right?'

'Thin as a pin she was. Dropped dead of a heart attack at fifty-nine. My mum was ninety-eight and built like a brick privy – she always used to say, "Ain't no belts in shrouds, darling!"'

I flattened three empty French Fancies packets for the recycling. I wasn't sure that was exactly the saying but Terry was already onto tales of his Aunt Shirley, who'd been an exotic dancer before she'd 'moved sideways' into wrestling.

He chatted away as I worked and didn't seem to mind that my replies were largely of the 'Hmm?' and 'Really?' variety. Apart from anything, keeping track of Terry's complex relatives took some doing; there were his three children (Jayne, Barry and Brian), seven grandchildren (Daisy, Rosie, Lily, Rowan … I think), their various partners … I tried my best to focus on the task in hand, but slowly Terry reeled me in. I'd always been fascinated by big messy families, since my own family tree was more of a family twig. I'd have loved a grandad who told outrageous stories like Terry. Instead I had Grandpa, Dad's dad, a retired electrician who pretended to be deafer than he was (according to Mum) so he could spend his time restoring radios in his shed, and Grandad, Mum's dad, who I hadn't seen since I was small – and of course, any further discussion of that side of the family was strictly *verboten*.

I had literally only stopped for one second to hazard a proper guess as to who the mystery soap star who'd had an affair with Terry's darts pal might be, when Jim appeared in the kitchen.

Oops. I glanced at the kitchen clock. Somehow it was two minutes to eleven.

He peeled off his Marigolds and said, 'You didn't make it through to the hall, Robyn?'

'No,' I said, 'but look at that hob!'

We looked at the hob. It was so clean we could see our faces in it. Jim's reflection didn't seem as impressed as mine.

'Well, that's us, Terry,' said Jim. 'See you next week!'

I held up a hand. 'Terry was just going to tell me how—'

'Next time!' said Jim briskly and ushered me out.

When I turned back at the door to wave to Terry, I couldn't help noticing that his expression wasn't as cheery as his goodbye.

And now I would never know who the soap star was.

We cleaned an already spotless house in Moffat Street (why, I don't know) and then Jim told me to grab some lunch in town before the next job. He disappeared, leaving only a warning to be back in half an hour exactly.

I bought the cheapest sandwich in the deli furthest away from anyone I might bump into, and ate it on a wall, out of sight. I'd put my jacket on over the Taylor Maid overalls, but there was still no reason for me to be wearing trousers this red of my own accord. No one would, apart from maybe Johnny from the office, or a children's entertainer.

I rang Mitch, and he sounded pleased to hear from me.

'My favourite negotiator!' Just the sound of his voice was a boost. 'What are you up to?'

'Temping for my sister. Helping her out.'

'Good for you. How's the job hunting?'

I told him about the jobs I'd applied for. 'It's still OK to give you as a reference?'

'Of course! I've put out some feelers – I'll let you know as soon as I hear anything.'

I started to ask about Lark Manor, then I got a reminder text from Jim that lunch was up. Great.

I walked back to where Jim had left me, and we drove across town to a most desirable area known to the local agents as The Poet Streets.

The Armstrongs' house on Coleridge Terrace was gorgeous: a three-storey, Georgian, stucco-fronted family home with a red front door big enough for an extra-large Christmas wreath. I'd marketed a neighbouring property a few months ago, and when the brochure for 33 Coleridge Terrace came back from the printers, the whole sales team stood around it, mentally calculating which body parts we could sell on the dark web for a chance of living there.

'Is two hours going to be enough?' I asked, as we carted the cleaning equipment up the steps.

'Yes,' said Jim.

'Really? These are big houses.' I knew for a fact that there were at least four bedrooms and three bathrooms in these properties. And most people had either extended into the attic or the cellar, or both.

Jim unlocked the door and jabbed at the burglar alarm. 'We're here twice a week. We focus on different areas on different days.'

'And what is it today?'

He ushered me inside. 'Today is kitchens and bathrooms.'

Of course it was. It was always bloody kitchens.

The first thing I noticed when we stepped into the tiled hall was that No. 7 didn't smell the way I'd expected. No. 33 had smelled of Jo Malone candles, wood polish and fresh coffee, even when they weren't expecting viewings. Whereas this house smelled of damp linen, blackening bananas and that faint, tart smell of boys. I noticed it when Alfie, Wes and Orson stayed over at Mum's for the weekend, detectable even above the smell of cleaning products. Not a *smell*-smell, just a tang of trainers and wet hair and farts and something under the sofa that hadn't been there before.

Jim was straight down to business, unloading cleaning buckets onto the stairs, scooping three stray socks and a gym bag up to make room, and dumping them straight into a washing basket.

'We need to get cracking,' he said, raking discarded clothes off the floor, 'because there's a lot to do, and Mrs Armstrong's back at three thirty with the boys. We need to be out by then.'

'The unseen staff, eh?' I said, feeling unexpectedly bolshy. 'Doesn't she like to see the servants at work? Frightened that the boys might be startled by the sight of a mop?'

Jim handed me the bucket. 'Quite the reverse. *I* don't want to be here when they come back. You make a start in the kitchen, and I'll take upstairs and work down.'

'Fine,' I said, and stepped into what should have been a showstopping double kitchen extension but was instead a heart-stopping mess.

A sensory overload of chaos greeted me. It was a jangling roar of colour and disorder: red and green Lego fragments scattered in irregular clumps on the rug, jaunty Emma Bridgewater bowls caked in dry cereal stacked on the side, a jammy knife sticking out of the crumb-speckled butter, ironing board still up by the window, shoes everywhere.

I took an involuntary step backwards. Straight into Jim, who was following me with the laundry basket he'd already collected from the first bedroom.

'Clean the sink and work out,' he said, with a nod towards the Belfast sink in the central archipelago of the kitchen.

'Can you give me a … list?' It sounds ridiculous, but my heart was bumping too fast and I fought down the strange urge to spin on my heels and walk out. Everything was out of place and I didn't know where to put it. And we only had two hours!

Jim filled the washing machine, slammed the door and said, 'Come on, it's surely no worse than you've seen at home on a bad day.'

It was … and it wasn't. That was my mess and I knew where everything went, and how it had got there – the straighteners were on the floor because I didn't have time to put them away because I was running late, the conditioner was upside down so I could get the last bit out of the bottle, and last month's gym kit was in a pile by the bathroom door because I didn't want to put it in with a whites wash. Etcetera. Etcetera.

But this was different. It set me on edge.

I turned to see Jim watching me. I'd noticed him doing that before: watching, saying nothing, *thinking*. 'Are you OK?'

I nodded, forcing myself to do my breathing: long breath in, hold it, long breath out. I'd learned techniques to deal with panic, and now did them almost instinctively, but new situations still threw me.

'It's always a bit challenging, this place – just life with kids, I guess.' He shrugged. 'Won't take long once you start.'

I nodded again, this time harder, but I couldn't move. A spark of impatience broke through Jim's carefully neutral expression, narrowing his eyes.

'What is it that you don't feel able to do?'

A mental image of Jim reporting back to Cleo flashed across my mind – '... and I had to show her how to clean the sink ...' – and I found my voice.

'I'm just ...' I shook myself. 'I'm deciding where to start.'

'Clear up the Lego first,' Jim advised. 'There's a dustpan and brush under the sink. Dump it in that box by the television.' He mimed despatching the Lego with a few brisk sweeps, and left me to it.

Come on, Robyn, I thought, visualising Cleo's expression if she heard I'd been broken by Lego. She'd *love* to be proved right about my inability to do this.

I squared my shoulders and went for the dustpan and brush.

Our last job of the day was a quick once-round-the-block for two dogs, Rambo and Nessie.

It was already twenty to five when we got there, ten minutes behind schedule; something Jim was quick to point out as part of his never-ending TED talk on the importance of time management. Now he'd started talking to me, he wouldn't shut up. I was a captive audience for his incessant lecturing.

'It's vital that we leave punctually at the end of each job,' he reminded me. 'Or else we risk the buffer zone.'

I couldn't take much more of Jim's managerial approach: wipe in this direction, don't smear that, hurry hurry hurry. It was irritating, especially since the one major detail he seemed to miss was that I had zero intention of becoming the Cleaner's Apprentice.

'And incremental lateness,' he went on, 'leads to a butterfly effect which is ...'

'Tasting with your feet?' I said, to wind him up. 'Or accidentally causing a nuclear war?'

He turned, giving me full Teacher Face. 'No, in this instance the butterfly effect is when …'

'I know what the *butterfly effect* is,' I snapped. 'I'm not stupid.'

He frowned, as if he couldn't work out whether I was joking or not.

We were saved from ourselves by the hysterical sound of two bored dogs trying to bark their way through the front door of 18 Macklin Avenue.

'I'll take Nessie, you take Rambo,' Jim instructed. 'The leads are by the stairs, grab them and clip them up. Deirdre should have harnessed the dogs before she left.'

'Why am I getting Rambo?' I demanded as I followed him in.

A Jack Russell shot out between Jim's legs like a cannonball and I grabbed its collar automatically. The momentum nearly carried me backwards down the steps.

'Rambo, stop!' Jim appeared with what looked like a small donkey. 'This is Nessie. Scottish deerhound.'

Rambo stopped long enough for me to attach a lead to his harness. He sized me up and I felt distinctly lacking. Dogs and babies could sniff out a lack of authority in a second.

'Right then,' said Jim, locking the door. 'Follow me, I've got a route.'

Of course he had.

After five minutes it became clear that getting the smaller dog wasn't necessarily the easier option. Rambo was freakishly strong, with Cleo-like levels of determination and a fixation with lamp posts.

'How long do we have to do this?' I panted as Rambo towed me down the street.

'Thirty minutes,' said Jim.

'What if we walked them faster and did it in twenty?'

'No,' said Jim.

'But that would be the same distance.'

'It's not the point. She's paying for thirty minutes.'

'We can't be flexible?'

'No.'

I came to an abrupt halt as Rambo made another stop, giving me the most outrageous side eye as he cocked his leg on his tenth lamp post, daring me to complain. By now, nothing was coming out, but it was clearly the principle that mattered.

Meanwhile, in stark contrast, Nessie was loping obediently by Jim's side, without need of any hauling or muttering. Every so often she glanced up at him, then returned her gaze to the pavement ahead, satisfied that everything was right with the world.

'Can you hurry him up?' Jim enquired.

'No,' I said, stubbornly. 'Marking and smelling is as important to the dog's sensory experience as walking.'

'You have a dog?'

'Not yet. But I've done a lot of research.'

I didn't want to tell Jim that it was more for any dog's sake than mine that I'd put off ownership: that I could wipe out a begonia in three days, two, if it was summer. However, I had a variety of hounds in my imaginary kennel and thanks to YouTube, I was a technical expert in everything from grooming to clicker training.

'Each lamp post is like an art gallery of smells,' I added, seeing Nessie raise her long nose to the air. 'It wears out their brains too, so we should let them stop.'

He grunted but couldn't argue with confidently presented facts.

'Do you have a dog?' I could see Jim with a dog; a self-poo-bagging black Labrador that told the time.

'No,' he said.

'Too messy for you? Too much smearing?'

He shook his head. 'I used to, but I … I haven't been in the right place for one recently.'

Wow. There was a lot going on between the lines there.

Jim must have realised he'd shared more than he meant to, because he said, 'Shall we move on?' and clicked his tongue at Nessie, who trotted forward.

Rambo seemed less interested in lamp posts now he'd been allowed a good sniff, and the rest of the walk was easier. Jim even allowed Nessie to stop a few times to investigate a flowerbed, which she seemed to enjoy. We managed some self-conscious chat through the dogs ('I see you don't care for cats, Rambo?' and 'Wow, did you bring a shovel, Jim?') and he seemed impressed when I shared the cleaning tip that tomato ketchup was an effective and natural way of neutralising fox poo.

Then we took the dogs back home – bang on time – said our goodbyes and, with some relief, I drew a line under my housekeeping career. The mystery of Jim's dog-unfriendly life would have to go on the list with Terry's soap star, to dance across my brain on one of my many sleepless early mornings.

7

~ You can wash children's toys, soap dishes, hair brushes, golf balls, bath sponges, dog collars, flip-flops and keys in the dishwasher.

I woke up on Saturday with a whole new set of aches and three unexplained bruises on my left hand, which were acquired either from Rambo's lead or extracting Lego from the Armstrongs' hoover. Or something I hadn't even noticed happening. It had been that sort of day.

But any thoughts of a recovery lie-in were dismissed by the arrival of two messages: one from Mitch, with a couple more LinkedIn contacts, and another from Mum, checking I was still on for 'coffee and a catch-up' with her and Cleo.

I'd forgotten about the latter, but I was so thrilled about the former that I was out of bed and into the shower before Tomasz even started his morning grunting.

Mum's brunch venue of choice, St Olaf's Church, was down an alley, off the main shopping street in town. It was Long-hampton's oldest church and, to fund the ongoing repairs, the rear half had been converted into a cafe from which you could admire the medieval stonework while eating an organic quiche. It appealed directly to Mum and Cleo's love of multitasking.

They were already there when I arrived, sitting with a coffee and a slice of carrot cake each.

'Sorry, I thought we should order, you know how slow they can be in here,' said Cleo, gesturing at a waitress who was definitely within earshot. 'Mum's appointment's at one, so we need to be out of here by quarter to.'

I bridled at the relentless timetabling, even on her day off. 'I'm not late, Mum said half eleven.'

'Did I say you were late?'

'Cleo's treating me to a haircut ahead of the awards,' Mum intervened. 'I've told her, though, nothing too dramatic.'

Next to her, Cleo did a half-eye-roll, which was her way of being affectionate.

I ordered myself a coffee – no cake, an economy that I pretended was diet-related – and resigned myself to hearing about Cleo's plans for Wes's eighth birthday party in a few weeks. Cleo prided herself on being a mother who could deliver top-quality parenting both on Instagram and in real life, and throwing memorable birthday parties for her three sons was a big deal. Over the years Orson, Alfie and Wes had seen many church halls decorated to look like indoor fairgrounds, as well as bowling alleys, indoor pirate ships, Build-a-Bear workshops, three Super Soaker parties (too popular in the end), the make-your-own-pizza party, laser tag, treasure hunts ... Cleo's parties were so successful that most years there were more uninvited siblings, and often parents, trying to gatecrash than there were guests.

This year, Wes had requested a trampoline extravaganza. Mum, Dad and I were expected to act as marshals, of course, as Cleo 'wouldn't trust Elliot to turn up on time, let alone stop a child from bouncing themselves into A&E'.

Personally, I thought this was unfair. I'd known Elliot Ryeland since I was eleven and as far as I knew, he'd never been involved in a trampoline injury. He'd driven his car into the cricket pavilion once, but that was over twenty years ago now and it had been for a dare. It was probably the last reckless thing he'd done.

'How are things with you, Robyn?' Mum asked me quickly, before Cleo could move on to Elliot's latest parental shortcomings.

'Good, thanks!'

'Recovered after your week of cleaning?'

'Two days,' Cleo corrected her.

I paused, cup halfway to my lips. *That* was the headline, not the fact that I'd mucked in and helped her out? Cheers.

'I've been doing some job applications this morning,' I said, with dignity. 'A friend of mine's put me in touch with some contacts, so hopefully I'll find something soon.'

'Which friend?' asked Cleo. 'Do I know her?'

'Him,' I said. 'And maybe? Mitch is a property developer.'

Cleo adopted an interrogative expression, but I never found out whether she had a query about Mitch's maleness or his property developing because Mum, ever alert to sibling conflict, interrupted.

'I'm sure something will turn up soon,' she said, 'but in the meantime, isn't it great that you can help Cleo out? What's she got lined up for you next week?'

'Nothing. Why would she?'

Mum glanced at Cleo. 'Weren't you just telling me that you're still down five cleaners?'

'Yes, but it's not like we're about to—'

'If you're not busy with interviews, it would help Cleo out,' said Mum. 'Wouldn't it, Cleo?'

Reluctantly, Cleo nodded. I think there might have been a kick under the table, I couldn't be sure.

'I don't think it's a great idea, Mum,' I said. 'I need to focus on finding another job in the property sector.'

'But I'd have thought this would be perfect for that!'

'How?'

'You're in people's houses, aren't you? Getting design ideas, seeing how people live, what sort of areas are coming up or going down. Isn't that useful for you?'

'Not really.'

Although she did have a point, sort of. While I was trying to restore the Armstrongs' kitchen-diner into something fit for human habitation, I'd had an idea for a home-staging business, helping clients to prepare their houses for sale. Boxes, basically. Buy a load of storage boxes, advise them what to throw out and rearrange what was left. Mum was a genius at it, and I'd picked up a few tips here and there.

But, I fully intended to get some interviews for proper jobs. I hadn't been lying when I'd told Mum I needed to keep my brain in estate agent mode: the same day, it had randomly occurred to me how nice it was not to have to answer the phone once *and* be able to wear trainers. I needed to find a job fast, before I lost the always-tenuous grip I had on my personal grooming.

'You're lucky that you have a sister who can give you flexible work at the drop of a hat,' Mum reminded me. 'What other employer's going to let you leave work early for an interview?'

Cleo had been checking her phone, but snapped back to attention. '*If* she gets some interviews, *then* she can ask me for the time off, like everyone else!'

'Mum ...'

'Oh, for god's sake.' Cleo stood up. 'Elliot doesn't even know what to get his own son for his eighth birthday. I've got to call him. If that waitress ever comes near us again, can you order me another coffee? Almond milk, treble shot.'

Mum waited until Cleo was safely ranting on the pavement, then gazed at me with the full force of her Guilt Trip Face. She didn't even need to speak.

'Don't give me that look!' I moaned.

'Oh, Robyn. Poor Cleo's having an absolute nightmare. She's short-staffed, and yesterday two more cleaners walked out on her to start their own company, and they've poached some of her best clients!'

'She never said anything about that.'

'Well, she wouldn't.' Mum sighed. 'Especially with this awards ceremony coming up. She doesn't want to look as if she's not on top of things.'

Even though I wished Cleo had confided in me, I still felt aggrieved on her behalf. Had the splitters been there at the Margaret Jennings' house clean? Did Jim know? I could picture his appalled face. He'd have them court-martialled.

'It's times like these that we have to pull together,' Mum continued. 'She won't admit it but she needs you. She needs *us*. You know she hates asking for help, and I worry that she doesn't tell us what's going on half the time. Maybe ...' She hesitated. 'Maybe she'd talk to you, Robyn? If you two were cleaning together?'

I stirred my coffee. As usual Mum had hit on my weak spot: Cleo hadn't needed me since … well, whenever her last English essay had been. And I did want to help her. I didn't even mind hearing more about Elliot, if it would make her feel better. I think she imagined we judged her for the relationship breakdown. We didn't. How could we?

'OK,' I conceded. 'I suppose I could do another week. But I *am* applying for other jobs.'

'Good girl.' Mum squeezed my hand. 'I'm sure you'll get a new job soon. Who wouldn't want you working for them?'

I managed a smile. Mission accomplished, Mum excused herself to go to the loo, and when she was a safe distance away, I signalled for the bill.

Cleo and I always treated Mum if we went out for meals. The older we got, the more we realised money had been tight when we were growing up: with the two of us so close in age, and no family nearby, there were no hand-me-downs or free babysitters. Mum dealt with our constant pestering for new clothes, school trips and so on by insisting she wasn't interested in clothes or make-up. Shamefully, it had taken me until I was about twenty-two to realise this was total bollocks. Mum *loved* shoes. And make-up. And interiors. She had an Instagram account just for following dramatic hair restyles. Once Cleo and I were earning our own money, we did what we could to make up for those mascara and shoe-less years, although it wasn't always easy to get to the bill before Mum did.

The waitress appeared at the same time as Cleo; Cleo had read the situation from across the room and was already rummaging in her handbag for her purse as she slalomed round the tables in an athletic effort to reach the bill before me.

Irresponsible Adult

'No, my turn, I'll get this.' I'd checked my current account before I came out, and I had enough, just. 'Thanks,' I said to the waitress, touching my debit card against the reader, thwarting Cleo at the final second, 'that was lovely.'

'Thank you!' We exchanged smiles and waited for the transaction to go through.

It didn't.

My smile stuck a little. The machine was taking a long time.

The waitress waved in the direction of the medieval church pillars. 'Sorry, it does this sometimes. It's the stone – seems to block the Wi-Fi.'

'Here, why don't I just—?' Cleo leaned over with her card, but I karate-blocked her arm.

'No!' I glanced towards the loos. No sign of Mum.

'I'll try it again,' said the waitress.

We stared at the machine and waited.

My stomach tightened. I was sure there was enough money in there: there were no bills due, and I'd cancelled everything I could. No Netflix, Spotify, gym membership – I was living the life of a Tudor nun.

The machine finally whirred and I breathed out. It was just in time: Mum was making her way back around the tables. When she saw the waitress next to us, she wagged her finger mock-sternly, but her eyes were happy and I felt a warm glow of generous adulthood.

I was also glad to have demonstrated to Cleo that I wasn't totally destitute.

'You shouldn't have,' said Mum, slipping back into her seat. 'Let me leave the tip, at least.'

'*I'll* leave the tip,' insisted Cleo.

'You can leave the tip,' I said, graciously.

'Sorry,' said the waitress, 'but this didn't go through.' She offered me the receipt; it said Transaction Cancelled. 'But it sometimes needs a PIN. For security?' she added, seeing my face freeze.

Mum and Cleo both started to speak but I stopped them.

'No!' I raised a hand. 'It's probably a security thing, let me put my PIN in.'

My fingers were trembling as I typed the numbers because I knew it probably *wasn't* a security thing. I knew what it was: the magazine subscription I'd meant to cancel in the Big Purge, but hadn't been able to find the login for. I'll do it in the morning, I'd thought, mourning the other comforts that I'd just sacrificed. It couldn't have been more than forty quid but that was enough to tip me over into public card shaming.

To add insult to injury, I hadn't even read most of the back issues. They were in a bag in my new flat, unopened. I kept meaning to have an afternoon of magazine indulgence, after which my career, my wardrobe, my skincare routine, my wellness and my gut brain (?) would be completely sorted, but somehow I never had. It was just too overwhelming.

Cleo was staring at me with what looked a lot like pity mixed with curiosity and a dash of triumph.

And meanwhile Mum had trumped us both by whisking out her purse.

'Don't!' said Mum, as I tried to apologise and Cleo tried to shove tenners at her. 'I was going to treat you anyway. I wanted to cheer you up!'

Cheer me up? Until recently I was a successful property expert who owned her own flat and was (outwardly, anyway) on top of things. Now I was an Internet laughing stock whose mother needed to 'cheer her up' and whose big sister was bailing her out by letting her scrub showers. And not even scrubbing them that well, according to Jim.

People on other tables were turning to see what the commotion was.

'I'll pay you back,' I muttered, hot with embarrassment. 'I just need to transfer some money … um, the bank …'

'Robyn.' Mum's voice was gentle. 'Are you sure everything's …?'

'Yes!' I insisted. 'Yes, everything is fine. Fine.' I turned to Cleo. Better to take the bull by the horns, grasp the nettle, etc. 'So, would you like me to do another week's work?' I asked with as much dignity as I could muster.

Cleo, the cow, took a couple of seconds to respond, in which I could happily have throttled her.

'I'll see you on Monday,' she said.

Mum beamed. So one of us was happy, at least.

On Monday morning, Jim picked me up for work from the corner of Worcester Road and Wye Street, outside Molly's Bakehouse, one of the few coffee shops in town where I wasn't a regular.

(I had been such a familiar face in Hoffi Coffi that they didn't even bother to ask me want I wanted; they just shouted, 'Hi, Robyn!' and started making a double shot oat latte, as if we were in *Friends*. Same in Espresso Bongo, opposite the office. When I'd gone through my bank statements it had literally sickened me to see how much I'd spent on hot milk, just to feel part of a gang.)

I suggested Jim picked me up there because – I know it's snobby, shoot me – I didn't want the neighbours seeing a Taylor Maid van pulling up and me getting in. I'd managed to keep myself to myself since I'd moved, and that sort of key detail would be on the local curtain-twitching spread-sheet before you could say Mr Sheen.

For that reason, I'd also decided to go to work in jeans and a T-shirt, and change into the red overalls when I got to the first job. Nothing wrong with being a cleaner but, as I'd told Mum, I needed to keep myself in a property-developing state of mind. To that end, my nails were now short, but still a glossy mulberry. On Sunday night, I'd sent my CV to both LinkedIn contacts Mitch had introduced me to and the four hours' fussing over the exact wording of the cover letter – charming but professional, concise but comprehen-sive – had given me time to do a great home manicure.

It was overcast, and my rumbling stomach felt as gloomy as the grey sky: I'd had to skip breakfast in the usual frantic rush to leave on time. Although my alarm went off at seven, I inevitably hit snooze once or twice (or thrice), and before I knew it, I was late. I leaned against the blue striped wall of the bakery and braced myself not to go in. The smell of the coffee and the baking croissants floating out of the door was so delicious that you could almost see it, ribbons of milky sweetness and toasted butter rippling out into the morning air. I stared up the road, looking for the Taylor Maid van while trying to inhale deeply enough to fool my brain into thinking I'd polished off a double latte and a pain au chocolat.

I wondered if Jim would bother to hide his annoyance that he'd been allocated me as a partner again. I'd made the point to Cleo, when she phoned me with my rota details.

'He clearly prefers working alone. Could I maybe pair up with someone more … fun?' I suggested. I'd seen the other teams at Margaret Jennings' house. Some of them looked as if they were even having a laugh.

'No,' Cleo had said. 'And don't ask me again, the rota is a nightmare.'

Spotting the Taylor Maid van approaching, I walked down the road so Jim didn't pull up right outside the bakery – again, not sure who might be in there. He leaned over and opened the door for me.

'Thanks,' I said, sliding in.

Unlike me, Jim was already in his overalls, pressed and smelling of Persil. I wondered if he'd ironed his own overalls. He suited the uniform; again, unlike me, he made it look clinical, rather than penitential. A clean white T-shirt peeped out underneath the first button, and his short dark hair was damp. He had that 'just been to the gym!' glow about him.

'You look fresh!' I said. 'Been to the gym?'

'Six a.m. spin class,' he replied. 'Gets the blood flowing.'

I stared at my thighs, relative strangers to a spin bike despite five years' direct-debited membership. Another reminder of money I'd forked out for the pleasure of imagining myself 'on a health journey' while never actually plucking up the courage to book an induction.

Five years. How many thousand pounds was that, exactly?

'Grabbing some breakfast?' Jim checked his mirrors before indicating and pulling away.

'No,' I said, then said, 'Yes,' because why else would I be asking him to pick me up from outside a bakery?

He glanced at me quizzically. 'Which?'

I decided on yes.

'What did you have?'

I shot him a side glance, but he was intent on the road ahead, maintaining a safe distance from the car in front.

'A croissant and a double latte,' I said, because that's what I used to have. In the Old Days when I happily splashed the best part of a tenner before I even got to work.

I don't know why I lied. I think my brain just wanted to be someone else.

'You must have eaten it very quickly.'

I felt my cheeks redden. 'What is this, Twenty Questions?'

'Indigestion is no way to start the day.'

'Where are we going this morning?' I asked, to change the subject.

'We've got a regular clean at Pembroke Terrace, followed by a quick hour at Macklin Street. Then forty-five minutes for lunch. Then this afternoon we've got two hours at the Armstrongs'.'

'Again? We were only there on Friday.'

'They have a twice-a-week booking.' A sidelong look. 'I did tell you that last week.'

I ignored the faint reprimand. 'How much mess can they make in two days?'

Messy didn't cover it. I reckoned they were only a few scribbles on the wall short of turning that lovely house into a kindergarten. It pained me, knowing how much repainting they'd have to do if they ever came to sell.

'All the details are on the sheet.'

He indicated towards the footwell, where there was a clipboard with several laminated cards attached. Cleo had paperclipped some notes to the top: *Check medication for Ivor, 30 min walk: Goldie and Badger; avoid park or roads with buses/cats.*

'Goldie and Badger?'

'Dogs. Ivor is a corgi. He has arthritis.'

'We're vet nurses now?' I asked.

'We do whatever needs doing,' said Jim, and pulled up outside 12 Pembroke Terrace.

According to the laminated sheet, 12 Pembroke Terrace belonged to Bill and Helena Corrigan and it required a whole raft of cleaning, from floor-mopping to dusting of light fittings to corgi medication. Everything was listed in room-by-room sections with a checkbox next to it. The laminated card was, I discovered, for me.

'Tick each task off as you go.' Jim passed me a pen. 'It's wipe clean. Make sure you do everything in each section before you move onto the next.'

I stared at him. For some reason I found the basic instruction of it weirdly insulting. First, I'd done this for two days already, and second, how hard was cleaning? 'Seriously?'

He stared back. 'Seriously.'

I didn't reply. I also refused to be the first to break the staring deadlock.

'Are you saying you don't think I know that you're supposed to …' I glanced down at the endless list of microtasks. '… *empty dishwasher* in a kitchen?'

He held up a hand. 'Don't take it personally. We give these sheets to all new starters, so you can get into a rhythm.'

I was still reading, outraged. '... or that I should dust from left to right?'

'Yes! It's so nothing gets missed.'

'But *left to right*? I didn't realise there were *rules*! What happens if I dust right to left? The world spins in the opposite direction for ten minutes?'

He sighed. 'Look. I've been watching you clean and it's ...' Jim seemed temporarily lost for words.

'It's what?'

'It's not normal.'

We were in the kitchen – where else? – of the Corrigans' house, being observed by their chunky corgi, Ivor, from the sofa. Ivor was basically a custard slice in dog form, and he took great delight in flipping up his water bowl. He'd done it twice already, just for the LOLs. And now he was giving us almost human levels of side eye.

'What do you mean by that?' I demanded.

'You've got absolutely no system. I was watching you mop the floor at the Armstrongs'. You were all ...' He mimed someone jerking a mop around as if chasing a rat. 'Like you were curling, not cleaning. Curling as in the Scottish ice sport, not ...'

'I know what *curling* is,' I interrupted. 'I'm not stupid. You don't have to explain everything.'

'It's just better if you learn to do it methodically.'

'Does it matter how I do it, as long as the floor's clean?'

'Yes, it matters!' Jim looked pained. 'Otherwise the floor ends up swirly. There are lines to help you! Squares! Just follow the tiles! Don't just swish the mop around and hope for the best – use the lines and do it properly. Have a bit of pride in your work, for god's sake. *Focus*.'

I flinched. It hadn't occurred to me that someone would actually pick me up on being bad at this job. It was one thing telling my mum I was a terrible cleaner; it was another thing being told by someone else that I wasn't coming up to scratch.

'I hadn't realised I was *annoying* you so much with my erratic mopping,' I said huffily.

'You're not annoying, you're just making life so much harder for yourself. And for me,' he added.

'For you?'

'Well, I couldn't leave the Armstrongs' kitchen looking like someone had skidded round it, could I?'

I stared at him in disbelief. 'Was that what you were doing when you said you were checking the locks? Re-mopping the floor?'

'Yes.'

'I spent half an hour on that! There was nothing wrong with it!'

'You honestly think that?'

'Yes! I do! It was fine!'

'Fine isn't good enough!' He stopped and ran a hand through his hair, as if controlling his temper with some effort. 'We're paid to leave the house spotless, not do the sort of haphazard bodge job clients can do themselves. It might be fine at home, but you're not at home. You need to lift your standards for work.'

There was a sharp edge to Jim's voice, and his criticism stung. Who did he think he was? We were both cleaners.

I placed the laminated card on the kitchen counter, ostentatiously ticked 'unload dishwasher' – and started emptying the Corrigans' dishwasher.

Ivor regarded me from the sofa, his soft mouth curled in apparent amusement. I couldn't believe I was trying not to meet the eye of a dog, but it seemed I was.

We worked through the rest of the day with An Atmosphere. Jim was cordial, but I couldn't shake my irritation, my feelings of inadequacy not helped by the fact that I was wearing a red jumpsuit with a cartoon of my big sister on the breast pocket.

This mood, I knew from bitter experience, could go two ways; either I slumped into a sulky, self-sabotaging spiral, or martyrdom drove me to productive heights of effort. Fortunately for Jim the latter kicked in and we exercised Goldie and Badger, of 20 Macklin Street, so efficiently that they ran and hid in their baskets after their seething, sniff-free power-walk around the block. I spent the whole day planning how I'd tell Cleo and Jim that I was leaving at the end of the week, possibly by writing SOD OFF in bleach on Jim's front lawn, then I worked my way through the bathroom list at the Armstrongs' to the absolute letter. The tiles sparkled. I got toothpaste out of cracks I doubt they'd even noticed it had got into. I barely had time to register the fact that they had a bicycle pump and a bottle of gin in their undersink cabinet. (Why? Why?)

At the end of the day, Jim informed me I'd done a great job but I had to pretend I'd done nothing I wouldn't have done otherwise. He dropped me outside Molly's Bakehouse with a terse goodbye and I couldn't even go inside to drown my sorrows in doughnuts because I hadn't been paid.

If I lasted the whole week it would be a miracle – but on the plus side, I had never felt more motivated to find another job.

8

The next day was Tuesday and, as Jim reminded me when I got in the van, we kicked off with an hour at Terry's.

'I see you've made it through the audition, Robyn!' he observed when we arrived.

'Doesn't everyone?' I asked.

'No, he's got high standards!' Terry followed me and Jim down the hall. He was looking dapper, in a shirt and tie. 'They don't call him the captain for nothing.'

'They don't call me the captain,' said Jim.

Terry winked at me. He had a very retro wink, the sort you only saw in 1970s sitcom reruns. I resisted the temptation to wink back, but it was hard. I was grateful, though, for his attempts to lighten the mood.

Jim handed me another of his wipe-clean cards. 'Kitchen, if you don't mind, Robyn. I'll do the bedroom and bathroom, and we'll finish in the sitting room.'

'Yes, sir!' said Terry, with a mock salute. 'I'll supervise in the kitchen. You can start by making me a cup of tea,' he added under his breath.

Terry had saved up several days' worth of conversation which he directed at me like a verbal water cannon while

I scrubbed baked beans off his hob. His oldest grandson had just had another baby, and that segued naturally onto him telling me about his seven grandchildren, and their complex family arrangements. Two of his sons had children with seven different mothers – it was like one of those riddles about getting foxes and chickens over the river in a rowing boat, but with wedding cake – and one of his daughters had married one of her brother's ex's ex. ('The black sheep, bless 'er.')

I did my best to keep up, but in the end Terry offered to draw me a diagram on the back of a French Fancies box, for which I was grateful. It was an impressive sight, and went across onto the front.

'How about you?' he asked, taking a welcome breather to finish his tea. 'You got a black sheep in your family?'

'Me,' I said.

'Nah! Can't believe that!'

'To be honest, there aren't enough of us to have one. Dad's family are totally normal and Mum only has her dad left on her side. They're not in contact.' I checked Jim wasn't looking, and took the Hobnob Terry was offering while I racked my brains for some – any – gossip. 'My sister's got a tattoo our mum doesn't know about. Does that count?'

'Nah, there's always some scandal if you look hard enough.' He winked. 'You need to dig around the family tree a bit. Ask your mum after she's had a sherry at Christmas!'

'I'd have a job, she's strictly tea and coffee only.'

'Ah! Now my Gill was the same – never touched a drop after that big night at the Ally Pally.' Terry nodded meaningfully. 'Maybe that's your story there!'

I *think* he was implying that Mum's abstinence was a result of a Pimms too many at a staff summer party, but Terry had unwittingly touched on something I'd been thinking about lately.

I'd recently had a routine check-up at the doctor's, and he'd asked me about any inherited medical issues – I had no idea. Dad had trained me and Cleo out of asking questions about Mum's family, but we were getting to an age where we might actually need to know stuff. I mean, *was* there a reason she didn't drink? Had anyone had cancer? Or cataracts? Or depression? Or a million other conditions that might suddenly rear their ugly genetic heads?

We were very familiar with the varicose veins and short-sightedness that were Dad's gift to the family. That was something to look forward to.

I heard a loud cough from the sitting room, and Terry wagged his finger.

'Get polishing, private!' he said.

And I did, but now my mind was half elsewhere, wondering what was worse, upsetting Mum or missing out on some crucial information about my own biology. And whether Cleo had ever managed to find a way to ask.

Jim didn't acknowledge the sparkling kitchen, not even when I finished it with time over to hoover the hallway. I reckoned I'd done a much better job than last time, but he said nothing, and I sat and stewed.

Jim's driving ground on my nerves. He checked his mirrors as if there was an examiner in the back seat, and he *slowed down* as we approached green traffic lights. At one point, we were being tailgated by a tractor.

Eventually, I snapped. 'I know you think I was talking too much at Terry's but I was cleaning at the same time.'

Jim shook his head, as if he'd been miles away. 'What? No, I wasn't thinking that.'

'I ticked everything off.' I brandished the card at him. A full line of ticks. 'See?'

'Well done. Great.'

'Are you being sarky? I can't tell.'

'No. Sarcasm's counterproductive, I find.'

I stared out of the window at a new development was going up where the old scout hut had been on Duck Pond Green. I wondered if Mitch was involved.

Discreetly I removed my phone from my overalls to check if he'd texted while we'd been at Terry's. He hadn't. I put my phone back in my pocket. Jim didn't say anything but I knew he'd noticed.

'Anyway, I think Terry benefits from the chat as much as the cleaning.' I pictured how Terry's wrinkled face lit up while he was rattling on about his youth, his adventures in the town. Did he have other visitors? Did he get out much? 'Must make a change when you live alone, having someone to tell your stories to. Someone to listen.'

'Tell that to your predecessor. She begged to be taken off his rota before she said something she regretted.'

'Well, I enjoy his stories,' I said, stoutly. 'He's led a very interesting life.'

'Good. Did he ever tell you who the soap star was?'

'Were you listening to our conversation?'

'Hard not to. Well?'

'No,' I said. 'He's making me guess. Two guesses per visit.'

Jim glanced across at me. Our eyes met and, although he didn't say anything, I knew what he was thinking: that it was a ruse to keep me chatting.

I didn't want to acknowledge that, so I said, 'Where are we going next?'

'St Anselm's.' Jim tapped his nose. 'Celebrity client! No clues but ... Ready, Steady, Clean!'

My heart sank. I knew exactly where we were going, and whose house it was.

My secret fear when I started cleaning for Cleo was about to come true.

It was inevitable, given the number of houses I'd sold and the amount of work I'd put Cleo's way, that eventually I'd end up scrubbing a sink belonging to an erstwhile client.

Not that they'd necessarily recognise me in my new persona, of course. I'd decided quickly that there was no point wasting contact lenses on mucking out messy houses (or on Jim), so I wore my glasses to work, and my glasses were *thick*. I'd abandoned my half-hour morning blow-dry in favour of maximum horizontal recovery time, and consequently, in just eight short days, I already looked like the 'before' photo in a very dramatic makeover.

It hadn't mattered what I looked like when I was degreasing the Armstrongs' kitchen or making a third cup of tea for Terry, but when Jim turned the van down a familiar tree-lined drive, towards a familiar stately property, now divided into eight luxury apartments, I suddenly felt concious of every unwashed hair on my head.

This was St Anselm's. And this was where Adam Doherty, the closest thing Longhampton had to a celebrity, lived, in the stunning garden apartment I'd sold him only six months previously. Casually, I checked today's laminated lists and yup, it was the garden apartment we were cleaning, for Mr A.C. Doherty ('Eco products, water plants, focus on the kitchen').

'Nice place, isn't it?' said Jim as we approached the house, and I nodded dumbly.

Adam Doherty was a farmer's son turned local fastfood entrepreneur who had spent much of lockdown posting on social media about his organic burgers, which he filmed himself cooking then delivering on a tractor. Somehow (well, not *somehow*: he did it in very short shorts and he was ripped) BBQAdam had exploded, netting him various sponsorship deals which he'd splashed on this flat and a new, bigger restaurant which he was currently away opening in Bristol.

Adam had invested his cash wisely, I thought, as we drew up outside. Its pointed Gothic windows gleamed in the morning sunlight, while varicoloured ivy crept along the sandstone, around the arched entrance and all the way up to the clock tower with the cockerel weathervane. Mitch and his team had done a stunning job on the conversion. Every apartment had sold for over the asking price, and I'd even had people asking to be put on a waiting list if a sale fell through.

And soon this will be me, I reminded myself. Lark Manor would be even smarter and more desirable than this. It gave me a warm Christmas Eve feeling inside.

'I know what you're thinking,' said Jim, cutting through my giddy imaginings.

'Do you?'

'You're wondering how much these apartments go for.'

I squinted at him. 'Why do you say that?'

'Because you always make some comment about this being a popular street, or that being a very trendy colour.'

'On trend. Not *trendy*.'

Jim ignored me. He counted off on his fingers. 'Or that house needing renovating or how much more saleable this place would be with a wet room.'

I didn't appreciate the expression he was pulling. Jim made it sound mercenary, though, not the professional insight that it actually was.

'I wasn't thinking that.' I lifted my chin. 'I was thinking … What an amazing place this must have been to go to school. Like Hogwarts.'

'It wasn't a school, it was a hotel.'

'No, it was a school first. Then a hospital during the Second World War. There was a bomb shelter in the gardens.'

Jim's pretend surprise turned to genuine surprise, and I realised normal people probably didn't know a building's CV in the sort of detail the agent who'd marketed it would.

'You didn't know that?' I shook my head, feigning the sort of 'surprise' Jim cast my way when I failed to recognise limescale. 'Wow. How long have you lived round here?'

'Two years,' said Jim. 'But I wasn't aware you had to take some kind of citizenship test.'

'Most big houses were requisitioned as hospitals during one war or another,' I said. 'Didn't you watch *Downton Abbey*?'

'Absolutely not. Anyway, just so you know, the client we're cleaning for today is a celebrity chef,' he went on. 'I don't think Mr Doherty's here, but just in case he is, no gawping, OK? And no taking photos of his flat to send to your mates.'

'Why would I gawp?' I followed him round to the back of the van to haul the green bucket of eco-friendly cleaning products out of the back. 'He's been on *Saturday Kitchen once*. He's hardly Gordon Ramsay.'

What Jim didn't know was that I'd met Mr Doherty on three separate occasions – to show him round the apartment, to discuss his offer and then to hand over the keys with the usual bottle of moderately priced champagne. He'd also patted my bum on occasion two. Just the once, though. Annoyingly I couldn't tell Jim that, on account of wanting to look discreet, but then I doubted he'd appreciate decent gossip anyway.

'I'm just saying,' said Jim. 'It's been a problem in the past.'

'Gawping?' I followed him up the stone stairs, banging the corrugated hose of the vacuum cleaner deliberately because I knew it annoyed him.

'Discretion. It's the main reason we have to let people go. You have to see everything and nothing in this business.'

We? Wasn't Cleo the one who did the hiring and firing? If he was a manager, maybe Cleo was making him work six months on the shop floor to learn the ropes. Ah. That would make a lot of sense.

'I have no interest in Adam Doherty,' I said confidently. 'Just his filthy cupboards.' But I checked my reflection in the age-spotted, salvage-sourced mirror over the fireplace in the entrance hall nonetheless.

There was no sign of BBQAdam when Jim let us in through the modern glass door to his apartment, and I was disappointed to see that his furniture choices hadn't lived up to the potential of the space.

Two bedrooms, two bathrooms, mezzanine study, and the star of the show: an open-plan kitchen-diner-sitting-room space with original herringbone parquet, double row of brass lampshades suspended from the vaulted ceiling and full-height windows giving a view out to the lawn, rolling down to the topiary shapes at the far end. Perfect for someone who loved cooking and entertaining, and filming themselves while doing so.

Adam hadn't exactly overwhelmed the space with furniture, and what furniture there was seemed to have been ordered in a job lot from World of Leather. There were two huge leather sofas, two full-size cowhide rugs and a couple of leather recliners, facing a television so big it might have come from a sports bar. I suppose it might have been a stylistic tribute to his farming heritage.

'Change of plan today.' Jim handed me the bathroom bucket. 'I'm going to do the kitchen, you can do the bathrooms.'

'Wow, is this a promotion?'

'No, the client's a chef. The kitchen's got to be spotless.'

How rude. 'And you think I can't get it spotless?'

Jim didn't dignify that with a response. He nodded at the bucket. 'I've put the bathroom checklist in there. Do everything in that exact order, top to bottom. Do you want me to show you how to use the Kärcher?'

'The shower hoover? I think I can work it out,' I said.

'Well, be careful with it, the tiles in the bathroom were extremely expensive.' Jim stared at the floor-to-ceiling units and vast expanse of marble and chrome and rolled his shoulders, like a man facing the foothills of Mount Everest. I'd say he was excited at the challenge of cleaning the kitchen of a professional. How totally tragic. 'We've got two hours. Let's go.'

I remembered Adam's bathroom from the viewings. They were the same throughout the development: French navy wet rooms with brass hardware, shower heads the size of a Le Creuset casserole, vast glass screens with flipper doors for easy access. Plants, plants, plants as far as the eye could see.

The interior designer had included wall brackets for trailing ivies and pothos to achieve that Instagram jungle look; Adam had kept the plants but most of them were on their last legs, so – after a quick peek in Adam's bathroom cabinet (Creed, very nice, but also Lynx Africa) – I put what I could fit in the sink to soak while I tackled the shower.

Jim's checklist was predictably forensic. I rarely cleaned my own bathroom, so I was grateful to have something to work down: for a start, it wouldn't have occurred to me to dust the extractor fan. It took me a while to identify it. But I got cracking: dusting, then wiping, then rinsing, then spraying everything in sight with the special eco-cleaning stuff.

From the kitchen, I could hear Jim's giant toothbrush going at the big range cooker – which looked unused to me, but what did I know? – then something caught my ear. Was he *singing*? I paused. Yes, he was. He was singing to himself, quietly, then whistling the guitar parts. Maybe he thought I had AirPods in and couldn't hear him.

Jim had a nice voice, bit wobbly in places, but he knew all the words. He was singing ... I strained my ears. *Guide me, O Thou Great Redeemer?* Really?

I turned to the shower, feeling like an eavesdropper. Although I'd extolled the virtues of the showers on viewings, I hadn't demonstrated them, and it was only when I went to rinse the tiles with the hand attachment that I realised I hadn't the first idea how they worked. There were three different levers, two different brass taps, every one blank – it was more like the workings of a steam train than a shower.

I turned to shout for Jim's assistance, then immediately thought better of it. No. I'd said I could do bathrooms. I'd do the bathroom.

So I started at the top and turned a tiny brass ship's wheel – nothing happened.

OK. I tried the next ship's wheel down, first one way, then the other. Nothing.

Recklessly I threw a lever to the left and a bucketload of freezing cold water was dumped straight onto my head.

I yelled out in shock – it was *freezing* – and flung the lever the other way, which stopped the water raining down on me for a second, only to divert the flow from the overhead to the handheld shower – which was pointing at my legs. A powerful jet of ice-cold water drenched my lower half and I shrieked again, while the force of the water pressure ('Really excellent, as good as you'd get in a five star hotel') sent the shower head skidding and spinning around the enclosure like a fire hose, efficiently saturating the rest of my overalls and misting up my glasses.

I grappled with the bucking shower head as best I could but whatever I'd done had set the shower to full force and I couldn't get a grip on it. Water was bouncing off the toilet and sink now, slicking down the walls, and in an effort to stop the bathroom flooding I reached out and grabbed for the biggest shower control, twisting it as hard as I could.

It came off in my hands. Literally. In one piece.

I stared at it in horror for one nanosecond as a horizontal jet of cold water shot out from the middle of the brass pipes with the force of a donkey kick straight into my chest. (That would be the enhanced water-pressure pump.) I stumbled backwards, slipped on my own cleaning sponge, and, reaching out for something to stop me falling, dragged the huge designer shower rack off the wall.

The sound of the clattering metal crashing against the tiles was only just louder than my own embarrassing screech of shock. My coccyx slammed against the shower tray so hard that my teeth felt loose in my head.

I think I might have concussed myself for a moment. Everything seemed to be underwater, thick and slow. And cold. Really cold.

'Robyn? Robyn? Did you break something?'

I heard Jim long before I saw him, since my glasses were now lost in the flood and my wet hair was plastered over my eyes.

He was going to go mad, I thought, and for a second I considered trying to act my way out of it, but with what excuse? And anyway, it was too late. Jim burst in with a startled, 'Oh my god!'

'I didn't do anything!' I wailed. Water was blasting out of the broken shower, hitting the tiles above my head and soaking me to the skin. I struggled to my knees just in time to see the shelf of plants behind Jim's head, now twice as heavy with a full load of cold water in the pots, start to pull away from the wall.

'Jim!' I yelled, as the shelf tilted and the plant pots slid.

He frowned – fair enough, I hadn't been very specific – and I gestured wildly over his shoulder. 'The shelf!'

It lurched to one side and I thought it was going to crash right onto his shoulder, but somehow, Jim spun and at the same time shoved the whole thing back against the wall with one hand, even managing to catch the mini cactus on the end as it slid off with his spare hand.

It was an impressive split-second reaction.

I fumbled around for my glasses, which thankfully I hadn't sat on, and the carnage around me came back into focus.

I vaguely registered the broken shower basket and the cracked bottles leaking expensive gels across the marble tiles, but it was hard not to stare at Jim, who was holding up the plant shelf as if it weighed nothing; I knew it must weigh a ton, because his sleeves were rolled up to the elbow for oven-cleaning purposes and I could see his bicep flexing under the strain. He didn't seem to notice, though.

'Are you OK?' He twisted round, trying to balance the shelf while assessing me for head injuries from a distance of five metres. 'Can you wiggle your toes and fingers?'

I dragged my attention back to my own predicament. 'Um, yes. I think so.'

'Nothing broken?' He seemed more concerned about any damage to me than the bathroom.

'Only the shower.'

'The shower?' he said, deadpan. 'Are you sure?'

'Yes!' I squawked, then realised he was joking. What a time for him to reveal a sense of humour.

'Good. In that case, can you give me a hand with this?'

I struggled to my feet and squelched over to the door. He handed me the cactus and said, 'This might as well come off,' calmly pulling the other side of the shelf off the wall and setting it down by the door. Then he grabbed a hand towel, wrapped it round the gushing shower pipe and thankfully, finally, the water stopped.

We both breathed out and stared around the bathroom. But not for long. The towel was darkening as it soaked up the water.

'Where do you even start?' I wondered, half to myself. Could we just leave? Could we pretend it had been burgled before we got here?

'We need to turn off the water at the stopcock.' Jim gave the towel tourniquet a last squeeze. 'I'm guessing it'll be in the kitchen. You hold that towel, I'll go and find it.'

I had a flash of memory, from a viewing with an exceptionally fussy client who wanted to see everything, up to and including the electricity meter, stopcock, water meter and fuse box. 'The stopcock's in the hall.'

'No, it'll be in the kitchen.'

I was too worried about the state of the bathroom to remember what I wasn't supposed to know. The towel was soaked and the pipe was shaking, as if it might come off the wall in another minute. 'I'm telling you, it's in the tall cupboard in the hall!'

Jim gave me a funny look but left and, within a minute, the pressure abruptly lessened, then went to a dribble, then stopped.

I breathed out. So there had been a silver lining to that seemingly wasted afternoon showing the Farrells around the designated bin areas.

Warily, I unpeeled the towel from the pipe and attempted to fit the valve back on. I tried every angle, including a basic jam-it-on-and-hope, but to no avail. It had sheered clean off.

Jim reappeared, drying his hair with a tea towel. 'Stop-cock was in the hall. What a stupid place to put it. How did you know that?'

'Um, a friend lives in a similar conversion.' I proffered the valve. 'Are you any good at fixing showers?'

'No,' said Jim. 'You?'

'No.'

We surveyed the damage to the bathroom. It was definitely a wet room now: water had saturated every crevice. The plant shelf had left ugly gashes in the plaster where the Rawlplugs had pulled away; there was standing water on every surface; and the vanity mirror reflected our shocked faces back at us, infinitely and with brutal lighting.

I braced myself for Jim to start firing off questions about how I'd managed to destroy a luxury bathroom. I had no idea how much this would cost to repair. Would I have to pay for this to be fixed? *How* could I pay for it? Would Cleo strangle me if Adam Doherty sacked the agency because I'd wrecked his house? No, that wasn't a question. Cleo *would* strangle me.

Jim peered at me. 'Are you all right? You look … dazed.'

'I'm fine.' My head ached, but I had more pressing things to worry about, like how I could fix this before Cleo found out and removed my head altogether.

He held up a finger in front of my eyes. 'Can you follow my finger if I …'

I swatted his finger out of the way. This wasn't the time for health and safety. 'I'm fine, Jim. We need to clean up this mess.'

For a second he seemed impressed at my motivation, but then he said something that tipped me over the edge.

'I need to give Cleo a ring before we start,' he said, and reached for his phone.

'No!'

We both looked down and acknowledged that I'd grabbed his wrist to stop him dialling. Self-consciously, I released it. Jim wasn't the sort of person you touched casually. I wasn't sure it didn't constitute a minor assault. 'Do we have to?'

Jim gestured at the carnage. 'It's damage to a client's property. And you've had a workplace injury. Cleo needs to call us a plumber.'

'She's so busy!' I gabbled. 'We need to prioritise the client! Look, I know lots of plumbers, I bet I can get one round here quicker than Cleo can.' I whipped out my own phone and scrolled through the list of trades.

For obvious professional reasons I took *everyone's* details: plumbers and electricians were about as reliable at answering phones as I was, so you needed lots of numbers. I started with Gary Allison and, miraculously, he picked up on the third ring.

'Robyn?' said Gary warily. 'This isn't about that septic tank in Much Martley, is it? Because it was definitely a sheep in there, not—'

'Nooo!' I said, in my most charming voice. 'I don't suppose you could do me a *massive* favour, could you?'

Jim raised his eyebrow, but disappeared to find a mop and bucket.

I'd never worked harder in my life, whipped on as I was by the knowledge that we only had forty minutes to hide the evidence of my carelessness, and by the time we left, the bathroom was almost back to normal. Gary the plumber managed to patch up the shower but there was no disguising the broken shelf, and as we drove away a feeling of acid dread settled in my stomach.

Cleo was going to kill me.

I'd destroyed a client's confidence in Taylor Maid, as well as a luxury wet room. It would cost a fortune to repair, Adam Doherty would find out who'd done it – the woman who sold him the flat in the first place, ha ha! – and then that would probably appear on the town Facebook page too. Which would help my property job applications *no end*.

But mainly, Cleo was going to kill me.

I was too stressed to speak, and Jim's silence didn't help; I guessed he was mentally compiling the report.

I shifted in my seat. The spare overalls in the van were too small, and the sensation of my thighs straining against the polycotton added to my humiliation. All I wanted to do was to go home and hide under my duvet, pretending none of this had happened. But I couldn't. I was trapped in a Renault Kangoo with my jobsworth line manager and his laminated checklists.

Was there any way I could persuade Jim not to tell Cleo what I'd done? My imagination shuffled the possibilities like a deck of cards. Was there a builder I could bribe to go round and fix the shelf before Adam got back? I'd need to steal a key. Could I do that?

Jim stopped the car (safely, in a lay-by, hazard lights on) and turned to face me. He started doing the 'watch my finger' thing in front of my eyes again.

'What?' I demanded. 'Why have you stopped?'

'Are you absolutely sure you don't have concussion?' He frowned. 'We can drive to A&E, it's not a problem.'

'What? No!'

Jim retracted his finger but maintained his concerned expression. 'You haven't spoken for ten minutes. We haven't been working together long, but even I know that's not normal.'

'I'm worried about Adam Doherty's bathroom,' I said, huffily. 'Do you think we did a decent job of cleaning it up?'

He seemed mollified. 'I'd say so. Well done on getting that plumber out so quickly. Shame he couldn't fix it but at least it's not going to leak.'

'Do you think … he'll notice?' It was a stupid question.

'Who? Adam?' Jim looked at me as if I'd just asked if Santa was real. 'Yes, I think even Adam might notice there's a space on the wall where his plants were. Although it might take him a while to work out what's different.'

'Is there any way …?' My voice trailed off.

'What?'

I couldn't believe I was even saying this. 'Are you going to tell Cleo it was me who broke the shower?'

Jim stared at me, as if he couldn't quite work out how to respond to the question. I could feel the judgement radiating off him and I shrivelled inside.

'Why wouldn't I?' he asked.

I bit my lip. There were several very good reasons why not, but unfortunately, I didn't want to reveal any of them to Jim because they made me look pathetic.

The truth was, I had been trying to pretend this entire unfortunate period in my life wasn't happening. I wanted to slither through it without leaving a mark, invisible in other people's houses, before emerging again as a re-employed estate agent. This disaster made it real. It would mean a showdown with Cleo, more evidence that I couldn't do something as simple as cleaning without screwing up, not to mention me damaging her business just before the big awards do.

Shame was knotting my innards. Everywhere I turned, I felt like a failure, with a bollocking waiting for me on all sides.

Jim was waiting for an answer. He reminded me of those teachers at primary school who were happy to sit 'for as long as it took' to get an apology. Maybe he *was* a head teacher. A disgraced head teacher, forced out of the profession for being too head teacherly?

I decided to go for the least embarrassing truth.

'I'm worried that Cleo will make me pay for the damage,' I said. 'I don't have ...' How could I phrase it so he wouldn't think less of me? (Why did I even *care* if Jim thought less of me?) 'I'm between jobs right now.'

'Hence the cleaning?' He said it as if it only confirmed what he'd already guessed.

I nodded, reluctantly.

I sensed Jim's satisfaction that he'd dragged an honest response from me. 'Well, I can set your mind at rest right there,' he said. 'It was accidental breakage. It'll be covered by insurance.'

Unfortunately, there was no insurance against your big sister.

'And in any case, didn't the plumber say the unit was faulty?' he went on. 'I don't think you *deliberately* meant to rip the shower off the wall ...'

'I didn't rip it off the wall,' I interrupted, 'the valve broke!'

'... even if you're maybe not the most, um, careful cleaner?' He smiled a little, to show he was joking – but also, not joking.

It was the way he said it. *Ngggh.* 'What do you mean, *not the most careful cleaner?*'

'Well, you're not, are you?'

I stared at Jim, furious even though it was true. Was that going to go in the report?

'Cleo will understand. These things happen. Although,' he added, thoughtfully, 'it's probably going to be the most expensive claim we've had to make, so be prepared for some grumbling. She can be a bit ...' Jim searched for an appropriate word, '*tricky* at times, but she's not a monster,

I promise. She's just got high standards, which is no bad thing.'

This wasn't the first time Jim had been mildly critical of Cleo. Another reason it was probably at least a week too late to reveal my secret identity. Although if he continued with the snarky comments …

'Is that it?' I enquired.

Either my sarcasm was lost on Jim or he chose to ignore it, which was equally irritating. 'That's it! In my experience, it's best to be upfront when problems arise.' He concluded his lecture, with the infuriating smugness of someone who'd probably never done anything more stupid than putting the wrong fuel in his car, once. 'There's absolutely no point trying to do anything else. Be honest, and then you never have to worry about what lie you've told.'

'Are you calling me a liar now?'

'No, I'm just explaining why I think it's important to own your mistakes.'

I slumped back into my seat. Was it too late to ask to be taken to A&E? I could sit there for a few hours with a coffee. I quite fancied that.

'Right then!' Jim rubbed his hands together as if he'd just solved world peace. 'Now we've got that out of the way, let's go and clean some houses.'

9

*~ Start at the top of a room and work downwards,
so you're cleaning away the dust and not smearing it
around. Similarly, when you're cleaning a room, start in
the far corner and work towards the door.*

Cleo texted me later that night, requesting that I drop by her office in the morning, before work.

> Jim will pick u up from mine 2mrw.

Textspeak was one of Cleo's rare inelegancies, but then she was nearly always doing two or three things at once.

> B here by 8.30 pls. U can hv breakfast!

It was ages since Cleo and I had had breakfast together – by which I mean a full pancakes and bacon, extra coffee and gossip job. But she was never going to suggest one of those mid-week. I had a sinking feeling that this would be about Adam Doherty's shower. Despite Jim's un-reassuring little speech I hadn't slept, replaying the scene over and over in my head, obsessing over what I could have done differently. And what Cleo might say.

As I approached, Cleo marched out of her front door, carrying a plate of bacon sandwiches and a massive coffee mug, with her mobile wedged under her ear. She nodded towards the stairs to the office. A deep pinch of annoyance was visible between her eyebrows, which were freshly laminated.

'It's his birthday, Elliot, you need to be there.'

Elliot. Oh dear. I followed at a cautious distance.

I'd expected a tongue-lashing from Cleo, so had prepared my defence on the way over – the shower was already loose, the fitting was faulty, I slipped on the tiles – depending on how mad Cleo was going to be. From her fierce expression, she was warming up by giving Elliot *his* daily tongue-lashing.

'Hardly his fault his dad doesn't know how to prioritise, is it?' Pause. 'Then *be* there.'

She indicated that I should sit down at the chair at the desk, then she slid into her own leather executive swiveller, pushed the plate towards me, got a notepad out of the top drawer, tore the lid off a pen with her teeth in the manner of a lion biting the head off a mongoose, spat it out, wrote, 'Doherty: Shower' at the top, underlined it, then rolled her eyes at the idiot on the other end of the phone. Or at least I hoped it was at him.

'Just be there, Elliot. It's a trampoline park, not base camp at Mount Everest. Yes. I'll see you then.' She dropped her phone in her bag, sighed, and took the bigger of the two sandwiches. 'God,' she said, through a mouthful of brown bread. 'It's been a morning. I haven't even had time to go to the loo yet.'

'Sorry to hear that,' I said.

Despite the furrowed brow, the rest of Cleo was perfect: freshly blow-dried Marilyn bouffant, flicked jet-black eyeliner, gold necklaces with her sons' initials in an artless and expensive tangle. She smelled of gardenias. This was what a morning routine could do for you, I reminded myself. *If you could get yourself out of bed on time.*

Cleo despatched her sandwich, sanitised her fingers, and turned her attention to the notepad. 'So, let's get this over with. Adam Doherty's shower. Go.'

I reset my face to 'serious'. 'I was cleaning the bathroom using the checklist Jim gave me. I'd worked through the initial section, first sanitising the ceiling fan then—'

'The shower. Just tell me about the shower,' said Cleo, impatiently.

'I had sprayed the wet room area with the recommended cleaner and was waiting the allotted time for the cleaning agent to work before proceeding to remove said agent.' I winced. I sounded as if I was giving evidence on *Line of Duty*.

'And?'

My pulse had begun to race as it always did when I had to deal with something uncomfortable. Why was Cleo stringing out the bollocking like this? Was she going to make me pay for it? I didn't have enough money for a Hansgrohe shower when I was in a job, let alone now.

'It wasn't my fault,' I blurted out. 'I was spraying the shower walls when the wheel thing came off in my hands, I didn't pull it or twist it or anything like that.'

'Finally!' said Cleo. She abandoned the pen and started typing, her nails clicking against the keys. She typed with a confident clatter. 'While cleaning the shower, the water-pressure knob broke away from the unit. My colleague located the stopcock and turned off the water, then called a plumber who made good the shower unit in the time available.' She looked back at me. 'Did I miss something?'

'It was me who called the plumber,' I said, hoping for a gold star. 'And he said it was probably defective to begin with. Almost certainly. Defective.'

'Anything else?'

'Um ...' Should I tell her about the plants? Cleo hadn't mentioned the shelf. Maybe we could just skim over that part?

Cleo made a spinning 'hurry up' motion with her finger. 'Sorry, I don't have time for you to re-enact the whole thing. It came off in your hands, that's the gist, right?'

'Yes.'

'I need to file an incident report this morning, get the insurance ball rolling,' Cleo explained, still typing.

'Oh, thank god,' I said with a laugh. 'I thought you were emailing Adam Doherty!'

'I'll give him a call later. I want to get this off to the insurer before I have to start dealing with the 101 other crises I've got scheduled for this morning.'

'What are you going to tell him?' I squirmed. 'The shower's fixed, isn't it?' I tried a nonchalant shrug.

Cleo didn't look up. 'I'll tell him what happened – that you were cleaning the shower and it broke.'

'Me? Are you going to tell him *I* did it? Me personally? But it was an accident.'

'No one's saying it wasn't. Breakages happen now and again. As long as we're upfront and make good, that's the deal. It's in the contract.'

'But ...' I squirmed. To be fair, Cleo didn't know the real reason why I didn't want Adam Doherty to know it was me, but surely the point of being a manager was standing in front of your staff like a human shield?

'Enough, Robyn, you have no idea how much I've got on today.' Cleo was still typing. 'Plumber's independent assessment was that the unit was faulty and should be replaced as it is likely to—'

She stopped, as if a thought had just occurred to her, and looked up at me. 'Robyn, if Jim hadn't filed an incident report, would *you* have told me about this?'

'Yes!' I said, unconvincingly.

My red face gave me away. Probably not, to be honest.

'Oh my. Two words.' Cleo pointed an accusing finger at me. 'Grandma. Viennese truffles.'

'That is *low*.' That was really low. And it was three words.

One Christmas – years ago – Mum had bought some chocolates and left them at Grandma Taylor's so she wouldn't be tempted by them before the big day. Grandma hid them, not very well, in the spare room where, I can't remember how or why, I happened across the box. Hands up, I have no willpower when it comes to chocolate and I had even less back then, so it only took me a couple of weekend visits to finish the lot. The sight of the empty box, when I'd swallowed the last sugar-dusted truffle, was a shock but, in a flash of criminal genius, I had the foresight to rip the box slightly to cover my tracks.

What I didn't know, being ten years old, was that Grandma was completely phobic about anything smaller than a guinea pig, and she and Grandpa had to move out for three days while Rentokil conducted a comprehensive extermination.

'Oh, come *on*. What's that got to do with the shower?' My face flushed even deeper red.

Cleo wordlessly arched an eyebrow.

She knew it was me, of course. I don't think she ever told Mum. But as it turned out, there was a sizeable family of real rodents hanging out in the loft, so some might argue that it was a good thing I inadvertently triggered the mousepocalypse.

'Because trust is everything in this business.' Cleo steepled her fingers and leaned forward, as if she were Lord Alan Sugar. 'Our clients trust us to go into their homes, to see their private lives and handle their most precious, valuable objects. They have to know we'll be honest if we make mistakes.' She paused, for effect. 'And I have to know my *staff* will be honest.'

'I am!' I protested. 'It's not like I tried to cover it up.'

She fixed me with that annoying big sister look I knew so well. Cleo didn't need to say another word; thirty odd years of cover-ups, excuses, tears and broken things hidden under our bed did the talking for her. Only now she had the opportunity to lecture me as an employer as well as a sister and I could tell she was *loving* it.

'Cleo!' I glared at her with real venom, but she just tilted her head as if to say, 'Tell me I'm wrong'.

This was worse than the shouting I'd been expecting, because this wasn't about me breaking the shower, it was about her judging me as a person. Cleo knew I needed the money, she knew I wasn't any good at cleaning, she knew she'd caught me out. And there was absolutely no point bullshitting her, because of all the above.

'I need to know I can trust you, Robyn,' she said, patronisingly. 'It's not just about you, it's about the reputation of my whole business.'

I bridled. First Jim treating me like an idiot, now Cleo.

'Don't give me a hard time just because you're pissed off with Elliot,' I snapped. 'I'm doing my best.'

'I'm not giving you a hard time. You should ask Jim what a hard time looks like. If I'm still sitting down, you're not getting a hard time, believe me.'

I glared at her. She glared at me.

Four more days, I reminded myself. That was all I needed to do. Four more days and then I'd get a job, *any* job rather than …

Cleo sent her document to print, then asked, unexpectedly, 'How are you getting on with Jim?'

'Why? Has he asked to work on his own because of this?'

'No. Should he have done? What else have you broken?'

'Nothing.' I couldn't stop myself. 'All he does is tell me how much I get wrong.'

'And? He's got high standards.'

'It's demoralising.' I knew that sounded pathetic, even as I said it. 'I think he'd be happier on his own.'

Cleo made a dismissive noise, then spun round and retrieved a piece of paper from her printer which she pushed across the desk for me to initial. It was only a few lines, and there was no mention of the spectacular job we'd done getting the place spotless afterwards.

'For god's sake, Robyn.' Cleo leaned over me as I read it through. 'Do you have *any* idea how much I have to do today?'

I signed, handed it back and she found a pen to sign it herself.

My gaze drifted across the desk to her 'to-do' list, which was, to be fair, an epic stack of tasks. Idly I tried to read upside down, to see if 'bollock Robyn' featured.

Car insurance.

Alfie report – query grades?

Detergents

Birthday presents

Jim – rehab Tuesday.

I squinted, intrigued. Did that say *rehab*? What kind of rehab? I leaned forward, angling my head to check I'd read Cleo's handwriting correctly. Rehab would explain a lot. Was Jim a reformed drinker? Or drugs? Or did he have an obsessive compulsive disorder?

'Right, that's you done.' Cleo snapped her fingers to get my attention. 'Dismissed.'

'Cleo, speaking of Jim, what's …?' I glanced back at the 'to-do' list and when Cleo followed my gaze, she immediately swiped the notebook away and flipped the page over.

'Speaking of Jim,' she said, 'shouldn't you be making a move? You don't want to add lateness to your charge sheet, do you?'

I left without my bacon sandwich, a sacrifice I regretted all the way to the first job.

Apart from one small dig (he allocated me the bathroom at our first job, with the jovial comment, 'Back on the horse, right?'), Jim made no mention of my shower-wrecking and there was no phone call from Cleo to say Adam Doherty had dispensed with our services. The day passed uneventfully: routine cleaning, a drop-in to Nessie and Rambo, who seemed delighted to see us, then more cleaning. I wasn't enjoying scrubbing kitchens any more than before, but I could now do half the kitchen before I needed to check the list for the next instruction. So, progress.

At half five, Jim dropped me at Molly's Bakehouse and I was walking back to my flat when Mitch called.

'Hey, Robyn,' he said, and my day improved instantly. In the space of two words, I went from mediocre cleaner to professional woman with property investments, and a deposit on an aspirational apartment in a luxe development. Also, he was calling out of office hours, which I hoped was a precursor to a drink. Ideally somewhere more exciting than Ferrari's.

'Oh hi, Mitch!' I tried to sound casual, though I didn't feel it. 'How are you?'

'Good, thanks! Listen, can't talk for long, I'm on my way into a meeting but I just had a rather interesting conversation and I thought of you. Are you sorted out with a new job yet?'

'Um, not yet.'

'Excellent! I had lunch with a guy who runs a property buying agency in Worcester, and he told me, on the quiet, that they're looking for the right person to expand their team. Someone with local knowledge, proven track record, excellent client service, problem-solver, star performer, soul of discretion – you, in other words!'

'Wow, really?' I hesitated. Property search was a slightly different kettle of fish to what I'd been doing so far; finding homes for clients – and sometimes finding them schools, builders, designers, movers, too – instead of just buying and selling properties. 'You know I don't have any experience, though?'

Mitch made a dismissive noise. 'Piece of cake. Client hands you a list of crazy requirements, you find the house. Want me to ping you their contact details?'

'Yes, please.' My mind was racing ahead. What should I prepare? How would I know what they were looking for? 'Is the job ad online?'

'Hmmm, no, it's not that kind of set-up,' he said, and I felt stupid because *of course* these kinds of opportunities never got advertised. You had to know the right people. Or they had to approach you. I wasn't in those sort of circles which was why, although I'd always fancied doing more bespoke, client-focused work, I'd never found a way in.

But Mitch moved in those circles. And he'd thought of me. I replayed his words with an inner glow. *'Great client service, problem-solver, star performer …'*

'See?' he said. 'I told you, you've got to keep moving forwards. Like a shark. If you hadn't had to leave Marsh & Frett, this opportunity wouldn't have dropped into your lap, right? Anyway, I said you'd get back to them asap. By which I mean tonight, OK?' he added, emphatically.

'I will.' I was smiling at thin air, even though my back was aching from a whole day mopping. 'Thanks, Mitch!'

'It's my pleasure. You can repay me in drinks,' he said.

'Absolutely! Let's make a date. And listen, while you're there, I've got a couple of questions about Lark Manor? I was wondering when you planned to start the—'

'Robyn? Robyn? Can you hear me?' The traffic noise in the background had increased while we'd been talking. Now the line had gone crackly too.

'Mitch? I'm still here!'

But he was gone.

Still, Lark Manor could wait; getting a new job was my priority, and I started my email before I got my coat off. I'd already sent five job applications and each one had taken me at least two days' worth of rewriting, agonising, second-guessing. This time, I didn't let myself overthink it. I copied Mitch's contact, wrote a short, friendly email to someone called Christian at Malvern Property Finders, and fired off my CV before seven o'clock.

This is what you can do when you get organised, I told myself. As usual, that both cheered me and depressed me at the same time.

It didn't take Malvern Property Finders long to get back to me. I was creeping around Michelle Nightingale's stunning kitchen in Swan's Row (she was working from home and pretending we weren't there, we were pretending she wasn't there, plus she'd emptied her own recycling bin before we arrived, read into that what you will) when my phone rang. I grabbed it before Jim heard. We weren't supposed to have our phones on at work, particularly not in Michelle Nightingale's silent Temple of the Blessed MacBook.

'Hello, this is Olivia from MPF. Is that Robyn?'

'Yes, it is!' I turned off the vacuum cleaner with a swift heel to the button and flung the hose towards the nearest soft furnishing; I was out of the back door before it even hit the sofa.

'Is this a good time to talk? Sure? Great! Thanks so much for getting in touch with us.' She had a voice like an animated Barbour jacket. 'Mitch said you were the best negotiator he's ever dealt with …'

Did he?

'Thank you,' I murmured modestly.

'… and that we should talk to you asap, so here I am. Would it be possible for you to come into the office for a chat next week?'

My heart soared.

'Yes. Of course!' I saw my free hand was shaking. I hadn't realised just how stressed I was until the stress suddenly stopped. Now I felt overwhelming relief in its place. Relief that my old life wasn't over, that this *was* just a blip. The feeling was so pleasant – like when the dentist finishes drilling, or when your upstairs neighbour completes his Peloton workout – that it was hard to keep focused on what the woman was saying.

What had she said her name was? Lily? Or Caro? I grimaced. I'd come out without a pen. Normally when I was in the office I wrote everything down as I was speaking; I had to, or else I forgot straight away.

'I've got Wednesday afternoon, late-ish?' Barbour Jacket Woman went on. 'Um, or I could squeeze you into Monday. We're hectic at the moment.'

'Wednesday would be great,' I said, to give myself maximum time to prepare.

I could see Jim through the kitchen window. He'd walked into the kitchen to see how I was getting on, spotted the abandoned hoover, followed the sound of my voice out to the yard and was now glaring at me over the sink. Which I hadn't got round to cleaning yet.

I pre-empted his query, pointing at the phone and panto-miming 'this is a serious phone call about something very serious' with a dramatic, sad face.

He tapped his watch.

I nodded and held up two fingers. Two minutes. It wasn't like I could achieve much in that time with a hoover.

Jim flinched.

Whoops. I reversed my fingers in a less offensive way of conveying two minutes, and he turned and left the kitchen. On his way, he automatically stacked the hose of the hoo-ver back into its slot so it stood to attention, tidied up and waiting for me.

'That's great, Robyn, shall we say four o'clock?' the woman was saying, and I flushed with embarrassment, knowing I should be making a positive impression by using her name, but I couldn't even remember the names I'd guessed at sec-onds ago. My head was jumbled with a mess of unhelpful thoughts, like what I needed to wash to wear for the interview and could I get my roots sorted out between now and then.

Milly? Katie?

'Sounds great.' I had a sudden brainwave and hurried back inside. 'Can I take your email? Just in case I need to, um, ask any background questions.'

'Sure, no problem. It's Olivia dot Collins at Malvern Property Finders – one word – dot com.'

I'd managed to find a biro and a Hello Fresh delivery slip, and jotted it down.

'Look forward to seeing you next week, Olivia!' I said, and put every single detail into my phone before I could forget.

Of course, what I hadn't done when I'd agreed to meet with Olivia at four o'clock on Wednesday was check whether I *could* meet with her then. I broached the subject on the way home with Jim.

'Have you got the rota for next week?' I tried to sound casual.

'You're going to be here next week?'

I ignored the faux surprise. 'Possibly.'

'It should be the same as this week,' he said. 'As far as I know.'

'Good, good. Um … would it be OK if I finished early on Wednesday?'

'I'm not the person to be asking. Check with Cleo.'

'I will. But … do you think it'd be a problem if I left at about three?'

We'd stopped at a traffic light, a long one at the cross-roads by the big Tesco. I knew we'd be here a while.

'Is this something to do with that phone call earlier?'

'Yes!' Now my life was about to get back on track, any former reticence about what I'd done before evaporated like steam off a heated mirror. I was no longer a sacked estate agent; I was a shortlisted property search special-ist. 'I've got an interview with a property search company. They're like estate agents but more bespoke.'

Jim didn't say anything and I found myself gabbling to fill the silence. I was very bad with silences. I'd done so many acting workshops at university on 'stillness' and 'letting my face speak', but I always cracked after about forty seconds. 'It's what I do, for my real job. I'm an estate agent. I mean, not that *this* isn't a real job, of course, it's a real job, definitely, ha ha, but it's something I was doing to fill a gap while I ...'

I trailed off. Somehow I couldn't think of a way around the word 'sacked' while Jim was examining my face like that. *He* was very good with silences.

'Uh-huh.'

Belatedly, it occurred to me that I could just have said I had a doctor's appointment for something gynaecological. It's what I'd always done at Marsh & Frett whenever I needed time off for a haircut. I kicked myself.

'Although I've learned a lot while I've been doing this,' I offered lamely. 'About ... houses. It's been helpful.'

Jim still said nothing.

I made myself stop talking. Had I offended him?

Why were these lights taking *so long*?

'Well, that explains a lot,' he said, finally.

'How do you mean?'

He tapped his fingers on the steering wheel. 'I'd narrowed it down to two options – either Cleo was taking you on as a manager, but wanted to make sure you spent a few weeks learning the ropes with the cleaners first.'

How weird, that he'd been assuming the same things about me as I'd been assuming about him.

'Why did you think that?'

'The office wear, when we met. Your lack of cleaning experience. Your black nails.' Jim had only paused for breath; he carried on before I could point out they weren't black, they were mulberry. 'The way you took offence at the checklists, your haphazard approach to cleaning, your low standards.'

That was a bit much. 'My shower screens are almost streakless!'

'Hmm,' said Jim, which wasn't yes or no. 'Oh, and the fact that you initially seemed to think you were the marketing manager.'

He'd stopped, but I waited, just in case there was more.

'And your other theory?' I prompted.

'That you were some friend of Cleo's in a tight spot. Someone she was helping out.' Finally, the lights changed and we set off again. 'Reasons, the above, plus I don't think she did a DBS check on you. She still should, even if she knows you. Legally.'

'I have one. All estate agents have to.'

'I'm pleased to hear that.'

'And which of those options were you leaning towards?' I asked.

He straightened his shoulders. 'Well, if Cleo was thinking of appointing a manager, I suppose I'd like to have heard about it before now.'

Aha! I thought. Jim assumed he was the obvious choice for manager – Cleo's 'most trusted operative', the one in charge of the office laminator. It would explain some of the grumpiness, if he'd assumed I'd been parachuted in over his head. 'She would have told you,' I reassured him. 'She says you're her most trusted operative.'

'Cleo said that? When?'

'It's what she told me at my interview,' I corrected myself. 'That if anyone could teach me how to be a decent cleaner, it was you. And anyway,' I went on, before he could examine that too closely, 'I *have* learned a lot of useful stuff doing this. Honestly. I swear I'll never look at tiles in the same way again. And I'll definitely buy a self-cleaning oven.'

We'd reached the blue and white exterior of Milly's Bakehouse. A baker in a blue T-shirt was winding down the striped awnings, signalling the end of the day. Jim checked his mirrors, indicated and pulled in behind their delivery scooter.

He paused for a moment, thinking of the appropriate thing to say, and in a flash I wished I could spin back the clock by a few minutes and be kinder.

Jim was a condescending neat freak, but I hadn't meant to hurt his feelings by implying his job wasn't 'proper', or sound as if I was relieved to be escaping his hygiene boot-camp. I mean, I *was* but ....

'Thank you for your patience,' I said. 'I know I've not been a much of a help.'

He tilted his head. It was a small gesture yet it conveyed everything: agreement that I'd been useless, acknowledgement of my thanks, kindness that he wasn't going to point it out. I couldn't help but admire its efficiency.

'You can say it, I'm not cut out for this cleaning lark. Everyone I know thinks I'm the messiest person they've ever met.' Gabble, gabble. Why couldn't I do eloquent silences? 'For me, cleaning is on a par with a vegetarian doing an internship in a haggis factory. Seriously, that's how hard it's been for me, and that's without working for—'

I was about to say, 'without working for my big sister' but I stopped.

'Without?'

Oh, why not tell him now? 'Without working for my big sister.'

Jim raised his eyebrow – again, enviably minimal.

'What? You knew?'

His mouth twitched. 'I knew the first time I saw you two together.'

'You didn't! What, because we look so alike? It's the eyebrows, isn't it? The nose?'

'More the way you—' He stopped, then shrugged. 'The way you're both so bad at pretending you don't know each other.'

I laughed. That was probably true.

Jim turned to me, and I abruptly stopped laughing and felt a cautious smile break out. He still gave off management vibes, but he didn't look quite as … intense. This was as personal a conversation as we'd had in all the hours we'd spent together.

'I'll have a look at the rota,' he said. 'I'm sure I can cope on my own for an hour or two on Wednesday.'

'Would you? I'd really appreciate it.'

'Is it to start straight away? This job?'

'I don't know. I think so.' I realised I didn't know anything about it at all. My stomach flipped. How could I prepare? I *hated* feeling underprepared for any new situations.

'But I won't leave you in the lurch!' I said.

'That's very thoughtful of you.'

I wasn't sure if Jim was taking the mickey. I *had* been rude. Implying his career choice was a last resort for me.

But then *was* it his career choice? He hadn't exactly reciprocated with an explanation of how long he'd been working for Cleo – and why. Maybe he'd been in rehab for prescription drugs, I thought. You could get an addiction to those, couldn't you?

I was racking my brains for a subtle lead into the question, but my phone rang and I grabbed it in case it was Mitch. It wasn't – it was Mum – but by the time I'd fumbled the phone and dropped the call, the moment had gone.

'So do you live over the bakery then?' he asked, as I gathered my things from the footwell.

'God no, that would be a nightmare, wouldn't it? Living over a bakery? I'd be the size of a house in no time.'

'So … which one? Isn't it worse to live over the off-licence?'

I glanced over to the row of shops, and realised that there weren't that many other houses along this stretch of road. I couldn't tell him where I really lived. Not just because it wasn't exactly aspirational, but because I'd have to come up with a reason for lying about it in the first place.

'Um, I live over the, er …' I scanned the shopfronts. Not all of them had flats above. 'The tattoo parlour,' I said, my gaze landing on Inkcredible: The House of Tatts.

Jim raised an eyebrow.

'You should see me from the neck down,' I said, deadpan. Then got out of the car, and cringed all the way home.

IO

~ All to-do lists should contain the instructions 'have a cup of tea'.

I spent the weekend doing as much research as I could about Malvern Property Search. When I focused my mind on a task I could get a lot done, and by the time Wednesday rolled around I felt confident that I was more than up to the challenge of finding perfect homes for extremely fussy, busy or wealthy people.

Obviously, there was more to it than that, but from the case studies on their website that seemed to be the gist.

Jim didn't mention the interview again, but on Tuesday night, as he was dropping me off after a long day (Terry had told me quite a sad story about losing his brother; I'd had to pretend I'd cleaned the oven to make up for the time I'd spent patting Terry's hand and trying not to cry), he said, 'If you want to leave at lunchtime I'll cover the afternoon jobs.'

'You don't need to …' I began.

'No, it's fine. It's just a quick whizz around Adam Doherty's and he's still away so there won't be much to do.' He tapped his fingers on the steering wheel. Was that a hint of a smile? 'Wouldn't want you to go to this interview soaked from head to foot.'

'*Thank* you,' I said. Then I turned, so he'd know I meant it, and said, 'Really, thanks. I appreciate that.'

Jim shrugged. 'If the oven spontaneously catches fire, I'll text you for an electrician.' He paused. 'Unless you know any firemen?'

I laughed more than I needed to in acknowledgement of his attempt at a joke.

But it was kind of him. And he even dropped me at the station. That, I surmised, was how keen he was to see me gainfully employed elsewhere.

Malvern Property Finders was located in a warehouse development in Worcester and the modern arrangement of creamy roses in reception telegraphed to visitors that it was a high-end operation, all glass and leather and a deferential hush. In an effort to counteract my habitual lateness I'd arrived way too early, and had had to spend forty minutes (and three espressos) in a nearby coffee shop; I could barely sign the visitors pass, my nerves were jangling so much.

But as soon as she walked in, I recognised Olivia Collins. She'd been at the launch party for the first release of the St Anselm's apartments. I was good with faces and names when they were combined with a handy name badge, and her horn-rimmed glasses and jet-black bob stuck in my mind. Olivia was also the only one who made a point of flushing every loo and checking out the drain rate on the showers, something I thought was a bit pernickety at the time, but now considered, knowing what I knew about Adam Doherty's shower, quite astute.

'Oh my god, it's *you*!' she exclaimed, pointing at me with delight as if we were old mates. 'Great to see you again!'

She ushered me into an elegant office with a view of the river and, after yet more coffee, the interview commenced.

Well, I say interview. We chatted non-stop for fifty-five minutes about local restaurants, heat pumps, the best place to source tiles, sourdough, the Hereford bypass, that sort of thing. As a result – *thank god* – there was no time for the usual 'tell me about a terrible mistake you made and how you rectified it' awkwardness so I had zero qualms about skimming over the entire sacking incident at my previous job. She didn't ask; I didn't tell.

At five to five, Olivia ('Oh, call me Liv.') abruptly said, 'Yikes, I haven't even mentioned the job, have I? *So*. It's a maternity cover, starting sooner than planned, unfortunately, poor Cordelia, so six months officially, but who knows, maybe longer. You'd be covering Cordy's client list, which is mainly relocators from London, some senior Forces personnel, nothing complicated. Is there anything you'd like to ask me about the role?'

I nodded. I'd prepared a few questions – commission, legalities, exclusivity, etcetera – but to honest, I was too wired on coffee to process Liv's answers. She seemed fine with my nodding, though. And then we were standing by the door and saying our goodbyes.

'Gosh, that flew by!' she said, and gave me a big hug. The weird thing was, the hug didn't seem weird. The interview had gone *that* well.

'I don't want to get ahead of myself,' Liv confided with a smile, 'but you would be a perfect fit for our team. I need to discuss with the directors, and they'll probably want you to pop back in for a chat but …' She hunched up her shoulders and made a thrilled 'squee' face. 'Are you free early next week?'

'Yes!' I said, without thinking. 'Yes, I am!'

I floated out of the office and into the street outside. That literally couldn't have gone better. Happiness was bubbling out of me: I needed to tell someone.

But who could I tell? I probably shouldn't tell Mum, not until there was a definite job offer. I nearly called Cleo, but then remembered it wouldn't go down that well, considering her staff shortages.

Mitch. I was calling him before I even had time to think.

'Hey, Robyn!' He picked up on the second ring, and I started burbling straight away.

'Thank you so much – I owe you a drink! I've just met with Liv Collins and I don't want to jinx anything but I think it went really, really well!' Should I say it? Why not? 'I think she's going to offer me the job!'

'That's so great, I knew you two would get on. They're a good bunch of people.'

'Aren't they? And it turns out that—'

'Sorry to interrupt, but where are you now?'

'Worcester.'

'Well, as it happens I am *also* in Worcester,' he said. 'Why don't you tell me about it over that drink? Unless you're in a rush to get home?'

I closed my eyes and smiled. The perfect job. A spontaneous drink with the man I really fancied. This was one of the best days ever. I couldn't remember the last time I'd felt so light, so weightless.

'No,' I said. 'I'm in no rush.'

Mitch was seated in the restaurant's prime spot with a view of the river, a chilly lager in front of him and his laptop open on the table. When I walked in he was on the phone to someone, but when he saw me he waved me over and ended the call almost immediately.

I let the waiter guide me to his table, mainly to have the pleasure of everyone seeing me joining the man in the suit who looked like he might be an actor or a footballer.

'Robyn!' He kissed me on both cheeks, letting his hands rest lightly on my arms and giving me a chance to smell the cologne on his warm skin. I privately thanked the date gods that our chance meeting had occurred on the day I was dressed for an interview, and not fresh from scrubbing someone's toilet.

I slipped into the chair opposite his and accepted the enormous wine list offered by the waiter. I'd decided on the way that I'd have a large glass of wine – no, two, I was celebrating – then move onto mineral water. I needed to leave by seven: there was a train I could catch that would get me home in a reasonable time.

I ignored the small matter of the taxi from the station. I was about to get a new job after all. Plenty of money for taxis in the pipeline.

Mitch waved away the wine list. 'No need for that. I think we know what we're having, eh, Robyn?'

'Do we?'

'Bottle of champagne!' said Mitch, signalling to the waiter.

There was something a bit thrilling and sophisticated about the way he just did that. The last date I'd been on

– a Tinder mistake – had ended shortly after my date had argued with the barman about whether I needed a single or double gin and tonic, and then demanded a receipt.

Mitch ordered some nuts and olives to go with the champagne, and I relaxed back into my seat, admiring the pair of swans gliding down the river outside. Swans, seriously. Could you wish for a more magnificent omen for a romantic night? The last traces of tension from my day vanished as a silver wine cooler arrived, and the sommelier solemnly filled our glasses.

Mitch wished me luck for my new job, then raised his glass to mine.

'Here's to you, Robyn,' he said, holding my gaze as we took our first sip, and my heart shimmered in my chest. I could see our reflections in the window, and we looked like the kind of attractive, successful young people I always envied as I hurried past restaurants on my way home to my messy flat.

Mitch chatted about the meeting he'd just come from, and I savoured the delicious sensation of bubbles firing alcohol directly into my bloodstream. It was a proposal for a complex of serviced apartments, complete with cinema, health suite and restaurants, built in the grounds of an old hospital. It sounded amazing: the properties were aimed at affluent retirees who'd sustained their social lives, and he'd already signed up key influencers to lead the design direction, including a couple of famous semi-retired musicians and a gnarly old thespian I'd met and mistaken for Sir Ian McKellen (it wasn't Sir Ian McKellen).

'And will this happen after you've finished Lark Manor?' I asked.

'We'll be running both projects simultaneously. I like to keep lots of plates spinning. You know me, I work best when the pressure's on!'

I nodded. I worked best under pressure too, but it didn't mean I enjoyed it. There wasn't usually another option. 'And how's that going? Has the planning department got back to you yet?'

I'd already started spending my new salary on imaginary curtains for my future apartment, as well as a huge sofa that I'd seen online. I didn't mind waiting a few months to build up my savings to pay for it, but it would be nice to be able to tell Mum where I'd be for Christmas.

I could invite Mum and Dad for Christmas, I thought, adding a proper dining table to my mental shopping list. And proper cutlery. I really wanted to be the kind of person who had a proper canteen of matching cutlery, not just a random selection of unrelated forks and teaspoons nicked from cafes.

'We've got outline permission which is a good start. A couple of issues to iron out with the architect but that's par for the course.' Mitch pushed the silver bowl of cashews towards me. 'Have you had some of these? They're incredible.'

'Is there anything I can do yet? Is there an interior designer attached? Can you commission mood boards yet? Or advance marketing?'

I didn't want to press Mitch too hard but how else was I going to learn if not by asking questions? It wasn't just impatience about my own flat; I genuinely wanted to be a part of the development process. One day soon, everyone who'd laughed at me in Marsh & Frett would be making brochures for *my* project.

Mitch pulled a 'yes/no' face. 'There's a fair bit of legal stuff to plough through first, which I leave to Allen, because he *loves* a complicated contract. If you want, though, I can set up a meeting with him and Nihal, and they can walk you through it? And then you and I can have another more interesting meeting with the architect in a few weeks? Talking about the design?'

'Sounds great!' I said. I didn't really want to have a meeting with Allen and Nihal, but I supposed I'd better now I'd asked for one.

'Remind me, I'll get onto that this week.' Mitch topped up my glass. 'So, how come you know so many famous actors? Did you sell their houses? You can tell me, I'm very discreet.'

'No, you're not!' I said, with a playful tut. 'You've literally just told me that …' I dropped my voice in case the next table was eavesdropping, 'Unnamed Famous Guitarist has shocking BO!'

'No, you're right, I'm not very discreet.' Mitch pretended to look contrite. 'But tell me anyway.'

'I didn't sell his house as it happens.' I sipped my champagne. It usually took a lot more than two glasses of wine to prise details of my more interesting past life from me, if at all, but Lark Manor had changed the playing field. Now I had the prospect of real business success in my future, I didn't mind talking about the past so much. I was no longer the failed child actor, I was a business success in the making – a smart investor, who also had an unexpected handful of amusing anecdotes about people you've heard of.

'When I was ten,' I said, casually, 'I was in a big film, and I met some household names.'

'What?' He sat up. 'Which film?'

I told him. His eyebrows shot up. I don't think I'd ever seen Mitch lost for words before. It gave me a pleasurable jolt of confidence.

'Wow! How come you never mentioned that?'

'Because people start doing impressions of ... No! You're going to do it now!'

He'd opened his mouth to start doing one of the famous quotes but closed it with a self-conscious laugh. 'You got me. Wow, though.'

'Imagine people doing that, every day, for about ten years.' I took another sip of champagne. 'But yes, it was a lot of fun.'

'So who else did you meet?'

I told him and I could see he was impressed. I knew I looked a lot more interesting with the reflected glory of celebrity shining on me. I just hated the 'so what went wrong?' conversation that inevitably followed. But Mitch wasn't interested in the fall from grace part, he was happy to stick with the fun stories. I kind of loved him for that.

'What an *incredible* experience you had.' Mitch leaned back in his chair, crossing one long leg over his knee. We were both in that nice, soft, third-drink state; he'd taken off his jacket, my hair was slowly falling out of its casual bun. 'Tell me more.'

So I told him a few more stories, about the television series I'd been in, and the Christmas ads that had got Mum more mince pies than she knew what to do with. (And which Dad found 'disappointing'.)

The evening started to speed up after that. I don't know how, but time seemed to compress in a blur of eye contact and laughter and some outrageous flirting. The second bottle of champagne might have had something to do with it.

I insisted on paying for the second bottle. Mum drilled it into me as a teenager: always go halves on dates so men don't think you owe them anything. I assumed she must have read that in *Just Seventeen* or whatever teenagers had for advice before Google because, as far as I knew, Dad was her first and only boyfriend. She worried constantly about what Cleo and I might get up to as teenagers, although only Cleo ever gave her reason to worry. Still, I felt empowered when the ice bucket was refilled with a fresh bottle of Veuve Clicquot, paid for by me.

I tried not to think about how many hours' cleaning it represented.

The conversation was flowing effortlessly, but still I made an effort to self-edit as I went along. Mitch didn't need to hear about the stress of learning lines that wouldn't stick in my head, or how crushed I felt when I bombed the auditions for drama school. The more I talked, the more I felt myself detaching from my body until I could almost see Robyn the actress, the professional storyteller, the person I thought I'd be now. And I noticed how easily Mitch brought her out, with his encouraging laughs and curiosity and general appreciation. He was the best company – because he made *me* feel like I was the best company.

He let the waiter refill our glasses, then leaned forward to touch mine, gently, so it barely clinked. 'Thank you,' he said, 'for such a great evening. I thought I was just meeting my favourite estate agent for a quick drink, but here I am with a legit celeb!'

'It's fate,' I agreed. Maybe we would tell our kids this in years to come. If I hadn't had an interview that afternoon and your dad hadn't had a meeting in town …

I'd gone from tipsy to definitely drunk, but Mitch's attention was making me feel much more reckless than the champagne. Somewhere, my inner prefect registered that I was now at least two glasses of wine over my self-imposed limit. I ignored it.

'So, what I need to know now is …' Mitch checked his watch. 'Oh. Do you want to guess what time it is?'

No, I didn't. He was going to say it was time to go. I didn't *want* to go. I wanted to stay in this happy bubble for as long as I possibly could.

'Seven?' I said, hopefully.

'It's *eight o'clock*. Time flies when you're having fun, eh?'

I nodded. I hadn't had this much fun in a very, very long time.

'Listen, do you want to grab something to eat?' Mitch suggested. 'We might as well stay here – by the time we've left and found somewhere …' He saw me hesitate, and grinned. 'Go on, live dangerously!'

My heart flipped over. This had turned into a proper date! And when had I last had one of those? Not one as enjoyable as this, anyway. I could always get the late train.

'Why not?' I said.

He beamed. 'Fantastic.'

Then he waved the waiter back and we were being shown into the flatteringly lit dining room, with thick white table-cloths and candlelight and very small tables. More wine arrived. My knees were touching Mitch's as soon as we sat down and, before long, my ankle was resting against his and little tingles were running up the inside of my thigh.

And we carried on talking and talking.

It took the waiter a couple of goes to get us to even look at the menus. In the end he more or less shouted at us to order.

What did we talk about? I can't remember, but my throat was sore from chatting, my cheeks ached from smiling into Mitch's face, and I barely touched my fish. The waiter hovered and left, hovered and left, and then eventually just took it away. In hindsight, I should have ordered something more substantial because that Dover sole wasn't soaking up any of the white wine that appeared on the table to go with it.

I know at one point we must have got onto siblings, because I found myself telling Mitch about Cleo.

'I admire her so much, everything she decides to do, she's amazing at, but she's such a tough act to follow. She always has been. Even when I was on television she was way more popular than me at school. Can you believe that? So I love her, but at the same time if she wasn't my sister I'd probably hate her. You know?'

Mitch nodded. I couldn't remember if he'd told me he had a brother or not. I think he had. He seemed sympathetic anyway.

'Mum always says she treats us both as individuals in our own right but she doesn't.' Somewhere along the lines, I'd stopped filtering what I was saying; I needed to open my heart to Mitch so he would understand the real me. 'Cleo's her favourite, she takes after Mum. They're so similar. I suppose I'm like Dad.' I took a sip of wine.

'That's not a bad thing, by the way. Dad's lovely. He's really good at sugarcraft.'

It took me a couple of goes to say sugarcraft, which made us both giggle.

'What does she do again, your sister?'

'She runs a cleaning agency.'

'A cleaning agency?' Mitch laughed. 'Sorry, I thought you were going to tell me she worked for the International Monetary Fund or Greenpeace or something.'

'It's a very successful business,' I said. 'She employs over fifty cleaners and covers the whole county.'

'Good for her,' said Mitch. Was he being sarcastic? I couldn't tell.

'So that's why it's so important for me to find something of my own that I'm good at.' I gazed at him, hypnotised by the sparkles of light in his brown eyes, the darkness of his lashes as he gazed at me. The focus of his attention, the invitation in his smile. His casual dismissal of Cleo, in favour of my own achievements. 'I'm so excited about Lark Manor. It's the start of everything I really, really want. Um, everything I want to *achieve*.'

'It certainly is.' Mitch reached out and took my hand, interlacing his fingers with mine. Something shifted in the atmosphere between us, and the silence took on a charged suggestion that neither of us wanted to break. We gazed at each other, waiting until the moment tipped from 'should we?' to 'where?'

The waiter returned with dessert menus, took one look at us and walked off.

When I woke up the next morning it took me a while to work out where I was. Partly because the room was dark, and also because my head was throbbing with a headache so bad I could see colours morphing like a lava lamp behind my eyelids. When I tried to swallow, my tongue clacked against the roof of my mouth.

I closed my eyes again. This wasn't good. The room smelled of starched cotton and air freshener so it definitely wasn't my house. I was under a duvet and when I ran my hands tentatively down my body I encountered nothing by way of underwear.

What? I froze. No. This wasn't good. Not good at all. A stale feeling uncurled at the back of my mind, a familiar shameful guilt, and I pushed it away.

Mitch's face, gorgeous and seductive in the candlelight. A long, delicious moment when the whole world seemed to shrink around us. Then a key on the table, with a stupidly massive key fob that made us both giggle uncontrollably for some reason. Him and me kissing in an old lift, which wobbled when I pushed him against the wall as if we were in a film. His mouth, warm and spicy. A red door. Someone shouting. A different red door. Then nothing more specific.

Nothing? For god's sake, I thought. I deserve to have *some* decent sexy memories to offset this hangover.

A more urgent thought struck me. Mitch *couldn't* see me in my morning state. I'd been presentable last night because of the interview but this morning I knew I'd look like a mole with Covid. Was there any way I could sneak out before he woke up? It would mean skipping the excruciating but necessary 'so …?' conversation which I never enjoyed anyway. I needed my wits about me for that.

I listened for sounds of breathing but could hear nothing. Slowly I turned my head.

The bed was flat next to me. No head on the pillow. No Mitch. I was alone.

I turned my head back, unable to decide if I was relieved or disappointed.

OK, I thought, trying to take tiny mental steps. It's dark, so it must be early. That's good. I need to get up. I need to stand under the shower. Then get to the station. Then get the first train home, and …

My phone rang on the bedside table. I winced at the shrillness of the ringtone, clattering on my tender ears, and reached out to drop the call. Unfortunately, my finger accidentally touched the answer button.

Oh god.

'Robyn? Robyn?' A tinny voice came from the phone.

It was Jim.

I really didn't want Jim intruding into this room right now. But there was no point hanging up. He'd only ring back. I reached for the phone, turning my head as little as possible.

'Hello?' I croaked. Why was he ringing so early? If our 9 a.m. job was cancelled he could just have texted.

'Good morning. Is there a problem?'

'How do you mean?'

'Well, I've been waiting outside your flat for fifteen minutes now and if we don't leave, we're going to be late.'

'What time is it?'

'It's five to nine. Are you still in bed?'

'Oh, you're kidding me.' I moved the phone away from my face so I could see the time. It was two minutes to nine.

I looked over to the window, protected by high-quality hotel blackout curtains.

'I'm really …' My tongue felt hideous so I sat up, hoping I'd been sensible enough to leave a pint of water by the bed, but the effort of moving made me dry heave. And there was no water. 'Ueegh.'

'Are you all right? You sound awful.'

'I *feel* awful,' I said. Not a lie. The room was swaying.

'Do you … do you want me to come up?'

'No!' I said quickly. 'I mean, no, it's fine. I'm not feeling great. I must have slept through my alarm.' Which was true. 'I was up half the night,' I added, for detail. Also not a lie.

'Sorry to hear that.'

I could picture Jim, sitting outside Molly's Bakehouse in the van, drumming his fingers on the steering wheel until his near-limitless patience finally ran out. For some reason I felt seedy, then I felt annoyed that he was making me feel like that.

'I'll be fine in an hour or two. I can get dressed and meet you at the next job,' I offered, then mentally kicked myself. That was a classic Robyn move: the worse mess I'd made, the more I overpromised. There was no way I'd be back in Longhampton in an hour. What was I *thinking*?

'Not if you're going to throw up on me, thanks.'

'It's fine, I'm sure I can be there in an hour.'

I closed my eyes. *Shut up, Robyn.*

'No, no, there are rules and regulations about sickness at work. You can't spread germs around clients' homes.' Jim was back on track now. 'Get a Covid test, then try to rehydrate. Lots of water, small sips, plain toast, take some paracetamol if you're feeling grim. Sleep if you can.'

The more concerned he sounded, the worse I felt. Hearing Jim's voice while naked was plain wrong.

'OK, well, you stay in bed and I'll check in with you at the end of the day. See how you're feeling. And if you feel worse …' He hesitated, then said, 'Give me a ring. I can bring you some supplies, if necessary.'

I closed my eyes. I didn't normally have a problem with white lies – I was perfectly happy with alternative truths, if they made a situation easier for everyone – but today I could feel the nasty taste of every untrue word on my tongue.

It's the hangover, I told myself. It's that booze shame people talk about.

'Right, I need to go. Don't want to be late for the Watsons,' said Jim, and rang off.

I dropped my mobile onto the duvet and allowed myself a brief moment of wallowing. Then I forced myself to get up.

Mitch had left a note on the desk, under a complimentary bottle of water.

'Sorry to leave early – site visit first thing. Thanks for a great night! Hope head not too sore. Will call! M.'

I stared at it for a long time, trying to process what I felt through my treacly hangover.

Obviously I was thrilled that nearly a year of flirting had now blossomed into something real. We hadn't just got drunk at an office party and ended up in bed (not that I'd done that for a while, I might add). We'd had dinner, and we'd *talked*. There was a connection there. It was promising.

But bloody hell. My head.

II

~ Dust first, then hoover, then mop.

I'd slithered home from Worcester on Thursday morning, convinced that I'd be spotted by Jim, Cleo or one of my parents. Hangovers always made me paranoid. Even more paranoid. As it happened, I saw no one, but after texting Cleo to tell her I had food poisoning, I spent the afternoon cleaning my own flat, very, very slowly. Partly in case Mitch called round to check on me; partly as an act of self-flagellation. I managed to get the sitting room respectable, before I remembered that the whole thing was a complete waste of time because Mitch didn't know where I lived.

Neither Mitch nor Liv called, but Jim did, as promised, at five o'clock. He enquired after my queasiness and recommended plain toast.

I don't know if he believed the overnight bug excuse. Obviously I couldn't see his face over the phone, but by now I knew the exact expression that would be on it: measured neutrality. I made myself stick to absolute facts to minimise the squirming of my conscience.

But to be fair to Jim, the toast trick worked, and I made a special effort to be on time the next morning, including a detour to the bakery for an apology croissant.

'Is this for me?'

Jim looked at the striped bag I'd dropped in his lap.

'Yes.' I slid into the car, carefully because I was carrying two cappuccinos in blue Molly's Bakehouse cups and the lids never fitted properly. 'Just a little Friday thank you.'

'What for?'

'For covering for me this week. I know I haven't been a great partner. What with, um, one thing and another.'

He peered into the bag. 'Wow. Is this an *almond* croissant?'

'It certainly is.' Now my financial crisis was all but over, it had felt good to splash the cash (one additional pound) to upgrade to almond. 'It's a *big* thank you.'

'That's very kind of you,' he said, 'but not necessary.'

'I've washed my hands,' I reassured him. 'I'm pretty sure it was just an upset stomach, not dysentery or anything.'

He turned to me and smiled, which came as something of a surprise. Jim had one of those smiles that completely changed a face, transforming his stern resting expression; it was crooked and a bit cautious, as if he wasn't completely sure it suited him. Not like Mitch and his gorgeous smile, which lit up his whole face and made you beam back automatically like a flower bending towards the light.

I pushed the thought of Mitch from my mind. I couldn't think about Mitch while I was wearing a pair of red overalls.

'That's most kind, if unnecessary,' said Jim. 'I will have it for my lunch.'

'You don't mind if I eat mine now?' I picked up my coffee and took a sip. Ah. Coffee. Glorious, extravagant coffee. How I'd missed it.

'Not at all. Just, you know … be careful, please.' Jim gestured at the immaculately hoovered footwell.

I adjusted the bag and the cup to minimise flaking and we set off. I couldn't say I was looking forward to another's day's cleaning, but now that I was re-caffeinated, with the end in sight, I found myself in something approaching a good mood.

'Can I put the radio on?' I asked, and Jim didn't object. So presumably he was in quite a good mood too.

Our first job of the day was at the Armstrongs' and, as we approached the front door, I could hear thudding, interspersed by the occasional muffled shout.

I glanced at Jim. 'Are they at home?'

'Sounds like it.' He rang the doorbell – something we'd never done before.

We waited, as the thudding continued.

'School holiday?' Having been out of the school system for nearly twenty years, I only had a vague idea of when holidays were, and only then because recently they'd signalled an upturn in Cleo's complaints about Elliot and his idea of what constituted childcare.

'Not for another month,' said Jim. Which made me wonder if he had kids? He was the type who'd make a point of learning term dates anyway. Like he probably knew bus times and where to park in town for free. 'Maybe one of the children is ill. It won't make a difference, just do what you can around them.'

I won't lie, while I was intrigued to discover what was causing the unstoppable trail of destruction in the house, I also felt self-conscious about cleaning in front of an audience.

A blonde woman about my age opened the door; she was dressed in a navy office dress accessorised with a gold chain and pearl studs. On her feet, though, she was wearing a stained pair of Ugg boots. When she saw me and Jim she looked blank, then said, 'Oh god, you're the cleaners. Come in, come in.'

The cleaners. Really? A bit dehumanising, considering we probably knew more about her intimate life than her best friend, thanks to my regular scrutiny of her bathroom cabinets.

We followed Mrs Armstrong into the kitchen, which was looking even more catastrophic than normal. A laptop balanced on four Ottolenghi cookbooks was open to a Zoom meeting, carefully angled towards the Shaker cupboards so no participants would see the Lego explosion, discarded trainers or half-finished cereal bowls spattered around the room. I assumed it was on mute because a small blonde boy was bouncing a basketball against the wall, perilously close to the massive television, in a regular 'thunk ... kerthunk' pattern. Over and over.

There was a dark smudge on the wall. It was slowly growing into a bigger smudge with every bounce.

That's going to be a right pain to get off, I thought, irritated, then remembered that I didn't need to have those thoughts anymore. Soon the cleaning of the Armstrongs' walls would be someone else's problem.

Well, Jim's problem. And he probably had a solution for it.

'So sorry, we're going to be in your way, aren't we?' Mrs Armstrong returned to her laptop and typed a rapid message, standing up. 'I've just got to send this ... Charlie, can you stop doing that?'

He carried on bouncing. 'I need to get to 150, then I can stop.'

'Where are you now?' she asked.

'Ninety-three.' *Thunk … kerthunk. Thunk … kerthunk.*

Jim and I glanced at each other.

Thunk … kerthunk. Thunk … kerthunk.

Mrs Armstrong chewed a hangnail on her thumb, watching her son intently but not attempting to stop him.

Thunk … kerthunk.

'Do two more in here, Charlie, and the next fifty outside,' Jim instructed, and contrary to everyone's expectations, Charlie did two more bounces, picked up the ball and ran into the garden. Pigeons scattered into the air as the ball thudded off the garage wall.

We took a moment to enjoy the silence that ensued, and Mrs Armstrong abruptly seemed to snap back to life.

'Gosh, that's better, ha ha! Um, I'm Sally, I don't think we've met. I don't think I've *ever* met the cleaners.' She pushed her glasses up onto her head, holding back her fine blonde fringe. She had an anxious energy that I recognised, and lilac-grey shadows under her eyes; from the way she kept rubbing her forehead, I guessed she probably had a crippling headache. 'We do appreciate your hard work, though. It's like magic elves come into the house twice a week.'

I smiled brightly. 'It's nice to put a face to the—'

'House,' said Jim firmly, before I could say 'recycling bin'. I had made a few comments to him about how interesting it was to guess family habits from the contents of their recycling. The Armstrongs got through a lot of Chablis. And I mean, a *lot*. 'It's good to put a face to the *house*. I'm Jim, and this is Robyn.'

'Hello!' Sally stretched out her hand. I spotted a faint pinkening of her cheeks.

I don't think he was expecting a handshake, but even in a boilersuit Jim gave off 'handshake' vibes. I can't explain it. The intelligent eyes? The square shoulders? Whatever it was, Sally was shaking Jim's hand a tiny bit too long, and laughing nervously. And pushing her hair behind her ear.

What? I tried not to react but made a note to mention it to him later.

Jim, obviously, did not react at all.

'I'll make a start on the bathrooms,' he said, using an upward gesture to extract his hand from Sally's enthusiastic shaking. 'Robyn, if Mrs Armstrong needs the kitchen, maybe do upstairs today and we can blitz the kitchen on Monday instead?'

'No, no, I'll just … Please carry on around me!' Sally picked up her laptop and swept a football, Sunday's newspapers and two jam-sticky plates off the sofa. 'Sorry, we're in a bit of a flap, I don't usually work from home but Charlie has a hospital appointment this morning.'

I adopted the 'listening and cleaning' expression I'd perfected for Terry's monologues, and opened the dishwasher, stacking the dirty crockery that had been abandoned around the sink area. Jim had gone through the 'correct' process for stacking a dishwasher – yes, there was one – and now I did it on autopilot. I even did my own dishwasher the same way now.

'This was the only appointment with Mr Shah we could get this side of Christmas, and I've heard of people waiting *years* to see him so I don't know whether to be worried or not that we've been fast-tracked, I suppose I should be relieved but ...'

Sally Armstrong was still talking, but in a gabbling rush that I recognised as one of my own habits – for me, it was a sure sign that anxiety was at the controls and running riot. I was half-listening but also conscious that if I stopped for even five seconds I would get behind; the Armstrongs' house required every possible moment of our allocated hours.

Someone had been making tomato sauce again, I noted, seeing fresh splodges welded to the hob I'd only got clean the previous visit. Always tomato sauce. Did they ever cook anything else? I sprayed it with the special hob blitzer and turned my attention to the grease-spotted toaster.

'... funny thing was, though – when I was going through the questionnaire with Charlie's teacher, I could have answered yes to so many of the questions myself. And I've read that it can be a hereditary condition, which made me think is it my fault, is it something *I've* ...' Sally's voice had been getting higher, and now the sudden catch, almost a sob, made me stop.

I turned and gave her my full attention. She seemed so distressed, it was the least I could do.

'I'm sure that's not the case,' I said, even though I had no idea if it was or wasn't.

She shook her head. 'Not necessarily. It's often missed in girls. You can spot ADHD more easily in boys – it's such a cliché, the uncontrolled energy, hyperactivity, loudness. Hard to miss. But in girls it's the other way around – it's all hidden.'

Sally had started to tidy up as she spoke, robotically scooping socks and toys off the sofa, plumping up cushions. 'The heartbreaking thing is that girls are too good at blending in. We copy our friends, we hide behind lists, we work three times as hard to keep up and still get distracted.' She laughed, but she obviously didn't find any of this funny. 'I mean, that's me right there. I've done a Ph.D.'s worth of googling this week alone when I should have been preparing a case study for work. Did you know casein is a problem for some kids with ADHD? So obviously we're screwed – the amount of dairy we get through as a family, you'd think we bathe in the stuff. Well, you know that, you've seen our recycling bin.'

Outside, I could hear Charlie's ball bouncing in the same repetitive pattern. *Thunk ... kerthunk.*

Sally stopped, as if mentioning the recycling had suddenly reminded her that I was a cleaner, not her friend. 'Sorry. Sorry. It's just been a lot to take in, and it explains ... so much.' She frowned, reached behind a cushion and removed an Action Man which she held for a moment, unsure what to do with it, until I stepped forward and took it from her.

'Thanks.' Her voice was wobbling again. 'Marcus is right, this place is embarrassing.'

I dropped the Action Man in the basket of toys, a jumble of plastic arms and legs, dinosaurs and tractors.

'I try to keep on top of it, but I don't get home till six and he works so late, and then the weekends are crazy, and I do try to make lists but I just …' Sally trailed off in despair and looked up at me. 'Be honest, do cleaners judge people for letting their houses get like this?'

'No,' I white-lied.

'I wish I could wave a magic wand,' she sighed, without specifying what she'd magic away. Everything, I suspected.

Sally's shoulders sagged and I wanted to tell her that everything she'd just said resonated with me – and that I too often felt as if I was suffocating in the same scary paralysis, when the world seemed deafening and demanding, driving me into a corner to hide. I couldn't even keep a small flat and a moderate amount of paperwork under control, let alone a house this size, three kids and a full-time job.

Outside, Charlie's *thunk … kerthunk* continued with metronomic regularity.

Jim appeared at the door. 'Robyn, if you're done in here, could you give me a hand moving the sofa in the sitting room? I think there's … ah, something underneath it.'

He always moved sofas to hoover underneath them. And rolled up carpets to mop floors.

His appearance broke the tension. Sally pulled herself together and managed a bright smile. 'I apologise now for whatever that might be.'

'Don't worry,' he said, reassuringly. 'We're here to clean it up, whatever it is.'

'As long as it's not a dead body,' I added. 'Apparently we have to report those.'

I don't know who looked more shocked, Jim or Sally, but at least it changed the subject.

'Did you hear what Sally Armstrong was saying?' I asked Jim.

'No, I was too busy scrubbing the bath. I don't know what bath oil they're using but it manages to catch *all* the grime and then somehow welds it to the enamel.' He overtook a cyclist, very carefully. 'It's probably got an industrial use, if they could patent it.'

'Charlie's been diagnosed with ADHD. That's why she was at home, to take him to a specialist.'

'Hmm.'

'What? Is that a "that makes sense" hmm, or a "that's a load of nonsense" hmm?'

'It's a "this is none of our business" hmm.'

I bridled. 'She *told* me. I had to listen, I was being polite. I was in her house!'

'I'm sure I've said this before, but we're there to clean, not chat.'

This was typical Jim, I thought. In an ideal world, he'd probably remove the people from the houses altogether. Stupid, messy people, undoing his good work.

'It was interesting, what she was telling me about girls and boys having the same issues but presenting completely differently,' I went on. 'Boys with ADHD symptoms are all outward energy, whereas girls turn everything inwards. Girls focus on control, because they feel out of control, and because organisation's seen as a *good* thing, no one asks why they're so obsessed with it.'

I could relate to that. As a teenager, I spent every Sunday night making detailed timetables of what I needed to do that week – not just homework, but what clothes I needed and which night to wash my hair. I didn't trust myself to remember everything, in the right order. If I lost the list, or if Cleo used up the hot water on Tuesday night, I went to pieces.

Like the time I left my diary on the bus.

I hadn't thought about it in years but as soon as I pictured the little red book with its three yellow elastic bands wrapped around it my chest hollowed out. Mum had assumed I was in hysterics because it was a *diary* diary, dangerously crammed with gossip about who I fancied and/or hated that week, but it was me that I'd lost: my life inside my planner, with five-colour highlighter and Post-its. Without it, I literally wouldn't have known what time to get up. And yet everyone used to tell me how much they envied my natural efficiency. They had no idea it was all utterly artificial.

'And?' said Jim, into the silence that had developed.

I couldn't shake the hollowness. 'And what?'

'It felt like there was going to be a punchline.'

I shrugged. The punchline wasn't funny. I'd nearly been sick, convinced that my diary was in someone else's hands, that some sixth-form mean girls had it and were pissing themselves laughing at my pathetic reminders to put my shirts in the laundry basket and shave my legs before PE. I'd begged Mum to drive me to the bus depot to get it. *Begged.* And she had – but only after she'd collected Cleo from Elliot's house, where Cleo shouldn't even have been on account of being grounded. Cleo always came first with Mum. We got there just after it closed and I had to plead with them, in tears, to unlock the door.

'Not everything has to have a label slapped on it,' Jim was saying, in his irritating Voice of Reason voice. 'Everyone's different. Like that whole left-brain, right-brain business. Would that perhaps explain why you go in big circles, not straight lines whenever you're called upon to clean a glass surface?'

'I don't think psychiatrists use window-cleaning as a diagnostic tool,' I said stiffly.

Jim glanced over. I knew I sounded grumpy; I wasn't really grumpy with him, it was delayed grumpiness at Mum and Cleo.

Hadn't anyone noticed how stressed I was as a teenager? Could my life have been different if someone *had*?

I slumped back in my seat. Up to that point I hadn't realised I'd been leaning forward.

Wisely, Jim switched tack. 'I've been meaning to ask you – how did it go?'

'How did what go?'

'Your interview on Wednesday. Now we're out of hours you can tell me, can't you?'

I looked at the van's clock: one minute past five. Jim had waited until the end of the working day to ask about my interview with another employer. Cleo would be proud.

'It went well. I'm meeting with the directors at the start of next week. But to be honest ...' Was this tempting fate? I didn't care. 'She more or less said she'd give me the job then and there if it was up to her.'

'Congratulations. When would you start?'

'It's a maternity cover so ... soon? They sound run off their feet, that's probably why it's been sorted so quickly.'

'Or maybe you're the ideal candidate.'

Cheesy, but kind. 'Maybe.'

I wasn't sure what to say next. Would I carry on working next week, if Liv offered me the job on Monday? I could do with the money.

It suddenly occurred to me that Jim wasn't even my boss; I should probably have told Cleo I'd applied for a job before I told Jim I'd got it. Which I actually hadn't, yet.

I kicked myself, imagining Cleo's reaction. Every time I resolved to be less impulsive and more discreet I did something like this. Not a big thing, but if Jim told Cleo before I did she'd go nuclear.

'Jim, do you mind keeping it to yourself for now?'

'You haven't told Cleo, have you?'

'No. No, I haven't.'

'You need to do that asap.' Jim signalled and pulled into a bus stop. 'Do you mind if I drop you off here tonight? I need to be somewhere at half five.'

Really? Where, I wondered? Jim hadn't given me a single clue about where he went at the end of the day, or where he came from in the morning. Who he went back to, or what he did when he went there. His entire personality began and ended in the Taylor Maid van.

'Anywhere interesting?' I asked.

There was a pause. 'Rugby practice.'

Rugby? I didn't know a lot about rugby other than what I'd seen on television but I had a sudden memory of the plant shelf falling down in Adam Doherty's bathroom, and the smooth way Jim had spun round, stopped it sliding and held it there as if it weighed nothing. The flex of his muscle, the speed of his movement had suggested someone with quick reactions, someone unafraid of physical contact. That was rugby, wasn't it?

I tried to imagine Jim streaked with mud, sweaty and shouting, but that was a step too far.

'Playing?' I probed.

'No, coaching. But have a good weekend. Thanks again for the croissant,' he went on, before I could even ask *where* or *with whom*, 'and watch for the bicycles up the cycle lane!'

He was definitely cutting the conversation short. How rude, I thought; I was only being friendly.

'No worries.' I grabbed my bag, checked for cyclists and got out. By chance, Jim had dropped me a few streets away from my real flat, and I was familiar enough now with the short cuts to sneak home without needing to change. If I walked quickly, I could be back by …

'Robyn? Robyn!'

I spun round.

Jim was leaning across the seat, looking up at me from the van. From that angle, I noticed his right hand resting on the wheel; it was strong, big enough to hold a rugby ball in one hand while he ran. I thought of the way he'd caught the falling plant as it slipped off the shelf; the satisfying trajectory of it, falling and landing safely into his hand.

Cricket. I could see Jim playing cricket.

'What?' I asked.

'Just wanted to know if this was a goodbye,' he said, simply.

I didn't know what to say to that. Was it? I hadn't thought about it in those terms; I was happy to draw a line under my cleaning career but in a funny way I would miss Jim, in the same way I missed books that I'd started but not finished.

Not because I'd lost interest, but because disorganisation had let them drift into a pile of papers and unread magazines, with the characters only half-met and the situations still unresolved.

There was obviously a lot more about Jim than I knew. The fact that he didn't share anything was, in itself, quite intriguing.

'I might do some more shifts next week,' I said.

Did he smile? I think he smiled, quickly and wryly.

'Good,' he said, his face serious again. 'See you on Monday.'

12

~ If you're really, really bad at sticking to a task, set a timer on your phone for fifteen minutes and focus on doing one thing – hanging up laundry, hoovering, emptying the dishwasher – until the timer goes off. Enjoy the school-bell feel of your task being 'over'.

Cleo phoned me first thing on Saturday morning and didn't waste time on pleasantries.

'Where are you?' she demanded.

I was in bed, obviously, idly stalking Mitch online while pondering which clothes I should buy for my new job, and where I might suggest he and I went for dinner to celebrate, when Cleo's voice blasted through my contentment like a foghorn.

Startled, I struggled to a sitting position.

Where was I *supposed* to be? Was it not Saturday? The last thing I'd done before falling into bed on Friday night was to shove my filthy overalls in a hot wash. They were still in the machine, damp and ready to be remembered in a panic in the early hours of Monday morning.

'I didn't know I was supposed to be at work today. Look, don't shout at me, but I don't have any clean uniform. You're going to have to—'

'What? No. It's not cleaning. I need you here to help get things ready.' Cleo paused, as if she couldn't believe she had to spell it out. 'For Wes's party?'

Wes. My youngest nephew. He was – I did some rapid mental arithmetic – eight today. I flopped back onto the pillows with a groan. Cleo's conversation with Elliot in her office had gone right out of my head, what with the job interview and the whole Mitch excitement.

This was going to be way more exhausting than scrubbing floors, and a lot noisier.

'Remind me,' I said. 'This year's theme is …?'

'Trampolining. Midday at Jumping Jumping. No jewellery, no sharp objects. Wear washable clothing.' Cleo sounded momentarily weary. 'Very washable clothing. I think that bug you had might going round the school.'

'Oh good,' I said.

I headed straight to Cleo's via Tesco Express to purchase a gift card for Wes; boring, yes, but I knew from fifteen years of buying presents for his brothers that a gift card would be preferable to whatever a thirty-something woman imagined an eight-year-old boy would want.

It was barely nine, but party prep was in full swing. There was a minibus on the drive by the house; Mum's Polo was parked next to it, and Cleo was checking things off a list, a clipboard in one hand and a travel mug in the other. She swigged and grimaced; it probably contained an octuple espresso.

'You took your time!' she said, by way of greeting, and steered me towards the garage, where Mum and Dad were at work assembling a production line of party bags.

'Morning, party people!' I said.

Mum smiled wanly over a catering box of Haribo and fake tattoos. Dad waved a whoopee cushion at me.

'*Not* the whoopee cushions, Dad!' said Cleo. She swung back to me with the clipboard, ignoring the prolonged sound of a flatulent cow reverberating around the garage. The boys' parties brought out a side of Dad I rarely saw. 'Robyn, I need you to text everyone on this list to confirm that they'll be bringing their child round here for eleven and if they're not here, they're not getting in. OK?'

I nodded. It seemed unlikely. One boy was already waiting in a car with his mum opposite the house. 'Where's the birthday boy?' There was no sign of Wes, or indeed Alfie or Orson.

Cleo's glossy pink lips compressed into a flat line. 'Face-timing Elliot.'

I seized on that: I'd been trying to work out how to bring up the Elliot issue on the way over. 'Will Elliot be joining us?'

Mum and Dad studiously resumed packing party bags.

Cleo snorted. 'It depends on his work commitments.'

This, I felt, was unfair. Elliot's workaholic nature had been there from the start. As is tragically the way, Elliot's ambition was one of the traits Cleo had loved most about him to begin with. But as we got older and Elliot rose in the breakdown world, business leeched all the fun out of him. He always attended his sons' parties, lurking in a corner on his work phone, a finger in his ear to block out the shrieking, while Cleo flew around spinning the plates, literally and metaphorically. Cleo's mood would build from muttering to hissing to snarling at Elliot, and he didn't always make it to the candle-blowing-out.

Which was really bad, in anyone's book.

Ironically, now Elliot and Cleo had separated, I thought he spent more time with the boys: he turned up at a pre-arranged hour, shoved them in whatever fancy car he was driving and then sat in McDonald's, fighting recovery-related fires while Alfie, Orson and Wes ate whatever they liked.

'Elliot's taking the boys out for food afterwards,' Cleo informed me, as if he was taking them to play on the railway lines. 'He's picking them up from here at four.'

'Will he be having a go on the trampolines?' I asked.

'I'll be bouncing him off the walls myself if he's forgotten a present.'

Dad made a forlorn parp with his whoopee cushion.

'Paul!' said Mum, under her breath.

The party mums started dropping off their boys right on time, almost as if they were scared not to, and by eleven fifteen we were on our way: Cleo driving the minibus and checking arrangements with the trampoline centre on her Bluetooth headset, with Mum and Dad in the seat behind her, Wes next to Orson, and me next to Alfie. Behind us were most of Wes's school class, in a state of collective excitement.

Despite the age gap, there had never been a question that Alfie and Orson wouldn't be coming with us to the trampoline park. The older two were close, and both treated Wes like a cross between a family Labrador and a science project. In front of me, Wes was telling Orson exactly how he planned to execute a triple pike backward whatever; I couldn't see Orson's face but he seemed to be listening. I turned to Alfie.

'Nice that you both want to go trampolining with your little bro,' I whispered.

Alfie removed one AirPod from his ear, made a 'cash' gesture with his thumb and fingers, and replaced the AirPod.

'Fair enough,' I said. Alfie was fifteen, going on twenty-seven, and had both his parents' eye for a business opportunity. He'd been born on the same day as my graduation so Dad had attended that, and Mum had gone to Cleo's bedside to hold her hand and keep Elliot's large and enthusiastic (and now largely emigrated to Spain) family out of the maternity suite. Orson arrived twelve months and three days later: Cleo initially intended to get the messy side of parenting over in one go. Depending on how many vodkas she'd had, she'd confide that Wes was either a 'wonderful blessing' or the result of the starlight and sambucas above the hot tub on the thirtieth birthday safari Elliot had arranged for her.

So, all those bonuses and overtime were good for *something*.

The party coordinators at the trampoline centre met us in the car park and from there they swept the assembled guests inside, where two hours of loud bouncing, interspersed with competitive wall-climbing and mini pizzas, commenced.

'This is nice, isn't it?' said Mum, as we sat watching from the cafe area.

I was checking my phone to see if Mitch had replied to my message about meeting for Sunday brunch at a new vegan restaurant that had just in town. He'd read it (good) but hadn't yet replied (hmm). 'What? Seeing the kids enjoying themselves?'

'That, yes.' Mum stretched her legs out. 'But mainly not being allowed to help.'

Dad and I nodded our agreement. Jake, Jack and Josh, the Bounce Kings, had directed us to the cafe and told us to help ourselves to complimentary coffee and focus on 'making memories'. From a safe distance, for reasons of insurance. Only Cleo was allowed to get anywhere near the trampolines, and that was only after an intense discussion about whether she'd be able to make memories without first capturing them on her phone.

Mum, Dad and I chatted about Wes's birthday present (a bike), and what Alfie and Orson had been up to, and when Dad went off to find more coffee Mum turned the conversation to me.

'So,' she began, in a not-convincing casual tone. 'How are things with you? Any news on the job front?'

'Actually, yes.' God, it was nice to say that and mean it. 'I had an interview this week and I think, touch wood, they're going to offer me the job!'

Mum's face lit up with relief. 'Have you? That's *great*, love. Who's it with?'

I regretted that immediately. Should I have told her, before I'd got official word? Probably not. Still, there wasn't much point rowing back now, and Mum looked so pleased I couldn't stop myself telling her all about it.

'Good for you, Robyn.' She beamed with pleasure. 'I never had any doubt that you'd find something else. So when would they want you to start?'

A cautious person would have stopped at this point, but I was not that person. 'Soon. It's a maternity cover.'

'So not a permanent role? Might they not make it permanent, if you do well?'

'Maybe, but actually that's OK.' I'd been thinking about this: six months was long enough to get the planning stages of Lark Manor underway, then I could start on the marketing and sales plan. It couldn't be more perfectly timed. But what with all the yelling and loud pop music going on behind us, this was hardly the time to explain that to Mum. 'I've got another project in the pipeline for later this year, so this is going to dovetail nicely.'

'Another project?'

I made a 'lips-zipped' gesture across my mouth. This, I *could* force myself to shut up about. I wanted to present Mum and Dad with the sales brochures, then tell them I wasn't just selling these apartments, I'd overseen the design and marketing, and – drum roll, please! – I owned one! The delight on their faces. The pride, the admiration, the …

Mum's voice cut through my daydream. 'Does Cleo know you've got this job?'

'Not yet. But she knows I'm looking. It's not like she'd want me on her cleaning staff long term, is it?'

'You should tell her,' Mum insisted. 'She's done you a favour, and you can't just leave her in the lurch when things are so …'

'Hang on, didn't you say you thought *I* was doing *her* a favour by …'

'Who's doing who a favour?'

I jumped. Orson, Cleo's middle son, had inherited his mother's ability to appear out of nowhere, despite now being nearly as tall as her already. He had Elliot's long lashes, Cleo's long legs, and, inexplicably, thick hair the exact colour of conkers. Genetics wasn't fair, I often thought. I'd have loved hair like Orson's.

'Shouldn't you be bouncing?' I asked.

'Not allowed. Too big. I might break someone. And I've done the climbing walls here four times already.' He picked up the top half of the cake Mum had been saving for last, the bit with the icing on, and shoved it in his mouth. He was also going through a startling growth spurt, consuming any food in his wake like an adolescent Pac-Man.

'Orson! That was Nanna's cake!'

'It's fine, love.' Mum gave me a reproachful look. She'd stopped telling the boys off for anything when Elliot left. They could have blown up the house and she would just have sighed.

'When's Dad coming?' he asked, through a mouthful of crumbs.

'Four,' said Mum. 'Maybe make that your last piece of cake?'

Orson rolled his eyes and sat down in the seat next to mine. I gave him a one-arm hug. My arm only just went around his shoulders; I could understand why the Bounce Kings had refused to let him bounce with Wes's relatively fragile friends.

'You know,' I said, affectionately, 'it only feels like yesterday since you—'

'Since I was a tiny baby and you accidentally left me in a Starbucks in my carry seat and Mum called the police,' parroted Orson. 'And it isn't yesterday, Auntie Rob, it's nearly fourteen years ago.'

'Where does the time go!' said Mum, right on cue, which made Orson roll his eyes again.

I looked at the strapping teenager slumped in his seat. Fourteen years had gone in a flash. Life was going too quickly. Even if I had a baby right now, I'd be well over fifty by the time I had a strapping teenager of my own. Fifty! And what if I wanted another? Was there even *time* for an accidental Wes?

My imagination wandered. Mitch was a couple of years older than me and wasn't married. (Not as far as I'd been able to find out, anyway.) Was he broody? I indulged a brief 'what would our baby look like?' daydream, then stopped, because Mum was giving me her 'tick-tock' look.

I hated that look. Mum and Cleo had got even closer since the boys were born, and while I'm sure Mum wanted me to join their little club, something about that sympathetic look made me want to protest that I was *fine*; that I was too busy focusing on my career trajectory, thanks; that children weren't the only signifier of a complete life – and several other arguments that I didn't necessarily believe.

'Did I mention,' I started, recklessly, 'that I'm also seeing a …?'

'Hey, Auntie Rob!' The smell of pizza and Fanta was suddenly very close to my face.

Wes.

'You're seeing …?' Mum prompted, but I wasn't going to tell her, not with Orson and Wes around. Our night of passion in Worcester would take some filtering for Mum's ears, let alone theirs.

I turned to Wes. 'Shouldn't you be on the trampolines?'

'Mum says I've got to let other people get a go. I need to be hospitable.' He grabbed a bag of crisps from Mum's bag of 'spare' food.

'Are you enjoying your party, Wes?' asked Mum.

'Yeah, it's great!' He turned to her with a serious look. 'Were birthday parties invented back when you were young, Nanna?'

I stiffened instinctively. Cleo told me she'd had 'the chat' with Orson and Alfie about never asking Nanna about her family, but maybe she'd forgotten to have it with Wes. Or maybe Wes didn't have the family 'under the carpet' gene.

'Of course we had parties. Same as you.'

'In what way?'

It was a phrase he'd learned from the teaching assistant at school. He used it a *lot*.

'Well, I had a birthday cake.' Mum blinked, twice. 'And we played games. Musical statues, musical chairs.'

'Did you *have* music in the olden days?' he asked, wonderingly.

'Wesley! How old do you think I am? It was the 1970s, not the 1870s.'

'She used to get the housemaid to wind up the gramophone,' I explained, trying to lighten the mood. 'And lift the needle off the record when it was time to stop.'

Mum spluttered, but Wes wasn't deterred.

'And did *your* grandpa make a cake? Like Grandpa does for me?'

We were well into uncharted waters here, and I knew I had to change the subject, but part of me was as curious as Wes. I literally had no idea who Mum's grandpa – my own great-grandpa – was. I only remembered meeting my grandfather once, when I was six. There was an awful strained mood the whole weekend. It ended so disastrously that we never spoke about it afterwards and, hands up, it was my fault. Mum and Dad left me and Cleo in the car while Mum said goodbye to Grandpa, and they were gone so long that I got bored. So bored that I let the handbrake off to see what it would do, and of course it rolled backwards and crashed into a wall. There was so much yelling and shouting I was sick every time I got into a car for a long time after. It also blanked out every other memory of that trip. Just the yelling and tears and the AA lorry.

Mum 'didn't get on with' her dad and, as with her mum and sister, Dad had been very emphatic that we weren't to ask about him either. I had a vague memory of grey hair, a sports jacket and the suffocating smell of tobacco. We got a lot of presents from our Taylor grandparents to make up for it.

'No,' said Mum. 'That's just something Paul – Grandpa – does because he likes watching *Bake Off*.'

'In what way?'

'Well, he likes the challenge of sugarcraft. And blowtorches.' She looked flustered. 'He used to work on a building site when he was younger.'

'Did he? I thought Dad always worked for the electricity board.' What a feast of family revelations this was turning into.

'When he was a student,' said Mum, cagily. She glanced over to where Cleo was dealing firmly with Willow Jones, demanding a prize for her forward tumble, even though there *were* no prizes. 'I think a space has come up on the trampolines, Wes!'

'What about you, Auntie Rob?' asked Orson, unexpectedly. He was at an age where anything to do with family was usually 'boring' or 'gross'. 'What were your parties like?'

'Oh, your mum and I *loved* our birthday parties as kids,' I said. 'Pass the parcel, Sleeping Lions, we had a great time! I'd have a party like that even now, if I could.'

'Would you?' Mum seemed touched. 'They were very basic, compared with this.'

'We had loads of fun.' I wanted to hug her with my words. 'I *loved* your Pin the Tail on the Donkey. Those amazing treasure-hunt maps you drew for us! And the pineapple hedgehog.'

We were the only family at school still enjoying a pineapple hedgehog in the late nineties. Mum made it because her mum had made it for her. It was one of the few things I knew about my grandma, a precious nugget of information Mum was happy to share, and so the pineapple hedgehog had become an unspoken grandmaternal presence at our parties.

'That sounds literally disgusting.' Wes screwed up his nose.

'I'll make you one later.' Mum patted Wes and Orson. 'Go on, you two, get bouncing while you've time.'

'We should do that more,' I said, as Alfie boosted Wes up onto a trampoline then pushed him over for good luck. I could hear Wes saying, '... *actual* hedgehog?'

'Do what more?'

'Talk to the kids about family memories.' I was thinking about Terry, who loved telling me stories about his sons and grandchildren, his kindly bruiser of a dad and his sainted mum. I felt I knew them better than I did my own family.

Mum's shoulders stiffened. 'No, they're not interested in that.'

'But I'd like to know.' I tried to meet her eye but she was busy tidying up the plates, scraping off the cake crumbs and stacking them for the waitress. 'A client of Cleo's asked me the other day how you and Dad met and I had no idea.'

Terry, again. He felt he had to ask me a question now and again, if only so he could tell me how *his* mum and dad met ('magistrates' court').

'Mum?' I pushed. 'I'm talking about you. You and Dad. *My* childhood.'

It hung in the air between us, the silent 'not your childhood, *mine*'.

She stopped tidying and met my gaze. Her expression was guarded, and I felt hurt, and a little uneasy. 'Mum?' I repeated, less certainly.

Abruptly, her expression brightened. 'Here's your father with the coffee! Come on, Robyn, move some of these empties.'

I frowned, but moved the plates so Dad could set down the tray of coffees and cake. He leaned forward and I realised he was rolling his eyes meaningfully towards the door as if he was trying to dislodge an eyelash.

'What's the matter with your eye, Paul?' asked Mum. 'You're not starting with that allergy again?'

'No! Have you seen who's here?'

We turned, as one, and saw Elliot standing by the door, holding three metallic balloons all in the shape of an eight. It was a nice idea but it made him look as if he was celebrating some sort of sales milestone, not his son's birthday.

'He's early,' said Mum.

'Good!' Dad selected the biggest slice of cake. 'He can watch his boy having fun with his pals. What's wrong with that?'

'He's gone off timetable, *that's* what's wrong with that,' I observed, as Cleo abandoned her trampoline awards and marched over to the door, where she embarked on a sotto voce lecture about timekeeping, going by the way she kept twisting her wrist to look at her watch with as much subtlety as a mime artist. Elliot's shoulders slumped further the longer she went on.

At work, he was a world builder. Cleo could reduce him to a nervous wreck in ten seconds.

'I feel sorry for the fella,' said Dad. 'I reckon it's six of one, half a dozen of the other with those two.'

'Have you forgotten what he did?' I still didn't know what Elliot had done, apart from work too hard. But I could guess. Mum was easy-going apart from three things: incorrect punctuation on signs, thank-you notes and people treating her family badly. She would have made a terrific Mafia boss. All the death threats would have been menacing *and* grammatically correct.

'We only get one side of the story.' Dad sipped his coffee, clearly going for a full set of cliches. 'They should kiss and make up, if you ask me. For the boys' sake.'

'*Paul*!'

'What?'

Mum's eyebrows jiggled. 'He's coming over.'

We simultaneously straightened up, which probably only made Elliot wonder what we'd been saying about him.

'Hello Mel, Paul,' he said, warily. His 888 balloons bobbed behind him like overkeen backing singers. 'Robyn.'

'Hello Elliot,' we chorused.

Cleo had told us, when they split up, that we were to be cordial with Elliot. 'He's still the boys' father,' she said, as if that was something she'd have preferred to have withdrawn, along with his house key and name on the deeds.

It wasn't a problem for me: I liked Elliot. But then I'd been at school with him, and had seen how much he'd had to put up with from Cleo over the years. Plus, everyone had a bit of a crush on Elliot, from his sexy highlights, courtesy of his hairdresser sister, Rhiannon, to his trainers, courtesy of his Saturday job cleaning cars in his uncle's dealership. I didn't exactly benefit from the halo effect of Cleo and Elliot's combined coolness but, put it like this, I didn't have to attend prom with my best mate like Shelley Collett and Sophie Roberts. Even twenty years on, I occasionally consoled myself with that fact.

'Everyone had a good afternoon?' Elliot asked.

I thought he looked knackered. 'They've had a great time,' I said. 'Hopefully they'll be worn out now for you!'

'Where are you heading off to?' asked Dad.

'The Beefy Boys. Then a film?' He sounded wary, as if it was a test.

That made me sad. He'd never been wary before; he'd treated us like members of his own sprawling family. A very small, rather uptight outpost of it.

'Fantastic!' said Dad, encouragingly.

'Sounds great!' I was conscious that Dad and I were being weirdly jolly, and Mum was saying nothing.

Personally, I didn't buy Mum's affair theory. For a start, Elliot was too busy for any malarky. Besides, look at the evidence – Elliot was hardly dressing like a man in the throes of a new passion: he was wearing an old Hard Rock Cafe T-shirt and a pair of cargo pants. Cargo pants! Cleo would never have let him out of the house looking like that. My money was on a row with Cleo about an entirely different matter. Maybe something she'd done? Something Elliot hadn't done? Or maybe just one of those rows that was about nothing at all. Cleo didn't always need a reason.

It seemed clear to me that neither of them was happy apart. None of *us* were, certainly. And whatever problems they'd had, surely it was worth trying again? But that would involve Cleo backing down or forgiving him, and neither of those options seemed likely. She wouldn't even discuss counselling.

'Have you had your hair done, Mel?' Elliot asked, uneasily. 'You're looking … very nice.'

I got the horrible feeling Mum was about to say, 'It's Mrs Taylor to you, Elliot,' but Cleo saved us from further conversational misery by arriving with Wes.

'Right, then, we're more or less finished here. Wes, get your things together, and we'll thank everyone for coming. Then you can go with your dad to … whatever he's got lined up.'

Irresponsible Adult

I exchanged glances with Mum and Dad but they were smiling politely, which meant nothing. We shepherded the guests into the changing rooms, checked they'd got everything and loaded them back onto the minibus, as Wes, Orson and Alfie trailed off with Elliot towards his BMW, parked, as usual, across two spaces in the car park so no one opened a door onto his paintwork.

I savoured one backward glance at the party area, which looked like a crisp bomb had hit it. I felt very sorry for the cleaners.

Mum and I were the last ones on the minibus, balancing cakes and presents in our arms. As we sat down, Mum coughed. 'We met at the pub,' she said. 'Karaoke night.'

She refused to be drawn further, and Cleo started the headcount just as my phone finally pinged with the message I'd been waiting for all day.

> Brunch tomorrow? Wheatsheaf 2pm – booked in my name. Mx

Yes, I thought, grinning at my own reflection in the minibus window. *Yes*.

13

I got about thirty minutes' sleep on Sunday night, but that wasn't unusual: besides, I had a lot to think about, both real and, in the case of Mitch, ridiculous flights of fancy.

Sunday's brunch was exactly as I'd hoped it would be, up to a point. Fun, flirty, easy. I drank three mimosas in quick succession, then became light-hearted and (I think) tremendously witty. Mitch revealed that he too had been to university in Newcastle – what were the chances of that? – albeit on a different course to me and three years earlier, and actually at a different establishment, but even so *that* was a lot to bond over, and my fears that I'd handled the whole Worcester situation badly evaporated like the bubbles in my glass. He smiled, he laughed, he leaned over to try my waffles, and found excuses to touch my hand. It was going so well, until Mitch got a phone call from Allen at work, and it wasn't good news. There was a problem with some contracts, apparently, too boring to go into, but it required Mitch's input before Monday's meeting.

'I am so sorry,' he said, lining up another call as he signalled for the bill. 'Do you want to stay and have another mimosa? I don't know how long this will take.'

I pretended I had some paperwork of my own to catch up on, and left too.

We shared a brief kiss at the door, Mitch's phone pinging *and* vibrating throughout with a series of urgent messages which he ignored for a gratifying minute or two, but was terminated by the arrival of his Uber. I bit my lip. Somehow we'd managed to skirt around the topic of last Wednesday night altogether. How exactly were we leaving things? Did the fact that our night together didn't require a Big Discussion mean he'd enjoyed it? Regretted it? Would I look needy if I asked him which? Would I look desperate if I admitted I could only remember bits of it?

'I'll call you,' said Mitch, as if reading my angsty thoughts, and leaned over to kiss me on the cheek. I was momentarily disappointed by the politeness of it, but he gave my earlobe a nibble in passing, and my insides turned to water.

Later that afternoon, while I was having a pre-interview glow-up session, my phone pinged and I hoped Mitch was messaging to pick up where we'd left off. It wasn't: it was Cleo, checking to see if she should rota me or not.

Why not? I thought, squinting as I repainted my toe-nails an aspirational shade of crimson. I'd need a wardrobe overhaul for the new chapter in my life, and it wouldn't be cheap. Not now I was going places.

Jim seemed pleased to see me again on Monday, which is to say he smiled briefly, and reminded me it was oven-cleaning day at the Armstrongs' place (joy).

I hadn't heard yet from Olivia about the interview with the directors. I kept checking my phone for missed calls under the pretext of going to the loo until Jim was forced to ask if I was feeling all right. Then *finally* it rang at half past two, just as we were loading the buckets back into the van and heading to the next job.

Olivia Malvern Property.

I took a deep breath, and tried to shift my brain out of house-keeping mode and into exclusive property finder mode. It was hard enough, on account of the overalls, but now there was so much at stake my thoughts scattered like startled pigeons.

'Do you mind if I ...?' I was already edging backwards and Jim nodded, shortly, and carried on slotting equipment into the special hooks and nooks that stopped them rolling around in the back of the van.

'Hello, Liv!' I said, trying to project boundless positivity. 'How are you?'

'Very well, thanks. Is this a good time to talk?'

'It's perfect timing!' I assured her. 'If it's about coming in, I can do—'

'That's what I was calling about. We don't need ... you to come in.'

'Oh. OK!' That was a good thing, wasn't it? 'So do we need to talk about starting dates? I can be available when-ever suits you.'

Liv cleared her throat. Her voice was strange, not the friendly warmth of last Wednesday. She sounded embarrassed. 'I'm afraid we won't be taking your application any further at this time.'

What?

My head suddenly seemed too light, as if it might float off from my body, and I sat down gracelessly on a garden wall.

'I'm sorry, I don't understand.'

'I discussed your application with our board of directors and they felt you, er, you weren't quite the right fit for our team.'

But that was literally the last thing she said to me as I was leaving the office – what a great fit I *was* with the team!

I tried to focus on the pavement cracks in front of me, struggling to get a grip on the conversation as my attention bounced from one random thought to another. What was going on? What had happened? Had I missed something? Stop, stop, stop.

But all I could hear was the buzzing of a million bees in my head, slowly crawling out to my whole body. I was frozen to the spot yet vibrating at the same time.

Liv was closing the conversation with some pleasantries I barely heard. '... really appreciate your time. And I'll definitely check out that restaurant you mentioned in Newent!'

Say something, Robyn. Say something.

But I couldn't say anything. My mind was blank.

'Thank you,' I croaked.

'All the best for your next steps, Robyn,' she said.

Was that a laugh in the background? I went cold.

Liv hung up. The conversation was over.

I stood there for a minute or two, trying to process what had just happened. This wasn't right. This wasn't how it was supposed to go.

Jim was back in the driver's seat, waiting for me. He wasn't the sort of person who scrolled through their phone to kill some time; he was staring into space, probably practising his times tables.

I walked towards the passenger side on autopilot. Seven minutes ago I was counting down the days until I started work again as a property search expert. My haircut was booked for Wednesday. I'd planned a summer holiday. Now, none of that was going to happen, and I didn't know why.

Part of my brain clung onto that comforting future feeling, refusing to let go. Was I still asleep, maybe? Was I having a very specific, very vivid nightmare?

Jim started to say something jovial about drains, then clocked my face. 'Bad news?'

I didn't want to tell him. That would make it true. So I just shook my head.

'So when do you start?' He checked his mirrors, signalled, and pulled away. 'Any chance of a few days off first? Recover from your short but illustrious career as a professional cleaner?'

I wasn't listening. Was it something I'd said to Liv at the interview? I replayed our conversation over in my head, but parts of it were now blurry, thanks to the champagne and two bottles of wine with Mitch that had followed. I couldn't remember saying anything obviously wrong, though. I'd laughed in the right places. I'd made sensible observations about mortgage rates.

Then a terrible, *obvious*, realisation struck me.

She'd seen Emma Rossiter's Internet roasting. Of course she had. It didn't matter that Liv wasn't local; Emma had tagged it so anyone who followed property or estate agents or, for all I know, cute baby otters, would have seen me being exposed as the shoddy negotiator that I was.

'Oh god,' I moaned aloud.

'What?'

'Nothing.'

'It doesn't sound like nothing.'

I made a noise that was supposed to quell further questions but instead sounded pathetic. A scared whimper.

'Don't tell me, your hairdresser cancelled?' Something about the way Jim asked – not unsympathetic, but confident that it couldn't be *that* bad – made the words flow.

'They're not giving me the job.' It felt like I'd been sacked all over again, but this time I hadn't even *worked* there.

I was expecting Jim to say, 'You said it was a done deal,' but instead he frowned. 'Did she give you a reason?'

'No.'

I swallowed hard. *Come on, Robyn. Don't cry.*

'Why don't you phone her back and ask?'

'What?' I wondered if he could sense my whole body cringe back into the seat. '*No.*'

'Why not?'

I stared mutely at him. Why not? *Why not?*

'And don't say it's because you're embarrassed,' he went on, reading my mind. 'She let you think you had the job in the bag last week, and now you don't. Don't you want to know why? What on earth have you got to lose by asking for feedback?'

Liv could tell me I'm useless, I thought, with a lurch of shame. She could tell me that they laughed about me when I left, and rewatched that TikTok over and over. That I brought the name of property sales into disrepute, and just stood there opening and closing my mouth as a client spelled out my failings.

'Ring her back, apologise for taking a moment to process her comments, thank her for the opportunity and ask her what you can work on for next time,' Jim went on.

'No!'

I realised I had my hands clamped underneath my knees like a little girl.

'How do you expect to get the next job if you don't ask where you can improve?' Jim finally turned to look at me. We had stopped at traffic lights, but even so. He was a conscientious driver; he rarely took his eyes off the road unless completely necessary. This was worthy of emphasis.

Jim probably saw through me just like Liv had, I thought, mentally lashing myself with one of those spiky religious whip things. He had every right to laugh at me, given how smug I'd been about this interview last week, but instead he was trying to help, setting me straight as if I were a badly made bed, or a stubborn coffee ring on a marble worktop. I was *that* useless.

'Come on, Robyn, you said yourself you're an experienced estate agent,' he added.

'Negotiator.'

He blinked hard, possibly to stop himself rolling his eyes. '*Negotiator*. So it's hardly going to be something terrible. Maybe they can't afford to match your last salary?'

'We didn't discuss salary.'

'Or maybe one of the directors wants his own candidate?'

'Maybe.' That was a possibility.

'So ask her. Find out,' said Jim. 'Then you can move on.'

'Yes,' I said.

'Good.' He paused. 'Well?'

'I'm not going to ring her now, am I? While you're driving?'

The lights changed and we set off again.

'Hold that thought,' said Jim. 'I'm looking for somewhere safe to stop.'

I asked to speak to Liv when the receptionist answered, and it took an excruciating couple of minutes before she came on the line. Her tone, when she answered, was stilted.

'Hello, it's Robyn Taylor again, I'm so sorry, I think we got cut off earlier.' My voice was too high, too keen. I took a deep, deliberate breath.

'It's fine,' said Liv. 'We'd covered everything we needed to say, though, hadn't we?'

I glanced over to Jim, who made encouraging bobbin-weaving gestures with his hands. He'd parked up in a quiet cul-de-sac and I'd got out of the car, for the fresh air and privacy. Jim had also got out of the car. He was standing a few discreet metres from me, next to a postbox. Like an unwanted stage prompter.

'I was wondering …' I stumbled. 'Um, this is awkward but I was wondering if I could ask where I, um, could …'

Why couldn't I do this? Cleo would have no trouble asking for feedback.

I closed my eyes and pictured Cleo behind her desk, dynamic, fearless, focused. *How would Cleo handle this?* Then the words flowed in an impressive stream. 'Liv, I felt we had a very positive meeting last week, and from what we discussed, it seemed as if I *was* a good fit for the team. I'm disappointed that the directors didn't share that view, and I wonder if you could give me some feedback on my interview and what I could improve on going forward?'

Wow. Where had that come from?

Jim gave me a thumbs up, and then, urgently, put a finger over his pursed lips and frowned hard. I think he meant, 'and now shut up'.

If I hadn't been so stressed, I'd have laughed at his ridiculous panto expression.

There was a pause, then Liv said, 'OK, well, since you ask ... For one thing, HR raised a flag about your references. We like to see the last two employers. And you didn't give either, just a developer you'd worked for.'

Blood rushed into my cheeks. This was what I'd dreaded.

'Did you speak to Mitch Maitland?' Cleo's borrowed confidence was wearing off fast.

'We did,' she said. 'He was very complimentary about your abilities. But we also did our own due diligence and ...' Liv hunted for the right words. 'There's no nice way of putting this, Robyn, but my boss saw that TikTok your client filmed in the Marsh & Frett office. The one where you admitted you'd crashed some chains and basically let your clients down rather badly.'

I closed my eyes. I'd guessed right. Emma Rossiter loomed up at me, her face red with fury, everyone blurred in the background, heads swivelling between me and her. This was some revenge she was having. She was going to haunt me for the rest of my career, a real life Woman in Grey.

'Don't get me wrong,' Liv continued, 'we've all had difficult clients. And I'll be honest, we work with people who have requirements that make them, um, more challenging to satisfy. But when we followed up with Dean, he confirmed that the allegations *had* been reasonable and that, combined with the fact that you hadn't disclosed it at interview ...' Her voice trailed off.

'Oh,' I said, weakly.

'It had over 300,000 views,' Liv added, unnecessarily. 'Which is great reach, but just not the kind of publicity we want for our agents.'

Jim hovered closer, expecting to see the positive fruits of his advice blooming in real time. He wasn't expecting to see me on the verge of tears.

I gestured for him to go away and he took a clumsy step backwards.

'I'm sorry, Robyn,' said Liv. 'Am I telling you something you didn't know?'

Either way I was stuffed: a liar, or a self-proclaimed social media expert who didn't even monitor her own social media tags.

I swallowed and said, 'I understand.'

'Good luck with your next projects though! I'm sure this will blow over soon enough.'

Now she sounded sorry for me.

I struggled to salvage a crumb of dignity from the conversation. 'Thank you for telling me that, I appreciate your frankness.'

'Not a problem,' said Liv, safe in the knowledge that she had never been called a dangerously incompetent, narcissistic, marriage-wrecking bitch of an estate agent in front of everyone she worked with, and now the rest of the Internet.

I ended the call and covered my face with my hands.

So that was that. Back to square one.

Although not square one, a mean-spirited voice pointed out. Square *minus ten*. Because this was going to happen again, and again, and again, with every job I applied for.

I'd effectively made myself unemployable.

If you regularly suppress emotions, a therapist once told me, it's like pushing down a jack-in-the-box. When the lid inevitably pops off, you're liable to take your own eye out with the force of the blast. I'd managed to block out that mortifying, public dressing-down with relentless cleaning, and I'd done it so well that it was a genuine shock to feel the shame again.

The consequences of my actions rolled out in front of me. I'd have to tell Mum and Dad that I hadn't got the job I'd assured them was in the bag. Mum would be so disappointed. Dad would worry about my rent. They'd ask questions about my flat money and I'd have to tell them that it was safe, but that Mitch's project was still at the planning stages and I didn't have a date for repayment.

And Mitch! If he'd spoken to Liv, she might have told him why they'd rejected me and probably send him a link to the evidence. I cringed, hard. He hadn't mentioned it so far, and I didn't want his attention drawn to *that*.

Shame – and disappointment, and guilt, and despair – crashed over my head like a massive wave engulfing a tiny surfer. I pressed my hands over my eyes to stop the tears, but I couldn't.

I was useless. A failure.

I turned away and struggled with myself for a good minute before I sensed Jim standing behind me. He didn't touch me, or try to hug me, but something about his calmness had a weird effect on my gulping breaths. He was obviously deploying whatever Zen calming vibes he used to stop Rambo the terrier going crazy at squirrels on our walks.

'Tell me what you're so upset about,' he said.

It took me a few goes to get it out. 'I didn't … get the job … because I'm stupid and careless.'

'Really?' He sounded doubtful. 'Random and easily distracted, maybe. But you're not careless, and you're definitely not stupid.'

'I am! I was sacked from my last job because I was so disorganised that at least one major chain crashed because of me, costing people thousands of pounds. Thousands!'

'Ouch.'

'Yeah. Ouch.'

'Everyone makes mistakes,' said Jim. 'I'm sure you were a decent estate agent most of the time.'

'I wasn't.' I told him about the video, the one of me getting publicly bollocked by a client whose marriage fell apart because she and her idiot husband were stuck in the house that I should have sold.

Jim refused to accept that either. 'Come on. If marriages fell apart purely because of bad estate agents, no one would risk buying a house.'

'She's suing the agency!' My voice was rising, but I couldn't stop it. 'I don't even know if I'm going to end up going to court!' I stared at him. Why wasn't he getting it? Why was he being so stubborn?

A woman walking her dog passed us on the other side of the road. Both she and the dog were gawping at us, and she had to tug its lead to move it along.

Jim made a 'honestly, she's fine' gesture over my head, and steered me back towards the van, which in hindsight probably wasn't that reassuring to the passer-by.

We sat inside. The artificial smell of pine and cotton was soothing. I took some more deep breaths and realised it was comforting because it smelled like Mum's house.

'So, you didn't tell them about this video?' asked Jim.

'No! If I can't see it, it can't see me.'

'That's not going to help you. You should have told them, but then used it to show how you've gained positive insight into your professional weaknesses and grown from the experience, that it was a turning point in your career, learning points, blah blah.'

'OK, fine. But we're going to be late for our next job.'

He ignored me. 'People make mistakes. It's what you learn from them that counts. And the biggest part of that is acknowledging you made a mistake in the first place. I guarantee you won't ever work for a boss who hasn't screwed up at some stage.'

'But if this client sues, it could finish the agency.' I hadn't dared search to see what people were saying about Marsh & Frett now. My imagination was doing a good enough job. 'And they might sue *me* for damaging their reputation.'

'Again, think about that for a second instead of catastrophising.' Jim passed me a tissue from the box on the dashboard. 'How many people watching that will be planning on buying a house in the next year?'

'I don't know.' He waited until I admitted, 'Not many, I guess.'

'I'd say a handful, if that. And how reliable a witness does the woman look?'

'No idea, I haven't watched it.'

'I'm only guessing, but I suspect she comes out of it as badly as you do. No one looks good airing dirty linen.'

I blew my nose. Mad as it seemed, that hadn't occurred to me before.

'Shall we have a look at it now?' Jim got his phone out of the glove compartment – of course he didn't have it on him during work hours – and started searching through his apps.

'No!' I swivelled in my seat. 'No no no!'

'You need to see it, so you can face it and let it go.'

A terrible urge to get out of the van gripped me. 'No. No, I'm not going to ...'

'OK, OK.' Jim raised his palms. 'It's what I would do but —'

'I'm not you,' I snapped.

We sat in silence for a few minutes.

'So what would you do?' I asked, eventually. 'After you'd watched it, obviously.'

'Not much you can do. You're not going to get that job. But there'll be others.'

'But that was such a *great* job,' I moaned.

'Life goes on. You can't get stuck on what might have been. You're growing as a person until you die. That involves the shovelling of manure and some rain.'

I turned to him. 'Can I ask you something, Jim?'

His normally guarded face was open, a little wary. 'Sure.'

'Did you read that in a fortune cookie, or were you a vicar in a previous life?'

'Management course.' A smile twisted the corner of his mouth as he started the van's engine. 'One of my better lines, I thought.'

'Why were you on a management course?' I asked, innocently. 'Did Cleo send you on one?'

Jim's expression returned to its usual impassive state. 'As you said, previous life.'

I waited for him to expand on that, but it was soon clear he wasn't going to. I sank back in my seat. 'Well, don't book the Edinburgh Fringe any time soon. Can we go home now?'

'Nope,' said Jim. 'It's time for the Armstrongs' oven.'

I texted Mitch as soon as I got home and didn't get a reply until lunchtime the next day, as Monday's meeting with Allen and the contracts had been 'complicated', but his reaction was gratifyingly sympathetic.

Mitch assured me it was their loss, not mine, and offered to take my mind off it with dinner in a new place that had opened by the canal, a modern wine bar that had recently been refurbished to look like a derelict Victorian warehouse it had never been. De-furbished, I suppose.

When I told him why Malvern Property Finders had declined to pursue my job application, he laughed out loud.

'That was *you*? Oh my god, someone forwarded that to me, I didn't realise it was you.'

'You've seen it?' I said, horrified.

It was a tiny sliver of comfort that he didn't recognise me. But then I'd seen Mitch fail to recognise Natasha, his old office manager, when we'd bumped into her in a bar the previous week, so maybe he just wasn't good with faces.

'It wasn't very funny at the time,' I said. 'Or now, actually.'

Mitch struggled to return his expression to something more serious. I could see it took some effort. 'I'm sorry. But you've got to admit, when she …'

I put my hands over my ears. 'I don't want to talk about it. Please.'

'Fair enough.' He grinned and clinked his glass against mine. 'Still, you've put Marsh & Frett on the map. The logo's visible in the background the whole time. Any publicity's good publicity and all that.'

Was it?

'But I'd have loved that job,' I said. 'I'm sorry if it reflects badly on you.'

'Nah.' Mitch waved a dismissive hand. 'I've done much worse than that.'

'How?' It was easy enough to spout platitudes. Jim hadn't shared his own mistakes to make me feel better, just delivered some corporate advice about Teachable Moments. 'I need *examples*.'

Mitch shook his head. 'How long have you got? Oh my god ... well, there was the time I borrowed a show flat because my lease had run out, and an agent started showing a buyer round while I was in the shower. That was embarrassing. And then one of my first projects, I signed it off without doing a proper check, and it turned out that the fitters hadn't plumbed the kitchen pipes into anything. So the dishwashers were emptying into the pond outside. We only found out when all the fish died. Never seen cleaner koi carp, mind you. And then the time that I had to ...'

He stopped. 'You're not laughing. Maybe I shouldn't be telling you some of these, eh? Look, it's not that bad. Malvern Property are great but they can be a bit up themselves. If Liv can't see the funny side, you're better off somewhere else. Forget about it. Move on. Tomorrow's another day, yadda yadda.'

If Mitch and Jim were both offering identical 'move on' advice, then maybe there was something in it. I sighed and tried to think positive.

I still had the Lark Manor project to look forward to. I still had my beautiful apartment in the pipeline. None of that had changed. No one would be laughing when I slapped that glossy brochure down on the table.

I looked up, about to suggest another walk around Lark Manor now I had some time on my hands to think about spaces, but Mitch nodded at my glass. 'Time for another?'

It was ten to seven, the tipping point between 'quick drink' and 'should we eat?'

'Go on,' I said.

In a way this was good, I thought, as his hand stretched out across the table, one finger stroking mine. Crises were bonding. And Mitch hadn't run a mile, even though he'd seen me both drunk and now humiliated on social media. That had to be a green flag.

He ran his fingertip around the silver ring Mum and Dad had given me for my nineteenth birthday. Back and forth on the metal, then up the knuckle to the back of my hand. Little electrical shivers tingled across my skin. I reached out my own hand, and found the knotted leather bracelet hidden beneath his shirt cuff. The contrast between the office cotton and the surfer bracelet was deliberate and, even though part of me thought it was a *tiny* bit corny, I still couldn't help finding it sexy.

'Do you want to get something to eat?' I asked.

'What do you suggest?' He raised an eyebrow.

I had a pleasantly dizzy sensation as the evening fast-forwarded in my head. There were a couple of decent restaurant options in town, not including Ferrari's, and I could imagine us sharing a bottle of wine, some tapas, laughing, another bottle of wine, flirting. *Intense* flirting.

Then maybe he'd pull me into one of the old Georgian doorways along the high street, out of the streetlights, and we'd kiss hungrily in the darkness and then hurry hand in hand through the streets of Longhampton, back to his flat where ...

I stopped, realising I didn't know where Mitch lived. And did I want to go to his place anyway? I didn't have anything to change into if I stayed over, and more importantly, I wanted to redo the night in Worcester properly. And by properly I meant decent underwear, at the very least.

I rewound back to the bit where we were kissing hungrily in the darkness, then hurrying hand in hand through the streets of Longhampton back to *my* flat where …

Again I stopped, abruptly.

I couldn't invite anyone back to my flat, not the way it was. My mind's-eye film continued with Mitch stubbing his toe on the boxes in the hall, seeing the weighted blankets (plural) dumped on the bed, judging me on my junk. I hadn't loaded the dishwasher for three days, and the bed needed changing. When did I last change the sheets? I frowned, trying to remember if I'd even brought a second set of bedsheets with me.

'Robyn?'

I looked up. Mitch was gorgeous, and he was sitting there on the other side of the table, practically inviting me to come up with a seductive plan. I'd wanted this to happen for so long, I couldn't risk him finding out what a walking catastrophe I was. It had to be perfect.

'Pizza?' I suggested. Then heard myself say, 'I can't be too late, I've got work in the morning.'

I wanted him so much. I wanted to have that first time over again, but this time I wanted to remember every second of it. But how could I say that, without suggesting I was too drunk to know what I was doing at the time? Or that I couldn't remember it?

I smiled stupidly while my brain struggled to find a charming way of putting that.

'OK.' Mitch sounded confused. 'In that case, I should be getting back – I've got a breakfast meeting with a couple of investors.'

We were getting up from our seats – *why were we getting up from our seats? I'd happily have stayed for another drink!* – and he was signalling for the bill.

'Sounds exciting,' I said. 'Which project is that?'

I wanted to say, Is it Lark Manor? But that was all I seemed to say to Mitch. Lark Manor, Lark Manor, like a child.

'The Jam Factory, it's a music venue.' Mitch paid, left a generous cash tip, grinned at the waitress, and slipped on his jacket, pretty much in one fluid movement. 'You'd love it. I'll put you on the list for the soft opening.'

'Sounds great,' I said. But it wasn't my stunning new flat. The Christmas tree slipped backwards, visible but now out of reach.

We lingered by the door, then lingered some more by Mitch's car, where we had an awkward kiss that thankfully turned into a longer, much less awkward kiss. He tasted of mint and lime, and as he pulled me closer, the smell of his skin triggered a buried memory – the kissing in the hotel lift, his cool hands confidently slipping under my shirt, my body responding to his.

And then some teens on bikes cycled past hooting, and that was that.

I walked home, hot and bothered, with only one thought in my mind. I would tidy my flat tonight. Definitely. I couldn't let my own slovenliness destroy my sex life.

I tidied mentally all the way home, even buying some storage boxes online, then fell asleep on the sofa.

14

~ A quick way to clean your (empty!) kitchen bin is to use it as the bucket for your squeegee mop when you wash the kitchen floor. Fill with hot water and disinfectant, mop, rinse out, and voila, clean bin.

Cleo asked me to call by the office before work on Friday, and I arrived at the same time as Elliot was leaving.

I could see Wes in the back of Elliot's car, in his school uniform and miles away, watching something on his iPad.

'Hey, Elliot.' I raised my hand in a wave. 'Recovered from the birthday celebrations yet?'

'Robyn!' He smiled but something about his smile wasn't quite right. 'Can't stop, I'm taking Wes to school. Cleo says go straight in.'

'Everything all right with you?' I wanted Elliot to know not everyone in our family thought the worst of him.

'All good!'

'Work good?'

'Yep!'

'Family OK?'

His face clouded and I regretted asking.

'Robyn, hurry up, I haven't got all day!' yelled Cleo, and I waved an apologetic goodbye to Elliot and headed up the stairs myself.

Cleo was alone in her office, but she wasn't on the phone or doing her emails. She was staring out of the window into the garden, and she looked upset.

'Cleo! Are you …?' I started, concerned.

'Before you ask,' she snapped, wiping an eye with the back of her hand, 'this is nothing to do with Elliot, and I'm *fine*.'

'If you say so.'

She turned away again, as if suddenly interested in next door's cat, which was stalking something in her rockery. Oh. It was next door's dog.

'Shall I make you a coffee?' I asked, as I fancied one myself. A latte from Cleo's bean-to-cup machine put a fiver on my day's wages, once you took tax into account. I was slowly chipping back at the pile of pound coins in my mind that I'd spent on coffee in the last year.

'Yes, please,' she said. 'You know how I like it.'

I did. Five sugars. She was too embarrassed to ask anyone other than close family to make her a coffee and even then she didn't say it out loud.

By the time I'd spooned in half the sugar bowl, she'd recovered her composure and was back behind her control desk, the district cleaning commander once more.

I handed her the cup. 'I saw Elliot on the way up. Everything OK with him?'

I was braced for a rant about how his present for Wes had fallen short of both educational and safety expectations, but it didn't come. 'No, not really. I might as well tell you now – Rhiannon's been diagnosed with breast cancer. She's come back to the UK for treatment. She and Kev are staying with Elliot.'

239

'Oh no! I'm sorry to hear that. Do the boys know?'

That was awful news. Elliot's sister, Rhiannon, was good fun and a great hairdresser. We'd all benefited from Rhi's balayage skills over the years, including Elliot and, controversially, Alfie.

'I've told them as much as they need to know. The tests caught it early so fingers crossed, but ...' Cleo sighed. 'It makes you think, doesn't it?'

'It does.'

She carried on staring into her cup, lost in thought.

I waited respectfully. I guessed this blew my non-job news out of the water. Was this what Cleo had summoned me to the office for? 'Have you told Mum?' I asked, to break the silence.

She shook her head, then said unexpectedly, 'Has Mum mentioned Grandad to you recently? Her dad, I mean?'

Grandad. It felt strange to call him that. He was more of a theoretical figure, more an 'our mother's father' than Grandad. 'No. Why?'

'I was collecting Orson and Wes last night, and her phone rang while she was upstairs getting their things. I answered it for her, and it was someone called Gwen Thomas. Wanting to talk to her about her dad.'

'Definitely *her* dad?'

Cleo nodded. 'I passed the phone over, but when I told Mum who it was she just said, "Sorry, wrong number", and hung up. It wasn't though. This woman wanted to speak to her.'

'Did she say what about?'

'Not to me. The woman didn't say where she was calling from, and Mum didn't give her a chance to speak.'

How weird. 'Did you try googling her name?'

Cleo gave me a boggling look that reminded me, rather endearingly, of the many 'Robyn, you are so stupid' looks she'd bestowed on me in the past. 'Gwen Thomas? Do you have any idea how many people there are called Gwen Thomas?'

'So what's your best guess? Who is she?'

'I have no idea. She could be his neighbour or his carer, or his second wife or his secret daughter. Literally, anyone.'

'Maybe Grandad's ill? Maybe he's died?' I paused. We knew so little about Mum's family that the possibilities were limitless. Nothing was too random. 'Maybe he's left Mum his massive EuroMillions fortune and a castle on the Isle of Man?'

'My money's on ill,' said Cleo. 'And that's what worries me.'

We stared at each other, gloomily. We'd overheard a few half-conversations in the past, but this time we were more than capable of filling in the missing parts with adult fears.

'I've thought for a while that I need to know if there's anything in our medical history, for the boys' sakes as much as anything,' she went on. 'Yes, it's painful for Mum, I get that, but her grandsons are here and now.'

'Have you tried to talk to her about it? Maybe coming at it from that angle?'

'I've tried a few times over the years. She just clams up, says there was nothing, everyone was very healthy.' Cleo huffed. 'But how would she know?'

'What about Dad? Might he know how to get in touch with … her dad?'

'He just says, it's up to your mum. Won't get involved. He's so protective of her. And it's not just the health side of things. I wanted to ask her about ...' Cleo bit her lip and looked away, and I knew there was something else she wasn't telling me. Something too private and painful to share.

'What?' I pressed her, but she shook her head.

What was so bad that she wouldn't share it with her own sister? Panic ballooned in my chest. 'Cleo, you would tell me if *you* were ill, wouldn't you? Or one of the boys?'

'What? No.' Cleo's attention snapped back. 'No, I'm fine.'

We held each other's gaze for a moment while she struggled with her own frustration, and I tried to think of something wise to say.

Then Cleo clicked her pen and resumed normal service. 'So! When were you going to tell me about *your* news?'

'My news?'

'That you've got a new job.'

'I haven't,' I said. 'Who told you that? Mum?'

'It slipped out.'

'Yeah. Right.' I put my cup down, ready for the onslaught. 'I thought I had a job, but it fell through. So, yes, I am available to clean for you for the foreseeable.'

Cleo frowned. 'Explain.'

So I explained, and when I told her I'd been publicly shamed on TikTok, she sniggered and said, 'What? Someone posted your Paddington screen test?' which I thought was below the belt.

'I'm applying for others,' I said, haughtily. 'I've got projects in the pipeline.'

'Fine, fine. Just give me warning if you've got an interview, please, don't take the piss, be upfront – all that stuff we've talked about before. Be honest with me, it's all I ask.'

'I will,' I said. 'Brownie's honour.' I did the Brownie salute for good measure, which was ironic given the provenance of half of Cleo's badges.

'I'm serious, Robyn.' Cleo fixed me with a piercing look. 'Honesty. I expect other people to lie to me, Elliot and those bitches who stole my client list, and people who swear blind they never pour fat down their sinks, but if *you and I* aren't honest with each other ...' She paused, and I saw a flash of the old Cleo, the big sister I'd loved to help in the rare moments she wasn't ruling the world. 'Then everything's gone to shit, frankly.'

It was one of the nicest things she'd ever said to me.

'I've learned my lesson,' I said, earnestly. 'You can rely on me, Cleo.'

'Good. Your job sheet's by the door. And wash the cups up on your way out.'

Jim and I didn't usually clean Nikki Nardini's holiday cottage but Cleo had added it to the end of our day's timetable. Nikki was a pal of hers from Women in Business, she'd noted, so we had to do it properly.

'You'll like it,' Jim told me, as we pulled up outside. 'It's so new that the dust hasn't had time to get in any cracks.'

Nikki provided a list she required us to tick off so she could say she'd met various hygiene specifications. It was even more detailed than the standard Taylor Maid checklist, but I'd stopped taking lists personally. They made things easier; you didn't have to think. I wasn't even offended that Nikki's had 'flush loos' on it.

'I'll start with the bathroom.' Jim nodded towards the stairs. 'You do the kitchen.'

I propped the list on the windowsill and began cleaning but soon found he was right about how immaculate the place was; my cloths didn't get dirty as I wiped the surfaces. The hob was like a mirror. Even the pans were shiny.

As Jim went past, I caught his arm. 'Look!'

'What?' He turned round.

I opened the pull-out bin. It was empty, with a fresh bag inside. Then I opened the dishwasher: empty and turned off at the plug. 'This place is spotless. Are you sure we're supposed to be here today? Don't holiday lets normally turn around on a Monday or Friday?'

My question was answered by the arrival of the flustered owner, Nikki, who was followed by a teenager wielding a camera. 'Hello, hello!' she said. 'I'm *so* sorry to interrupt. Is this a good time?'

People were always apologising for interrupting my cleaning. I don't know why. I never minded stopping.

'Have we got the right day?' Jim enquired. 'Everything seems to be clean already.'

'Didn't you get the message? I thought I'd explained to Cleo.' She turned to the teenager. 'Paige, do you want to take over from here, love? I'm very much in your hands, so to speak.'

Paige didn't need to be asked twice.

'Hi, I'm Paige. I'm the photographer.' She held out her hand and shook ours. 'Nikki's tasked me with creating some seasonally directional content for her website.'

Nikki nodded as if that was exactly what she'd told Paige.

'So … you want us to light the log burner?' Jim guessed. 'Move some tables around? Set up some coffee?'

'Yeah, exactly that.'

Perfect, I thought. What a nice end to the day, making coffee and moving a table.

'Actually,' Paige went on, 'what would be awesome would be if I could use you in some shots? We need something to give guests an idea of what they might use the space for, you know, catching up with friends, romantic weekend in the countryside …' She waved a hand around.

'Do you mind standing in for that?' Nikki enquired. 'Cleo said it would be all right.'

'Did she?'

I glanced at Jim. He didn't seem to be acknowledging the major problem, which was that we were both wearing red boilersuits.

'There would be a model fee,' Nikki added, in case that was the problem. 'Bottle of wine each?'

'We're not exactly dressed for it,' I pointed out. 'Unless you want your holiday cottage to look like it's also an indoor tyre-fitting centre.'

Nikki laughed more than that joke deserved.

Jim turned to me. 'You've got your clothes in a bag in the van,' he pointed out, which was true. I didn't leave my home dressed like I'd escaped from the Crystal Dome. I had standards. 'I've got a change of clothes too.'

'Have you?' Jim was always in his overalls. If I hadn't seen him in the office that first day, I'd assume he slept in them. 'Why?'

'I'm going somewhere after work.' Jim looked evasive, but before I could ask him why, my phone rang.

It was Cleo. I went outside to take it, and Jim followed me.

'Everything going OK with Nikki's shoot?' she asked.

'You might have warned me,' I said.

'I didn't want to give you the chance to say no,' she said breezily. 'Anyway, you two are the best team for the job.'

'What makes you say that?'

'Because you know about angles and lighting and what-not, and Jim looks like the sort of person who can afford to rent Nikki's overpriced holiday cottage. Have you seen how much she charges? It's outrageous.'

I frowned. 'You're on speakerphone.'

'I'm not offended,' said Jim.

'But I am,' I said in a Nikki Nardini voice. I think she was from Edinburgh or thereabouts. Which was good because that was the only Scottish accent I could do.

'I know that's you, Robyn,' said Cleo.

Paige appeared at the front door. 'Can we start with the sitting room? I need some help with the sofa.'

'Sure!' Jim seemed relieved to have a task, and I volunteered to arrange the board games. Making an artistic mess was something I was good at.

Paige buzzed around taking different photos of the furniture then instructed me and Jim to pretend we were playing Trivial Pursuit as part of a fun weekend away.

'You'll need to get changed,' she reminded Jim, and pointed to the downstairs bathroom.

I made another pot of tea – for set-dressing purposes, obviously – while he was changing. I'd already taken off my overalls and was back in my jeans and a white T-shirt, fortunately one that didn't need ironing. Nothing I owned needed ironing.

Nikki had done a great job with the cottage, I thought, admiring the dove-grey walls punctuated with original oak beams and tasteful engravings. The sort of country nest you'd enjoy pretending was yours for a weekend, without the stress of wondering how you'd cope with no storage or mains drainage.

'Is this OK?'

Jim reappeared in the doorway and it took my brain a moment to process that it was actually him, and not some passing stranger.

It could have *been* a stranger. It wasn't the Jim I mopped floors with nor the Jim I'd met in the office on my first day. This Jim was wearing dark blue jeans and a checked shirt, unbuttoned at the neck, with a pair of dark suede trainers. Everything fitted him well, and somehow the clothes changed his whole face. He looked years younger, for a start. I noticed for the first time that his eyes were blue, not grey. A slatey blue.

Where did he go to wear those clothes? I wondered. Why were they in the van? Was he going somewhere or was that just his off-duty wardrobe? Was there someone at home who'd chosen that shirt, someone who'd bought him that belt for Christmas? Something twisted inside as I tried to imagine Jim's girlfriend.

Paige interrupted my train of thought. 'Great, can you sit there?' She began arranging us. 'So, pretend you've just got a question right. Hold this.' She handed me a mug. 'And you, you're asking the questions.' She shoved the question cards at Jim, and stood back. 'OK, go.'

Where was the light in this room? I angled my face to find the most flattering light and started improvising Fun Weekend Away with some pretend quiz answers. 'Is it "Daydream Believer" by the Monkees? 1977! Anna Mae Bullock!'

Jim looked at me as if I was mad. I nodded for him to smile and he adopted a nervous rictus grin. The clothes hadn't changed him entirely: he was still about as far from relaxed as it was possible to be.

'Come on!' I said, gaily. 'Ask me another! This weekend away was a great idea! I'm having enormous fun.'

'Why are you moving around like that? You're making me feel seasick.'

'It's to keep the photos natural,' I said. 'It helps, try it.'

Jim shuffled on the sofa as if he was trying to dislodge a wedgie without using his hands.

'Stop, stop, stop,' said Paige. 'One of you's having fun, the other's just heard their dog's died.'

'I'm smiling,' Jim protested. 'This is my normal face.'

'Really?'

We tried it with me asking the questions, Paige shooting from behind Jim, but it was no use. His shoulders remained tense, his arm lay stiffly along the back of the sofa. He winced when she showed us the thumbnails so far.

'I'm going to make some tea.' Paige eyed Jim critically. 'See if that helps.'

When she'd gone, we made 'wtf' faces at each other. Jim seemed crestfallen about what he'd just seen on Paige's camera.

'Do I really look like that?' he asked.

'Like what?'

'Like …' he winced. 'Like someone's weird uncle. Why is it so hard? You look like a normal human being.'

'Thanks.' I offered him a biscuit from the tin Nikki had provided. 'Just pretend to be someone else. OK, here's a game we used to play …' I was about to say, 'On a new set', but changed my mind at the last minute. That wasn't a conversation for now. 'I'm going to ask you a question, but you have to answer it with another question. Don't think too hard, just say whatever comes into your head. Loser has to eat a biscuit. Right, I'll start, where did you get those jeans?'

'Why? Is there a problem with them?'

'No! I mean,' I racked my brains for another question that maybe didn't sound so loaded. 'Are those your favour-ite jeans?'

He regarded me quizzically. 'How many pairs of jeans do you think I have?'

'Would I be in the right ballpark if I said you had … one pair of jeans?'

'Would you judge me harshly if I said I preferred chinos?' Jim parried my questions smoothly, like a table tennis player.

'Don't you think you're a bit young for chinos?' .

'How old do you think I am?'

'Were you born in …?' I did some quick mental maths. If Jim was about thirty-eight, minus five years to be flattering, that would make him born in … '1990?'

He screwed up his face. '*What* grade did you get in your Maths GCSE?'

'A C,' I admitted. 'But I missed a few lessons.'

Jim pointed at me. I realised I'd fallen into my own trap.

'You got me.' I ate a biscuit from the plate. They were good biscuits, oaty and buttery.

'1985,' said Jim, while I was trying to think of a new question.

He didn't have to tell me that. He wanted me to know.

'Too young for chinos,' I said. 'You should get another pair of those jeans, they suit you.'

He looked pleased. Flattered.

It took me by surprise.

'Much better,' said Paige out of nowhere. I hadn't even noticed she'd started shooting again. 'Can you give me some breakfast vibes now?'

'Breakfast vibes?'

I shrugged. Something was keeping me and Jim on the sofa. 'I think she means she wants us to make toast,' I said, and forced myself up.

We followed her into the kitchen and started messing around with the toaster and kettle.

'What did Cleo mean when she said you had experience with cameras?' asked Jim.

'Are you asking for the game, or because you want to know?'

'Is there a difference between those two options?'

I offered him a plate with a croissant on it. Should I tell him? Mitch loved hearing about the famous people I'd met (and had asked more than once now if I was still in touch with any of them), but I knew Jim would focus in on the career progression. Why I wasn't acting any more? What went wrong? He might even offer me advice on fixing it.

'Here's another game,' I said. 'You tell me three facts about yourself, two made up, one true, and I'll see if I can guess which is which.'

'OK.' He frowned. 'I represented the Isle of Wight at U11s cricket, I was on *Mastermind* with the works of Tolkien as my specialist subject, I used to be a model.'

'Seriously?' I could believe any of those to be true. 'Erm, the *Mastermind* one is true?'

Jim seemed affronted. 'What? I look like someone who reads Tolkien? Thanks.'

'The cricket?'

Paige was moving around us in the background, no longer giving us instructions.

'Too slow for me.'

'You were never a model! How come you're so bad at this then?' That sounded a bit rude. 'I mean, what were you modelling?'

'I was at a conference in California with colleagues, and the hotel asked if they could use us in publicity photos.' Jim leaned on his elbow; it wasn't very convincing 'relaxing'. 'I had to pose in the hot tub with my boss's wife as if we were on honeymoon.'

'No!' Jim. A hot tub. A boss. California. A portal had opened into Jim's other life and information was flooding in. My mind reeled, trying to process everything. 'Where was your boss?'

'Right there next to us.' He grimaced. 'Apparently, they "didn't look like a couple".'

'And you two did? In the hot tub? How did that work out?' Jim, in a hot tub, pretending to be on honeymoon. What an ... *unsettling* thought.

'It went about as well as this is going.'

'And how was the flight back?'

'Terrible,' said Jim. 'Absolutely terrible.' There was a pause, then he flashed me a brief grin that hinted at a mischief that I'd never imagined, let alone seen in him.

Then the smile was gone and serious Jim was back again.

I missed the smile already.

'This is great,' said Paige. 'Can you sit down at the table now?'

Jim pulled out a chair for me and said, 'OK, your turn. And it has to be as embarrassing as that, please.'

'Ah ...' I pretended to think. My heart had sped up. 'My voice has been dubbed into forty languages, I can juggle fire sticks, I'm banned from every Starbucks in the west country.'

'Wow. One of those is *true*?'

I nodded, delighted – despite myself – at the intrigue in his expression.

Jim scrutinised my face, as if the answer was in my eyebrows, my nose, my lips. I had to drop my gaze as his eyes slowly travelled over me.

'OK. So, I'm going to go for ... Starbucks?'

I shook my head.

'Really? OK, um ... the ... fire sticks?'

I was vaguely aware of Paige moving around but I think we'd both more or less tuned her out.

'Nope.' I pointed at the biscuits.

'I don't get it.'

'I was in a film and my voice was dubbed into forty languages.'

'Get away!' Jim looked curious. 'What kind of film?'

I told him. He laughed. I felt pleased.

'I feel like there's a bigger story there.' He tilted his head, encouragingly.

'Upstairs?' said someone behind us.

We turned round.

'Upstairs,' said Paige. 'We need to do the bedrooms.'

We moved upstairs, and Jim started the question game again, with an opening, 'Is this the weirdest job you've ever done?' Mostly we were trying to catch each other out or make each other laugh – 'If you were an animal what would you be?' (me, squirrel; Jim, stag) 'What's your favourite smell?' (me, fresh bread; Jim, rain) – but now and again I caught him looking at me curiously, and wondered whether his opinion of me was changing.

I'd always had a weakness for quick-witted men and Jim volleyed my questions back with elegance, barely giving me time to think. It was properly fun, so much so that I didn't really notice what Paige was doing until she thrust some fluffy white dressing gowns at us, and said, 'Here, put these on.'

That brought us to an abrupt stop. 'What?'

'I'd like some shots of you bringing her a breakfast tray in bed.'

Wow. Weirdly, tea in bed felt more intimate than if she'd asked us to pretend to cosy up on the sofa.

I turned to Jim, trying to laugh it off. 'What's the chances of that, eh? Two fake romantic holiday photoshoots.'

'I'm not sure...'

'You don't have to take any clothes off,' said Paige, impatiently. 'Just put the dressing gown on. Please. We're almost done.'

Jim and I exchanged glances. For a moment, I thought he was going to refuse. Was he wondering if I was going to refuse?

'I'll go and make a pot of tea,' he said.

While Paige took photos of the blinds up, then the blinds down, I slipped into the bathroom and checked my face in the mirror. My mascara was smudgy but my eyes were bright and I had a glow out of proportion to the quick touch-up job I'd done on my make-up using whatever I had in my bag.

I wasn't expecting to see Jim already back upstairs – and also in a dressing gown. It was shorter than mine, finishing just under his knees, and his legs and feet were bare. He had really attractive calves, long and muscular. Lightly tanned.

I dragged my gaze away, then glanced back, then looked away again, making a point of admiring the wallpaper.

'I tried it with him in clothes but it looked weird,' Paige explained. 'Like you were ill, not on holiday. Right, you perch on the side of the bed and he'll bring the tray over.'

I smiled up at him for the camera, but that made me feel even stranger – Jim, bearing down on me with breakfast in bed – and my eyes dropped back to his ankles, leading down to long, strong feet. Normal feet. Bare feet. For some reason I kept picturing them wet in the shower, walking through sand on holiday somewhere hot.

Jim lowered the tray onto the crisp white duvet; there was a chintzy teapot, two mugs and a vase with a rose in it.

'Is this how you normally serve tea in bed?' I asked, trying to sound light, but my imagination was stuck on an image of Jim's feet on a sandy beach, his legs in Bermuda shorts. A Panama hat, a long unbuttoned linen shirt.

Stop it, I told myself. Come on, a question about … tea? Milk in first? Or …?

He beat me to it. 'Is there anything nicer,' he asked, 'than a cup of tea in bed?'

'Someone bringing it to you?' Oh wait, that sounded a bit suggestive. Too late.

'Having someone to bring it to?'

Our eyes met and I couldn't look away. Neither could he. A smile, cautious yet devastatingly confident, played at the corners of Jim's mouth. We didn't move for a moment, as if neither of us was completely sure what had just happened.

'That's great,' said Paige, unwittingly coming to our rescue. 'I've got everything I need, you can get dressed now.'

I gingerly hopped down off the bed while Paige moved the furniture back into place. Jim had already departed with his tray.

I let out a long, silent breath.

In the course of my acting career I'd pretended to be a Victorian detective, a trainee witch, a chorister and various kinds of dead. *Nothing* had been as weird as that.

Thank goodness it was Friday night.

15

~ De-pong a stinky bin by putting a tumble-dryer sheet at the bottom, under the bin bag.

On Saturday morning, Mum turned up on my doorstep with the latest weapon in her arsenal in her war on grime: a carpet cleaner. Cleo was, she explained, thinking of investing in them for Taylor Maid but was far too busy to road-test one herself.

'Do you mind if I give it a go in your flat?' Mum asked, eyeing my dingy hall. 'I'm not sure it's working – it barely picked up a thing on ours.'

There was an obvious reason for that – Mum's carpets were cleaner than most people's work surfaces – but I wasn't going to look a gift horse in the mouth.

'Be my guest.' I swung open the door as far as it would go, which wasn't very far on account of two bin bags of clothes and a fan heater.

'Oh, Robyn.' Mum sighed. 'I thought you were going to take a carload to the charity shop last weekend?'

'That's why they're there! Just waiting to go,' I lied, but I lugged them into the bedroom and began tidying up the sitting room.

It turned out that the carpet cleaner did work. Horrifically well. Mum, who had once admitted her secret dream was to present cleaning products on QVC, steamed one demonstration stripe down the middle of the room, like a red carpet from the door to the window. Well, a beige carpet. My sitting-room carpet was camel, not brown, it turned out.

'Can you see how the rolling brushes are *blasting* away the built-up grime?' Mum demanded, euphorically, 'and how the multi-jet head is *drenching* the fibres in detergent?'

I watched as the carpet slowly surrendered years' worth of filth. The room visibly lightened. It was compelling, if also revolting at the same time.

'And just *look* how the powerful vacuum *sucks* back the dirty water!' Mum enthused to the imaginary director in her head. ('Can you be more excited, Melanie? Even more excited? Like it's growing wings in front of you.')

I was starting to feel nauseous at the sight of the tarry water in the tank, so I left her to it and went into the bedroom to unpack a box of junk. Candles, mugs, things I'd bought to make my house look better when in fact what would have made it look better was a massive declutter. I found some earrings I thought I'd lost, and an old Quality Street tin full of bits and bobs that weren't even mine. It must have fallen into a packing case when Mum and Cleo were carting my junk over: I'd had so much stuff in Mum's garage that it was hard to tell what belonged to who.

I packed up three charity shop bags for Mum to take home, then made two cups of tea and took them into the sitting room, which now smelled different.

'This machine really works!' she said, with a theatrical 'behold the freshness!' sweep of the hand. 'Do you want to help me move the furniture back?'

Together – Mum was subtle but firm with her 'suggestions' – we shifted the sofa so it faced the view and moved the lamps round so the lighting would be softer. Mum had a knack for knowing what went where, and by the time she'd finished, my sitting room was unrecognisable. Maybe I'd risk a new house plant, I thought, admiring the harmony of my surroundings. What plant wouldn't like living here?

'That looks a bit nicer, doesn't it?' she said, satisfied.

'Understatement of the year,' I said, offering her the better of the two mugs. 'Mum, I don't know how you do it.'

She seemed pleased. 'I know you're not planning on staying here long, but you might as well make it as nice. Have you found anywhere yet? Or are you going to get settled into your new job first before you start looking? Is it a good time to buy a new house?'

Her voice was breezy but there were at least three different Mum Worries concealed underneath the breeziness. They stuck out like the piles of unironed clothes Helena Corrigan shoved under her duvet before we arrived.

'Actually, Mum, that job's not happening now.' I tried to sound unconcerned.

'What? Why?' She went to put her tea down, couldn't find a coaster and flapped in panic. 'Oh no, I've spilled. Where are your coasters?'

'I've never had coasters.' I slipped an unread Women's Prize shortlisted novel under the mug. 'It's fine. I'm over it. Onwards and upwards.'

'But Robyn, what happened?' Mum's face fell. 'You were so sure!'

Maybe it was the sunlight flooding the room, or maybe it was the flirty exchange I'd had with Mitch about booking a romantic break later that month. Or maybe it was because my flat no longer smelled of rancid dust, or because Tomasz had put my bin out for me or … whatever it was. I had moved on from the Malvern Property Finders disaster. I could learn from it and grow.

'It didn't work out.' Mum didn't need to know exactly why it hadn't. 'But I've got other things in the pipeline. And the *other* good news is that I've got in on the first phase of a really amazing—' I stopped short.

Mum was fidgeting nervously with her rings. I decided not to tell her about Lark Manor right now. She'd only zone in on the risk involved, and it was hard to explain that there really wasn't any, not in the way she was thinking. I did sometimes get cold sweats thinking about that huge lump sum I'd invested, but reminded myself it had only moved from one piggy bank (the bank) to another (property). And I had a document in a file that confirmed all that.

I made a mental note to get it out and re-read it once she'd gone. Just to reassure myself. I was sure I'd seen some dates in there.

'I'll get you some coasters for your birthday,' she said.

'That would be great, Mum.'

She did look stressed about something, I thought. More than my failure to get a job warranted, anyway. Was it poor Rhiannon's news? One of Mum's book-group friends had only just recovered from cancer, and she'd done a lot of batch cooking to help out the family. Or had Cleo's mysterious Gwen Thomas phoned back? Had Grandad himself called?

I longed to reassure her – such an adult thing to do, re-assuring your own mother – but Mum tended to shut down quickly if you didn't judge your approach right. How could I coax her into telling me what was wrong?

I had a sudden brilliant idea, a cunning sideways approach that might elicit some spontaneous sharing where Cleo's 'tell me now' tactics had failed.

'I think I've got something of yours,' I said, and went to get the Quality Street tin.

It was only kitchen-drawer flotsam and jetsam, cotton reels and gift shop pencils, but for someone like me, des-perate for any fragments of the past, it was a treasure trove. Some of the old bank cards were in Mum's maiden name, Melanie Davies, and I'd spotted what looked like baby pass-port photos of me and Cleo. If I could just lure her out with a few anodyne memories about her first teaching assistant job or something.

I offered it to her with a smile, but when Mum saw what was inside her face changed and she recoiled as though there was a dead mouse in there, not a jumble of old loyalty cards, coins, keys, badges.

'Mum?'

She got up, reaching out a hand for the tin. 'Thanks, Robyn. I should probably make a move. Cleo's got the mobile hairdresser and make-up artist booked. You know it's her awards do tonight?'

I'll be honest: I'd forgotten about it.

That was probably why Mum had come over, I realised. She was evening things up. Attend one child's awards ceremony, clean the other child's carpet.

I wasn't ready to hand the tin over, not without getting some history in exchange.

'Is this your student railcard?' I waved an ancient photo-card, so old the photo had peeled away from the backing. 'I didn't know you had glasses.'

'You won't forget to ring Cleo and wish her good luck, will you? You know how important this is for her.' Mum held out her hand for the tin. 'I'll take that, thank you.' She paused, and said, more pointedly. 'Robyn?'

There was a firmness in Mum's expression that I rarely saw. Her jaw was set, and as she frowned, her dark brows lowered over her eyes, transforming her whole face. I was so used to Mum-who-never-said-no that it was unsettling to suddenly see her as Mrs Melanie Taylor, independent of me, refusing to bend to my wishes. Even more unsettling, determined to keep something of herself separate from me.

She reminded me of Cleo in that moment.

'Is there something in here you don't want me to see?' I demanded.

'No! It's just ... junk,' she said. 'I'll bin it when I get home.'

It clearly wasn't junk. It was a box of fragments of the life she'd had before me and Cleo, part of a story that started before us, and would end after us. And I really, really wanted to know what had happened before us.

'Then I'll bin it.' I held her gaze. What the hell. 'Mum, Cleo said someone called wanting to talk about Grandad the other night. What was that about?'

'Nothing. Please.' Mum looked almost tearful. 'Give me that.'

Maybe I should have pushed her, but I hated seeing her upset. Mum's pain always cut me deeper than my own. Nothing was worth that. Reluctantly, I handed the tin over, and my chance to talk about Grandad slipped away with it.

But only for the time being. Cleo was right: we needed to have an adult conversation with Mum about our family history. I'd just have to find the magic words.

To cut a long, looong story short, Cleo came Runner-Up in the Small Businesswoman of the Year category. She still managed to make herself more prominent than the winner in the press-release photos, though. So, you know, still a result.

To celebrate, she graciously awarded her whole squad a bonus and then, on top of that, Jim and I won the monthly team award, which I didn't even know was a thing. Apparently it was assessed on client satisfaction, and Terry, Sally Armstrong and the Corrigans had sent complimentary feedback.

I knew this because Terry had shared said feedback directly with me in the kitchen at the end of our Monday session. I could tell he'd spent a while composing it and he read it aloud with his customary relish.

'In conclusion, these two smashers should be called Batman and Robyn,' he finished, turning over the second sheet of ancient Basildon Bond notepaper. 'They fight grime and banish dust, germs and clutter – kapow! Jim is a top-drawer cleaner and Robyn is a ray of sunshine.'

'Is that a kind way of saying I'm not a good cleaner?' I deadpanned.

'There's more than one way of cleaning. You two brighten up my flat, and my day,' he said, with his gappy smile.

'Aw, Terry,' I said. 'You brighten up my day too.'

Jim pretended he was only interested in providing a quality service, not 'monthly popularity contests' but I knew him well enough by now to spot the involuntary back-straightening of pride as I read highlights from Cleo's email, containing key snippets of client feedback.

'You know who else thanked us for going the extra mile? I'll give you a clue – they mean it literally.'

Jim didn't take his eyes from the road. He was back in uniform, and there was no trace of the man who'd pretended to bring me tea in bed on Friday afternoon. You wouldn't even have thought they were related. 'No. Tell me.'

'Nessie and Rambo! They said we were the best walkers they'd ever had. Oh, and Ivor the corgi says thank you for his medications. I think you should take credit for that.' I glanced over, hoping for a glimmer of a smile, but … nothing. 'Are you OK? Something on your mind?'

He'd been distracted all day. Not distracted from his work, which was as thorough as ever, but distant, as if he'd been engaged in a conversation raging on in his head.

'What? No, nothing.'

That wasn't true, I thought, covertly watching him in the reflection of the windscreen. He was different.

The door to the real Jim had opened a crack the day he'd patiently coached me through that excruciating call to Liv Williams. He hadn't needed to get involved but he had. We'd spent hours and hours together, cleaning or driving, talking not talking, and though he rarely offered up any

263

facts, I'd started to sense what he might be like as a person: he was practical, professional, observant. Kind, occasionally funny in a dry way. I had relaxed into his company; I no longer rushed to fill silences.

And then that bizarre but hilarious photoshoot had swung the door into Jim's psyche wide open and it turned out his inner life had a chandelier in the hall. I couldn't help but be curious as to what else was in there. Upstairs, even.

'Did you have a good weekend?' I asked. 'Were your team playing rugby?'

'My team?'

'The team you coach.' I paused. It was like getting blood out of a stone, but we'd worn matching dressing gowns, for heaven's sake. I'd seen his shins. 'Where do you play? Somewhere in town?'

Jim turned and, while his expression was pleasant enough, there was a formality in his voice. 'Robyn, don't take this the wrong way, but work is work. I don't like to talk about my hobbies during work hours. OK?'

I felt stunned. 'Yes, but …'

'It's better to keep things separate. No offence.'

'OK.' I wasn't sure what he meant, but I heard, *Shut up*, so I did.

I turned up the radio so we didn't have to talk, and Jim didn't turn it down. And then I texted Mitch and didn't bother to hide my smiles when he suggested dinner.

I spent half my bonus on a haircut and the other half on an aspidistra for my Mum-improved flat, which I called Astrid, just to up the emotional stakes for both of us.

Astrid was a symbol of my determination to keep my life as tidy as my domestic quarters. I bought her a brass plant stand, invested in plant food and put a watering schedule into my phone. Astrid wasn't going to die on me. Not now she had a name.

Then I did the same for myself, metaphorically speaking. I looked honestly at my CV and created a version I didn't have to cross my fingers and hope no one looked too closely at. I workshopped my 'how I learned from my mistake' story until it was fluent and honest. I made a meal plan with proper food, I did a budget and I bought some vitamins. Mum even sketched out an amazingly detailed plan for rearranging my bedroom into a more relaxing space.

For the first time in I don't know how long, I managed to get nearly six hours' sleep a night, which for me was a lot. The first baby green shoots of new growth started to appear on Astrid, and something started to sprout in me too. Hope, and confidence. Not huge new leaves, but promising buds.

It took a while for the changes to register with the universe but finally, just as the first proper hints of summer warmth were softening up the morning air, I got a call on my way to work.

It was for a negotiator role at Hastings Laidlaw, a new agency in town looking to expand their sales team; a bit of a step down in salary terms but I wasn't in a position to be fussy. Anna Hastings sounded keen to see me, as soon as tomorrow; not a maternity cover this time, but a 'health issue' that meant an immediate start.

'Can you do a morning appointment?' she asked. 'Say, ten?'

I had to be at Terry's for nine thirty, my first call of the day. Jim was off all of Tuesday morning – no reason offered, just that he wouldn't be in – and Cleo had reshuffled the schedule. I was supposed to be flattered that she trusted me to clean Terry's house alone, but I knew it was because she was still short-staffed. She'd sent me the job list, then phoned me twice to make sure I'd got it and fully understood it. And made me promise that I would be there on the dot of nine thirty.

'Any chance you can make it earlier?' I asked Anna. 'I have a meeting at nine thirty.'

'Um, can you come in before the office opens? Say, eight forty-five?'

Hastings Laidlaw was on the far (currently unfashionable) end of the High Street, down by the market place. Terry's flat was at the other – ten minutes' fast walk away. Longhampton wasn't a big place, but if the interview went even slightly over half an hour, there was a risk I'd be late.

I wrestled with my conscience. I was sure Terry wouldn't mind. It wasn't as if he was going anywhere. And I could make up the extra time by skipping my lunchbreak and getting back on track by the afternoon. Jim wouldn't know, and Terry wouldn't tell, especially if I agreed to make him some lunch before I left.

No, I decided. It was a matter of principle. I said I'd be at Terry's by nine thirty, so I'd be there. I'd made that promise to Cleo. Anyway, it would make me sound organised, needing to leave for another appointment.

'Can you do eight thirty?' I asked.

'Perfect,' said Anna. 'We'll see you then.'

'Perfect!' I said. 'I'll see you then.'

When I arrived (on time!), Anna Hastings herself welcomed me into her office, and although it wasn't as self-consciously luxe as Malvern Property Finders, everyone there was busy, and that was a good sign. I put my phone onto airplane mode so I wouldn't be distracted.

'Graeme is the Laidlaw,' she said, showing me into a meeting room. 'He's our financial director.'

A bald forty-something man in a proper suit was sitting at the table with a pen, pad, cup of coffee and a glass of water arranged in perfect alignment in front of him.

'Hello!' I said, already sensing that this was going to be a good cop, humourless cop type of interview.

Anna opened the batting with some straightforward questions about my recent sales and what I enjoyed most about selling houses, which I was able to answer with enthusiasm. She'd seen my virtual viewings and liked them.

Then it was Graeme's turn, and he wasn't messing about. 'Can you tell us about a time that you made a mistake and what you learned from it?'

I swallowed. It had been so easy in my bathroom mirror but now I had to get it right: I didn't want to go into too much detail and if I messed it up …

Graeme was observing me closely. Anna had mentioned my social media work for Marsh & Frett, so maybe she'd seen the Emma Rossiter rant. Was this a test? My armpits prickled with sweat as my courage wavered. Should I make up something less … horrendous?

In my mind's eye I saw Jim's shrug; his 'own it and move on' advice. Maybe Graeme did know. What could I do about it now?

'I love finding and selling homes for people, but admin isn't my strong suit.' I chose my words carefully. 'I wasn't proactive enough with one client's sale, and that caused delays that led her to lose her onward purchase, as well as her own sale. She was understandably angry. That was a low point for me, as well as horrible for her, but the experience made me address my tendency to take on too much, and also commit to managing my time so I don't rush important communication.'

There. It was out. When I put it like that, I knew I'd deserved that bollocking from Emma Rossiter. I'd been useless. But I would be better. So much better.

'You lost the sale?' Graeme clarified. 'And that impacted a whole chain?'

'Yikes,' said Anna. 'Big lesson, right?'

'It was a big lesson,' I agreed.

'Reliability is obviously key to what we do.' Graeme seemed less amused, and I nodded harder.

'It's my main priority now.'

'And how did you leave the situation with the client?' he went on, but someone knocked on the meeting-room door behind us with an urgent query about a transaction, requiring both Graeme and Anna's attention. By the time the junior left, the moment had passed. I glanced at the clock. Seven minutes past nine. Perfect timing.

'I think that's about it!' Anna smiled and swung in her chair. 'Do you have any questions for us?'

We'd covered pretty much everything I needed to know in our chat – hours, salary, area – but I felt I had to ask *something*. And we had a few minutes in hand. So I said, 'What's been the most interesting property you've brought to market recently?'

Irresponsible Adult

It was a question Graeme and Anna obviously hoped I'd ask, as they immediately started rattling on about a luxury development in an old marmalade factory, oh, but also that fabulous Arts and Crafts property down by the river with the original wallpaper, and no, wait, what about the Cider Barn, the award-winning Passivhaus project …

I could talk about houses and their owners all day, and the more we talked the more I wanted to work there. Unlike my friendly chat with Liv Collins, it didn't feel like a test of who I knew or where I'd been. They both clearly loved being part of people's stories, loved the way buildings told the history of the town. Just like I did. I *really* wanted them to like me.

We were still talking when the junior knocked on the door again. 'Sorry to interrupt, guys, but Anna's nine forty-five's here?'

What? I looked up at the clock.

It was nine forty-eight.

Oh no. I was *so* late for Terry.

I powerwalked faster than I thought possible to Terry's street, ignoring the buzzing of my phone and the dead feeling in my shins, then jogged up the stairs to his flat and rapped the letter box. 'Terry? It's Robyn.'

No answer. I was so late that maybe he thought I wasn't coming, and had gone back to bed. Or was in the loo.

I hunted for the key safe that Terry's daughter Jayne insisted he install under the letter box for emergencies. The code was easy to remember – 1966, 'so her old dad would remember, greatest year in our history, shall I tell you why,

Robyn?' – and found a key inside. When I tried it, the front door wasn't locked.

Did he have guests? Ugh, late, in front of guests.

'Terry, it's Robyn, I'm letting myself in, so I hope you're decent!' I called out. 'I'm sorry I'm late, I got held up at the—' I stopped short. 'Oh shit.'

Terry was lying between the hall and the sitting room, one of his legs at a worrying angle. His eyes were closed and his skin was a blotchy beige, like porridge.

A punch of adrenalin walloped me in the chest, but instead of moving, I froze. What was I supposed to do? I'd never seen a dead body before. If he was dead. Was he dead?

My voice seemed to be coming from somewhere else. 'Terry, are you all right?'

I'd had no first-aid training, but I did watch a lot of *999 Emergency*-type programmes when I couldn't sleep and something must have lodged in my subconscious. Nothing medical, unfortunately, just the importance of the recovery position and reassuring chat until someone arrived who knew what they were doing.

'It's OK, Terry, I'm here. What are you doing, giving me a scare like this, eh?' I dropped to my knees, and tried feeling his neck for a pulse but the loose skin above his shirt collar was chilly to the touch.

He was wearing his good shirt, the 'bespoke cotton' one he'd got on a long-ago holiday in Hong Kong. Terry always wore a proper shirt and tie, even when the only people he'd be seeing that day were me and Jim. The effort it must have taken to keep himself so smart, I thought, always shaved and pressed

… It suddenly dawned on me that maybe he only wore the shirt and tie *because* we would be in the house that day.

Oh, Terry.

I winkled my phone out of my pocket. There were several missed-call notifications and voicemails. Mostly from Cleo. Shit. *Shit.* I ignored them for now, and dialled 999 with my thumb, trying to keep talking at the same time.

'Now then, Terry, this is a first for me, calling the emergency services, let's hope they haven't got the camera crews in … Hello? Ambulance, please.'

At some point I was connected to a calm woman who started talking me through how to check if he was breathing or not. I don't know how long it took or what I did. I kept talking to Terry at the same time, even though there were no signs of life. If I stopped talking, then it was like admitting there was no one there to hear me.

'I'm going to roll you into position now, as this lady's telling me, so if you don't mind … this is one to put in the Christmas round robin, isn't it … something to tell the grandchildren …'

The words tumbled out because I didn't want to think. I didn't want to think about how I was the only one here. I was the one who'd have to save Terry by forcing my own breath into his lungs.

Please, I begged silently, please blink. Please don't be dead.

'Now she's telling me to get you flat on your back …'

Laid out in front of me on his patterned carpet, Terry's body seemed so small. In his chair, chatting and laughing, I'd always assumed he was taller, the way he filled the room with his personality. That 'big man in the pub' energy. Now there was an echo in the flat, an ominous emptiness.

I knelt over Terry's chest, fingers knotted, ready to start chest compressions.

'I'm scared I'm going to break his ribs,' I blurted out to the phone, on speaker by Terry's head.

'Don't think about that, Robyn, just follow my instructions. Are you ready?'

I looked down. He didn't look alive. It was too late. I was too late.

Why hadn't I checked my watch? All those times I'd wished I could turn back the clock just a few minutes to stop a disaster, yet it had been in my power to stop this one.

'I'm sorry, Terry,' I half-sobbed, 'I hope this isn't going to hurt you, this is ... oh!'

Without warning, Terry's eyes snapped open and he choked on a half-breath.

The calm woman instantly shifted her advice to recovery positions and blankets, and then, miraculously, there was a knock on the door: it was the paramedics.

I fell back onto my heels, numb, as they went into their routines. I couldn't tear my eyes away from Terry. He had gone limp again. They were loosening his shirt to stick on the ECG pads and wiring up his finger to a different machine, and every bit of exposed skin was the same pallid texture. His shirt seemed far too big for him.

'Hello, Terry, mate, my name's Kyle and this is Martin. We're going to run a few quick checks then ... what?' Kyle turned to his colleague, who pointed to something on the machine. 'No, we're going to do that in the ambulance now, Terry. We need to get you into hospital quick smart, all right? Stay with us, pal.'

He turned to me. 'Are you a carer? Relative?'

'Cleaner,' I said dully.

'Done a great job, love.' Kyle was packing up his equipment. 'Are you coming to the hospital with us? Any family you can call?'

I thought of Terry's family. I knew so much about them: Jayne and her grandchildren, Holly, Lily, Rosie, Daisy ('daft names, I get them mixed up, called one Tulip by mistake, didn't half get an earful ...'), his sons Brian and Barry, one a policeman, the other 'gone the other way, if you know what I mean', the various junior footballers and tap dancers. Terry was so proud of them.

'They're not local,' I said, 'but I can call someone.'

'Yeah, if you could do that.' Kyle nodded. 'They'll probably want to get here.'

I knew what that meant. My heart sank.

'He's got an address book somewhere.' I'd seen it by the telephone while I was cleaning. An old-fashioned address book, decades old, with tatty Christmas cards and Post-it notes sticking out.

'Bring that with you, eh?'

I heard the other paramedic say, 'Think he's trying to speak, Kyle!'

We crowded round as Terry's breath rattled in his throat. It was the most upsetting thing I'd ever heard.

He opened one eye, bloodshot and unfocused. His voice was barely a whisper and I had to lean close to hear the words but I couldn't. They were lost in a scratchy breath. I think he said 'Robyn'.

Then he closed his eye, let out a final ragged breath and the paramedics sprang into action.

16

~ Throwing salt or white wine on a red wine stain is more likely to make things worse. Instead, rinse with fizzy water (the bubbles help lift the stain) then blot and spray with carpet shampoo.

One minute I was in the back of the ambulance, mechanically discussing the relative merits of biscuits with Kyle, the next I was sitting alone at the hospital while the rest of the world rushed past around me at high speed.

Terry's heart was still ticking over, but only just. His left leg and left wrist were not so good. More worrying was his hip. We were met at the door by two nurses, who whisked him straight off to ICU.

His battered address book was on the cafe table next to my cup, an incongruous piece of his resolutely twentieth-century flat in the bright, clean hospital cafe. I had to phone Terry's closest relatives and tell them what was happening, possibly the worst phone calls I would ever have to make. I had no idea how I was going to find the words, yet I couldn't avoid it. My brain was in full *defer, defer* mode, but I couldn't – I'd been late for Terry once, I couldn't be late again.

I opened the address book and turned the pages in search of familiar names. Gillian, his calorie-counting late wife,

274

hadn't bothered with surnames, but I remembered some of the family from the elaborate tree he'd drawn me on the back of the French Fancies packet.

Who was the daughter who'd fitted the key safe? Jayne. I'd start with her.

Jayne had four different Wolverhampton addresses, three written in Gillian's curly handwriting and the last in Terry's poignantly wobbly old man biro. That wobbly biro alone nearly set me off.

I dialled the number, my heart beating so hard I could feel the pulse in my throat. It rang, and rang, and then I got her voicemail.

Beep. Speak. I swallowed. 'I'm so sorry to bother you, but I'm your dad's cleaner and I'm afraid he's had an accident ...'

I didn't get through to Brian, or Barry, and I was starting to panic that maybe I wouldn't get through to anyone, but eventually I spoke to Nicola, Barry's oldest daughter, who lived nearest, in Birmingham.

'Thank god he had a friendly face with him,' Nicola sobbed, turning her car round from a shopping trip to drive straight to the hospital. 'Thank you, thank you, Robyn. You've saved his life.'

I hope she didn't mind that I was too choked to reply.

Once family support for Terry was on the way, I had no reason left not to deal with the pile of missed calls and messages.

The first was from Cleo, at 8 a.m. *8 a.m.!*

'Robyn, just a heads-up. Terry's left me a message to say he's not feeling too good and that he's left the door open for you. If you don't think he's up to having you clean, tell him we can come another time. I'll fit him in somewhere. Thanks.'

And another, 9.10 a.m. Cleo again.

'Robyn, I've just had a call from Terry's number but he didn't speak, which is a bit worrying. Can you call me when you get there to let me know he's OK?'

Ten past nine? Had he fallen then? How long had he lain there, alone?

I took the phone from my ear. There were three more voicemails from Cleo and I didn't want to hear them. I knew what they'd be saying: update me, what's going on? And *where the hell are you?*

My instinct was to delete them without listening – something I did a lot when my imagination informed me that the message was likely to cause inner distress. I sometimes bribed Johnny or Katie at work to screen my client voicemails at times of high stress.

God, I thought, disgusted with myself. What a *baby* I am.

'Get a grip,' I said aloud.

Then I braced myself and called Cleo back.

She picked up immediately, furious. 'Where the hell are you? I've been trying to get hold of you since eight o'clock! You've *got* to answer your phone if you're working, it's not like your personal life where you can just ignore people until you think fit to—'

'I'm at the hospital,' I said flatly. 'With Terry.'

There was a short, sharp intake of breath. Cleo's indignation evaporated instantly. 'Oh no. I knew something was up! Is he OK?'

'I don't know. He's been taken off for assessment. I wasn't sure if I should leave or not.' I bit my lip. 'There's nothing I can do but I just didn't want him to come round and not have anyone here.'

'What happened?'

'I don't know. I got there and he was … lying in the hall. I called the ambulance and the paramedics came and …' I couldn't say it. There was every chance Terry could still die, and it would be my fault: he'd lain there without medical attention for those critical minutes.

'Thank god you were there,' said Cleo. 'Oh, Robyn. Are *you* all right?'

'I'm fine.'

'Really, though? You must be in shock.'

'I'm fine,' I repeated.

'Don't worry about the rest of the day,' she said. 'Go home, have a brandy. And ignore my arsey messages, obviously you couldn't phone me back if you were in an ambulance with Terry. I must have called when you were dealing with the paramedics, did I?'

Should I tell her? I felt an urge to confess, to admit to Cleo I'd only just got her messages, but an equally powerful force swept up against it. I *couldn't*. What good would it do to have Cleo go ballistic at me now? No one knew what time it had happened. It might not make a difference.

Only me. I would know. I shrivelled a bit inside. I'd just have to swallow this awful knowledge. It would be my punishment.

'I'm going to ask Jim to come round to get you,' Cleo was saying.

'Jim?'

'I've just spoken to him, he's not far from the hospital. He'll pick you up and bring you back.'

Oh no. No, no, no. Jim was the last person I wanted to see. He'd see straight through to my guilty conscience. 'It's fine, I'm honestly fine.'

But she wasn't having it. 'He's on his way. And Robyn?' Cleo's voice cracked. 'I've always said that our cleaners go above and beyond, and you've proved that today. I'm so proud of you. And not just as a boss, as your sister. You've saved a life.'

I couldn't reply. It was something I'd always wanted to hear from my big sister, that she was proud of me, but I'd managed to ruin it for myself by burying an appalling lie at the centre of it.

Yeah. Well done, Robyn.

I don't know how long I sat there, but at some point I heard a familiar click, click of purposeful steps.

I looked up. There was Jim, in a very un-Jim black T-shirt, but I was so dazed I barely registered his clothes or even wondered where he'd been. His expression was concerned.

'Are you OK?' he asked, pulling up a chair next to mine. 'Can I get you anything? Sweet tea? Another coffee?'

I shook my head.

'So what happened?'

I couldn't speak for a moment, but to his credit, Jim said nothing else until I pulled myself together. Then he coaxed out the whole story with simple questions, and didn't patronise me with any 'it'll be fine' platitudes.

When I finished, he said, 'You did everything you could.'

I didn't respond. I really hadn't. My conscience kept zoning in on the fact that I'd been so eager to impress Anna and Graeme that I'd hadn't bothered to check the clock. I'd abandoned my responsibilities, just like that. I didn't think I was that sort of person, but here was the evidence.

And what about the other times?

I liked to think I had self-respect and good boundaries when it came to relationships, but I'd ended up in bed with Mitch in a hotel after *one* dinner that I barely remembered.

I saw myself as a professional, but my casual inefficiency had cost people time and money. Surveys wasted, movers cancelled, plans spoiled, lives altered. Because of me.

I thought I was a good sister but I didn't really know what was going on with Cleo, and I hadn't spoken to any of Dad's family in months, despite it being my Auntie Bex's fiftieth birthday recently.

Just look at yourself, I thought, disgusted. *Who are you?*

'Robyn?' Jim's voice sounded a long way away. 'Are you OK?'

'No,' I said. 'I'm not OK. I'm the worst person I know.'

'I find that hard to believe.'

'I am.'

He refused to react. 'What have you done?'

I didn't look up, but I knew exactly what Jim's expression would be. He thought I was in shock about seeing Terry so close to death – which I was – but it was the sudden shock of how much terrible behaviour I'd managed to ignore that was making my head throb.

'I just …' I began, and I knew if I started I would tell Jim everything. Not just about Terry, but how useless I felt, my talent peaking at thirteen, how jealous I was of Cleo, for her family and her business and her *drive*, how utterly desperate I felt at 3.15 a.m. when I couldn't sleep because time was trickling away, and my options were narrowing before I even knew what they were.

'Robyn?'

It was pathetic. I didn't even have age-appropriate anxieties.

'I …' I began, then a pair of sensible black shoes appeared in my line of vision.

'Robyn Taylor?'

I looked up. A nurse was standing in front of us with a clipboard.

'You came in with Terry Gilchrist?'

'Yes.' I jumped up, and my legs wobbled. I put a hand out to steady myself and grabbed Jim's shoulder; I was so focused on the nurse I barely noticed him put his own around my hip to steady me.

'I don't have a full update, I'm afraid, but he's stable. The doctor's waiting for some test results which will tell us more.' The nurse's expression was careful, deliberately not giving too much hope. 'Would you like to see him?'

'Are his family here yet?'

'No one so far.'

I glanced at Jim. I wasn't sure what I should do.

'Why don't you pop up and say hello?' he suggested. 'Let Terry know the family's on the way.'

'Will you come with me?' I hated how pathetic that sounded.

'Of course,' said Jim.

Terry was as fragile as a sparrow in the ICU bed, surrounded by wires and machinery and drips. He was asleep, but his skin seemed less porridgey than it had done when I'd found him on the floor.

Remorse speared through me. A broken hip could take months to heal at his age, maybe even a year. If Terry pulled through, would he be able to live independently again? Would his confidence have shattered, along with his bone? Was that the end of his flat, and the French Fancies and the cupboard of mugs?

I sat down on the chair by the side of the bed. 'Hello, Terry,' I said.

He didn't respond. But then I'd have been more freaked out if he had.

I wasn't sure what to say next. The ward was open-plan with three other beds and the nurse was busy with the man in the far corner.

There wasn't much to inspire me, amid the grey metal and white wires. I racked my brains, and leaned my forehead against one cool metal arm.

'I'm sorry I was late,' I confessed in a whisper. 'I will never be late again.'

Jim approached, cautiously. 'We can go now, Terry's daughter's on her way in. What? Don't look like that.'

But it was too late; there was Jayne, steaming into the ICU ward with a nurse close behind – the golden-child daughter

I'd heard so much about. I'd have known her anyway; she looked exactly like Terry but with a silver pixie cut.

As soon as she saw her dad lying there, her face collapsed in grief and she rushed over to kneel by his side.

I started to move away, but Jayne got up and flung her arms around me, hugging me so tightly that her nose pressed hard into my shoulder. 'Thank you, I'm sorry, I don't even know your name,' she sobbed into my overalls. 'But he wasn't on his own!'

'Least I could do,' I mumbled, and let her sink into the chair to hold Terry's hand while the nurse brought her up to speed.

As we left, I could hear Jayne half-talking, half-crying. '... Got here as soon as I could ... should have moved nearer ... my dad ... feel so bad ...'

Jim put his hand on my shoulder. I could feel the weight of his palm against my shoulder blade. I wondered if he could feel the guilt burning in my chest.

'Come on,' he said. 'Your work here is done.'

It was nearly six o'clock by the time we got back to the town centre, and we didn't speak for most of the journey.

Jim pulled up outside Molly's Bakehouse and it took me a moment to remember why he was doing that. It was because I'd lied about where I lived.

Cleo was right: I told such stupid, pointless lies. Why on earth did it matter if the neighbours saw me? The thought of the long trudge home made me feel weary, plus I'd left my bag with my interview clothes at Terry's flat, so I'd have to walk through the streets of Longhampton in my overalls. All I had was my phone, my purse and my house keys.

But I was too exhausted to care. The sooner I set off, the sooner I'd be back in bed, under a blanket.

'Cheers, Jim.' I got out of the car. 'I'll see you tomorrow.'

'Robyn?'

'What?'

Jim looked up at me from the driver's seat, his brow furrowed. I'd thought he looked like an eagle when I first met him, but now I thought he was more like an owl. A wise owl. 'Are you *sure* you're OK?'

'Yes,' I said.

'Because ...'

'Because what?'

'Because you haven't had anything to eat and you look shattered.' He paused. 'Do you want to get something now? McDonald's or KFC or whatever else you can drive through?' he added, as if I'd worry he was asking me out for dinner.

I gestured towards House of Tatts, where I 'lived'. 'Honestly, I'm fine, I've got something in the freezer.'

'If you're sure ...'

I couldn't keep up this facade much longer. It was a half an hour walk home from here, and the first few drops of rain had started to fall.

'See you tomorrow!' I said, and waved.

Jim hesitated, and I flapped my hand in a 'get on with you!' gesture. He tipped his head, a regretful tilt, then waved back, checked his mirrors, indicated and drove off. He might not be dressed in the uniform but he still drove like a Taylor Maid employee.

I waited until the van disappeared around the corner and sank down on the bench outside the bakery. I dropped my head into my hands and listened as the bakers dragged the sign indoors, heard the squeak of the awnings being wound in for the night. There was still a faint smell of almond croissants in the air.

Keep Terry with us, I bargained with the universe, and I will clean his mug cupboard and laugh at his terrible stories, and *not* laugh at his dodgy theories about the moon landings.

I will try to be a much better person.

I will *be* a much better person.

The rain started falling properly, but I didn't have the energy to move.

I got myself home, somehow, and sat on my sofa until night fell around me.

My phone rang a few times but I didn't answer it. I didn't want Cleo's sympathy or Mum's praise.

Someone knocked on the door, but I ignored it.

Whoever it was knocked again.

And again.

And again.

And again.

And again.

Then Tomasz upstairs banged on the floor and yelled, 'Open the fricking door!'

Dully, I supposed it might be Cleo with my bag from Terry's – or worse, the police, coming to check what time I'd found him, but that thought only occurred to me as I was opening the door and it was too late.

It was Jim, standing there with a carrier bag in each hand. 'Before you say anything, Cleo asked me to come round,' he said. 'She's at some sort of concert tonight.'

'Wes, nephew, trumpet. Why are you here?' I asked, too exhausted to feel embarrassed that he'd caught me out.

He was still in his off-duty clothes but there was an air of on-duty efficiency about him, as if he'd arrived to tidy me up.

'I've brought you supper. You need to eat.' He lifted the bags. 'I've got soup and some rolls. Shall I pop them in the oven?'

I thought about protesting – hadn't he been the one to insist on keeping work for work? – but Jim raised one eyebrow just enough to make it clear that resistance was futile. So I swung the door further open and let him in. Some further cleaning up meant the hall was now empty, and Jim was able to move freely to the kitchen, where he commenced unpacking his bags.

I followed him, but he steered me back to the sofa. 'You stay there,' he said, draping my weighted blanket back over my shoulders. I melted gratefully into the cushions.

After a while he returned with a bowl of tomato soup, which I spooned into my mouth, reluctantly at first, then much faster until its warmth spread through me. I wasn't hungry until I started eating, then I realised I was ravenous. There was a soft white roll too, buttered. He brought me a second one, while I was finishing the first.

Jim sat quietly watching me, and I felt my guilt build and build until I blurted out, 'Jim, I was late for Terry. If I'd been there when I should have been, he might not have ended up in hospital. If he dies …' I made myself say the words. 'If he dies, I don't think I'm ever going to be able to forgive myself.'

'Don't be so dramatic. There's every chance he'll pull through.'

'But I'll still know it was my fault.' I stared at Astrid the aspidistra in her beaten brass pot. She'd put out a new leaf in the last week, a tightly furled spear in the heart of her foliage. I'd been so proud of that. A sign I'd turned a corner. 'I'm not the person I want to think I am. I want to think I'm kind and smart, but I'm not.'

'So you made a mistake,' he said. 'Good people some-times do bad things. Terrible things. Clever people do stupid things. One mistake doesn't change who you are. What you learn about yourself might, though, if you inter-rogate yourself honestly about your motives and actions.'

'Don't do that management fortune-cookie talk, Jim,' I said. 'It might work in whatever self-improvement seminar you used to run but I'm talking about real people.'

'I *mean* real people,' he said.

'Well, I'm talking about me.'

Jim paused. 'So am I.'

We were sitting in the half-light of the table lamps; it was cosy but I couldn't quite make out the expression on Jim's face.

'Go on,' I said.

He cleared his throat. 'I used to work for a big pharma-ceutical company, specialising in … actually, that's not important. Basically, I was head of a sales division, lots of travelling, lots of targets – weekly, monthly, quarterly. Constant stress, but I got used to it after a while. And of course, the salary made up for a lot.'

He paused. I wondered if I was supposed to say well done or something, but my imagination was already at work, racing to reach the conclusion before he did.

Although, it was obvious now, wasn't it? Jim had been a workaholic and had turned to alcohol, or maybe cocaine – hence the rehab – to deal with the pressures of international pharmaceutical sales, whatever that was. (I didn't think it was the fun kind of pharmaceuticals.) He'd hit rock bottom, let his fridge get mouldy, jacked in the job, headed to the Priory, and was rebuilding his life with low-stress cleaning.

I could see where this was going, and I wasn't sure it really applied to my own situation, but I did him the courtesy of listening. I was mostly curious about what he'd been addicted to. It was hard to picture Jim letting his hair down with a crate of Jack Daniels. Single malts, maybe. Reckless bets on the Masters golf?

'I was young, and people don't always like being managed by someone younger, so I had to develop a work persona to get anything done. I was the perfectionist. Not really me, just something I put on every morning with my suit. And that was fine, for a while, but the more responsibility I got handed, the less and less time I had away from that,' he went on. 'No time to have a relationship that wasn't about meeting once a fortnight for dinner. Or a dog.' He turned his head, showing me his rueful smile.

'That's responsible dog non-ownership,' I confirmed.

'Thanks. Anyway, I had one commitment that always made me feel like myself again ...'

'Your family?' I suggested.

Jim looked momentarily thrown. 'No, rugby. My family are all right but they tend to make things worse, not better.'

'Oh. Right.' I wasn't sure where this was going now.

'I've always loved rugby, not just playing it, but the camaraderie and the tactics, the beers afterwards. Everyone's got a job to do, everyone relies on each other. I didn't have to be the leader there, I was part of the team.' He squeezed his nose. 'So. About eighteen months ago, the business hit a rocky patch. Share price crashed, I had to sack people. People I'd worked with for years. I had a meeting at head office in which *I* nearly got sacked, then flew home on Saturday morning, still on this massive stress high, and went straight to rugby without getting my head straight.'

Jim's voice became muffled, then stopped.

I turned to look at him and had to hide my double take. He had his head in his hands, psyching himself up for something.

'First tackle I made, I wasn't concentrating, I went in too hard,' he went on. 'Bam. My mind was still in that meeting. All my frustration ended up in that tackle. Everything you're not supposed to do. It happened so quickly, and there was some confusion but I knew it was me. I knew as soon as it happened, I heard the crunch right in my ear. I could have got away with it, but ...' He shook his head slowly, side to side.

'What happened?'

'I broke the opposition flanker's back.'

I sat up. God almighty. I hadn't been expecting that. I noted the way he phrased it. I would probably have said, 'The opposition flanker broke his back.'

'But it was an accident, right? You didn't mean to hurt him?'

'Of course not. But ultimately ... my anger made it happen. I was out of control.'

We didn't speak for a moment. I was shocked. I couldn't imagine a violent, angry Jim, capable of paralysing someone. And yet he was. I thought of his strong hands, the burst of strength I'd seen under the mild exterior. How close to the surface was that anger? How good an actor was he?

'Chris – the man I hurt – was in hospital for months. He was incredibly generous about it, insisted it was one of those unlucky breaks. His family, not so much.' Jim's face twisted with shame and effort. 'I committed to help his recovery however I could, and I still volunteer for a sports rehab charity. Patient support, fundraising, whatever they need.'

'Is he ...?' I didn't know how to phrase it. 'Did he ...?'

'Did Chris recover? Yes, he did. Not enough to play rugby, but he's back on his feet.'

'That must have been such a relief.'

Jim turned his head. 'For whom?'

'Him, I mean, good for him,' I corrected myself. Then I said, 'And you.'

'Totally. A *huge* relief for me. But that moment changed everything. I realised I didn't know myself at all. I wasn't coping, I wasn't getting good advice. I wasn't the sort of person I'd want to be around.' I heard the understatement. 'I resigned, so I could try to fix things. Start again.'

'Hence the cleaning?'

'Hence the cleaning. Sorry, I don't talk about this a lot, I find it hard. That's where I was this morning, the rehab centre. I volunteer with their fundraising team, transport, whatever's needed. There's a lad there right now who looks exactly like Chris, but he won't walk again. I often think how lucky I was that I wasn't standing a centimetre to the left.'

'But you weren't.'

Jim's eyes met mine. They were still shrewd, but I saw a vulnerability in them now. 'And you weren't ten minutes later for Terry.'

I knew what he was getting at, but did it make me feel better? Not really.

What were you supposed to say now? I always thought I'd know, when I was 'older'.

'So …' Jim slapped his thighs awkwardly. 'I guess what I'm trying to say is that is when good people do bad things, which they sometimes do, they take responsibility. I don't think you're a bad person. A bad person wouldn't feel as terrible as you do now.'

'But I should be better,' I said.

Jim's smile was sad. 'We could all be better, Robyn.'

His story hung between us for a moment, then he said, 'Right, I'll be off now you've had your supper. Don't get up,' he added, as I feebly tried to push off the weighted blanket. 'You look so comfy under that … whatever that is. I'll see myself out.'

'Thank you,' I called, as he left, and I heard him say, 'You're welcome,' as the door closed.

I closed my eyes and tried to empty my brain, but all I could see was Terry.

17

~ Tomato ketchup will lift rust from garden furniture and copper pans – dab it on, rub off, try not to think what it's doing to your insides.

The image of Terry collapsed on the hall floor hovered just on the edge of my waking mind for the next few days.

Cleo informed us that he was stable, but I flinched whenever my phone rang, in case it was the hospital or, worse, his family calling to 'establish a timeline' of his fall. At night, when my brain couldn't be slowed down with cleaning, I lay awake, examining every tiny one of my shortcomings like a forensic scientist.

I didn't tell anyone, because I had no one to tell. Mitch was away on business, and it wasn't something I wanted to discuss with him over the phone. I thought about what Jim had said about taking responsibility, and as penance I went back to Terry's flat after work to collect my bag, and cleaned on my own until the place was immaculate. I got the tea stains out of the cups, and put a shine on the windows. While I was hoovering, I tried not to meet the eyes of the children and grandchildren on the wall.

That said, I did feel better as I let myself out, replacing the spare key in Jayne's lockbox.

My brain was in such a mess that when Anna Hastings called me at the end of the week, it took me a second to remember who she was.

'Hi, Robyn! Is this a good time?' she asked.

'Um, yes.' I'd been cleaning a mirror at the Corrigans', trying to avoid looking at myself as I polished, but now I stared at my reflection; I looked miserable. Not the sort of upbeat professional you'd buy a house from. Bad roots, dark circles under my eyes. And spots. I hadn't had spots in *years*.

From the sofa, Ivor the corgi regarded me with his ever-judgemental side eye.

My lack of enthusiasm seemed to wrong-foot Anna. 'Good! Well, Robyn, I'm ringing with some good news – we'd like to invite you to join the Hastings Laidlaw team!'

I forced a huge smile onto my face. 'That's … tremendous.' The smile was making my cheeks sting. It didn't reach my eyes.

I turned away from the mirror. 'That's *brilliant* news!'

Better. Just.

Ivor tilted his head, intrigued.

'So that's a yes?'

I nodded. 'Yes. It's a yes.'

'Great! We've just had the go-ahead to bring a couple of new projects to market, so it's all hands on deck,' Anna went on. 'When could you start, ideally?'

I almost said tomorrow but then I caught sight of Jim down in the hallway, finishing off a perfectly straight hoover line.

If I bailed it would mean shuffling the timetables around and Cleo was running low on emergency cleaners. I'd seen what they were like, and I didn't think Jim's blood pressure would stand it.

'Next Monday?' I suggested.

A week. One more week of cleaning.

'I think we can just about cover till then. Tremendous!' Anna sounded relieved. 'I'll email the paperwork to you now and if you have any questions in the meantime, you've got my number. Call me any time.'

'Thank you,' I said. 'I will.'

We said goodbye, and I let my smile fall. My cheeks really did ache with the effort of sounding upbeat for that long.

I stared at Ivor, who stared back. Come on, Robyn, I told myself. This is what you were praying for! A job! With a new agency! A chance to get back to your real life!

It *was* good, wasn't it? I'd been chosen ahead of other candidates, I'd been *approved*. I fanned the flame of enthusiasm with the thought of some shopping. I'd treat myself to something new to wear for my first day. I'd rebook the haircut I'd cancelled, and – I looked down at my ragged, unpolished nails – definitely restore my hands to their former glory.

Jim came in with the hoover, ready to create stripes in the sitting-room carpet.

'What was that?' he asked.

'I got the job,' I said.

'What job? Have you had another interview? You didn't say.'

Oops. I kept forgetting I hadn't told anyone I'd been at an interview on Tuesday morning and now I spoke carefully, as if picking my way across broken glass, stepping on the tiny squares of safe truth.

'I had an interview with another agency in town.' There was a pause for him to ask, 'When?' but he didn't.

He knows, wailed a voice in my head. He's not stupid.

'Which one?'

I swallowed. This was the moment to tell him. Should I tell him?

My mouth refused to move.

'Well, that's good news,' he said, mildly. 'An estate agency? Or have you been poached by a *cleaning* agency?'

'No, no, definitely an estate agency. Hastings Laidlaw. It's new, on the High Street.'

'Uh-huh.' He nodded as if he had a mental top ten of estate agents and Hastings Laidlaw was at least in the top three. 'So when do they want you to start?'

'Next week.'

'So soon!'

I nodded and he smiled. 'Congratulations.'

'Thanks!'

'I mean, *this* job's definitely happening,' I gabbled, to fill the silence. 'I told them about the TikTok and Emma Rossiter and they were very understanding, so thanks for the advice on that.'

Jim nodded. 'Good for you.'

'So, you know, if you ever need to buy a house, you know where to come, ha ha!' I didn't know where Jim lived. I wished I knew where Jim lived.

'I'll bear that in mind.'

And I'll miss you.

The clarity of that thought startled me. Particularly since only that morning Mitch had forwarded me a link to some hotels in Paris and asked how I felt about oysters.

I had to stop myself blurting out something emotionally incontinent and embarrassing us both. 'Not too late for you to teach me the secret to hoover lines, though! And everything else you know about stain removal.'

He shook his head. 'You've only got a week left. Stains are a complex field.'

'I've still got two visits to the Armstrongs left,' I pointed out.

Jim smiled, the tentative smile that made his eyes crinkle. It couldn't possibly be because of my lame joke.

In the kitchen there was a sound of a water bowl being tipped over my freshly mopped floor, followed by a yap of delight, and I realised I hadn't even noticed Ivor sneaking out.

I rang Mitch on my way to collect Orson from his junior league football match. My call went to voicemail, which I'd half-expected it to, as he'd told me he had a full day of planning meetings, but he called back just as I was getting out of the car.

'Amazing news!' he said. 'They're lucky to have you on board. We need to celebrate!'

From the background noise, it sounded as if he was somewhere celebrating already. 'Where are you?' I put my finger in my other ear to see if I'd hear him better. It didn't help much. 'I thought you were away somewhere?'

'Finished early,' he shouted over the sound of cheering. 'We've got the green light from the planning, at bloody last, which means we can start focusing on Lark Manor.'

'I thought you *had* planning?'

'No, different project. Listen, where are you now? We've got a table booked at the Ledbury for eight. Join us!'

I didn't know who 'us' was; Allen and Nihal? I wanted to see Mitch, but not in a crowd. I couldn't yell, '… and I was sure he was dead!' across a pub table.

'I can't,' I said. 'Why don't you give me a call when you get home?'

The noise increased, and I couldn't hear his reply, so I hung up and trudged over to the pitch where a 0-0 match was in its final turgid stages.

Football, for me, ranked somewhere between ironing and watching paint dry, but I dutifully summoned up my enthusiastic face for Orson, who often seemed to fall through the gap between Alfie's teenage dramas and Wes's baby-of-the-family indulgence. There were a few parents on the side line, some bellowing 'encouragement', some disguising AirPods with unseasonable bobble hats.

As I got nearer, I spotted a familiar figure, standing alone by a corner flag. It was Elliot sporting a team hoodie, and he was clapping and shouting loudly enough to be heard from the footpath.

'Good touch, Orson! And again!' he shouted and as he turned to follow Orson's courageous but short-lived break, he spotted me.

I decided I wasn't going to make this difficult for either of us, since Cleo wasn't around to give me a hard time, and I raised my hand in a friendly greeting.

'Didn't expect to see you here,' I said. 'It *is* my turn to collect him, isn't it?'

Elliot nodded. 'Yeah. But I come to his home games anyway. I remember how much better I played when my old man was there to watch.'

'Does Cleo know?' She made out Elliot missed nearly everything: football matches, parents' evenings, concerts.

He shrugged. 'Orson's probably mentioned it, it's not a secret. I suppose she told you different?'

I could hardly deny it.

He sighed. 'I know she's your sister, Robyn, but Cleo always rewrites history to suit herself. I'm not saying I'm the world's best dad, but I haven't missed a football match in a few years. Even before we split up. I do my best with Wes and Alfie too.'

'She's in a funny place,' I said, unwilling to badmouth my own sister, but at the same time, wondering what else Cleo hadn't told me and Mum. It hadn't made sense to me that Elliot would go from busy but engaged dad to absent father so quickly. Anyone who willingly stood through a game of football this tedious had to be driven by that very undiscriminating parental love.

'A funny place? You can say that again.' He shook his head. 'I don't know what's going on with Cleo, Robyn. I don't even know if it was me. I mean, yes, I work long hours. But I've always worked long hours! She never had a problem with it before. One minute she was, you know, standard Cleo ...' We both knew what that shorthand meant: a broadly benevolent whirlwind. 'And the next she was angry *all the time*. With everyone, about everything. I did wonder if it was something to do with ...' Elliot raised his eyebrows meaningfully. 'Her, you know ... time of life.'

'Jesus, Elliot, she's only thirty eight!'

'Yeah, well, she put me straight on that. Good job, Orson!'

'Yes!' I waved a fist as Orson hoofed a ball straight to an opposing player. 'Good job! So what do you think she's angry about?'

Elliot frowned. 'All I can think of is that it's something to do with our holiday to Mauritius. She was in a mood the whole time, and the fights really started once we came back. Went downhill from there.'

'Bikini shopping will do that to anyone.'

He turned to me, bewildered. 'She's the same size now as she was when we first met.'

That was true. Had Cleo met someone while they were out there, someone who made her feel she was more than a mum? Had she had an existential moment on the beach with the turtles? I couldn't see Cleo having an existential moment, but stranger things had happened.

Another, sadder, thought struck me.

'I'm so sorry about Rhiannon,' I said, and the pain on poor Elliot's face made me want to hug him. He'd been my brother-in-law for nearly half my life.

So I did hug him. And then the whistle blew for full time, and we were all released from the football misery.

Cleo had instructed me to deliver Orson to Mum's, from where she would collect both him and Wes, who Mum was taking swimming. Wes had recently moved up to Newts. Or Water Rats. There didn't seem to be a logical progression.

Orson headed straight to what had been my old room to rehash the football match with his mates online while I went into the kitchen in search of cake.

Dad went to Cake Club once a month and practised the showstopper at least once before the big night. The mixer was roaring away and Dad looked to be in the middle of something involving a tonne of icing sugar, going by the unusually Georgian appearance of his hair. Mum and Wes still weren't home.

'Do you want a cup of tea?' he shouted over the sound of whisking buttercream. 'Put your feet up next door, you can tell me what you think about this red velvet. I can't get the crumb right.'

I didn't need asking twice. Mum's sofa was the sort you can sink into, and she had the full Sky package. I immersed myself in a large slice of red velvet cake and a terrible show called *Train Wreck Cleaners*, and the first thing I knew about Cleo's arrival was the abrupt smell of her perfume and the swift removal of my half-finished cake.

'Hello Cleo,' I said.

'Hey.' She stared at the women on the screen, entering a hoarder's house wearing full Hazmat suits. Cats were perched on anything that wasn't swaying. 'I think I'd just set fire to that and start again. How was football?'

'OK, I think. You'll have to ask Orson.' I glanced over cautiously, trying to gauge her mood. Might this be a good time to put in a word for Elliot? 'Guess who I saw there?'

'If you're going to say Elliot, don't,' she said, without moving her eyes from the screen.

'But he was—'

'Don't. Please. I've had the day from hell. It turns out those missing hamsters in Jellicoe Road aren't under the floorboards, they're in next-door's snake. And we've had a

VAT inspection. Thank your lucky stars you'll never need to understand VAT.'

There was always something Cleo had to worry about, and I didn't. Boyfriends, VAT, children, pension plans. I think she intended to be reassuring rather than belittling, but still.

Since she'd brought up the topic of work, and we were in the safe space of Mum and Dad's house, I thought I'd tell Cleo about my new job and get it over with. She might be less furious about the short notice, sitting underneath a collage of photos of us in Brownie uniforms.

'I've got some good news,' I said. 'I've been offered a job with an estate agency in town, so I guess I'm handing in my notice.'

'Congratulations. When do they want you to start?'

'Ideally now. But I said next Monday. To give you time to rearrange the rotas.'

'Thoughtful,' said Cleo. 'Who is it?'

'Hastings Laidlaw.'

She raised an eyebrow, which I think indicated approval. 'Anna Hastings?'

'Yes, she's very nice. Do you know her?'

'Mum and I were on her table at the Women in Business Awards.' Cleo pressed her finger on the remaining cake crumbs and tidied them up. 'She's very involved in local animal charities. Likes to tell people she's got five rescue donkeys in her back garden which, if you ask me, is just a subtle way of telling everyone how big her garden is.' She got up. 'Do you want another cup of tea?'

'Please. Listen, while we're both here, if you wanted to talk to Mum about this Gwen Thomas woman, we could do it together? United front? Dad could show Wes how to ice a cupcake and turn the mixer up really loud.'

Cleo paused at the door. She considered it, then shook her head. 'Maybe at the weekend. I've had enough for tonight. But, thanks.'

'You're right, though, we need to talk to her,' I said. 'Together.'

She gave me a smile that made me glad I'd mentioned it. 'Yeah. And it's good news about Hastings Laidlaw, honestly. I'm happy for you. But they've messed you about, haven't they? You need to keep an eye on that.'

'How do you mean?'

'Well, last week you told me you hadn't got the job. Now you have. What happened? Did their first choice drop out?'

'No, this is a different place. They've been pretty quick, actually,' I said, without thinking. 'I only went in for the interview on Tuesday and Anna called me today ...'

'Tuesday?'

I blinked. 'Um ...'

'When on Tuesday?'

Shit. Shit, shit, shit. I didn't want to speak. Whatever I said was going to land me in trouble.

Cleo's confusion cleared, as if she'd answered her own question. 'Well, that's even more impressive, Robyn. To do an interview after you'd been through that drama with poor Terry – wow. I guess an interview must have felt like a doddle after that.'

I stared at her, frozen with panic. *Don't say anything, Robyn. Don't say anything.*

But my silence began to speak for itself. Slowly, Cleo's friendly expression changed. I didn't need to see the cogs in her brain turning; she didn't have cogs, she had microprocessors.

'Oh, wait,' she said. 'You had the interview in the morning, didn't you?' Her voice was crisp, every word articulated as the truth unrolled in front of her. '*That* was why you didn't answer my calls. You were with Anna Hastings.'

'I specifically arranged the interview before work!' Which I had.

'What time did you get to Terry's, Robyn?' Cleo pointed at me. 'And don't lie to me.'

'I …' I stopped, unable to lie *or* tell the truth.

She hit her forehead with her palm. 'Oh my god. I spent nearly an hour this afternoon talking to Terry's family about how grateful they were to us, the way we'd looked after him over the years. You know they wanted your address, so they could send you flowers? For saving his life?'

'But …'

Cleo stopped my words with her jabbing finger again. 'Terry *called me* to let me know he was feeling ill, and *I called you* to tell you to get there early in case he needed some help. And you ignored me because you were in the process of trying to get a better job. What time did you get there?'

'Ten past ten,' I whispered.

It *had* been ten past ten. I'd convinced myself it was quarter to, because that was when I'd last checked my watch. Walking down the high street, desperately trying to manifest a taxi.

Cleo glared at me with disgust. 'So that call Terry made, when he couldn't even speak, was at ten past nine. When you were supposed to be there. He lay there, alone, for an *hour*.'

I shrank back in my chair, hugging my knees. She didn't need to spell it out.

'Why do you do this, Robyn?'

'Do what?'

'Bend the truth as if no one will notice.'

I wasn't prepared for a row with Cleo. 'I'm not ...'

'You've always done it. You just say whatever suits you. What's wrong with you?'

'That's not fair,' I protested, and immediately we were back in our childhood bedroom, Cleo towering over me, even though she was two inches shorter, me struggling to keep up with the relentless torrent of her words.

'Don't give me that!' Cleo spat dismissively. 'You've only been working for me for a few weeks and I've caught you doing it so many times!'

'Not *so many times* ...'

'Adam Doherty's shower! You wouldn't have told me about that, would you? And before you say it, lying by omission is just as bad. It's deception, either way. It makes you untrustworthy.'

'I ...'

'You're completely untrustworthy!'

'You can't talk!' Finally the words shot out of me. 'You haven't been honest about what's going on with Elliot, have you? You don't want us talking to him, because you don't want to deal with the fact that you've treated him—'

'How dare you talk to me about Elliot?' Cleo took a step towards me, her eyes blazing, and I took a step back, scared.

Lucy Dillon

Why didn't Dad come in? How loud did that mixer need to be?

I heard the front door open, and Mum's voice sang out. 'Here we are! Sorry we're late, we might have stopped at the milkshake machine …' Her voice trailed away as she entered the sitting room. The fury on Cleo's face and the tears on mine told its own story. 'What's going on?'

'Nothing,' snapped Cleo.

I saw Wes mouth 'nothing' to himself. His eyes were round, and as Cleo spoke he shrank behind Mum.

Cleo held her hand out towards him. It wasn't the reassuring maternal gesture she hoped it was. It was more like Mary Poppins at her most petrifyingly militant. The light glittered on her diamond rings, bought by Cleo for Cleo, and her immaculate red nails gleamed. I'd always envied Cleo's ability to defy chips. 'Come on, Wes, time to go home.'

'Grandma got us milkshakes,' he said in a small voice. 'She said we could froth up the chocolate one and put marshmallows on it.'

'No, we need to get back,' said Cleo. She shot out her Mary Poppins hand again, and Wes took it, even though I hadn't seen him hold her hand for a while.

'Cleo!' I didn't want us to part like this. I hated confrontation, but arguing with Cleo was like fighting with myself; she knew every terrible thing I secretly thought about myself and wasn't afraid to give them a voice. A loud, mean voice that still wasn't quite as mean as the small one in my own head.

'What?' She turned, her eyebrow raised.

304

I just needed to hear her say she hadn't meant the cruel things she'd said about me.

'You can't make me feel worse about this than I already do,' I said, pathetically. 'About Terry.'

She shot a quick glance at Wes, then at Mum.

'It's not just Terry, it's the lack of trust.' Her voice was icy. 'I expect to be lied to at work. And I expect to be lied to by my ...' She was obviously about to say Elliot, but since Wes was only one arm-length away, she managed to correct it to, '... by people who only ever have their own interests at heart. But if I can't trust my own family, then I can't trust anyone. And that is ...' Again, she struggled not to swear in front of Wes. '*Very sad.*'

'Cleo!' Mum let out a moan.

'Come on, Wes,' said Cleo. 'Let's say goodbye to Grandpa.'

When she left the room I half-expected the door to slam behind her – as it had done for most of our teenage years – but she had evidently grown classier in her adulthood. All she left in her wake was a painful silence.

I slumped in my chair, adrenalin pumping through my veins. I wanted to cry, from shock, not sadness.

It had been years since anyone had shouted at me like that. Maybe never. My skill at avoiding confrontation meant that situations with even a whiff of awkwardness – break-ups, bad holidays – had either happened via text or were left to fade away. It was shameful, I knew, but being criticised made me hyper anxious, to the point where I felt like a balloon being inflated too fast, too much.

Mum too seemed shaken by the force of Cleo's fury. She sank onto the arm of Dad's leather armchair, winded.

'Mum?'

She looked up at me. 'What was that about? What have you done?'

I noted it was *me* who had done something, not Cleo.

'I was late for a client.'

There you go again, observed the voice in my head, minimising.

Mum nodded, as if it wasn't anything new. 'Oh, Robyn. You know what you're like about timekeeping. You need to set an alarm.'

Be honest. 'And it was … Well, there was a bit of a situation.'

The penny dropped. 'Not that poor man who went to hospital?'

'Mum, please don't. I've been beating myself up about it since it happened.'

'So what did she mean about lying?'

'I was late because …' I swallowed. 'Because I was at an interview. I hadn't told Cleo because she gave me such a hard time about the other one.'

'Oh …' Mum sighed, as if she didn't know whether to be reproachful or not.

'Do you want a cup of tea?' I offered.

Mum nodded. 'Go on.'

In the kitchen I heard the mixer slow down, as if the operator was trying to gauge whether conversation had returned to safer waters.

'It's fine, Dad,' I shouted. 'We're all done.'

18

~ Clean up stained teapots with a couple of denture tablets dropped inside, with hot water. And buy a spout brush.

I suppose if I'd been petty, I could have shoved Cleo's bucket where the sun didn't shine, but I didn't want to let Jim down, plus I needed money for clothes, so I arranged for Jim to collect me as usual on Monday morning. Still outside Molly's Bakehouse, though. I still didn't want to be seen in the overalls.

The week went by without any major drama. My last job as a Taylor Maid was at the Armstrongs' and it felt appropriate to finish there, since of all the houses I'd worked in over the past weeks, it had taught me the most. There had been such a challenging variety of chaos to smooth out: food-pocked work surfaces, scribbled-on walls, sticky floors, Lego clumps on every surface, unpleasant smells that had to be sourced and then eradicated … The list was endless, and the temporary order we achieved collapsed back into chaos between each visit. It was like some sort of mythological punishment, the Constant Tidying of Coleridge Terrace.

Still, now I knew how much Sally Armstrong relied on our efforts, I couldn't judge. We were making a difference, not just in her house, but in her head.

'Last job!' said Jim, as he unlocked the door.

'So kind of you to save the best for last,' I said. 'Something to remind me that no matter how messy my own house is, I'll never have to scrape pancake batter off my light fittings.'

'Never say never,' he reminded me, and pushed the door open.

I could tell something was wrong before we even set foot in the black and white tiled hall.

The house smelled ... different.

I took a deep breath. No damp laundry, no soggy stir-fry left in the wok from the previous night.

No bikes thrown against the wall, no bags of cricket kit, books or broken umbrellas.

Well, one bike. But the helmet was in a bag, not abandoned on a doorknob like a black skull.

Was this definitely number 33?

I looked at Jim. 'Did they have someone in this morning?'

'Not as far as I know.' He pointed under the stairs. 'Was there a shoe rack there on Monday?' Three rows of shoes were lined up in demure order, tiny trainers to giant football boots.

Jim and I commenced cleaning in what I can only describe as a wary fashion, just in case a hidden camera team leaped out at us. Instead of tackling half the house, we managed to do nearly all of it in the hours allotted. As usual I was left with the kitchen and had time to get a nice shine on the stainless-steel range instead of throwing everything into baskets and hoping I wouldn't have to poke mouldy bagels out of the hoover nozzle when I probed under the sofa.

The only clutter was a pile of leaflets that had been left on the edge of the counter top and, as I swept it up, I noticed that it was mainly pamphlets about ADHD. Curious, I started reading the top one, focusing on diagnosis in adults. There was a checklist of symptoms and yet again I thought, this is so me.

Inability to finish tasks? Yes.

Impulsive behaviour? Yes.

Restlessness, stress avoidance, mood swings, forgetfulness …

'Hello!' Sally Armstrong appeared through the back door, and I jumped.

'Hello!'

'What do you think?' She swept a hand around proudly.

'This is a lovely house,' I said. I almost said, 'Did you hire a secret second team of cleaners?' But as I'd just been reminded of my poor impulse control by the pamphlet, I was able to stop myself in time.

'Thank you.' She beamed. 'I took some annual leave to get on top of things, and once I started cleaning I couldn't stop. Quite therapeutic, isn't it? I've taken four carloads to the tip!'

Only four carloads? Still, they had a big car. 'You've done a great job,' I said. 'Not much left for us to do!'

Sally saw the pamphlets in my hand and there was no point pretending I hadn't been looking at them.

'Oh, gosh.' She pulled a face. 'Last time I saw you we were going for Charlie's assessment, weren't we? I'm so sorry, I was very stressed. I hope I didn't ramble on too much.'

'How did it go?' I thought it was safe to ask, since she was no longer looking like a woman on the verge of a breakdown.

'Better than I could have hoped. Just having someone *explain* what was going on in Charlie's head made such a difference, to everyone. We'd been blaming ourselves for being bad parents, Charlie was so sad about being naughty … Now we know where we are, what we're dealing with, we can work out how to live with it.' She waved a hand around again. 'Even the house feels happier, don't you think?'

The house was probably happier not having balls bounced off its internal walls, I thought, but there was a calmer, lighter feel to the place. I wouldn't say it was open-house ready, but the 'walk-in' feel was a million times better.

It was a happy ending, I thought, as Jim and I said goodbye and closed the door behind us. Or a happy beginning.

'One more call,' said Jim, pulling out cautiously from Coleridge Terrace. For once I didn't blame him: you had to be cautious in Coleridge Terrace. One false move and a passing Chelsea tractor speeding to make a last call at Waitrose would have your wing mirror off.

I checked my watch. It was well past half five now. 'I thought we were done for the day?'

'You've got somewhere else to be?'

I hadn't. But that wasn't the point.

'It won't take long,' said Jim, and set off towards the High Street.

I wondered if he was maybe taking me for a goodbye drink, and was surprised by the flicker of hope that he was.

I wondered if I should have suggested it first, to say thanks. I wouldn't see Jim again after today and, despite our chat the night Terry had been taken to hospital, there were still things I was curious to know.

In my dating experience, when men avoid discussing where they lived (with their wives) or what they did at the weekends (with their kids) it made me suspicious, but I didn't think Jim was hiding anything. He'd willingly shared his lowest moment with me, but glossed over the parts that anyone else would have enjoyed showing off about – the high-powered career, the success, the travelling. Driving between jobs, I'd tried to lure him out with some open-ended questions about holidays or places he'd loved, but he smoothly turned the conversation on its head, and I found myself telling him more than I meant to about myself.

It was too easy to talk to Jim. He was just determined not to talk about himself, for whatever reason.

Disappointingly we drove through town, past many suitable bars and a couple of very unsuitable ones, including Ferrari's, until we were turning down Hildreth Street, and the penny dropped

Oh no. We were going to Terry's flat, weren't we?

I turned to Jim, ready to ask, but he was there before me.

'Someone asked if they could have a word,' said Jim, mildly. 'With you particularly.'

I squeezed my knees together as my imagination went into overdrive: Terry and his entire, accusatory family, lined up on Terry's leather sofa like a jury. Armed with a printout from the paramedics and ready to question me about my timekeeping. I'd definitely intended to check in on Terry, but when he was a bit further along the road to recovery.

I turned in the passenger seat to look imploringly at Jim. 'Do we have to do this?'

'Do what?'

I desperately wanted to leave Jim with a good impression of me, but the sight of Terry's flat reignited the smouldering embers of shame burning in my chest. Seeing Terry's family, and worse, being thanked by them, would be confirmation that I was an unreliable, terrible person. I really, *really* didn't want to go in.

'Do we have to see Terry? Is he well enough for visitors?

'You don't have to,' he said, evenly. 'I mean, this is your last day. I could tell Terry you had to dash off. But knowing you, as I think I do by now, you'll obsess about what you should have said for the rest of your life. It'll grow out of all proportion. Boom.' He mimed something mushrooming. 'Go in, apologise that you were late, say you're glad he's recovering. Take control.'

'I cleaned his flat,' I said in a small voice. 'On Wednesday night.'

'Did you? That was kind. Why don't you tell him?' Jim's expression softened. 'He likes you, Robyn. He probably likes you more than you like yourself right now.'

Whatever Terry thought about me, I realised, would be no worse than what I thought about myself. And Jim was right: I would shove it in my mental cupboard of guilty fuck-ups and it would slowly grow and grow until the pus-filled boil of shame engulfed the (relatively) tiny splinter of offence inside.

'I'll come with you, if you want,' he offered. 'If Jayne comes at you with Terry's crutches, I'll see her off.'

'OK,' I said, and got out of the car before I could talk myself out of it.

Terry was in a wheelchair in the sitting room, a more elaborate hospital version of his usual model, with a saline drip and a protective frame around his leg. He was wearing a box-fresh M&S dressing gown which was too big for him and a pair of sheepskin slippers, also brand new. He didn't look great but, I was pleased to say, he was no longer easy to mistake for a dead person.

'Robyn!' His craggy face lit up as soon as he saw me.

The relief nearly made my knees buckle.

His daughter Jayne followed us in, fussing. 'Dad, no moving, remember what the doctor said about that drip.'

Terry winked. 'Any chance you can put some tea in this drip for me, Robyn?'

'He's been a right monkey,' Jayne said. 'I honestly don't know how you put up with his nonsense.'

Jim asked how he'd been getting on, and Jayne told us about the diagnosis (Type 2 diabetes, plus heart condition, broken leg and wrist), and the treatment (no French Fancies) and the outlook (fair, 'if he takes better care of himself').

'The paramedics got there in the nick of time,' Terry told Jim. 'Another minute and I'd have been a goner.'

That did it. I blurted out, 'Terry, I've got a confession to make. I was late. The day you ... the day you went into hospital. I was at a job interview.'

There. Done. Out.

I dropped my gaze, not wanting to look at Jayne. Out of the corner of my eye I could see Jim fold his arms. Terry had already managed to get crumbs on the carpet I'd spent an hour cleaning, and had compounded it by crushing them in with his wheels. Not that I cared.

'Not as late as I nearly was,' said Terry. 'Main thing was you got me to hospital. If it had happened any other day that week I'd have had no chance. Could have been lying there for days.'

'Dad,' said Jayne. 'Don't say that.'

She looked even more uncomfortable than I felt. I realised that she probably was – it was the same remorse I'd seen on Sarah Jennings' face, the day we'd blitzed her mother's neglected home. My first day as a Taylor Maid. Now that seemed a long time ago.

Terry wasn't deterred. 'Good job I don't have a dog, eh, Robyn, or else it'd have had half my leg eaten! Did I tell you about an old Navy pal of mine who woke up to find his Doberman—?'

'Dad! No! Please!'

He winked at me. I suspected he knew Jayne wouldn't let him finish.

'Dad's going to come and stay with us while he recovers.' Jayne pulled her shoulders back, recovering her composure. 'We're looking into finding him somewhere easier to manage. There's some very nice sheltered accommodation not too far from my brother Brian ...'

'We'll see about that.'

'We *will*, Dad. Need to make sure you're being looked after properly.' She patted his shoulder. 'Need to keep you with us a bit longer.'

'When are you off?' Jim asked Terry.

'Tomorrow morning. Soon as madam here packs my bags.'

'Got to get back for my grandkids.' Jayne indicated the family group on the wall, the four red-headed children I'd dusted very carefully. 'Rosie, Lily, Rowan and Holly.'

'Husband's a keen gardener,' said Terry.

Jayne frowned. 'No, Dad, I've told you before, Gavin's a *doctor*.'

Jim laughed, but Jayne looked at me and made a 'you have to worry' face. 'Anyway, Dad wanted to give you this.' She handed me a gift bag and I started to open it, but Terry waved his free hand.

'No, wait till you're home. Don't want any waterworks, I'm on a heart monitor whatsit here.' He beckoned me forward. 'Just a little thank you, bab. You ringing all those people from my address book – never had so many messages. Been like a family reunion.' He patted my hand. 'You're a good girl.'

'Thanks, Terry.' I couldn't say much more.

'No, thank you.' Jayne folded me in a big hug. 'Thank *you*.'

I looked over her shoulder to where Jim was sitting on the sofa.

He gave me a very discreet thumbs up, and I allowed myself a crooked smile in return.

'I tell you what,' Jayne said, wiping tears away with the side of her finger so as not to smudge her eyeliner, 'this flat is spotless. You two are marvellous.'

'The work of my colleague here,' said Jim. 'She's not bad.'

I waited until we were back in the van before I looked in the bag.

'So what's he given you?' Jim asked.

I lifted out a faded mug. Terry's *Bullseye* mug, a classic 1980s colour change one. When you added hot tea, a speedboat appeared. When your tea went cold, the speedboat disappeared. A lesson for us, Terry liked to say: drink your tea while it's hot.

There were also four packets of French Fancies. I suspected they were less a gift from Terry and more Jayne clearing out his secret stash.

'I reckon he's going to be OK, you know,' said Jim. 'He's a tough nut.'

'Jayne's not giving him the option. I hope she's ready for a lot of stories about his darts team.'

'And do you feel better?' he went on.

Actually, I did. I felt as if a weight had been lifted from my shoulders. No, that was a cliché. I had that unexpected heart-lift you get when a brown envelope turns out to be a tax refund, not a speeding ticket. Or when someone cancels a party you didn't want to go to and you can stay in with a takeaway and a boxset instead.

I turned round to face Jim, my knee jammed up against the handbrake. The van was inevitably an intimate place; we were sitting much closer than we would in a bar. I wasn't going to see Jim again after today, I reasoned, so it didn't really matter if I was a bit gushy now. 'You were right, what you said about facing up to mistakes. I really appreciate you sharing your own story, to get that into my thick head.'

He nodded, slowly, and I tried not to notice an aftershave that I didn't think he'd worn before. It was clean, but subtle. It made me think of salty air and blue skies.

'I *have* learned my lesson,' I added, half-joking. 'I will address my chronic avoidance. And my timekeeping and my disorganisation, and some other things that now point to me having faulty brain wiring. I've made an appointment to see my GP after work next week.'

After what Sally Armstrong had said about ADHD presenting differently in girls, I'd done some research of my own: three Internet diagnostic tools said I should probably get some medical advice about adult ADHD. How much easier could my life have been if someone had checked that out before now, I'd thought, staring at my laptop one sleepless night. The stress I'd had learning lines, meeting everyone's expectations, the endless, endless lists. Why hadn't Mum spotted that? She was quick enough to take Cleo to the specialist when they thought she was dyslexic.

'Good for you,' said Jim. 'Nothing wrong with asking for help.'

He smiled, and the lightness in my chest increased. I felt floaty. Bright and light, without the guilt that had been following me around like a rain cloud.

'Have you got time for a Friday drink?' I said, impulsively.

Jim paused, and in that instant I felt the absolute disappointment of him saying no. My mind flung up the unknowns – the girlfriend, the wife, the *boyfriend* – I felt as if I was on the crumbling edge of a cliff, staring at the crashing waves below.

Please don't say no, I thought.

Then he said, 'Yes. That would be nice.'

Jim suggested a pub that he'd found near where he lived, which turned out to be in the properly old part of town near the cathedral, where properties rarely came on the market.

'My house used to be an almshouse,' he said, over his pint. 'I think there might be a ghost but it's quite a benign one. It turns down the heating.'

'Seriously?'

He nodded. 'I come home to find the heating's been turned down. Not off, *down*.'

'You're sure it's not someone else in the house?'

If Jim spotted my artful attempt to flush out a partner, he didn't let on. 'No one else to do it, unless you count next-door's cat. And even he's stopped coming round now it's so cold.'

I would have to tell him about the Doom Barn, I thought. 'Did they tell you that when you bought it?'

He shook his head. 'Bloody estate agents, eh? Fortunately, I'm only renting. I downsized when I resigned. Wanted to keep my options open.'

'Snap! I sold and now I'm renting too. Temporarily.'

'So you're not staying there long?'

'You say that as if you're relieved for me.'

'What? No, it's a nice flat.' He pushed the bag of crisps towards me; he'd opened the bag neatly down the seam and flattened it out so it made a plate. Even in the pub, Jim didn't make a mess. 'Maybe not what I imagined you in but still nice.'

'And where did you think I'd live?' I asked casually, as though the very idea of Jim speculating on my whereabouts after hours wasn't itself an intriguing thought.

'I don't know, somewhere old, with nooks and crannies. Fancy windows. You always point out fancy windows. And stairs. Even though they're annoying to clean.'

'Well, funny you should say that ...' I helped myself to some crisps. 'That's exactly where I will be living in the not-too-distant future. I've invested in the redevelopment of a country house just outside the town, and as part of the deal I get first choice of the apartments.'

'And what have you picked?'

'I've picked the garden flat.'

'Why's that? Are *you* a keen gardener?'

I fidgeted with the crisps because I wanted to look at Jim, and I didn't. It was the end of a long week and I'd had half a glass of wine, but that wasn't what was making me feel so relaxed. Now we were out of work time, he'd switched into that conversational mode I recognised from the holiday cottage, or the night he brought me takeaway. Talking to off-duty Jim was like being swept down a river, effortless and scenic. I also realised that what I thought was his permanent judgemental expression was just the way his face fell when he was listening properly. He had Judgy Resting Face, I realised. A bit like Ivor.

'I want to get a dog,' I admitted. 'Eventually. If I can take it to work. I'm starting off with plants – I've got an aspidistra called Astrid that I haven't killed so far – and when I can take care of plants, and myself, I'll be ready for a dog.'

'What are you talking about? You're a grown woman. What makes you think you couldn't look after a dog?'

The fact that Jim had to ask that meant either he was being polite, or he clearly hadn't noticed much about the real me. But he'd asked, so I answered.

'I don't always look after *myself* that well. I don't sleep properly, I forget to have meals, it's months since I last went to the gym. Dogs deserve better than that. But I would love one. I like the way they listen to you.' I took a sip of wine, suddenly self-conscious. 'Anyway, I've started with Astrid. If I can keep her going for six months I'll know I'm on the right track.'

And if I kept the dog alive for ten years, then I got a gold adult star, or something.

Jim regarded me over his beer. 'That's your main goal in life? To keep your plant alive and then maybe get a Nessie of your own?'

'Is there anything wrong with that?'

'No!' He turned his glass round and round. 'Old habits die hard. Where do you see yourself in five years' time? What would you say is your main career goal? Sorry.'

I pretended I was thinking but something in his words struck a nerve. What *was* my career goal? Where *was* I going to be in five years' time?

I didn't know.

The realisation made me sit up straighter. Jim had accidentally put his finger on something that had bothered me for years.

I didn't *have* a destination. The last ambition I had was to get into drama school after university and when I'd failed to do that I'd just drifted into my adult life, looking backwards instead of forwards, all the while getting twice-yearly reminders that I'd failed, in the form of dwindling repeat fee cheques, floating past me like wreckage from the ship I'd sunk.

But until I knew what I wanted to do, that was always going to be inevitable. I just needed to find a new destination. Face the front, not the back. Although wasn't that what the property development with Mitch was meant to be?

'Did I say something wrong?' Jim asked.

'No, no.' I'd spilled my drink, but now had the excuse of mopping it up. 'I'm just glad they didn't ask me that in my interview. I don't actually know.'

'It's a stupid question – none of us know. How can we? If you'd asked me five years ago I wouldn't have said that I saw myself being the best cleaner in a small housekeeping business.'

'But you still had to be the best cleaner.'

Jim's eyes twinkled. 'Of course. My mum would have laughed her head off.'

'I suppose in five years' time I'll be an estate agent. A partner,' I added, to sound ambitious.

'You don't have to be. Travel, go and work somewhere else for a bit. Someone I worked with retrained as a paramedic, he loved it. Changed his life. Maybe that's Terry's gift to you.'

I'd been dying for the loo for at least twenty minutes but hadn't wanted to break the conversation to excuse myself, in case Jim thought it was an exit strategy, the end of the drinks. However, now I had no choice about excusing myself. 'Hold that thought,' I said. 'I just need to …' I nodded towards the Ladies.

'No problem,' said Jim. 'I'll get some more crisps.'

The toilets were right at the back of the pub, and I was weaving round the tables when I spotted someone at the bar that I really didn't expect to see.

Mitch.

I stopped dead. What was he doing here? We'd spoken only that morning about meeting up at the weekend; I'd suggested Friday night cocktails to celebrate my final day as a cleaner, but he'd apologised, explaining he wouldn't be back until the small hours of tomorrow morning. He was away dealing with some urgent problem on site (I think he said Ireland) and was on the last flight out.

As ever, seeing Mitch leaning on the bar, chatting animatedly to another bloke in a suit, gave me a quick swoop of lust, but not as much as normal. Possibly because I didn't understand why he'd told me a deliberate lie.

He turned to order another drink from the barman and in turning saw me, and – was that a momentary hesitation? – waved me over. If he was embarrassed to be caught out, he didn't show it.

'Robyn! How are you, gorgeous?' He kissed me on the cheek, and introduced me to the people he was with, whose names I promptly forgot. The introductions included their property companies, anyway, and I didn't like the up-and-down look they gave me.

'This is a nice surprise,' I said. 'I thought you were in Ireland?'

He slung his arm around my shoulder and gave it a squeeze. 'Did I say that?'

'You did.'

'Hey hey, Mitchell,' said one of the men. (Steve, probably. Or Chris.) 'What are you up to?'

I could tell from the rapid movements of Mitch's eyes that he was thinking fast, and then he said, 'I've been in Leominster, babe. Did you think I said Leinster?'

'I don't believe you specified a place.'

I was playing along with the ooohs from Mitch's companions but in truth I was ticked off. He knew this was a big deal for me, moving on from Taylor Maid, and he'd been so enthusiastic about my new job. Why hadn't he wanted to celebrate with me? And now he knew he'd been caught out, why wasn't he admitting it?

Mitch turned back to his companions. 'Robyn here is one of our best local agents, and she's celebrating a fantastic new job with a new agency. I should be celebrating with her right now, not talking shop with you guys. But we can put that right, can't we? Prosecco all round?'

I didn't want to celebrate with random men. I wanted to celebrate alone with Mitch. And this week hadn't just been about the new job; there was so much more I needed to talk to him about.

I politely removed his arm – more 'oooh!'s – and said, 'Thanks, but I'm here with a friend. Great to meet you, but I'll leave you to it.'

'Bring her over!' said Steve, or Chris. 'We'll get a bottle!'

I could see Mitch scanning the pub for this friend and I was glad that he'd see Jim, not some single girl who could be brought over to flirt with his mates.

But there was no one at our table. Had Jim gone?

I felt a grip of disappointment.

'She gone?' Mitch made a sad face. 'Never mind, join us. I've been telling Andy here all about Lark Manor, but you paint a much better picture than I do.' He turned to them. 'Robyn is amazing when it comes to communicating a property vision. When we found Lark Manor, she was the first person I wanted on board, not just for the sale but for developing the concept of what aspirational millennials really want.'

The two men looked impressed, and any other time I would have been thrilled to hear Mitch say those words – and even more excited to discuss Lark Manor – but not tonight.

I managed a quick, unconvincing smile. 'Sorry, guys, don't want to abandon my friend for too long. Love to chat about Lark Manor another time though?' I glanced at Mitch. 'We're pencilling in a meeting about that in the next week or so, aren't we?'

I said it casually, but I meant it; Mitch might be used to having his money tied up in projects but I wasn't. I didn't need a binding timetable, just an update on how the sale was going. In an effort to calm my nerves, I'd dug out the contract Allen had sent me, but it was the most complicated document I'd ever dealt with, full of clauses and technical phrases I hadn't come across before. It took all my concentration to unpick single paragraphs at a time. And there were no dates.

Mitch squeezed my waist. 'Absolutely! But come on, it's Friday night.'

I extricated myself, much to Mitch's evident confusion, but by the time I'd wriggled through the packed pub, there was no sign of Jim. Friday evening drinkers had spilled onto the pavement outside, but he wasn't one of them.

I stood there, feeling strange.

Did Jim think I'd stood him up? Had he seen me with Mitch, Mitch kissing my cheek, putting his arm round me?

My phone pinged with a message.

> Sorry to dash off – Cleo texted with an emergency at Welbeck Street. Good luck on Monday! J

And that was it. I stared at my phone. No more Jim.

Back in the pub, the Friday night atmosphere was ramping up and I glanced back, debating whether or not to join Mitch and his friends.

Reluctantly I decided to go back in for one drink. If only because listening to Mitch wax lyrical about Lark Manor to his property mates reassured me that it was going to happen.

19

*~ You can lift greasy fingerprints from walls using a
piece of white bread to rub away the marks. Also use
white bread to check the area around a broken glass, to
ensure you pick up all the tiny shards.*

Hastings Laidlaw was, I'm pleased to say, a fantastic
place to work. Not just because the office was bright
and clean, and the chairs were Danish and ergonomic, and
there was a living plant air purifier in the reception, but
because Anna Hastings was keen on work-life balance,
made a point of checking that I was settling in well, and
was generous about sharing the clients around so everyone
got a fair crack of the whip.

In addition to me and Anna in the sales department there
were also Caelen, Tia and Katie. Caelen was from Dublin,
Tia was from London and Katie was from Marsh & Frett.
I spent the first day on pins in case she took one look at me
and spilled the beans about my Drawer of Shame to Anna,
but she greeted me like an old friend, and when we were
alone in the kitchen asked me, sotto voce, if I wouldn't mind
keeping that 'whole thing with Dean and me' to myself.

I had no idea what she was talking about. I nodded discreetly anyway.

I wanted this to work, so I made myself a new series of
lists and felt the benefits immediately. Both my alarms,

phone and radio, went off at seven. I leaped out of bed straight away and ticked off shower, hair, healthy breakfast, so I was on the bus by half eight and in the office on time, clutching my Hoffi Coffi VIP travel cup. It was exhilarating, that blank-page feeling of a new start. I wanted to keep it that way for as long as I possibly could, even if it meant concentrating for the rest of my life.

I did miss Jim's daily lectures about contaminants, but his cleaning tips stayed with me. I watered and fed Astrid and the other plants, and carefully wiped any dust from their leaves. I emptied the crumb tray of my toaster regularly and made a point of spraying my shower screen after each use, instead of letting the soap scum build up to a frosty pattern.

Jim might not have transformed me into a star cleaner in his image but he'd indirectly made my flat a much nicer place to be. The plants seemed to like it too.

And like the plants, I started to flourish.

'I think this one's right up your street.'

Anna dropped a valuation request on my desk, and the address jumped out at me.

St Anselm's Court.

'Nice development,' she went on. 'Quite recent. I don't think this guy's been in it very long.'

'It's not … Adam Doherty, is it?' I asked.

'Do you know him?' Anna seemed impressed. We'd had a few of those crossed wires conversations where I'd unintentionally made myself sound better connected than I really was, and now every time I tried to set her straight she thought I was just being discreet. 'You *do* know everyone, don't you?'

'Mmm.' I decided not to tell her I'd sold Adam the apartment in the first place. Well, not until I'd established why he was selling up.

'Can you pop round and have a look at it this morning?' Anna went on. 'He seems keen to get it on the market asap.'

The first thing that crossed my mind was that it was a Wednesday, and therefore a Taylor Maid cleaning day. I wondered if Jim would be there, or if a different team had taken over.

The second thing that crossed my mind was whether Adam would remember me. I'd managed to return my appearance to something near its pre-housekeeping state but I'd ditched the false lashes and smoothed-out blow-dry because, when it came down to it, I decided I preferred the extra minutes in bed each morning. A fair trade-off, but one which made me look a bit less like my old self in photos.

'Sure!' I said. 'I'll head over there now.'

The Taylor Maid van was parked outside when I arrived, but I couldn't tell which cleaners would be working inside.

And no, Adam Doherty didn't recognise me. He didn't even realise I was the estate agent he'd summoned until I explained that I was the agent from Hastings Laidlaw. He wasn't the sharpest knife in the block, Adam.

'Yeah, so I'm putting this on the market.' He ushered me into the centrepiece dining area that I knew better than he did. 'Basically, new restaurant's taking off, need to be closer to Bristol, not really spending as much time here as I'd like. Blah blah blah.'

'That's a shame,' I murmured. I knew I should be taking notes but I'd only written a description of this place a few months ago, so it wasn't going to be a stretch to redo it. Adam had barely had time to change the loo rolls, let alone the layout. I gazed around at the expensive Corian work surfaces. They looked amazing in photos, but were an absolute pain to keep smear-free, I knew now. 'It's a stunning apartment.'

'Yeah, not bad.' Adam was squinting at me, as if he was trying to place me, but then his phone rang, saving me from explaining that we'd already met at least three times. I hoped he wasn't remembering me from my Internet shaming.

'Sorry,' he said, already answering it. 'Gotta take this … Yeah, Eddie, what's up? Nah, man, ignore the paramedics, that's not a reason to close the kitchen …'

I took the opportunity to wander round the open-plan space, checking to see whether Jim was keeping up with the dusting. It was spotless, but I noticed there were several flaking areas where the screws were coming through the plasterboard; they'd need touching up. And – I trod on a floorboard a second time to check the squeak wasn't my imagination – yes, that was loose.

Still. Squeaks wouldn't show in photographs.

Adam was still talking, so I carried on towards the full-length windows and the view out towards the lawn where small boys had once played cricket and local grandees had taken afternoon tea. Not that Adam was interested in that. My eye was drawn by a flash of red against the grey stone and I saw Jim walking down the steps with a bucket and a hoover; he was with a woman, mid-twenties, black hair wrapped in a scarf.

What was that I felt? Relief, I told myself. Relief that I'm no longer having to clean these windows.

I don't think that was exactly what I felt.

Adam had dealt with the kitchen issue and returned, still texting. 'So, yeah. How long do you reckon it'll take to find a buyer?'

I dragged myself back into slick professional mode. Bright smile. Confident attitude. 'Not long. There was a waiting list for viewings on these properties when they first came to market. Still very popular, with the location and the premium specification on the interiors.'

'Hmm,' said Adam.

'Have you had any problems?' We were standing in the middle of the lounge area. By now I'd usually have put the vendor at ease, got them chatting about how much they loved the house, how sorry they were to sell and so on, until tea had been offered and we were having a cosy heart-to-heart about the real reasons they wanted to move. Adam was having none of that. He just seemed keen to get rid.

'Not problems, as such …'

I tilted my head, inviting him to go on, but internally I was flipping through possible reasons, some problematic, some not.

Fallen out with neighbours over massive barbecue.

Fallen out with neighbours over massive sound system.

Couldn't afford mortgage payments on top of new restaurant.

New girlfriend who didn't want to sleep in a cupboard while Adam's massive television got more storage space than he did.

'It's just … crap!'

I stopped flipping. I hadn't expected that.

Adam seemed to have startled himself by his outburst too. He wasn't a sweary type of chef; at heart, he was a good country boy who (according to Johnny, who knew Adam's landowning dad) had been Tractor Driver of the Year twice in the local Young Farmers' Club.

'Crap?' I repeated, in case I'd heard wrongly.

'Crap. Take the shower,' he said. 'It never worked properly. And then the cleaners broke it, so it had to be replaced, and the plumber said the original shower was a cheap knock-off, and it had been installed the wrong way round, so we had to redo the entire wet room. I mean, I didn't fork out nearly a m—' He seemed embarrassed to mention an actual figure, although of course I knew exactly how much he'd paid. '… all that money for a knock-off shower.'

'I see. Wow.' I felt slightly less bad about breaking it now.

'And the oven's never been right.' He eyed it contemptuously, then had a thought. 'Should I be telling you this?'

'Best to be completely honest with me,' I said. 'Any buyers will get their own survey done.'

'Do I have to tell them the shower's shit?'

'Not if you've replaced it and it works,' I reassured him, but I wasn't feeling quite as reassuring as I sounded.

What if all the showers in the development had been plumbed in backwards? More to the point, what if none of them were the brand listed on the particulars? How much would that cost to sort out? I'd have to tell Mitch. Those plumbers were going nowhere near Lark Manor.

I took some more details from Adam, to show willing more than anything else, and he walked me out to the door, where we bumped into Jim and his cleaning partner.

It was strange, seeing him in his overalls while I was wearing my smart negotiator outfit. I'd gone big city shopping for my new look, trying to lock in an organised personality with some neat and tidy jackets and simple dresses. I hadn't been able to resist a pair of statement boots, though: oxblood leather with a silver flash on the heels. The funny thing was, I didn't feel as different as I'd expected.

I smiled. Jim's replacement colleague smiled back.

'Hello!' said Jim.

I had a split-second choice: did I know this man or not, and if so, how?

Really, there was no choice. My face was giving me away. 'Hello, Jim!'

Although Jim didn't smile, his eyes twinkled. 'Can't keep away, I see.'

Adam looked between the two of us, unsure of whether Jim was part of the valuation process or not.

'These are your cleaners, Adam,' I said. 'I don't know if you've met them before? Jim and …?'

'Gracie.'

'Jim and Gracie.'

Jim and Gracie waved.

'No need to introduce *you*,' said Gracie to Adam.

Adam raised his own hand in acknowledgement, with the faint but thrilled modesty of the Instagram celebrity, then his expression changed. 'Wait a minute, you're the cleaners? So you're the ones who broke my shower?'

Gracie instantly went on the defensive. 'No, that was …'

'Actually,' I said, keeping my eyes fixed on Jim's. I'd show him how far I'd come! 'Actually, that was …'

'Me,' said Jim, firmly. 'That was me. It came off in my hands. Can't apologise enough.'

I opened my mouth to say, 'No, it was me,' but Jim shook his head imperceptibly.

Adam made a tsking noise. 'Well, don't mess about with the oven. I don't want to replace that before I sell.'

'I'll be in touch with some draft particulars,' I told him. 'Someone will be round to take measurements later this week, if that's OK?'

'But it'll be on the market as soon as, yeah?'

I nodded. 'Of course.'

'Cheers.' Adam turned to Gracie and Jim. 'Yeah. Cheers.'

And he closed the door on all three of us.

I retracted my Young Farmers' Club approval. Rudeness to cleaners was not acceptable.

'So,' said Jim. 'Does it look very different, now you're viewing it from the other side?'

'Ha ha! I'm certainly not telling them how hard the counters are to clean.' Duh. Was that really the best I could come up with?

I racked my brains for something witty to say about the shower but all I could come up with was more gormless smiling.

Gracie cleared her throat and pantomimed looking at her watch.

'We're running late,' she told me, 'and we haven't finished upstairs yet.'

'We're cleaning for a client upstairs first,' said Jim, gesturing towards the sweeping staircase. 'Slowly taking over the building.'

'But you've finally got a punctual partner!'

I needed to get out of there before I said something really stupid.

We mumbled some goodbyes and that was it, Gracie was marching up the stairs with Jim following. He was probably happier working with someone even more focused than him, I thought, and felt a twisty-turny sensation in the pit of my stomach that I couldn't pin down.

When I was back at my desk, trying to find another way of saying 'disproportionately massive sitting room', my phone pinged.

It was a text, from Jim.

> I can't believe you walked those boots across a floor we only polished last week. How soon we forget. J

I looked at it for a second, trying to gauge the seriousness of it, then texted back:

> Many apologies. Next time I'll take them
> off. R

As soon as I sent that, I panicked. Oh god, what if he wasn't joking? What if that sounded too flirty?

I stared at my phone for a full five minutes before it pinged with Jim's reply.

A laughing emoji.

I smiled at the screen. Then wondered if Orson would tell me that emoji meant something I wasn't aware of.

Jim and I had only chatted in the pub for an hour or so, but our conversation lodged in my head, particularly the bit where I'd admitted I didn't know what I wanted to do with my life. I fell down a research rabbit hole, exploring everything from gap years for adults, retraining as an interior designer, volunteering at the local dog rescue, even going abroad to qualify as a real estate agent in the US. I hadn't realised how many other people were in the same boat, and it made me feel less stupid.

Two things stood out from my brainstorming: one, I would need to embrace change, which I wasn't good at; and two, I would need money. I *had* money, of course, albeit tied up in the Lark Manor development. But investing in myself, I reasoned, was just as important.

Financial planning induced peak anxiety in me, but I needed to know from Mitch's own mouth where I stood. Either development was underway, in which case I wanted a timeframe for a return, or, if nothing had been finalised, I hoped he'd be able to arrange for me to get some money back. I'd been a bit rash, in hindsight, investing everything I had, but Mitch would be handling way bigger investments than mine. How hard would it be for him to find a way to release a small chunk? I couldn't find anything in the contract about a cooling-off period, but there had to be one, didn't there?

I decided I'd raise it at the weekend, when we were meeting for a lazy day at the annual food festival. I mean, who doesn't feel relaxed when surrounded with cheese and cider? Mitch was in a particularly good mood, bubbling with excitement about the project he'd been discussing with the two investors I'd seen him with in The Ram. It seemed they were converting an old bank in Cheltenham into a steak restaurant.

'We're in talks to get Adam Doherty on board as a meat curator,' he finished, triumphantly. 'BBQAdam, it's going to be amazing!'

I let 'meat curator' go. I wasn't sure Adam Doherty would be that keen when he discovered who was behind the project: the man who'd fitted his knock-off shower. 'You know he's selling his flat in St Anselms?'

'Really?'

'He's had some issues with the finish.' I studied Mitch's expression carefully. He was wearing sunglasses so it wasn't easy. 'Significant problems with the plumbing, for a start. Can we go with a different firm for Lark Manor? And stress-test the showers before the launch?'

'Sure! Do you want to be in charge of sourcing the bathroom fittings? You've got a great eye for it. We could stress-test them together …?'

I tried not to be distracted by that thought. 'Who actually does the final checks?' I asked. 'Is that an external company? I mean, you'd know if the builders didn't use the materials they'd...'

'Robyn, can I stop you for a second?' He touched my arm. 'Sorry, we just need to grab that waitress before she vanishes again. What did you want? Pimms? What about something to eat?'

It was warm and the food was great, and we had a very gratifying discussion about our Paris minibreak, the places we'd go, the hotels Mitch had stayed in. But I knew I had to ask about the money, and better sooner than later.

Emboldened by a second glass of Pimms, I brought up the issue of getting some of my investment back, but Mitch cut me off before I was halfway through my carefully rehearsed request.

'Ah, Robyn, I was going to tell you about that. Good news! The sale's literally just gone through and we've made the downpayment to the architect and the builders, for materials, so we're on the way!' He stopped when he saw my shocked expression. 'Oh, what? If you'd asked me last week... God, I'm sorry. Ask me again in a couple of months and I'll see what I can do. What do you want it for?'

'I'm thinking about taking a course in Interior Design,' I said. 'Or maybe an immersive language school. Or Drama Therapy, something where I can use my skills.'

'Sounds fascinating, good for you.' I suspected Mitch wasn't listening; he'd already pulled out his phone and was scrolling through images to show me. 'Speaking of interior

337

design, I wanted to ask your opinion on something. It's the steak place I was telling you about, we're workshopping Feather and Blade as a potential chain name. Tell me what you think about this tableware.'

As he leaned over to share the image on his phone, I looked at the sunlight gleaming on his thick dark hair, the soft skin just behind his ear and felt the pressure of his thigh against mine: the usual surge of physical attraction raced through the sensitive parts of my body, and I glanced up to see a woman on an organic kombucha stand giving Mitch an appreciative once-over. When our eyes locked, she made a 'lucky girl' face at me and turned back to a customer.

I dropped my gaze to the phone and watched Mitch's finger, swiping the images across and across and across. Forks, forks, forks, forks.

The finger stopped swiping; he reached up and touched me on the nose. 'You don't have anywhere to be first thing tomorrow, do you? I've been invited to this new Sunday night speakeasy, I said we'd drop in later tonight. It's a friend of a friend who's behind it, and I know they've got a pretty interesting guest list ...'

This was everything I'd wanted – the flirtation, the social life *and* Mitch involving me in his business plans. It was the entire wishlist that I'd begged the universe for.

'Sounds great. But I've got a pre-work viewing booked in for eight on Monday.' Why had I agreed to that? 'I can't cancel, she's a cash buyer.'

He frowned playfully. 'Of course.' His fingertip dropped to my mouth, tracing the outline of my lower lip. 'You don't have to be out late. I'm sure you could persuade me to come home early.'

It was hard to resist Mitch when he gazed into my eyes like that. Not hard, impossible.

Mitch leaned forward and slowly kissed me. The sun was warm on my face, and the sound of a live band, the smell of hot barbecue coals, the sensation of his lips on mine and the strawberries and the first weekend of summer merged inside me like a wonderful, common-sense-suppressing cloud.

I would just have to get up very early, I told myself. And drink a *lot* of water before I went to bed. Even though I already knew it was a very very bad idea.

20

~ Add a drop of dishwasher rinse aid to the water when you're washing windows, and you'll get a lovely streak-free finish.

I'd promised Adam Doherty that I'd have his flat listed asap, and the new Robyn was as good as her word. Or, at least she was aware of her word and let people know in advance if she was running late with it. I only wished Jim was around to see how very diligent I was being.

Despite my private misgivings, I created a persuasive description of Adam's flat and asked Anna to have a look at the listing before I hit send. The photographer had visited not long after Jim and Gracie had departed, and the resulting sheen on the flat was so striking I assumed multiple filters had been deployed. But no. It was pure elbow grease – and probably bicarbonate of soda, knowing Jim.

'Great-looking property,' said Anna. She skimmed my copy and suggested a few tweaks here and there (I'd overused the word 'stunning', to be fair). 'Did you check the nuts and bolts?'

'How do you mean?'

'Well ...' Anna jiggled her hand. 'It's one of Mitch Maitland's developments, isn't it?'

'Yes? Why do you ask?'

She stopped jiggling and squinched her nose. 'I've got to be honest …'

'Go on.' I had a sinking feeling I knew what she was about to say.

'They always look *fabulous*. I mean … fab-u-lous. They're just never constructed to a standard that I'd be happy buying myself. The finish is tremendous. The boring bits underneath, not so much.'

I felt dull inside. I'd only been working with Anna for a short while but she was easily the best boss I'd ever had. Her buzzy personality was what made the office so welcoming to clients, but there was no question about who was driving the business, and where she intended to take it. She was smart and insightful, and I was learning new things every day from her.

So as soon as Anna mentioned Mitch, with that eloquent squinch of her nose, I knew I had to listen, even though I didn't want to. 'So what are you saying? We shouldn't work with him?'

Anna leaned against the desk opposite mine. She was wearing a blouse printed with Granny Smith apples. I made a mental note to find out where she'd got it. I needed more apple blouses in my life. 'Mitch approached me recently about a development he's bringing to market next year.'

My stomach flipped. Should I tell her? No, I wanted to hear what she had to say first. 'Lark Manor?'

Anna paused, thinking, then shook her head. 'I don't think so, it's what used to be the metalworks? I did a bit of digging and I don't think he's even got funding for it yet. Sounds like he's just casting a few lines to see who bites. It's how he works, one step away from crowdfunding, if you ask me.'

I didn't remember Mitch mentioning a metalworks. So there was that *and* the steak restaurant. How far down the priority list was Lark Manor? I'd done a bit of digging around myself, and discovered that despite what he'd told me at the weekend, there was no record of a sale in the Land Registry; OK, the records might be taking a while to update, but it introduced the very real possibility that he hadn't even secured it yet. It wasn't being sold on the open market, so there were no sites to check to see if it was under offer.

I tried to tell myself that Mitch probably had lots of irons in the fire. It was how developers operated.

'I told him we weren't interested, anyway,' Anna went on. 'Not until I could have a look round the finished property. I mean, Mitch talks a great game, I'm not denying that, and there's always a waiting list for his properties, but I don't want to be remarketing after six months because the client feels they were sold a pup. What? Why are you looking like that?'

'I sold this pup last year,' I said. There was no point lying to Anna. I didn't want to, in any case.

Her blue eyes widened. Anna had very expressive eyes.

'Yup. And the client told me that one of the reasons that he wants out is because the plumbing's bodged. Which I obviously didn't know at the time.'

Anna's eyes widened further.

'I can confirm that with first-hand knowledge. And,' I added, raising a pre-emptive hand, 'before you jump to conclusions, I know the shower's rubbish because I broke it myself when I was working for my sister's cleaning agency. It literally came off in my hands.'

Anna laughed. 'The undercover estate agent! I love it! Did Adam give you a hard time about selling him a shoddy bachelor pad when you went round last week?'

'He didn't recognise me,' I admitted. 'I could have been wearing a T-shirt with "I Was Your Estate Agent" printed on it, and he wouldn't have recognised me.'

That was the thing about men like Adam, I'd realised. When they wanted your attention, they couldn't take their eyes off you. When they didn't, you might as well be invisible. But maybe I was being mean. Maybe it was just a bloke thing. Mitch wasn't great with faces either; he'd walked straight past another ex-colleague at the food festival, this time an in-house solicitor called Danni. I supposed it was better than the alternative – she certainly seemed delighted to have bumped into *him*.

'Well, make sure everything's perfect before you start showing clients round.' Anna wagged a finger. 'And if Mitch Maitland calls in with his big brown eyes and his big sexy property portfolio, you say no thanks, you hear me?' I nodded, and said nothing. I was happy to be honest with Anna about selling the flat, and also breaking the shower, but that didn't mean I wanted to reveal the full extent of my involvement with Mitch Maitland. Not yet anyway.

Jim had given me a great piece of advice early on in my cleaning journey. It wasn't even a cleaning-related tip; it was just something he'd intoned in the car driving between jobs when I was moaning about the mess in my flat.

'Just time how long a task takes,' he'd he'd informed me, like some kind of internet self-help guru. 'It's never as long as you think. You'll do it before you've even stopped making up excuses not to.'

This was so true I felt like getting it embroidered onto scatter cushions for family Christmas gifts.

For example, it took me twenty minutes on the phone to book an appointment with my GP, and then about three minutes for the GP to confirm that most of my adult personality, and the struggles I had with it, could also be a symptom of ADHD.

I'd probably done too much Internet research, but it had helped to compile a full list of my possible symptoms beforehand, so I wouldn't be overcome by a misplaced sense of not wanting to bother anyone. I told Dr Keyes the truth: that my disorganisation, lack of concentration, fear of failure, inability to complete tasks, and so on, was more than I could control alone. Once I started articulating everything I'd struggled to keep in check my whole life, I couldn't stop. I cried a couple of times, and it was embarrassing to admit the worst of my past behaviour, but Dr Keyes listened patiently, as if I wasn't the worst person in the world. He reassured me that the rest of my life didn't have to be as chaotic or stressful, and referred me to a specialist. I left with a handful of the same leaflets Sally Armstrong had had.

It wasn't a silver bullet but it was a start. And I'd done it myself.

Back home, I'd also timed how long it took to sort and empty the boxes I'd lugged from my old place. Thirty-five minutes, on average. Even I could concentrate that long, and now the flat was almost clear of them.

Who knew that chucking unwanted possessions away would be so easy, or that it could dissolve any lingering regrets faster than you could say 'misplaced nostalgia'. I'd despatched my university notes and books without so much as a backward glance – goodbye Pinter, Chekhov and the Method Actors! Goodbye, Meredith, Zara and the other students I shared a house with nearly twenty years ago and felt bad about losing touch with! Hello, space and light and air.

I had reached the final box which had only survived because I'd placed Astrid and her friends on it to enjoy better sunlight. Still, it had to go. I moved the plants off, unfolded the top and stopped, because I didn't recognise anything inside: a jean jacket, flip-flops, a bucket hat. It seemed too old to be Cleo's. Which meant … it had to be Mum's. My heart bumped with excitement, as I reached down and took out a shoebox that someone had covered in Christmas wrapping paper.

I removed the lid, and it released a fragrant cloud of magnolia soap.

Inside was a familiar jumble of unfamiliar things: birthday cards, a cassette tape with handwritten track listing, photographs, newspaper cuttings, a velvet jewellery pouch, a bead bracelet. I laid it out slowly on the floor around the box. A train ticket to Manchester, a Young Person's Railcard, single earrings, folded-up notes on lined A4 paper, postcards from Majorca, Paris, Dublin.

The Young Person's Railcard belonged to Kirsty Davies.

It took me a second. Kirsty. Mum's sister!

I lifted the photocard nearer. It was eerie to see a face that was almost but not quite me, almost but not quite Cleo. Same dark eyes framed with dark brows, same small rose-bud mouth, no make-up, round gold-rimmed glasses that had been in and out of fashion twice since she'd worn them.

I had a sickly sense that I was snooping on something I shouldn't be, but at the same time I couldn't stop looking. This was a past I'd never even been allowed to imagine, and I had to consume every detail before the box was snatched away. Kirsty was a stranger but she was also my auntie, my flesh and blood, the shadow at the heart of our family.

My heart beat quickly, faster than it ever did at the gym, as I examined each fragment of evidence, trying to absorb any decades-old traces of Kirsty or Mum that might be lingering on the surfaces, putting each piece together to see if I could make a complete picture of a girl I'd never meet.

The cassette was an old-fashioned mix tape; I didn't know whose handwriting it was, but it was pretty, each title printed, each artist in capitals. True Faith, NEW ORDER; April Skies JESUS AND MARY CHAIN; Build, THE HOUSEMAR-TINS; other bands and songs I didn't recognise. Who'd made this? For whom? Had it gone in a Walkman, on a bus, on a train? Was it the soundtrack to a holiday?

The postcards were mostly from Mum to Kirsty. Mum seemed to get about a bit: '*Having an amazing time in Galway, met some fit lads who took us to a great pub with live music. I got a penny whistle! Hope revision going well and you're not working too hard! xxxxx*'

'*Having an amazing field trip in London – we were supposed to do two art galleries but we got postcards in the shop and went to Camden Market instead! Mum says you got all As in your mocks which is BRILLIANT. SO proud of you. Don't forget to sleep! Xxxxx'*

'*Just a postcard to say congratulations on the county hockey trials. I am crossing everything for you!!!*' I turned over the card; it was a hand-drawn black cat surrounded by lucky shamrocks. Had Mum made it herself, I wondered? She was good at drawing, always making us treasure maps as kids, and I knew she'd been to art college – but it was part of the family folklore that we never asked about, as her time there coincided with Kirsty's accident, so it fell under the embargo. She certainly never mentioned it.

There were sketches in here, though: vivid drawings of Kirsty posing with her hockey stick, a sweet, good-natured expression caught in a few clever dashes of pencil. A Labrador – I hadn't realised Mum had a dog. I'd never seen a more Labrador-like Labrador.

And what were these? I lifted out a tiny doll with a blue dress and – I spotted a stray leg under a scrunchie – another in a red dress. Why were they familiar? Oh! I covered my mouth, as if my emotions might escape. Of course. They belonged with the family in our doll's house, the one Cleo had demarcated with tape as a protest against my mess. I'd always wondered why the family was as small as ours, just a toy Mum, Dad, a little boy and a dog. Cleo and I had had to supplement it with a diverse selection of adopted Weebles and Playmobil nurses and doctors. These were the missing girls.

So that was Mum's doll's house? I marvelled at my own lack of curiosity. And then I marvelled that she'd never told us, in all the years we played with it. Had she never wanted to tell us how we were exactly like her and her sister, making up the same stories, the same arguments? She probably had wanted to, I thought, with a sudden pang of insight. It probably broke her heart fresh every time but she'd held the pain in silence.

I laid the photographs and postcards, dolls and jewellery, notes and trinkets around the box, and tried to sense Mum and Kirsty's blood in my own veins. Mum's love for her sister jumped out of the postcards. I thought of how close Cleo and I had been once. Even now, even with this storm cloud between us, my first instinct was to share this with her.

I need to tell Cleo, I thought. What if something happened to her before we had a chance to hug and make up? I shrank at the thought of how unexpectedly, how permanently life could change. Jim and his mate had expected their rugby match to end in the bar, not in an ambulance. Terry had woken that morning with no inkling of how close he'd come to dying.

A horrible thought struck me. What if Mum and Kirsty had been in the middle of a stupid row when Kirsty was killed in the car accident, the same way Cleo and I were now? What if *that* was the reason she was so desperate for us never to fall out? Was she to blame for the row, was that why she couldn't bear to look back? Was that why we weren't allowed to remind her of it?

Slowly, and very carefully, I replaced everything in the box and put the lid back on top. This had gone on long enough. I knew Mum was in on her own on Friday night, when Dad was at Cake Club. I'd take the box of memories round to her when I could spend some time with her alone. If it was just her and me, she might open up.

I arrived at Mum and Dad's house just as Dad was leaving with his challenge bake, the one he'd been rehearsing the previous week.

As far as I could make out from the transparent cake container he was lifting into the car, moving in that careful, *careful* slow motion so beloved of *You've Been Framed*, it seemed to be a marzipan spaceship.

'Princess cake, love,' he explained, bending slowly at the knees so he could slide the box horizontally into the back of the Polo. 'Swedish speciality, very complex construction, cream, custard, genoise, jam. High technical tariff.'

'I'll take your word for it,' I said as I edged my way into the house.

'You can clean out the bowl!' Dad shouted behind me, as if I'd ever asked for permission.

Mum was even more pleased to see me than usual. It turned out Cleo hadn't asked for any childcare at all since she'd taken Wes swimming, which was breaking Mum's heart, as well as giving her unprecedented amounts of free time to think about what she might have done to upset her.

In other words, Cleo's plan was working exactly as she intended.

'It must be something to do with Elliot,' she said, before I'd got my jacket off. 'Do you think they've got back together and she doesn't want to tell us? I don't mind if they have. I know we said he wasn't treating her well enough when she kicked him out, but if she wants to be with him, who are we to get on our high horses? She knows him better than we do. And there's the boys to consider.'

'I don't think she's getting back with Elliot,' I said, licking the custard spoon. It had occurred to me that Cleo might be playing a cunning long game of laying so much blame at Elliot's door that no one would notice potential bad behaviour on her part. Although this theory fell down when I tried to calculate when she'd actually fit an affair in to her diary.

'Then what is it?' Mum threw up her hands. Poor Mum. She looked tormented. 'I want to help her. She's obviously unhappy. Why won't she tell us what's going on? We're her family, she shouldn't keep secrets from us.'

I carried on licking the spoon. This was ironic, coming from Mum. I hoped she'd bear her words in mind when I produced the shoebox later.

Mum sighed. 'And I worry about her. I worry about you both, obviously, but Cleo has the boys to look after and that's not easy. When you're a parent you don't stop worrying from the moment you wake up to the moment you go to sleep.'

I sensed this could go on for some time, so I turned to the rest of Dad's bowls. There was a cream bowl, a cake bowl and some leftover marzipan in the shape of tiny pink roses. Mum must have been worrying away for ages if Dad had deliberately chosen such a complex cake to get away from it.

'... I said, if you need us to look after the boys more so you can spend time with Rhiannon, I don't mind, but she didn't return my call ...'

I nodded, and moved on to the cream bowl.

Eventually she ran out of steam, and offered to make me some supper.

'It'll be omelettes,' she apologised. 'Your dad overestimated how many eggs he'd need for his cake this month so we need to get through a few boxes.'

'Fine by me.' Mum's omelettes were legendary.

'You relax in the front room, and I'll shout when they're ready.' She bustled away, leaving me to enjoy the luxury of a full-service diner with hundreds of television channels and an electric recliner.

I was engrossed in a programme about someone training dogs to speak using buzzers when the phone rang. I had to look around to see what was making the noise at first; Mum was one of the last people I knew who still had a landline. She and Dad kept it 'in case of emergencies'.

'Mum, phone!' I yelled.

'Can you get that for me?' she shouted through from the kitchen.

When we were small, Grandma Taylor had taught me and Cleo to say our names and the phone number but now, of course, that was tantamount to offering someone your front door key and your bank details, so I just said, 'Hello?'

'Hello?' The voice on the other end had a Welsh accent. 'Is that Melanie?'

'No, this is Robyn,' I said.

'Would it be possible to speak to Melanie, please?'

'Who should I say's calling?'

'Gwen Thomas.'

My pulse quickened. Gwen Thomas! I was going to handle this *much* better than Cleo did.

'One moment.' I covered the mouthpiece of the phone and mumbled, 'Mum, it's Gwen Thomas for you.'

I said it deliberately quietly, and right on cue Mum said, 'Who? Oh, just take a message, would you, love?'

I returned to the call. 'I'm sorry, she can't speak just now, but you can give me a message if you like?'

'Are you a relation of Mrs Taylor's?'

'Yes, I'm her daughter.' My heart was right up in my chest, pulsing hard. *Tell me, tell me.*

'Her daughter? Well, in that case ...' Gwen Thomas cleared her throat. 'I'm sorry to be calling with bad news, but I'm afraid your grandfather is very poorly. We've had the doctor out to see him twice this week, and he advises that Mr Davies be admitted to hospital this evening.'

Your grandfather. Gwen Thomas's tone was kindly and concerned, as if this might come as a terrible shock to me. I tried to summon him in my head; I could see grey hair, a tie, a red sleeveless jumper, but no face. An angry voice, stale tobacco. Mum's strange quivering energy.

'Where are you calling from?' I asked, reaching for my phone to start covert Internet searches.

'The Ferns Nursing Home.' Gwen Thomas belatedly realised she might have made a bit of a data protection blunder. 'I'm sorry, maybe I should call back ...'

But I needed to know *now*; Mum wasn't going to repeat this precious information. 'When you say poorly, what exactly do you mean?'

'Well, Gordon is ninety-four at the end of the day, so we're dealing with a very elderly gentleman with multiple health issues.'

What multiple health issues? Mum hadn't even mentioned the fact that he was in a home, let alone ill. Did she know any of this?

Recent events with Terry had made me hypersensitive to medical euphemisms. 'Are you saying he's ...?' There were so many bland ways of putting it. I scrabbled for the least awful. 'That he's reaching the end of the road?'

'I think so, yes.' Gwen Thomas sounded relieved that I'd gone there first. 'He's very weak, poor man. He's been asking for Melanie and Kirsty, over and over, very agitated, and I've got to be honest with you, this is the first time he's spoken about his family to our care team. I appreciate the family has asked for contact to be restricted to emergencies only, but we do often find that when our guests reach this point of their lives ...' She left me to fill in the blanks.

I didn't know what to say. It was as if she was telling me about a complete stranger. Well, she was; I couldn't remember if I even knew my Grandad was called Gordon.

'Could you perhaps ask your mother to call me back at a moment that suits her?' Gwen Thomas asked. 'As soon as is convenient, if you don't mind. Shall I give you a direct line?'

I wrote down the number on the back of the Neighbourhood Watch magazine, my hands shaking with the pent-up energy of this unexpected revelation. Mum could hardly refuse to discuss this. It felt too big for me to handle alone – no Dad, no Cleo – and yet I was excited because it *was* just me here, for once.

Mum entered the room as I was hanging up the phone. She was carrying a tray with two big fluffy omelettes, cheesy and delicious, and a pot of tea with two mugs. One was the Mum mug Cleo and I had given her for Christmas in 2016.

'Who was that then?' she asked.

'Gwen,' I said. 'Gwen Thomas?'

'From the Parish Council?' She put the tray down on the table. I watched her, fascinated by this bombshell trembling invisibly between us, waiting to go off. 'Did I tell you next door is planning to extend their house *again* and your dad and I are going to put in an objection? It's ridiculous, your dad thinks they're trying to build a sneaky granny annexe …'

She was pouring the tea as she spoke, adding the exact amount of milk and three-quarters of a spoon of sugar, my tea requirements since childhood, and I thought, the man who held you in his arms as a newborn baby is dying, the man who is a quarter of my genes is dying, and he is just a name to me. How can that have happened?

'No, Gwen Thomas from the Ferns Nursing Home,' I said.

Mum's back straightened instantly but she didn't turn round.

'Grandad is very ill.' Were her shoulders moving? Was she crying? 'She says that if we want to say goodbye we should think about going very soon. Can you call her back, please?'

Mum didn't speak. I tried to see her reflection in one of the family portraits around the room, but she wasn't in the right place.

'Mum?' Maybe I'd been too blunt. He was still her dad, no matter what had happened. I went over to put my arms around her. 'Mum, I'm so sorry. She says the doctor's recommended he go into hospital tonight. I didn't realise he's ninety-four. Ninety-four! Do you want me to drive you there?'

I realised I hadn't even asked where the Ferns Nursing Home was.

'Where is Grandpa living now? I thought he was up in Scotland.'

Mum still hadn't said anything. I assumed she was in shock.

If Cleo were here, she would be in the car by now, I thought. Driving and organising the funeral on her hands-free.

I probed my own surprisingly calm reaction. Should I be more upset? I didn't feel anything. I'd felt more distressed when Terry had been rushed into hospital. Maybe this was how responsible adults felt all the time.

'Mum?' I repeated.

'I have to think about this,' she said.

'Well, don't think about it too long.' What was there to think about? Her dad was dying, surely she should be jumping in the car, even if they hadn't spoken for years? 'It doesn't sound as if there's a lot of time.'

She raised a hand. Was it a warning hand? A 'give me a moment' hand?

'Do you want me to call Gwen back?' I asked. 'Do you want me to call Cleo? Or ask Dad to come back from Cake Club?' I racked my brains for more people to call. But that was it. That was all the family we had.

'No!' Mum's voice snapped out of her. 'No! I just need to think! I need some time. On my own. To think! Not do what everyone else wants me to do for once.'

It wasn't the reaction I was expecting, and the force of the feeling behind the words shocked me. Mum's hands were balled into tight fists. I'd never seen *that* before. It started a knot of worry twisting in my chest.

'Mum?'

She lifted her head then looked at me. Her face seemed older, but her eyes were scared and young, brimming with tears. She was that unfamiliar woman again: Melanie, not my mum. A woman who might say or do things I couldn't predict. In the thirty-six years I'd known my mother, I'd never ever not known what she was thinking and it was scary.

'I'm sorry, Robyn, but I need to be on my own. Two minutes. Do you mind?'

I did mind, if I was honest. OK, I was hardly known for my emotional rock status (now partly diagnosed as having an actual mental-health issue) but I was her daughter. Her adult daughter.

'I don't want to leave you on your own,' I said. 'You've had a shock. Let me get you a brandy, Mum. Is it still in the drinks cupboard?'

That was what people did in films. They offered brandy, or sweet tea. I knew this for a fact because, again, I had watched a lot of very bad Hallmark movies while unable to sleep.

'Robyn, please. I need to be on my own.'

If Mum wanted to be on her own, what could I do? I decided I'd ring Cleo from the kitchen. We'd work something out together.

I picked up my bag and, as I did, remembered the reason I'd come round in the first place. Maybe it would help her decide what to do about Grandpa. Or maybe not. It was a risk, but she could decide.

'I think this is yours,' I said, taking the wrapped shoebox out of the bag for life I'd brought it in. 'It was in with the things I left in your garage.'

As soon as I passed it to her, the expression on Mum's face changed. Shock at first, then sorrow, then she crumpled onto the sofa, holding it tightly, her head bowed.

God, this wasn't going well at all.

'I think it's Auntie Kirsty's,' I added, spooked into gabbling by her silence. 'There was some other stuff, clothes, mainly. I had a quick look once I realised it wasn't mine – do you think we could go through it together some time? I'd love to know the stories behind ... Mum? Oh, Mum, are you all right?'

Her head had fallen forward, her hair hiding her face, and two fat teardrops fell on the lid of the box, blotting the old wrapping paper dark red. Another teardrop, then another, then her shoulders began to shake.

I'd only seen her cry like this once, when our cat Misty died, and she'd tried to hide the tropical storm of her grief from me and Cleo. It had frightened me, the intensity of her emotion breaking through the familiar shell; Mum was so constantly cheerful and normal. She'd had Misty since she was a kitten, before we were born; we'd never known a Misty-less house. We were both inconsolable, but Mum's grief was something else. It made us strangers to each other.

'I'm going to call Cleo.' I reached for my phone. 'Don't worry about this, Mum, she and I will deal with the nursing home and find out what's going on. And if you want to go up and ...'

'No!' She raised her head. 'No! We're *not* going up, we're *not* calling back and we are definitely not giving that vile man one more second of our time.'

Vile? 'Why?'

'Do I have to tell you why? Do you need a reason other than I don't want to?'

'What if I want to? What if I want to know something about my grandfather?' I demanded. 'Don't I have the right to say goodbye?'

'No!'

'That's it? Just no? No explanation? Just no?'

'Oh ...' She stared at me, then stared at the wall as if she couldn't bear to think.

I struggled to find something, anything, that would make Mum's reaction make sense and I automatically turned on myself. 'It's not ... it's not something that I've done, is it?' For a second I was the scared child who'd let the handbrake off the car again. Had I killed that Labrador in the sketch, without knowing? Had I done something worse, and blocked it out? Was it somehow my fault?

'What? No! No, of course not, it's nothing you've done.'

'Then what? Mum, you're freaking me out.'

She breathed in through her nose, a long, shuddering angry breath. 'I haven't spoken to that man in half a lifetime,' she said. 'Do you think I'd have cut us all off with-out a very good reason? Do you?'

Oh Christ. A stomach-turning thought occurred to me. Had her dad abused her? Had he abused Kirsty?

'Why don't you tell me what that reason was, and I'll be the judge of it?' I dropped down to my knees next to her. 'Mum, whatever it is, whatever's happened, you don't have to deal with it on your own.' I hugged her, scared of how inadequate I felt. 'I love you so much. I would do anything for you. Anything at all.'

Mum had been staring over my head at the various fam-ily photos in their silver frames on the sideboard. Lots and lots of us, and a few Taylors. Now she dropped her gaze to me, and I was startled by the fierce challenge in her eyes. 'Are you sure about that?'

'Yes,' I said.

Mum closed her eyes as if she was summoning up the very last of her strength. Then she opened them.

'Fine,' she said. 'I'll tell you. But you're not going to love me the same afterwards. You might not love any of us the same.'

21

~ *Clean your microwave every so often by heating a bowl full of water with some lemon slices until it gets steamy inside. Leave to cool, then wipe away any residue with a cloth or kitchen roll.*

Before Mum could start her story, the front door opened, and Dad's voice floated in from the hall. He sounded positively jubilant.

'Say hello – or should I say, say *Hej hej*! to the man with the finest princess cake in the Midlands! Ta da!'

He appeared in the door holding aloft his green space-ship, which now had a wedge cut out like a gaping mouth. It really did contain a lot of cream, so much that the marzipan was barely sagging despite being structurally compromised. Or that might have been Dad's expert construction skills.

He read the room instantly.

'What's happened?' he said, looking between our strained faces.

I spoke before Mum could. 'Grandad's care home called, he's not expected to live much longer. If we want to say goodbye, we have to go now. He's asking for Mum.'

'And I'm not going,' said Mum, in the same flat tone.

Dad put the cake down on the coffee table. He wasn't a domineering man, nor was he a pushover. He trod the path of moderate resistance, the sort of British man who would express triumph or disaster with the same 'not bad, considering' attitude. But sometimes he took a stand.

'We should go.' He said it as if he'd considered everything and reached a conclusion he was confident was the correct one. I supposed he'd had about thirty years to think about it.

'But, I don't—' Mum was protesting but now Dad was here, something had changed in her. She was still tense, but her back had slumped, and she seemed less scared, more resigned to whatever horrible experience was ahead. I wasn't sure if that didn't unnerve me more.

'We'll set off, Melanie.' Dad stood behind her, his hands on her shoulders. I remembered him doing it to me when I'd had a bad test, or been upset. It was comforting in a low-key 'I know you think this is the end of the world but I'm here to reassure you it's not' way. 'You can decide what you want to do when we've driving, but let's set off. We can always turn back. Robyn, phone your sister, tell her what's happening, and we can pick her up, if she wants to come.'

Would Cleo want to come?

I answered my own question. Of course she would. Regardless of how awful this journey might be, or how furious she was with us, for whatever reason she wasn't sharing, Cleo wouldn't want to be left out.

Ten minutes later we were waiting outside her house, where she was on the doorstep issuing Elliot with instructions about something or other. I could see Wes's face upstairs in his bedroom window. He looked excited, but that might have been because his dad had turned up for an unexpected sleepover. One window across, Alfie was peering from behind his curtains, thinking no one could see him. His face was creased with anxiety and my heart ached for him.

My heart ached for all three boys. First Elliot moving out, then Rhiannon's illness, now this. I tried to imagine telling a child their auntie was seriously ill, or that their dad was leaving, and my whole body recoiled. How did anyone do it?

Dad honked the horn and Cleo gestured at him, then turned back to Elliot for a final word.

I couldn't hear what she said, but Elliot suddenly wrapped her up in his arms and Cleo burrowed her head into his neck, and I thought, well maybe something good will come out of this. But then she turned away, her face thunderous again, and she was ramming herself and her huge expensive designer handbag into the back of the car with me.

I hadn't seen her since our showdown at Mum and Dad's, when she told me I was a compulsive liar who didn't deserve to be trusted. Since then, nothing. I'd texted a few times, hoping for a response, but she left my messages unread, which hurt.

'Hello!' I tried a smile.

'Hello,' she said, getting her phone out without meeting my eye.

We both slid down into our seats.

I hated being in the back of the car. I'd hated it when I was a child, and I hated it even more now. Even though Mum and Dad had had several cars since the ancient Volvo estate of our childhood ('You can't argue with the safety record ...'), Dad's tatty AA Road Map had been ceremoniously transferred between each one, despite every subsequent new car having a satnav. This ancient map was currently tucked into the seat pocket in front of me, along with the hand wipes Mum still kept in the back, just in case someone became eight years old again and needed to wipe their hands after an ice cream. They would still be there, I reckoned, when Wes was having his midlife crisis.

I turned to Cleo to point out the road map but she was staring daggers at her phone, texting importantly.

'So where am I setting the satnav?' asked Dad.

Mum inspected her phone and silently typed in a postcode.

We watched as the satnav thought about it, then flashed up a route into west Wales.

'That's not the way I'd have gone,' said Dad, predictable as clockwork.

'Should we tell them we're on our way?' I asked.

No one reacted. Cleo had sent her text and was now checking her voice messages, frowning. Dad was fidgeting with the settings, to see if he couldn't come up with a better route than the car. Mum was staring dead ahead. I could see her reflection in the window and her expression was as eerily blank as a shop dummy.

I looked at the little dot on the map, and the white line tracing our path to it. Not as far as I thought it would be. Grandad had been within a few hours' drive all this time?

I used the back of Mum's seat to pull myself forward. 'Why is he there? Why west Wales?'

She shrugged. 'It was recommended as being good for dementia care.'

Had Grandad had dementia? She'd never mentioned that. 'But it's miles away from where he lived. And it's not that near us.'

She shrugged again and I realised she'd done it on purpose, isolated him as far away as possible. A cold feeling shivered over me.

'Right then,' said Dad, and we set off.

A few times I racked my brains for a conversation starter. We couldn't drive the entire way way in silence. Surely we needed to have a conversation before we got there? Shouldn't Mum give us some background? Prepare us for what we might be about to see? In a way, a car was ideal for an uncomfortable conversation, given that it was impossible for anyone to look anyone else in the eye.

Every so often, I saw Dad glance at Mum, watching for the sign that she wanted to stop or turn back. None came.

Cleo. I glanced sideways at her. She remained focused on her phone.

The tension was making me feel sick. But being in the back seat was making me feel sick too.

I fought the terrible urge to ask if we were nearly there yet.

We drove on in silence, our family unit moving slowly along the satnav's route. I checked my own phone, hoping Mitch might text, or even Jim. A few times I tried to catch Cleo's eye, but she deliberately didn't acknowledge my attempts to communicate.

And then, after forty minutes, Mum's mobile phone rang.

We all took a simultaneous in-breath.

It rang twice, three times, and I was on the point of leaning over and grabbing it out of her hands when she answered it. She didn't put the caller on speaker.

'Hello? Yes, it is.'

Cleo and I craned our ears. This time I caught Cleo's eye, and she looked impatient.

'Yes, we are, probably about an hour away.'

There was a long pause. Medical detail, probably.

'I see.'

Another long pause.

'I see.'

Mum wasn't giving away much in her answers. This was excruciating.

'Well, thank you for your efforts, Gwen. I appreciate it. Yes, I will pass on your condolences to the family.'

Condolences. So that was it. I sank back into my seat, deflated. He was gone. We were too late. Whatever my grandfather was like, whatever he had become, I wouldn't know. Ever. A link to the past, snipped. Stories, images, memories, floating out of my reach into the ether, unknown.

Cleo opened her mouth to speak, then sank back in her seat too.

We both waited for Dad to say something to break the tension filling the car; that was his job. I stared out of the window at the passing cars. The feeling reminded me of that moment just after the final climactic mega-firework explodes, leaving fading plumes of smoke and echoes in the air, and someone has to be the first to break the spell with a brisk, 'Shall we make a move then?'

It was Mum who spoke first.

'Paul,' she said, in a tone I couldn't place. 'Could you pull off at these services, please?'

'Can't you wait until the next one, Mum?' Cleo piped up from the back. 'This is a Burger King and there's a McDonald's in another …'

'At these services, please, Paul.'

Dad obediently indicated into the left lane and drove us around to the car park area, where we sat for one unbearable minute, waiting for Mum to reveal whatever it was that was so bad we wouldn't be able to love her again.

Finally, she spoke. 'There's something I need to tell you. About me. About our family.'

'Here?' I glanced over at Cleo. I wanted to be able to see Mum's face. I didn't want to hear whatever this life-changing mystery was while staring at an old copy of the *AA Guide to Great Britain and Ireland*.

'Well, I need something to eat first,' said Dad. 'There's a Greggs. Who wants a sausage roll?'

I flicked my eyes towards Cleo. Dad had always used holidays as an excuse to treat himself to a Greggs sausage roll, a food item Mum wouldn't allow in the house. I wanted to laugh (it was nerves), and I wanted Cleo to show she remembered too, that she shared this past with us.

She grunted, shoved her phone in her bag, and got out of the car.

We trailed into the services, bought coffee and sausage rolls, and went to sit at a table by the window, well away from anyone else. It was past midnight now, so we had plenty of choice.

Mum didn't touch her coffee. She sat for a while, then reached down for her handbag, taking out some photographs which she put on the table in front of her, like a fortune teller. I hadn't seen them before.

'My dad, your grandfather, Gordon Davies, was a town councillor, in charge of finances,' she began, as if she was telling us a bedtime story. 'He was a popular man, he was on the church council for years and years, president of the golf club, Britain in Bloom organiser – but he wasn't a nice man.'

'Not nice, how?' I asked.

'He was a controlling bastard.' Her words were sharp, snipped off. 'Everything revolved around him and what people thought of him. What people thought of us. He wouldn't let my mother go back to teaching after we were born, he wanted her to do volunteering instead, projects that he could get into the local paper, with him next to her, taking the credit, of course. Our house had to be spotlessly clean. Kirsty and I had to be top of the class. We weren't allowed to wear make-up or have boyfriends. It would make him look bad. One summer he decided I'd got too fat, so he made Mum weigh me in the sitting room every Sunday night until he decided I was the right weight.' She looked pained. 'I've always had a sweet tooth, so that was miserable.'

'Bloody hell,' I muttered.

Dad muttered something else under his breath.

'It was fine when we were younger, we just went along with it. I thought everyone's dad made them read their school reports out loud. But I started pushing back when I was about fifteen, and he didn't like that. I wanted to go to art school to do a Design degree. Dad thought I should do Law. I mean, it was ridiculous – he told me he'd spoken to one of his golf club cronies who had a law firm and he'd already arranged work experience for me in the holidays. I'd never shown any interest in law, but Dad decided it was appropriate, so that's what would happen.' Her lip curled. 'And I'd never have worked for his friend. He was well-known for feeling up the waitresses at the golf club. They called him Handsy Harry. I kneed him in the balls when he tried it with me. Dad was furious. *With me.* That tells you everything.'

I couldn't take my eyes off Mum. Her face was the same but her energy, her voice was different; I could only compare it to the times I'd seen the best actresses go on set and, in the turn of a head, transform into another human being.

'Anyway ...' Mum pushed a hand through her brown curls. 'I had a great art teacher who could see what was going on, and she encouraged me to apply wherever I wanted. I filled in one UCCA form with the universities Dad approved of – UCL, Durham, St Andrews – and another with the places I wanted to go. Most of them as far away as possible. And I posted the art school one and tore up the other.' She managed a smile. 'Rebellious, eh?'

'Brave,' mumbled Dad and squeezed her hand.

'I got a place at Goldsmiths.' Mum finally pushed a photograph across the table to me and Cleo. 'This is me in Freshers Week.'

If she hadn't told me, I'd have assumed it was Cleo. The same candyfloss cloud of peroxide hair, dramatic eyebrows, but with ripped 501s, black DMs, a leotard that skimmed her skinny white shoulders, and a bold handprinted scarf wound around her hips. She – *Mum* – was toting a bottle of Newcastle Brown and eyeing the camera with a hungry gaze, as if she couldn't decide whether to eat the photographer or save him for later. Confidence shone off her like a lighthouse beaming in the darkened club. Confidence and the sheer elation of being herself, in that moment, in that place.

I was sure it was a he behind the camera, by the way. No question.

'That's *you*?' asked Cleo. It was the first time she'd spoken since we arrived.

'Yes!'

'Wow.' Cleo studied the photograph. I don't think we'd ever seen a photograph of Mum without one of us in it. 'What did Grandpa say when he saw your hair like that?'

'He went ballistic. Not that he could do anything 400 miles away though.'

'How did he know?'

'Kirsty must have shown him this. I sent it to her.'

'It looks like you were having a good time,' I said, with deliberate understatement.

'Oh, I was.' Mum nodded emphatically. 'I mean, I was in New Cross in the late eighties, I went to gigs, I went to the Hippodrome, I stayed out all night doing my fair share of ...'

'OK, Mum, we get the picture,' I said. This was a lot to take in about a woman who still took her library books back on time, even though the librarians weren't issuing fines anymore. I shot a glance at Dad, who seemed surprisingly unruffled by these bombshells. I dreaded to think what revelations were coming up about him. I couldn't cope with discovering Dad had been Mum's dealer or that they met in the back of a police car or something.

'I was *happy*,' said Mum, and the simple emphasis broke my heart. 'I was really, really *happy*, for the first time in my life. The only thing that made me sad was that I couldn't share it with Kirsty – I missed her, but Dad was never on her case the way he was with me. She was a straight-A student, academic, she actually wanted to study Law. Dad paid for her to have golf lessons so she could follow in his footsteps at the golf club. He set up a junior girls' competition so she could win it. And she did, twice.'

Suddenly Cleo slapped the table and our heads swivelled in her direction.

'Look, Mum, can we cut to the chase?' she demanded. 'I know what you're going to tell us.'

'Do you?' Mum raised an eyebrow.

'*Yes*. I've known for a while now.'

I stared at them both, bewildered. I had no idea what they were talking about. How could these two people, as familiar to me as my own hands, have had some secret knowledge that I didn't even know that I didn't know?

'What?' I demanded.

Cleo looked at me with pity written across her face, then turned back to Mum. 'Dad's not my dad, is he?'

'What?' I repeated, foolishly.

'He's not my dad.' She shook her head at our slowness. 'I found my original birth certificate a couple of years ago. It had Mum's name on it, but there was a gap where the father's name was supposed to go.'

No one spoke.

Oh my god, I thought, staring across the table at their downcast eyes. Mum *and* Dad. Did that mean it was true?

'And it made sense,' Cleo went on. 'I don't look anything like Dad, do I? Makes even more sense now, after what you've just said. You got pregnant when you were at art college, your dad went ballistic and cut you off from the family, which is why we never saw them.' She lifted her chin, sharp like Mum's, the point of her perfect heart-shaped face. 'Is that it? Was it a one-night stand? Did you even know who my real father was?'

Mum flinched and I threw myself into the silence to defend her.

'What are you talking about? I've seen your birth certificate.' They were in Mum's admin file; I remember poring over them when Mum sent off our passports for our first trip abroad, such official evidence of *me*. 'And Dad's name *is* on it. I swear it is. Are you sure you didn't imagine it?'

Cleo had always been tidying something or other when we were kids. She loved going into drawers, pulling out boxes and peering into cupboards. I'd sometimes joined her, more for the treasure-hunting fun of unearthing 'unwanted' lipsticks or maybe even a family photo, but if this was true, Cleo's constant tidying took on a different feel. Was she looking *for* something the whole time?

'He's on the new one,' she agreed, then looked at Mum. 'But it's an amended copy, isn't it?'

Dad looked at Mum, who was staring into her coffee cup.

'No offence, Dad,' said Cleo. 'But I'm not stupid. I'm nearly forty, it's about time we discussed this. For the boys' sake, if not mine. There are medical implications.'

'When did you find it?' he asked.

I stared between the two of them. What? He wasn't going to deny it?

'Two years ago. I needed Wes's birth certificate to renew his passport and I thought it might have got into your admin files by mistake.'

Oh. So that was why she'd been so weird on that holiday to Mauritius. Then it clicked. Cleo wasn't angry with poor Elliot, or me, or any of the other unfortunate souls who'd got the sharp end of her tongue these past few years. It was *Mum*. The one person she'd never yell at. Which meant she'd yelled at us instead.

I stared at her. Why hadn't she said anything? And how could Mum have lied about something so important?

I tried to think what I would have done, and my brain shut down, instantly. When were you meant to reveal something like that? The truth would have taken a sledgehammer to our family. Of course it was easier to shove it under the carpet and carry on. Even if there was now an awful lump in the carpet. I would have done the same.

Mum didn't speak. Her eyes were closed and I thought she might be crying. Dad's arm was round her now, the other holding her hand tight. The concern on his kind face made me want to cry too.

'Mum?' I reached across the table and took her hand. 'Mum, are you OK?'

I heard Cleo make a dismissive noise, and it sparked anger in me. She'd had a lot longer to get used to this than I had. Wasn't she thinking about how *Dad* might feel right now?

372

'Shut up, Cleo. It's not always just about you.'

'It *is* about me,' she retorted. 'That's the whole—'

'Stop it!' Mum's head lifted, and she looked at the pair of us, her eyes red. 'Stop it.'

In the ensuing silence, the small voice in my head whispered, *what about me?*

I tried to ignore it. I was the spitting image of Dad. I had Mum's personality. And yet …

I heard myself speak. 'Is Dad not my dad either?'

The question hung between us on the table. The next word could change our family forever.

Dad broke the silence. It was a Dad job, after all, shouldering the burden of family conflict. Like lighting fireworks and dealing with rats.

'Just tell them the truth, Melanie,' he said. 'There's never going to be a right time.'

'But …' Her eyes pleaded with him, and he took her hand again.

'If you can't, my darling, I will. This is the right time.'

I'd never heard Dad call Mum darling before. Now he was half a stranger too, a man who loved his wife with a special tenderness that they'd kept private, their own relationship hidden beneath their parenthood.

'All right,' said Mum. She paused and took a deep breath. 'So that's only half of the story. This is what happened …'

And then everyone's world fell apart.

22

~ A ball of newspaper will leave your mirrors clean and magically streak-free.

Mum reached into her bag again, brought out the velvet pouch I'd seen in the shoebox, and emptied the contents onto the metal table with a clatter.

There was a blue enamel prefect badge, a gold lapel star, a hockey captain badge, a silver treble clef. 'This was Kirsty,' she said simply, pushing the star towards me and Cleo. 'She had these on her blazer. The star was for general excellence. And she was. She was a generally excellent person. But she was also very funny and incredibly kind. She taught herself astrology. She trained the dog. She was a lot nicer than me.'

Mum stopped, as if remembering was causing her physical pain, and pressed her lips together before she could carry on.

I held my breath.

'I missed her when I went to art school. We wrote to one another, postcards mainly, but she was busy with her GCSEs and I was having too much fun, to be honest. I didn't want to go home. There'd only be arguments. Anyway, Kirsty rang me one Sunday evening. I was in halls and we had a pay phone on the landing. Awful shrill ring. I didn't answer it at first because I had a hangover. But it kept ringing and ringing so I answered it just to make it stop. I had no idea it would be Kirsty. She'd never rung before.'

I didn't want to interrupt, but my mind was trying to set everything in order: Mum was a first year, so eighteen? Nineteen?

'Kirsty said she needed me to come home. I asked her why and she wouldn't tell me. I thought maybe Dad was putting pressure on her about her exams. I said I'd get the first train in the morning but she said that was too late, I had to come *now*.'

I glanced at Cleo. Her face was impassive.

'So I drove there,' Mum went on. 'I'd just passed my test and I'd never driven on my own but something about the way Kirsty begged me to come … She never asked for help. So I got in the car and drove. I only had one tape, that mix tape there, and I listened to it over and over on the motorway. We lived on the edge of a village – well, you've been to the house, you know where it was – and when I pulled up outside, the lights were on upstairs. I just knew something bad had happened.'

Mum stopped. 'Let me get this in the right order.' The story had been folded up in her head like the press cuttings in Kirsty's memory box, safe but untouched for years and years. The facts hadn't got blunted or softened by retelling. The pain remained sharp, an unused knife.

'The door was open, so I went in and I could hear someone crying. My mum. Mum was crying and Dad was talking, not shouting, but talking in this awful bullying way he had. I couldn't hear Kirsty. I ran up the stairs and Mum and Dad were standing outside the bathroom. Dad said Kirsty had locked herself in.'

Mum stopped and put her hand over her mouth.

'And what?' I thought I knew what she was going to say and my whole body was braced against it. Had the story about the car crash been a cover for something else?

Mum looked at us, her eyes bleak with grief as if it had just happened. 'Kirsty refused to unlock the door until Dad and Mum had gone downstairs. So I made them go and then she let me in.' She paused. 'I thought everything was fine at first, then I saw the blood. In the bath. And Kirsty was in the corner with this tiny baby in her arms. It was bright pink and silent, wrapped in her T-shirt.'

No. A baby? That wasn't where my mind had been going.

'Kirsty said she'd started to feel ill that evening and that's when she'd phoned me. It happened suddenly – once her waters broke, she'd locked herself in the bathroom and ...' Mum made a frustrated gesture. 'I don't know exactly what happened. *She* didn't know what happened but somehow there was a baby.'

'How *old* was she?'

'Sixteen. Just.'

My head was spinning. So many questions. 'And who was the father? Did she have a boyfriend?'

'Not that any of us knew about. She didn't have time. Sports, music, homework. The only thing she did on her own was the golf lessons.' Mum picked up the golden star, pressing the sharp edge into the pad of her thumb. 'At the golf club where Dad's sleazy friends hung out.'

I stared at her. 'You think ...?'

Mum shook her head. 'I don't know. I begged her to tell me if it was who I suspected, but she was in absolute denial about everything. Even the baby. I didn't want to push her because ...' She raised her palms. 'She'd been through enough. I thought there was plenty of time to find out later.'

'So what happened?'

'I cleaned up the bathroom.' Mum looked anguished. 'I scrubbed and scrubbed and tried to work out what to do. I thought if I could make everything normal again, then Mum and Dad would start behaving like parents and look after Kirsty. Except they didn't. Mum was in shock. Looking back, I think she knew something horrific must have happened to Kirsty at the golf club. And Dad was blustering about, threatening to kill whoever had done this, but I could tell from his face that it was probably someone he knew.

'So, I had to take charge. Which was ironic, given that I was supposed to be the disgrace who'd gone off to take drugs and sleep around at art college. I didn't, by the way,' she added, quickly. 'That's just what Dad told me everyone was saying.'

I nodded. If teenage Mum had wanted to take drugs and sleep around that was fine by me. I just didn't want to imagine it. And it sort of wasn't the point right now.

'I said Kirsty and her baby had to go to hospital to be checked out. Dad refused to let the baby leave the house. He said it would be better if we got someone to come to us. Better, as in not so many people to see Gordon Davies's underage daughter walking into the hospital with a baby.' Mum's lip curled. 'While he was getting himself a brandy, I persuaded Mum to take Kirsty to hospital. I told her if she didn't, Kirsty might bleed to death and it would be her fault.'

I grabbed Mum's other hand, the one Dad wasn't holding, and wrapped my own hands around it. I couldn't hold her tightly enough.

'She wouldn't go in mine, and Dad's car only had two seats. It was a Jaguar, Mum wasn't usually allowed to drive it. All I could think was that if they didn't *go*, Dad would stop them. I said I'd follow behind with the baby in my car and we'd see a doctor together. So they left. Dad was still in the sitting room, messing about with the brandy. I put the baby in a laundry basket, ran outside and locked him in the house. Then I got into my own car and I—'

Mum stopped, as if she'd finally come to words that were too painful for her mouth to speak. She squeezed her eyes shut and tears spilled over the lashes as her chest shook with one silent sob.

Dad gently kissed her on the side of her head, as if she'd done enough, then looked at me and Cleo. 'There was an accident,' he said, simply. 'Wet roads. Unfamiliar car. They think your grandmother lost control going round a bend, and she hit a tree. There was nothing anyone could do. She and Kirsty both died instantly.'

I couldn't hold back the moan of shock. 'Mum.'

We sat in silence, trying to imagine the pain of discovering one horror, only to be thrown immediately against another. People died in car accidents, young women had unexpected babies. It was horrific, but not unheard of. But to deal with both, one after the other? That was beyond cruel.

'And the baby?'

Dad started to speak for her, but Mum put a hand over his. 'No, Paul. I have to take responsibility for this.'

She looked me and Cleo straight in the eyes. 'I arrived just after the fire brigade, who tried to cut them out. I still had the baby in my arms, I wouldn't let go. At the hospital, Dad got me on my own and told me we had two choices. We could register Kirsty's baby as hers, no father on the certificate, and let everyone gossip about what a little slag she'd been on the quiet. Or ...' She paused and shook her head, as if she couldn't quite believe what she was about to say. 'Or I could register her as mine, because – as Dad so charmingly put it – who'd give it a second thought if someone like me gave birth without even realising I was pregnant?'

I struggled to understand how this was even possible. 'But don't you need medical records?'

'There weren't any. Kirsty had told no one. Either she had no idea what was happening, or else she wanted to pretend it *wasn't* happening. And Dad knew so many people at the council, paperwork wasn't a problem. Poor widowed Gordon, doing his best losing his wife and child, and now this silly girl of his to deal with too. I thought ...' Her face twisted with grief again. '... I'd let Kirsty down. I should have *known*. And afterwards I just couldn't bear the thought of people gossiping about her. That wasn't who she was.'

Mum opened her handbag, and took out a square of faded newspaper from the inside zipped pocket. She unfolded it on the table. It was from a local newspaper: Star student dies in horror smash. Kirsty's shy smiling face below the headline, her last school photograph. '*Tributes have been paid to a popular student who was tragically killed alongside her mother in a crash early on Monday morning ...*

representing the county at both hockey and athletics, Kirsty was "clearly destined for great things", according to her shocked head teacher, Malcolm Townley ... Friends are holding a vigil for her ...'

'That's how I wanted everyone to remember my sister,' she said. 'As the perfect girl she was.'

'And the baby?' The anger in Cleo's voice sliced through Mum's words. 'You keep saying, the baby, the baby. Who is the baby?'

'You.' Mum turned to her, and her face was wet with tears. 'Who else would it be?'

'So I'm not your daughter,' said Cleo, flatly. 'And Dad isn't my dad. I'm nothing to either of you.'

'No!' Mum's voice cracked with pain. 'No, Cleo. You are everything to me. *Everything.* From the second I picked you up and felt you move in my arms, I was changed. I knew I'd walk through fire for you, just like I would for Kirsty. I had to protect you both. I thought, I'm not going to be the person I thought I was. Everything is different now. And then ...' Mum swiped her tears away with her hand. 'Afterwards, I swore I was going to love you *for* her. I was going to love you as much as Kirsty and me put together.'

Tears were rolling down my face. Dad was crying too.

'I'd never seen a baby before. You were perfect. Tiny curled-up fingers like shrimps, and toes like beads.' Mum let go of my hand so she could reach for Cleo's. 'But your eyes were exactly the same as they are now. You looked straight at me as if you could see inside my head. I swore I'd never let you down. I know you think I have. But I never wanted to. You have to believe that.'

None of us spoke for a while. It was late but still a few people drifted in and out of the cafe area, avoiding our table. It could have been midnight or 3 a.m., I had no idea.

Dad picked up the story for Mum. 'Your grandfather gave your mum some money and she came back to London with you,' he said. 'She wasn't the only student on the course with a baby so it wasn't such a big deal. Although you dropped out after your first year, didn't you?'

Mum nodded. 'I didn't mind. You were the only thing that mattered to me. Then one evening my housemate offered to babysit so I could go out for my birthday, and that's when I met your dad. At a karaoke night.'

'I Got You Babe,' supplied Dad.

'And, well ... You know the rest. We fell in love, I found out I was expecting Robyn, and we got married in a regis-try office.'

'That's all very happy ever after, but when were you planning to tell me?' Cleo demanded.

Mum and Dad exchanged shameful glances. 'I always planned to tell you on your fifth birthday, when I thought you were old enough to understand that I was your mummy but you hadn't grown inside me. But then when Robyn came along ...' She flushed. 'You two grew up so close, like peas in a pod, I just couldn't do it. I couldn't tell you that you were different, not when I loved you both exactly the same. So I thought, fine, I'll tell her when she's fifteen, when she's old enough to understand why I did what I did.'

'And then fifteen came and went.'

'Well, be honest,' said Dad, 'you weren't having the best of times then, were you? We didn't think it would help.'

'It never occurred to you that I acted up *because* I never felt like I fitted in?' Cleo shot back. 'I always felt like something was wrong with me, but I didn't know what. I guess now I do.'

Mum flinched as if Cleo had slapped her. 'There's never been anything wrong with you. I knew I had to tell you, but the longer I left it, the harder it got. I didn't want to upset you before your wedding, or when the boys were born ...' She swallowed. 'Especially not then. Seeing your baby for the first time is such a precious memory. I couldn't spoil it.'

'Oh god, Mum,' I groaned. What a mess. I wondered when I would have told Cleo, if I'd been in Mum's shoes. When could you? When did 'it's not the right time' suddenly disappear into the rear-view mirror and become a timebomb?

'We know we should have told you sooner,' Dad added. 'But we knew you'd have so many questions we couldn't answer. We didn't know if that was fair.'

'So who is my dad?' Cleo demanded. 'Who is it?'

'I don't know.' Mum's voice cracked. 'The only person who might have known was Dad, and he claimed he didn't know, insisted it was better to draw a line under the whole sorry business. I tried to make him tell me. He refused. So in the end I cut him off. He wasn't someone I wanted in your lives. You deserved better. I'm so sorry, Cleo.'

Dad stroked her back. 'And you, Melanie. *You* deserved better too.'

Mum looked choked. Cleo wasn't the only person who'd lost someone. Mum had lost her mother, her sister and her father – and we'd lost the grandparents and aunt they'd have been, the happy family that could have shared our childhood alongside her and Dad. All gone, in one violent act.

I couldn't be angry with Mum. We'd been the focus of her life from the very beginning; she turned her back on art and student life and parties and painting, and become an expert in packed lunches and homework help, channelling her creativity into making our home the nest it was. But it wasn't up to me, was it?

I was almost afraid to turn my head to see how Cleo was reacting. She was no different to the sister I'd walked in behind, blonde hair bouncing, heels clicking as she strode. I felt nothing different in my heart, in my head, when I looked at her. She was still Cleo, still the person who knew me best. But how would it feel now for her, inside?

Was I different? Was I not her sister any more? Was that for her to decide, not me?

Cleo was silent. Around us, the service station swished and beeped, strangers passing through oblivious while we sat motionless, half in the fluorescent lights of the present, half in the blurry colours of the past.

When she spoke, her voice was bitter. 'Did she choose the name Cleo? Or was that your choice?'

'Cleo was the name of Kirsty's doll. From the doll's house we had when we were kids. I asked her what she was going to call you, and she said, "I should call her Cleo," and we laughed.' Mum squeezed her eyes tightly shut against a sharp surge of memory. Her lashes glistened again. 'It was the last time I heard her laugh. So I thought, Cleo, yes. You looked like a Cleo.'

'Was your doll called Robyn?' I hoped it was; it would be my own link with the auntie I'd never met.

Mum's eyes remained shut. 'No, my doll was called Suzi. After Suzi Quatro.'

'Oh.' I didn't know who Suzi Quatro was.

Cleo got up without saying a word and strode off in the direction of the toilets. Mum half stood to follow her, but Dad caught her arm. 'Melanie, give her a moment.'

She sank back into her seat and he put his arm around her, cradling her bowed head into his shoulder, murmuring soothing words I couldn't make out into her hair. The moment they'd dreaded for nearly forty years had finally come, and gone. It was done.

I watched them comfort one another, and suddenly saw how much Mum must have depended on Dad; they'd carried this huge burden of secrets together. He'd known from the start what was in store, one day, and he'd loved Mum enough to shoulder it with her. Not every husband would have done that. He kissed her forehead, quietly, and she leaned against him, exhausted.

I turned away to give them a moment too.

Shocking as it was, I felt relief. I had a secret question of my own that had finally been answered: Mum's focus on Cleo growing up wasn't favouritism, it was fear. I'd spent so many years wondering what I had to do to be the centre of attention, whether there was something wrong with me. Why Cleo was excused and forgiven time and again, even as she was stamping on every boundary. There was nothing wrong with me; Mum was just trying to give Cleo 100 per cent more love, and Cleo was struggling to articulate a difference that didn't make sense.

A few truck drivers wandered in, glanced incuriously towards our table and wandered on towards the KFC counter, unaware of the tiny ripples of emotional aftershock surrounding us.

Dad disentangled himself briefly, looking up over Mum's shoulder just long enough to nod towards the toilets. 'Why don't you go and talk to your sister?' he suggested.

Cleo had locked herself in a cubicle at the far end of the toilet block, but I could see her red handbag in the gap under the door.

It was nearly two in the morning and we were the only people in there. The strip lighting hummed, and I tried not to meet my own eyes in the mirrors. I knew I'd look ghastly; my skin felt raw on my face.

'Cleo? It's me,' I said.

She didn't reply.

'We are *never* coming to these services again.' I tried to sound jokey, but failed. 'That's literally the worst muffin I've ever had.'

No reply.

What could I say? I couldn't begin to imagine what Cleo was thinking right now. Nothing had changed for me: she'd always be my big sister. But everything had changed for her.

I walked over to the cubicle, conscious of my overloud footsteps in the empty space, and sat down on the floor outside, back to the door, waiting. Cleo had done something similar when I had my first ill-advised encounter with happy hour cocktails on my sixteenth birthday. Guarded my cubicle against furious queuers for half an hour, then gone in to hold my hair back until I'd thrown everything up.

Was she crying? I strained my ears. Nothing.

'I love you,' I said. 'I will always love you.'

After a couple of minutes, the door moved and I scrambled to my feet.

Cleo stood there. Her face was drained and dejected, her eyeliner smudged.

'Don't say anything,' she warned me.

'I ...' I began, but stopped. I wrapped my arms round my sister, and we just stayed like that for a while. Hugging. This was a silence I could only fill with love, not words.

23

~ Coffee grounds are full of antioxidants, potassium, phosphor and nitrogen which can boost your plants, so recycle (dry) used grounds in the soil.

Cleo asked to be dropped off at the Travelodge on the outskirts of town, where Elliot had already left an overnight bag for her.

Of course he had. He was a logistics specialist. He texted me to let me know the detailed arrangements he'd made for the boys, the time he'd taken off work to be there for them. Was there anything he could do for Cleo? Or us? We only had to say.

'I need some time on my own to get my head around this,' she said, and we didn't argue.

Dad drove me home. I didn't take up their kind offer of a night in my old bedroom because I needed to be on my own too, and I sensed they did. I'd never been so glad to get back to my temporary flat, where everything was bland and new, and exactly what I thought it was.

I turned off my phone, watered the plants and opened a bottle of wine, then spent the next six hours flipping through makeover programmes while my brain whirred away in the background, trying to process this new information while I thought about absolutely nothing.

On Sunday night Cleo sent a message on the family WhatsApp to let us know that she was going away for a few days to think, and attached a list of arrangements for us to implement.

Elliot was to carry on looking after the boys, with Mum and Dad to cover certain meals and clubs. I was to be on standby, whatever that meant.

I don't know whether she intended to, but Cleo also attached the memo outlining the temporary cover for the Taylor Maid offices. I read with interest that Jim was now acting manager, and would organise cover for himself accordingly. The email she sent him – which put her sudden absence down to 'unexpected family matters' – was a lot more charming and apologetic than the one she sent us.

Mum texted me to ask if she could come over on Monday night for a chat 'to answer any questions I might have' and it broke my heart a bit that she felt she had to ask. I wasn't sure what more she could tell me, and the questions I had weren't ones she could answer. I expected that she'd come round, we'd cry, then she'd clean my kitchen, but she wanted to *talk* talk.

I hadn't thought there could *be* any more surprises, but it seemed Mum was doing a major spring clean of her conscience.

'I had post-natal depression when you were little,' she confessed. 'I couldn't deal with the unfairness of how Cleo had come into the world, compared with your start in life. I wanted my mum, I wanted my sister, but in order to keep your childhoods the same, I had to pretend Kirsty didn't exist. I couldn't ever talk about her, I couldn't ever tell you how wonderful she was, how much I loved her. She only existed in my head from that moment on.'

'But you could have, if you'd just *told* us,' I pointed out. 'Dad said never to mention Kirsty because it would upset you too much.'

Mum looked tormented. 'But then I'd have had to tell you about your grandfather, and how Cleo was born, Kirsty's secrets. You know what kids are like – why, why, why? I had no answers! Keeping this inside me was a sacrifice I could make, for her sake as well as yours. I thought I was protecting you.'

'You gave up a lot for her. For us.' I grabbed her hand, trying to fit this sad woman in a cardigan with the blonde man-eater in the photograph on the cafe table. 'Did you never want to go back to art school? Finish your course once we were older?'

Mum shook her head. 'I couldn't be that person again. I blamed myself for going so far away – if I hadn't been so determined to escape from Dad I'd maybe have realised ...'

'You can't think like that,' I interrupted her. 'Maybe Kirsty didn't even realise herself.'

She shrugged. 'That's been the hardest part, accepting there are things I'll never know.'

'I can imagine.' I squeezed her hand. 'I'm sorry, Mum.'

'I know you're angry that I didn't tell you sooner,' she said. 'But ...'

'Don't. I'm not angry. How can I be angry?'

We sat for a moment, then she said, unexpectedly, 'You know what did annoy me?'

'No?'

'When everyone was so surprised that you had creative abilities.' Mum frowned. 'I had to say, oh yes, so creative, don't know where she gets it from, blah blah blah.'

I regarded her curiously.

'I got an art scholarship,' she added. 'I could have been a classically trained portrait painter.'

'Oh,' I said. 'Whereas the acting performance you kept up for the last thirty-seven years was just what? Another string to your bow?'

Mum was a better actress than I'd ever been, I thought.

'It's not too late,' I said. 'Enrol in a course here. There are loads at the art college. Finish your degree. Do a different one.'

She sighed. 'I don't know. It feels pointless somehow.'

'Do you want to help me clean my bathroom?' I asked, solicitously.

Mum pressed her lips together. 'Not really,' she said. 'But why don't we paint your bedroom a more interesting colour?'

Elliot gladly accepted my offer of help with teatimes and homework, and whereas the old me would have started making pre-emptive sickie noises to cover the school pick-ups, I came clean with Anna from the start.

'My sister's had some life-changing news this week,' I told her, 'so I might need to take couple of days' holiday this week to do some emergency childcare. I'm sorry, I know I haven't been here long enough to accrue holiday, but I'll make up the time however you need me to. I can do weekend viewings, if you want?'

Anna didn't even let me finish. 'Don't worry about it, these things happen. If you can work from home that would be great, but do what you have to do.' She raised her eyebrow. 'That sales pitch for your St Anselm's apartment worked a treat. You know we've already got ten viewings booked in now? Three cash buyers. I reckon we'll have a deal in place by the end of the week.'

'Good news,' I said.

Anna didn't seem too thrilled for someone about to make a quick sale. 'Just don't demonstrate the shower for them, eh?'

'No,' I said. And that was something else that was giving me sleepless nights.

For the last few nights, my first thought on walking through the door of my flat was, 'It's good to be home.' *Home*. I never thought I'd feel that about something that was only ever meant to be for a few weeks.

It wasn't the biggest flat or the most elegant, but it smelled of clean tiles, not mould, and now Mum had painted a few walls a soft thistledown beige, it was cosier too. The plants were flourishing on a hanging rail Dad had put up for me in the bathroom, and the kitchen was big enough for the minimal cooking I attempted.

Plus it was cheap, which was important to me now, even though I had a job. Money still kept me awake at night. If Mitch couldn't release my investment, I needed to save up some cash to put my year-out plan into action, so it made sense to save as much as I could on rent. This flat was a short bus ride from my office, and close to every delight Longhampton had to offer.

In short, I started to question whether committing to buy one of the Lark Manor apartments was the best idea after all. Especially now I knew Anna wouldn't touch them with a barge pole.

Mitch called me during the week but I hadn't been able to pick up; the first time I was driving Alfie and Orson to football and didn't need them listening in on my private conversation, and the second time I was at work, going through some paperwork with a client. Paperwork, in my new regime, didn't enter a drawer or file until it was complete. A tactic that so far seemed to be keeping my admin under control.

When I got a quiet moment to return Mitch's call, I found myself hesitating. What would I tell him had been going on at home? It was impossible to condense into a chatty conversation and I wasn't even sure I wanted to discuss it with anyone outside the family yet. I hadn't minded confessing my work disasters to Mitch, but this was different. I didn't know how he'd react, or how I'd react if his reaction wasn't the one I hoped for.

So I texted him to say I was in the middle of a family crisis, apologised for being hard to get hold of and promised I'd explain everything in a couple of days.

He sent a sweet, if short, reply, saying how sorry he was to hear that, to call him if I needed cheering up, and the following day a bunch of roses arrived in the office.

I didn't tell Anna who'd sent them, and dropped them off at Mum's on my way home.

My clean Taylor Maid overalls had been sitting on top of the laundry basket for a few days, long enough to risk them being reabsorbed into the washing cycle. So I used the excuse of taking them back at Taylor Maid HQ to see how the business was running in Cleo's absence.

By which I mean, I wanted to see whether Jim had dared to implement any structural changes while Cleo was away.

I climbed up the stairs to the office and found Jim sitting at her desk, talking to someone on the phone while making notes, his white shirt sleeves rolled precisely up to the elbow and his dark grey jacket slung over the back of the chair. It was a halfway house between his overalls and his relaxed off-duty wear. I wondered if that was the suit he'd worn in his previous executive life, when he was stressed and angry.

This Jim didn't look angry now, or stressed. He looked almost relaxed, as if he was operating in his comfort zone. Like one of the more erudite sports pundits on the BBC. No tie, top button of his shirt undone. Just the top one, though.

He glanced up as I came in and smiled, gesturing for me to take a seat while he finished the call. I gathered it was his new cleaning partner, Gracie. She was having trouble opening a key safe.

'To what do I owe this pleasure?' he asked, when he'd finished guiding her through some basic code-breaking, the very model of patience. 'Are you here on estate-agency business or are you looking for some extra hours? We can always find work for well-trained housekeepers.'

'Trained by you, you mean?' I said, handing over the bag. 'Neither – I'm here to return my overalls. I've washed and ironed them, before you ask.'

'Ah, they're an audition piece. Look at those creases!'

'I did them inside out, to avoid scorching the printing.'

'Fabric conditioner?'

'Of course.'

We were skirting around the elephant in the room, and predictably it was Jim who grabbed it by the trunk.

'I'm sorry to hear Cleo's taking some time off,' he said. 'I won't ask why, but you know that if there's anything I can do, you only have to ask?' He gazed at me; I detected genuine concern. I understand personal crises, Jim was saying, wordlessly.

'I know. It's ...' I felt Jim deserved to know more than the office round robin, but I didn't know how to phrase it. 'It's a family thing. But thank you. Knowing her business is in safe hands is a weight off her mind right now. I'm not being sarky. It really will be.'

'Good.' He pressed his lips together in a 'that's good' smile. Not a happy gesture, more an acknowledgement.

'Can I get you a coffee, now you're here? You can tell me how the new job's going.' He gestured to the machine. I didn't particularly want a coffee but it was nice that Jim obviously saw it as an excuse for a chat.

'It's funny how different houses look now I'm seeing them from a cleaner's perspective. I was doing a viewing this week and the clients were raving about the feature bath which was located in the *worst* place in the bathroom. All I could hear was your voice telling me what a pain in the arse it would be to clean behind it, no room for a mop, terrible for the grouting, etcetera. And then same house, stainless-steel surfaces everywhere. They have small kids.' I pulled a face. 'And you know what that means.'

'Fingerprints?' Jim looked up from his milk frothing. He'd mastered the microfoam already, of course.

'And the rest. It'll be like Coleridge Terrace in no time.'

'Such a shame,' said Jim. 'Still, I'm glad I'm bedded into your subconscious. Did my voice in your head really say pain in the arse?'

'No, it said annoying.'

He looked relieved.

'And how about you?' I swivelled from side to side in Cleo's chair. 'Is this a permanent move for you? Back into management?'

He laughed. 'No, but it's, ah … It's rather nice being back in a suit. Just relieved it still fits. I've actually had a couple of interviews myself this week.'

'I hope you've told Cleo. Have you been headhunted by a better housekeeping agency?'

'No, by management consultants.' He handed me a text-book cappuccino. Someone – Jim probably – had acquired a foam stencil with the Taylor Maid logo on it. 'A couple of people I used to work with are setting up a consultancy and they want me to be part of it.'

'Great!' I sipped my cappuccino. The microfoam was perfect, thick and smooth. 'Whereabouts?'

'Singapore.'

'Singapore?' I spluttered on my coffee, swallowing it the wrong way.

Jim's back was to me as he made his own coffee, and he didn't see my reaction. 'Yes, I worked there for a while a few years ago. Fantastic place, incredible restaurants.'

I struggled to wipe the chocolate powder off my face before he turned round. I wasn't expecting Singapore. I thought he'd say Slough. I realised I'd *hoped* he'd say Birmingham. Or nearer.

'So no more cleaning?'

Jim returned, stirring sugar into his cup. 'No more cleaning, as of next month. That was more of a …' He hunted for the diplomatic word. 'Practical therapy. I needed to do something simple, something structured but undemanding, so I could focus on myself. Ask myself some hard questions.' He paused, rolling his eyes at his own easy slip back into management speak. 'And, if I'm being brutally honest, to begin with, anyway, I was looking for a hair shirt. The weird thing was that I ended up enjoying it.' Jim shrugged.

Why wasn't I surprised by that?

'And I thought you were a natural. Or at least a career cleaner.'

'Nope, never so much as scrubbed a toilet a year ago,' he admitted. 'But if you're going to do something, do it to the best of your ability, that's always been my attitude. It was a challenge, working out the best techniques, developing productivity strategies.'

'You are insufferable,' I said.

'Thank you!' Jim put his coffee down. 'Actually, the one thing I hadn't appreciated about cleaning was the human impact. You were the one who taught me that.'

'I taught you *nothing*.'

'You did. You made me notice the houses with roses or wisteria outside, because you always stopped to smell it before we went in. I know I said you were time-wasting, but ... it's not a waste of time to smell roses. You moved things round at Terry's to make it easier for him. And I miss the debriefs in the van afterwards, when you pointed out the details I didn't see. Like the mysterious snowshoes at the Corrigans. Or the 2020 calendar at Tara Hunter's.'

Our eyes met.

I didn't miss cleaning. I did miss Jim.

'I'm sorry if I overdid the work versus home boundaries at times,' he went on. 'I was trying too hard not to make old mistakes. I shouldn't have.'

'It's OK. Well, we should have a drink before you go,' I suggested. 'I think I still owe you one from The Ram, the other night? We never finished our round.'

He started to smile, then said, 'Oh, yes. Was that your boyfriend you bumped into? The bloke at the bar?'

'Um, yes, well, no, he's ...' I fumbled for the right words but was saved by loud honking from outside.

Jim nodded towards the door. 'Would you mind holding the fort for a second? One of the cleaning teams needs to drop off a broken carpet cleaner and pick up another one – I said I'd action a drive-by.'

'No problem,' I said. 'Must have been a big job.'

He looked askance. 'The worst. I'll tell you when I get back.'

Obviously I waited until Jim's footsteps had clattered down the front steps before going through Cleo's desk drawers. They were disappointing. Little trays of clips and pins, a bag of the expensive chocolate mints for leaving on pillows, nothing interesting.

I helped myself to a couple of mints and scrolled through the tabs Jim had open on the browser. One was the listing for Nikki Nardini's holiday cottage. Curious to see how the photos of us had come out, I clicked on it, and there we were: me and Jim, pretending to have a romantic game of Trivial Pursuit. And there again, by the log burner, me leaning on the sofa, him looking up at me from an expensive Scandi-chic chair, his head resting on one hand.

Wow, I thought. How relaxed we looked in each other's company, as if we were a proper couple. What were we laughing about there? Was that when we were playing the questions game? Despite his acute self-consciousness, Jim was surprisingly photogenic; those strong cheekbones came out well on camera, I thought. And I don't think I'd ever noticed how well-proportioned he was.

There we were again, this time in the kitchen. I was pretending to make a cappuccino without revealing the milk-less cup, and Jim was leaning against the counter, chatting. We weren't that close, but the way we were smiling at each other, you'd believe we really were honeymooning in the cottage, not two cleaners posing while a photographer shouted, 'Don't do that thing with your hands!' at intervals.

I clicked through the shots of the bathrooms, an arty close-up of a brass tap, an orchard view, an en suite toilet, until I was confronted by Jim and me in bathrobes, and an unexpected warm sensation bloomed in my chest, like a flower opening its petals. Wow. Jim – who didn't resemble the Jim who'd instructed me in the art of streak-free hobs – leaning over the bed as if he was about to kiss me. I zoomed in on his eyes. He had *gorgeous* eyes. I definitely hadn't noticed him looking like that at the time. Paige had caught me at an unusually flattering angle too; I was positively glowing as Jim placed the tea tray on the bed next to me.

The way I was gazing up at him, you'd almost think …

'Robyn, you're not going to believe what I've just found in this carpet cleaner …?'

I closed the window hastily – too hastily – and swung away from the computer.

There was Jim in real life. Fortunately he was in office mode, and therefore exuding nothing more seductive than Febreze. He was also holding up the lower half of a set of false teeth. Or half a jaw. Hard to tell.

'Wow.'

'So, about that drink …' I said at the same time as he said, 'Anyway, I hope Cleo's feeling more …'

We both stopped, suddenly awkward, then the phone rang.

'You should probably get that,' I said.

'Yes. Absolutely.' Jim's hand was on the receiver; he hadn't lifted it. 'Thanks for dropping off your overalls.'

'My pleasure.' Phone still ringing. I made a 'call me' gesture. 'Give me a …'

'Sure.' Jim's eyes were locked with mine, a half-smile on his lips, as if he didn't particularly want this conversation to end either. 'Let me know about any flats needing cleaners. Nothing with badly fitted showers, ha ha!'

'You'd better get that,' I said, then added, 'Might be Cleo?' We both stopped smiling.

'Yes, quite. Um, OK.' Jim lifted the phone and said, 'Taylor Maid, this is Jim,' but he was watching me as I left, his gaze following me out of the door as if he wished we were still chatting.

I made the 'call me!' sign again, felt stupid, grinned, felt more stupid, then left.

Cleo texted on Thursday morning to invite me for a coffee in the park. And 'a chat', obviously.

I hated scheduled 'chats' at the best of times. It made me worry that she'd have an itemised agenda to work through. I spent the morning running through the things I wanted to say, searching adoption websites and groups to make sure that none of them were insensitive or could cause upset, trying to find resources and guidance until, in the end, I gave up. It was *Cleo*. I'd known her my whole life. All I could be was honest.

She'd suggested meeting on the bandstand, and that filled me with mixed feelings. The bandstand was one of our teenage haunts, along with everyone else who grew up in Longhampton. It was the backdrop for snogging, breaking-up, pre-drinking, inept smoking, and a hundred other adolescent rites of passage.

Cleo was waiting there with two coffees and two cinnamon buns from the coffee stand by the park gates.

'I came prepared,' I said, offering her one of the two coffees and two cinnamon buns *I'd* brought.

'Mine are better,' she said. 'They're organic.'

I let her get away with that. My cinnamon buns were actually better on account of being free: Hoffi Coffi were so pleased to see me and my caffeine dependency back in town they'd upgraded me to a Gold VIP card.

'Just so you know,' said Cleo, peeling the lid off her coffee to add more sugar, 'you're third on my list, so please don't be offended if we keep this to the basics. I've already explained how I feel to Mum, and then Dad separately. I've still got to talk to Elliot, then Alfie today, and Orson, then Wes.'

'It's a lot.' I was flattered to have come in third on her list.

'It is.' Cleo sighed. 'I'm starting to understand how you must have felt, delivering the same lines over and over again. I can see now why you sounded so robotic all the time.'

'Thanks,' I said.

We sipped our coffees and I waited for her to start.

'I'm basically just glad it's finally out in the open,' she began, 'My whole life, I've felt as if people were lying to me. I thought it was because I was just a suspicious kind of person – which is not a nice thing to think about yourself, by the way – but I found it so hard to trust anyone. I was always second-guessing, triple-guessing. And now ...' She let out a breath. 'I mean, I wasn't wrong, was I? Everyone *was* lying to me. About who I was. Even if they didn't know they were doing it.'

'I'm sorry if I was part of that,' I said.

'I don't blame you for any of this, Robyn. It's turned your childhood on its head too.' She turned to me. 'How are *you* feeling?'

'I don't know. I don't know whether I have a right to feel different, it doesn't affect me the same way. You're still my big sister. I'm only heartbroken that you might feel ... further away from me.' I struggled to articulate the feelings that drifted around inside me like clouds, some dark, some rainy. 'Are you going to try to find out ...?' Dad's face rose up in my mind. It was hard to form the words. 'Who your real father is?'

Cleo let out a long breath. 'I've thought about that a lot. Getting a DNA test. I keep going round in circles. Probably not. I have a father. But then I think maybe I have a responsibility to the boys to find their real grandfather. Or is it my responsibility to shield them from him? I don't know.' She shook her head. 'It's like being trapped on a rollercoaster. Just when I think I can get off, because I've worked out how I feel, it sets off again. I wake up crying because I'll never see my real mother's face, then I think, well, *Mum* is my mother, then I get angry, then I'm swamped with regret that I've lived nearly half my life thinking I'm someone I'm not ...' Her voice trailed away.

'I don't think it's something you can resolve overnight.'

'No. It's just weird, not being who I thought I was. But then ... How am I different, really?'

I thought about telling Cleo about my new ADHD diagnosis, and the fact that I too had spent half my life thinking I was stupid and chaotic when that might not be the whole story, but I decided that could wait for another day. I'd stopped being angry at Mum for not noticing. She clearly had a lot on her mind.

'You know who's been amazing through this?' said Cleo.

'Who?'

Go on, I thought, *say 'You, Robyn'*.

'Elliot.' Cleo's expression softened. 'I know, I know. Elliot's had to deal with my insecurity, my anxiety … I know I've been hard to live with at times. He's been hard to live with too, though,' she added quickly. 'We've come second best to his job for years, expecting me to deal with the kids, the house, the laundry, everything, just because I was working from home. But he's taken time off this week to be with me if I need him. He listened, Robyn. He really listened to me.'

Privately, I thought it would help if she could listen to him too, but I didn't want to spoil the delicate balance of the mood.

'So you're talking? You think you might give it another go?'

'Maybe. Elliot wants us to have a serious talk once I'm in the right place to think about the future. Which is sensitive, isn't it, not putting too much on me now?'

'It is,' I agreed.

'He knows me.' Cleo leaned on the railings and gazed out at the park, where a teenage couple were snogging on a bench, much to the disgust of the pigeons. 'He's known me since I was eleven. That counts for a lot. Especially now.'

I nodded.

'Anyway, I'm bored of talking about me.' She tore a strip off her bun. 'What's happening with you? What happened to your plans to buy a fancy new flat with your Hollywood nest egg?'

I sank my forearms onto the railings next to her. Doubt had got stuck in my head like a fly trapped against a window, buzzing away since Anna Hastings dismissed Mitch as someone she wasn't keen to do business with. Maybe Cleo would have better stories to put my mind at rest.

'I'd appreciate some advice on that, actually.'

'Go on. I wouldn't mind talking about something else.'

So I told her about the investment, what a genius solution it had seemed at the time, but also how I'd realised I needed to stop and have a life audit, so committing every penny of that money, plus more to furnish an expensive apartment, suddenly didn't seem such a great idea.

I didn't tell her about me and Mitch. I couldn't face two lots of advice at once.

Cleo listened, thoughtfully, then said, 'You've got a written contract, haven't you?' as if I might have impulsively handed Mitch a big bag of cash.

'Yes.'

'And what does that say about cooling-off periods? Or returns? When did you sign it?'

I had to confess that despite reading the contract several times now, I didn't have confident answers to either of those questions. I'd even had to put some phrases into Google to see if they made sense. And yes, I had signed it without giving it to a solicitor to check over. Because Mitch was helping me out, not trying to rip me off.

Cleo stared at me in horror, then said, 'OK. Right. You need to write to the company, stating clearly that while you're happy to leave your money in the project as an investment with the agreed return, you no longer want to treat it as a down payment on the apartment.'

'I can do that?'

'I don't see why not. I can ask my solicitor to go through the contract with you if you want?'

'Would you?' I felt a surge of relief. 'I've tried to talk to him about it, but a letter puts things on a better legal footing, doesn't it?'

'Him? So you have discussed it with someone?'

I went red.

Cleo interpreted my discomfort with her usual accuracy. 'You're not …? Oh god, you are. Is it that property developer Mum said you were seeing? Oh, Robyn.'

I pushed myself away from the railings. 'I know. I know! But I think he'll be all right about it. He's a good guy, you'd like him.'

'Hmm,' said Cleo. 'Send me the contract.'

We finished our coffees and watched the dog walkers circling the pathways, and the teenagers slouching in packs from one end to the other, clumps of boys, then girls following giggling behind. Then back the other way, but reversed.

'Time's a bastard, isn't it?' said Cleo. 'One minute you're you, getting on with your life, then one day you look in the mirror and you've become someone completely different. And my teenage self probably wouldn't even recognise me now. Or she'd be horrified, probably.'

'That's the whole point of siblings,' I said. 'It doesn't matter to me who you *think* you are, you're still my big sister. That's never going to change, I'm afraid. We're stuck with each other.'

She turned, and her expression was intense, the same sharply defined, confident attitude that I'd known all my life. I knew those eyes under bowl-cut fringes as a child, ringed

405

with Rimmel kohl as a teen, behind her sunglasses as an adult. Always Cleo. 'And you're still my little sis.'

I held out my arms and we hugged in the bandstand, breathing in the familiarity of each other, her expensive Jo Malone Roses, my whatever-I-walked-past-in-Boots, her gym-toned shoulders, my messy hair.

We hugged, then bounced up and down very slightly, still hugging, the way she used to pretend she was going to lift me up when I was little but never did. Just like it had always been. And probably always would be.

24

~ To remove labels from jars, soak first in warm water to peel off the label, then use nail varnish remover to rub off any stubborn glue.

I thought that would be it for drama for a while, but over the course of the next couple of days I made two distressing discoveries.

Neither of them was in the same league as other recent distressing discoveries, but in any normal week I'd have classed them as catastrophic.

First, having consulted with Cleo's solicitor, a helpful woman, I sent an email to Mitch's company, outlining my request to withdraw my reservation on the first phase apartments. Within an hour, I got a brutally formal reply informing me that this would be impossible. Cleo's solicitor, Wanda, warned me that there were some 'irregularities' in my contract, but advised that I find out exactly how far the work had progressed on the project so she could prepare a response. I launched into research mode and managed to track down Lark Manor through one of Anna's property scouts, who put me in touch with Simon, the same agent who'd shown me and Mitch around. And he told me it was very much still on the market.

'There's been a lot of interest,' he lied down the phone. 'We're currently in an auction situation with several significant offers on the table.'

'But nothing finalised?

'Not as yet.'

Then I turned my increasingly jangling attention to the council planning portal.

I located Mitch's various applications; there were several in progress, which was good. But I didn't recognise the name of the company making the applications, nor the names of the agents, architects or builders attached to the projects. Everything slithered backwards into a labyrinth of parent companies. Worst of all, I discovered that this wasn't the first time Lark Manor had been purchased for redevelopment, and then mothballed.

I sat in horror, reading through the many objections raised by the parish council, local residents, the Highways Agency, the ecology officer, the bat people, the badger people, and the conservation officer, aka, Listed Buildings. No decision had been made, but the redevelopment of Lark Manor clearly wasn't going to go ahead any time soon.

If ever, whispered a voice in my head. I'd worked in property long enough to know that once the Listed Building people started objecting, you were stuffed. Mitch had to know that too. Or was that the plan? Gather up the cash, 'fail' to get the necessary permissions, move on with the money safely salted away?

I stared at the screen, struggling to process what I'd learned. I was such a gullible idiot. Why hadn't I investigated this sooner? But I'd had no reason to think Mitch would lie to me. Part of me still wanted to believe I was missing something obvious, that I just didn't know enough to understand the machinations of property development.

I couldn't concentrate on anything else, so I left early and drove home via Lark Manor. I had a masochistic urge to see it again, in the hope that I'd find builders there, starting work. I'd even have taken a conversation with someone from English Heritage, if it meant my suspicions were wrong.

The elm-lined carriage drive up to the house was as romantic as I remembered, sweeping around to give that breath-taking view of the facade as I approached. Early summer had brought out some tangled pink roses in the unkempt beds, and my hopes lifted when I saw there were two cars parked outside by the fountain. The architect, maybe, or someone from the council? It wasn't a builder's van, but then the builders I knew all drove brand new top-of-the-range BMWs.

I checked my reflection in the rear view mirror. Presentable enough. I decided I'd go in and have a chat with whoever was there, see what I could learn from an innocent chat. I wouldn't necessarily tell them I was an investor, I thought. I'd say I was someone from Mitch's office. A marketeer. Vague enough.

Pleased with my cunning plan, I was getting out of the car when I saw Simon the agent emerging from the front door, and quickly slid back in, ducking down so he couldn't see me.

Was he showing someone else round? Was he doing viewings?

Before I could think what to do next, two more people followed him out, standing a few paces back from the door so they could admire the stonework above the entrance arch. A tall blonde woman in tight jeans and a gilet, and with her, his hand resting on the small of her narrow back, was Mitch.

I stared, confused.

The three of them said their goodbyes, then Mitch escorted the woman back to a Range Rover with blacked-out windows, and when they were discreetly hidden from Simon's view – but not mine – he leaned in and kissed her goodbye on both cheeks. After a moment's hesitation, she grabbed him by the waistband and pulled him in for a very passionate kiss which he happily returned.

I wanted to tear my eyes away but I couldn't. I watched as Mitch proceeded to slip his hand into her hair, the exact spontaneous way he slipped his hand into *my* hair, and then, after a while, when her hands started roaming, he pulled himself away, as if struggling gallantly with a desire he had to keep in check. As he had with me.

She said something, Mitch smiled and cupped her cheek with his hand, and that was enough for me.

I slammed the car into reverse, my feet jerking on the pedals, and drove home, where I threw myself on the sofa and sobbed, first with humiliation and then, when the full financial ramifications of what I'd seen sank in, fury laced with the acid taste of fear. Every useful new technique I'd learned to control my emotions went out of the window as I spiralled into total panic.

Everything pointed to a scam. I'd fallen for a scam that had wiped out my life savings, and my self-respect.

I had nothing left financially, and once word got out that I'd been so easily taken in, Anna would understandably question whether she'd want someone so stupid working for her.

I went through to the kitchen to make myself a coffee, in the hope it would kick-start my brain. How had I ended up here? What had Cleo said about the younger you walking past the current you, and neither recognising the other? What would the ten-year-old me think if she could see herself at thirty-six, a gullible estate agent, not the star everyone said she'd be, living in the same town she'd grown up in, mocked on the Internet ...

I closed my eyes, letting despair drown out any vestiges of logic, and begged the universe for help.

Nothing came. Just the sound of Tomasz upstairs doing sit-ups.

Despondent, I scraped a black flake of baked-on onion off the hob while the kettle boiled. It left a smear, so I got a cloth and wiped the smear away. Something about the clean space on the hob created a clean space in my brain, enough for a tiny voice to break through.

What would have happened if I had got into drama school? Would I have enjoyed it? Learning lines wouldn't have got any easier. Auditions wouldn't have got any easier.

I might have turned to drugs to cope, or ended up in terrible films. I might have realised I was okay but nothing more.

There was more onion on the other side of the hob that I hadn't noticed. Might as well do the other side too. I got the spray out from under the sink and spritzed the whole thing, running hot water for my cleaning cloth. I began to clean.

I still had those same creative abilities, I reminded myself as the crumbs lifted. I could empathise with people. I improvised every single day. I was great on camera. Those were positive skills I'd taken with me.

The hob was grubbier than I'd first thought. I lifted the metal frame off so I could really get at the gas burners. Might as well soak them too. No point putting greasy frames back on, was there?

It struck me that I'd spent longer as an estate agent than I had as an actor. Why was I letting one failure define my adult life? That wasn't just crazy, it was self-destructive. But also crazy.

The hob was clean now, if smeary. What had Jim used to get it streak-free? Window cleaner?

Maybe I should do one more acting project, I thought, watching the smears disappear under my cloth. I could audition for a local play. Or create something online; some reels would be a great way of reclaiming my Instagram account after the Emma Rossiter shaming.

But I needed to get my money back from Mitch first. I couldn't do anything without that money, and he wasn't going to give it back without a struggle.

And then it occurred to me. The perfect solution to everything.

I would get my money back. I would say a final farewell to my acting dreams.

I stared at the hob, which was now so clean I could see my face in it.

And I smiled at my reflection.

Anne-Marie Musgrave still couldn't believe her luck in winning so much money on the National Lottery but her dad had always told her that you couldn't go wrong with bricks and mortar, and that was why she was thinking about putting some of her £8.2 million in a restaurant. Something local, like the one she was sitting in now, with her partner Jim and the developer she'd arranged to meet to discuss a joint venture investment project.

'I like the idea of supporting local businesses,' she said, earnestly. 'My family back home are farmers, so I thought maybe ... a steak restaurant?'

Mitch opened his eyes wide as if she'd said something both miraculous and hilarious. 'You're joking, right? Did someone tip you off about Feather and Blade? Come on, I don't mind.'

I shook my head, a picture of small town innocence. 'No? Feather and Blade? What's that?'

'It's a project I'm working on right now. My partners have acquired a stunning bank conversion in Cheltenham and we've got Adam Doherty on board to curate the meat offer.'

'The meat. Offer,' repeated Jim, as if they were words he didn't understand in that combination.

Mitch turned to him as if he'd only just remembered he was there. He hadn't been giving Jim much attention throughout our meeting thus far but that might have been because, in order to distract Mitch from the fact that Anne-Marie was his own girlfriend dressed up as someone else, I was wearing a leather miniskirt and my new boots. The frequent approving glances Mitch kept directing at my legs was proof that my eyes hadn't been deceiving me when I saw him kissing that woman outside Lark Manor; he wasn't behaving like someone who had a girlfriend.

Was I even his girlfriend? I'd thought I was, by any of the usual criteria. But Mitch obviously didn't see us that way.

I let the shame fuel my anger.

When I'd told Cleo how I planned to get my money back, she laughed and insisted that Mitch would recognise me immediately. I hadn't been so sure. For one thing, I was a professional actress, who had been convincing in at least one role. But for another, I'd begun to suspect Mitch, like Adam, only registered people when they were in front of him, being useful. Particularly if they were female.

'If I wear a wig and coloured contacts, and have a different accent, and talk about money,' I'd told her, 'I think it'll work.'

Cleo had considered this. 'And wear a short skirt. It'll distract him from the hidden camera.'

I'd pointed at her. 'Good thinking.'

The hidden button camera had been Cleo's idea, along with the second hidden camera currently positioned right in front of Mitch, waiting for him to say something actionable or embarrassing. Not that Cleo had ever used a hidden camera in a fake coffee cup to catch dishonest cleaners in the act. No. Definitely not.

'The meat offer means the menu,' Mitch told Jim with just a hint of condescension. He turned back to me. 'We're in the early stages of development, but if you want to come on board for that, then we'd be more than happy to show you around.'

'Did you say Adam Doherty was involved?' I crossed my legs to stop Jim asking more questions. 'My mam *loves* him. Is he as nice as he seems on the Internet or is it a bit of an act?'

I held my breath. This was where I needed Mitch to say something he might later regret.

Predictably, Mitch obliged. He never could resist a name drop. 'I'm not going to lie,' he said with the confidential air of someone sharing prime gossip, 'Adam's a lovely bloke and he knows his steaks, but when it comes to anything other than meat he's a bit …' He rapped his knuckles on the table. 'Don't tell anyone, but he managed to pull his own shower off the wall washing his hair! Or at least that's what my source tells me. He does have quite an active social life, if you know what I mean …'

'Really?' I giggled, encouragingly. That probably wasn't enough. 'What else have you heard? Has he got a girlfriend?'

'He's got a few!' Mitch glanced left and right, to indicate even juicier gossip was incoming. 'Don't repeat this, but his parties have been known to get a bit wild. I was at the launch for his restaurant and there were some young ladies who should probably have been in bed much earlier, if you know what I mean. On a school night!'

I felt Jim straighten his shoulders next to me, as if he was about to say, 'Steady on, mate' or something similar. The last thing I needed was for Jim to come over all honourable and stop Mitch being a blabbermouth.

Jim had insisted on coming with me to the fake meeting. He'd been in the office when I'd collected Cleo's never-used-honest-guv surveillance equipment and, naturally, wanted to know what I planned to do with a pretend coffee cup with a camera inside.

So I'd told him, and he'd looked horrified. 'Can't you just send him a legal letter?'

'She's done that,' said Cleo, checking the batteries. 'No joy. This is Plan B.'

'What about your boyfriend?' Jim went on. 'Isn't he a property developer? Can't he step in?'

Cleo looked up at Jim with a 'you weren't meant to repeat that' glare.

'One, I want to deal with this myself,' I started, primly.

'And two, this *is* her boyfriend,' Cleo finished.

'Ex-boyfriend,' I corrected her. I avoided Jim's eyes as I said that. I didn't want to see his reaction, either way.

'Then you shouldn't go on your own,' Jim insisted. 'What if he turns nasty?' ('He *is* nasty,' Cleo muttered.) 'I could be on a table nearby, I won't say anything.'

'But you're working?'

'I could ask my boss for the morning off,' he said, with a side look at Cleo. 'Are you sure you need to be so cloak and dagger about it, though? There's nothing wrong with a solicitor's letter.'

'It's about settling some ghosts,' I said. 'I want to do it.'

'Go with her,' said Cleo. 'I'll be the getaway driver. I could do with some light relief.'

And so here we were, naive lottery winner Anne-Marie and her boyfriend Jim. We decided not to give Jim an alias. Too much to remember. The trouble was, I sensed Jim had sussed Mitch for a wrong 'un as soon as we'd shaken hands, and it was going to be difficult to keep him as a supporting actor.

'Are you suggesting that Adam Doherty is a ...?' Jim began, and I grabbed his hand to stop him.

The sudden grip distracted Jim, and he turned towards me, to see what I was doing. I squeezed his hand harder, trying to telegraph *shut up*, but he missed my meaning. Then the penny dropped, he squeezed back and did a flickering half-wink. I nearly blew the whole thing by laughing aloud at Jim's useless undercover skills.

We had to get Mitch to admit, on record, that he was reselling the same deal on a house that wasn't even his, ideally with some gossip that he wouldn't want forwarded to the person in question and then suggest, politely, that this might go away with one swipe of the finger in return for my investment.

'Ah, those wild party days are behind us, eh, love?' I said with a sweet smile. 'Still, all publicity's good publicity when it comes to restaurants, right Mitchell?'

'We love working with Adam because he's a local boy with local connections, and we've got a great relationship with his brand.' Mitch was back on his sales pitch. 'But obviously, with Adam's lifestyle and everything, we need contingencies. We've approached Luke Holly, another up-and-coming burger chef, or Theo Fano, who's a local rugby player. So whatever happens, we've got a plan.'

'Sounds sensible,' I said. Which it did. But it seemed very unfair on poor Adam who definitely wasn't the brightest but, as far as I knew, had a girlfriend called Eva, an influencer.

Mitch tipped his head and regarded me curiously, and for a wobbly moment I thought he'd recognised me under Cleo's auburn wig.

'If you don't mind me asking, whereabouts is that accent from?' he asked. 'Don't tell me, I've got a good ear. Is it …' He put a finger on each temple, like a stage hypnotist. How had I ever thought he was sexy, I wondered. The man was an idiot. 'I'm going to say, Yorkshire?'

'Very close,' I said. 'Cumbria!'

'Ah! Scotland.'

Jim tutted.

It was a shame so few people could recognise a Cumbrian accent because I could do a good one. Izzy, the junior Miss Marple I'd played on the kids' detective show, had been from Whitehaven, so I'd spent weeks listening to tapes to get her accent spot on. It seemed appropriate to wheel her out now, for a farewell performance.

I squeezed Jim's hand again. He hadn't let go. I supposed it added to the authenticity.

'Are you only interested in restaurant investment?' Mitch asked. 'Because if you're looking to build a property portfolio, we're in the first stages of a significant project just outside Longhampton, luxury two-bed apartments in a historic country house.'

Was he about to pitch Lark Manor to me?

He was. I stared in disbelief as Mitch started to pitch my own pitch to me.

'… so atmospheric, you can really *feel* the history as you walk through it. It has the sort of magnificent staircase you want to sweep down like Lady Downton, and as for the lawns ...'

Fury began to flicker in my chest. Mitch was using my vision, my creativity, as bait to reel in another mug, so he could take their money for a project he knew would never get off the ground.

'First stages means what?' said Jim, sensing I was unable to speak. 'How advanced are you?'

'We've secured the property, we've got permissions, contractors are ready to go, but it's not too late to get on board if you can make a decision quickly. And I would recommend you do, between you and me. This will be a fantastic return on your investment.'

'You've already bought the property?' I repeated, for the tape. 'And you've got the permissions?'

I turned to look at Jim, pretending to be interested in his response. I was glad Jim was there as backup, but I hadn't expected to find myself feeling more and more contemptuous of Mitch, purely by seeing him in close proximity to Jim. Mitch's charm felt synthetic, especially seeing the way he was deploying it now on two strangers. The chat that had made me feel like the only person in the room now seemed glib, the compliments too quick to be real.

'All sorted,' said Mitch, confidently.

'What sort of investment would you be looking for?' I needed to hear him say this. 'Ballpark?'

'However much you want.' Mitch didn't blink. 'If you wanted to reserve one of the units for yourself, either as a rental opportunity or to live in, we could arrange that.

There would be some fitting-out on top of that but we'd give you first choice. The garden flat's going to be the one to go for – I can secure that for you.'

I nodded, encouraging him to tell us more, but inside I was howling with rage. I let Jim talk about heat source pumps and solar panels while I forced my brain to stick to the plan.

I wanted it all back now. No discussion. I wanted to run far, far away from this man and his entire business.

Jim was asking questions to keep Mitch talking, but his increasingly frequent glances at me suggested he knew something was up. I was supposed to be leading this conversation, steering it towards the evidence I needed to leverage what I wanted, but the longer we sat at the table with Mitch, the grubbier it felt. The grubbier *I* felt.

When the plan had originally unfolded into my head it seemed flawless. Flexing my acting skills would prove to myself that my short career hadn't been a fluke. Using Mitch's own scam against him, his own inability to resist flirting with an attractive woman, would remove the splinter lodged in my pride.

But sitting here now, next to Jim, it felt stupid. Yes, it seeme to be working, but I was better than this. If there was one thing I'd learned recently, it was that it was better to be honest sooner rather than later. Easier, too.

'... up to fifteen electric cars on the same ...'

'Stop,' I said, in my own accent. 'Shut up, Mitch.'

Mitch stopped, mid-sentence, his mouth open.

I thought about ripping off my wig but that was a bit melodramatic. Besides, I knew what my hair looked like underneath, flattened in a flesh-toned wig cap, and it wasn't pretty.

'Mitch, it's me.' It came out as a sigh, not a roar. 'Robyn.'

'Robyn?' He squinted. '*Robyn?*'

I ignored the shame of having slept with a man so easily baffled.

'Everything you've just said to us is a lie. You know it is. And what you said about Adam Doherty is slander. He'd be pissed off to hear you spreading rumours about him, by the way.' Mitch tried to interrupt me, but I held up a hand. 'It's all recorded, before you try to deny it.'

Mitch stared, then swallowed, glancing around him as if trying to spot the hidden camera. He really wasn't that bright. He hadn't even looked at the unbranded coffee cup right in front of me. 'Isn't that illegal?'

I ignored it. 'I know you haven't bought the property. I don't think I'm the only person who thinks they've invested either. In fact, my solicitor thinks Action Fraud would be very interested in the contract Allen sent me. But I just want the money back.' My voice was so level, I barely recognised myself. 'I'll give you until five o'clock to think about how you're going to do that. OK?'

'Are you serious?' Mitch tried to laugh it off. 'Come on, Robyn. You've got the wrong end of the stick, you don't understand how the business operates. Your money's safe!'

'I don't think so.' I'd been back to Cleo's solicitor. Wanda had gone through the contract and concluded it was cleverly written to guarantee almost nothing. She also made some depressing guesses about where my money might be, and it wasn't in a high-interest savings account. If it came to it, Wanda reckoned I could maybe claw back something in court but warned it could take a long time. But then she leaned across the desk with a very non-Law Society glint in her eyes. Maybe I could do a deal directly, she suggested. If I played my cards with a bit of chutzpah...

I could see why Wanda and Cleo got on so well.

'You're trying to blackmail me?' He squinted, any pretence at charm gone. 'I wouldn't. That's not going to be good news for you.'

I looked him squarely in the face. 'Mitch, just do the right thing.' I fought to control the rising tide of panic inside me but kept my face poker still.

'You wouldn't go to the police, though.' A flicker in his eyelid gave him away. He was rattled.

'Wait till five and you'll find out.'

I was running out of confidence and adrenalin. One more minute and I'd turn back into a despairing estate agent.

I turned to Jim. 'I think we're done here.'

Jim squeezed my hand again. 'Shall we go?' he said, and I nodded.

Mitch had made a move for the coffee cup, but I snatched it away and Jim and I walked out of the restaurant. I didn't look back to see how Mitch was reacting. I couldn't let go of Jim's hand. It was keeping me upright.

My heart hammered but something inside me was soaring, stretching, reaching up into the afternoon sky. I had gone in there scared, and I'd come out scared, but in between I'd felt an excitement I'd forgotten, the same fizzing 'what happens now?' anticipation I'd had walking on to a set when I was young and pretending to be someone else was just a game. Under the weirdest pressure I'd discovered it again, like a long-lost treasure buried at the back of a drawer.

I didn't want to do that again. But I was glad I still could.

We crossed the road heading for the car and I glanced over at Jim. 'You're still holding my hand,' I observed.

'Just staying in character. Do you think he's still watching?'

'I don't know. I'm not going to look back.'

'Do you think that went well?'

'Why don't you ask me again at five o'clock?'

He laughed. 'Are we playing that questions game again?'

'Do you want to?'

Jim swung my hand. 'Why didn't you warn me you were going to do an accent?'

'Are you glad I didn't ask you to do one?'

'Do I look like the sort of person who enjoys party games?'

I laughed. 'Are you good at Twister?'

Jim glanced at me, and before I could think of another question to ask, he said, 'Why is it sometimes easier to say what you feel in the form of questions, rather than statements?'

'Might it be because there's a fifty-fifty chance of getting the answer you want?'

'Would you like to have dinner with me sometime?'

My heartbeat skipped. 'What day would suit you?'

'Would it be rude to ask you if you're free tonight?'

'No,' I said, and stopped. I stopped walking, I stopped asking questions, I stopped fighting the fact that I was falling in love with Jim. 'It wouldn't be rude at all.'

We'd been walking along the high street, and I stepped back from the pavement into the cobbled space under a tree where horses had once been hitched, according to the town plaque. We stood, our faces shaded from the sun by the soft clouds of pink cherry blossom, and I took Jim's other hand in mine, turning so we were facing one another like two people about to start a country dance.

I looked up at him. His eyes were searching mine, as if he was making sure this was the right thing to do, giving me time to change my mind.

I smiled up into his face. I wasn't going to change my mind.

And then Jim bent his head and very slowly, he kissed me. Outside Lakeland's Spring Cleaning Window Display, where the mops made a lovely line of bridesmaids behind us. And I finally felt like the Robyn I was supposed to be. The extraordinary, unpredictable Robyn that I'd been all along.

Epilogue

*~ To dust venetian blinds, put an old sock on your hand
and wipe along the slats until they're clean.*

It's surprising what property developers can lay their hands on at short notice when they're feeling legally vulnerable.

I got a phone call at exactly five o'clock that afternoon from Mitch, in which he offered me a deal: he had no spare cash, but he would sell me a renovation property he'd bought at auction earlier in the month for a quid. I said I'd get my solicitor to have a look at the paperwork and – in return for a deep clean of her kitchen – she scanned it and told me to bite his hand off. Wanda also got him to return some money, I don't know how, so I had (just) enough to stop the roof leaking.

And that is how I came to own Pear Tree Cottage, a two-bed Victorian farmhouse on the edge of the perry orchards five miles outside town. It needs a lot of work, but there's an outbuilding and a garden with an old quince in the corner, and when the breeze blows through the pear blossom on a spring afternoon, it smells like heaven. As you'll know from watching property programmes, such things are much more valuable than space for a second dishwasher. If you can find a builder to teach you how to insulate your outbuilding, and then use it to store your plastic containers full of house-staging equipment for the side hustle you've set up with your mother, then that helps pay for the first dishwasher.

(Anna was a big fan of mine and Mum's house-staging venture, especially since it had such an impact on my sales. I'd shifted three 'challenging' properties after Mum had gone in, painted some walls and moved the furniture around. One client even bought and framed the sketches Mum had thrown together to illustrate her ideas. Mum didn't think she'd done anything particularly special, until I transferred her share of the cash. Then she did.)

That week changed me forever. Not just dealing with Mitch – that was confidence boosting – or telling Jim how I felt – that was … well, that was great. It was the realisation that the past was important but it didn't have to dictate the rest of my life. Evolving didn't mean rejecting what had gone before. I just had to be honest, with myself and with everyone else, and push forward with my life.

I made a pact to try something new every month. I did some silly acting workshops for Orson's scout group, and some singing therapy at the wellness centre in town. It wasn't easy but now I was getting treatment for my adult ADHD, stress didn't control me the way it used to. Instead of being under a dark duvet I was forever trying to fight my way out of, it slowly became something I found I could negotiate with. Baby steps.

The big changes had to start with my family, obviously. Mum took me and Cleo on a road trip back to the places where she'd grown up, so she could share her memories with us. We huddled in the biting wind on the beaches where she and Kirsty had built sandcastles, paddling in the same chilly grey waves they'd paddled in, and walked around the town they'd trailed around as teens, the loop of Top Shop, Woolworths, Dorothy Perkins that were no longer there. We tried to imprint the landscape of Mum and Kirsty's childhood somewhere in our own subconscious. It was a bittersweet visit. I won't pretend it was all sweetness and light – Cleo's moodiness hadn't just vanished overnight – but we saw flashes of a different Mum as the week went on. She'd started sketching us, I noticed. Recounting stories she said she'd forgotten, she seemed lighter, less anxious, as if she was no longer smuggling a secret through life.

Cleo and I wanted to do something symbolic to say goodbye to Kirsty and the grandmother we'd never met, so Mum gave us a pair of plastic daisy earrings that had belonged to her mother and another diamante Top Shop pair that she'd 'borrowed' from Kirsty and never returned. We said we'd drop them in the sea but we didn't. We each took one, and fastened them together to make a pair.

'One day some poor grandchild will find these in a drawer when they're clearing out my stuff, and they'll wonder what the hell they are,' observed Cleo.

'I'll make sure they know the story,' I said. Stories slipped beneath the waves too easily. I wrote an explanation on a brown luggage tag, tied them to the earrings and hid them at the bottom of a box I'd bought to keep my valuable documents in. (No more pre-flight passport panic for me!) On the back, I wrote where the other half of the pairs could be found, in case someone wanted to reunite them.

Dad and I scattered Grandpa. Quickly, and without much joy, in the drizzly memorial garden of the crematorium.

As Mum said, you can only refuse to go to something if it actually happens, so Dad and I went so Mum and Cleo could snub the event. What can I say? That's our family mentality in a nutshell. I bought Dad a Greggs sausage roll on the way back, and we ate them together in the car with the windscreen wipers shunting the pouring rain from one side to another.

What a hero that man had been. He deserved all the sausage rolls in the world.

It's ironic, isn't it, that the disasters that you think will blow your family apart often end up bringing you closer. Rhiannon's chemo forced Cleo and Elliot to spend time together as they shuttled backwards and forwards with meals and lifts, talking honestly about how they could help Alfie, Orson and Wes understand what was happening to Auntie Rhi.

As Cleo said, it was easier to talk about how *they* felt about their relationship, what had gone wrong and what could be fixed. I didn't need to know the gory details of their marital MOT but, in her new spirit of openness, Mum told me everything Cleo had told her, who had shared in *her* new spirit of openness. I'll be honest, we went through a corrective period of collective overshare, which sent poor Dad into the kitchen for days on end to avoid being urged to stand in his, or someone else's, truth. For a while the Kenwood was rarely off.

The only condition Elliot insisted on before he and Cleo relaunched their relationship was that she moved the offices of Taylor Maid out of their garage and into an empty shop on the high street. He'd got a new job managing a deli in town and had become evangelical about protecting family time (I wondered if he'd been talking to Jim, but didn't like to ask, in case he had).

Epilogue

'Fine by me,' said Cleo, and immediately secured a prime spot between the homewares store and the florist. I was helping her move in over the weekend so Taylor Maid could start the week in a brand-new place.

She'd summoned her best cleaners to give the place a thorough scrub, and then once she was satisfied that not a trace of the old chemist's shop remained, she and I had painted everything a bright, fresh white, from the original pine floors up to the ceiling. It reminded me of the time we'd painted our room at home as teenagers: the music was up loud, we got paint in our hair, had a squabble about who'd splashed who. Just as we had all those years ago, we ended the day on the bandstand eating chips with salty fingers, knackered and happy.

Now, first thing on Monday morning before the shops opened, I stood outside and took a moment to appreciate our hard work. It looked less like a cleaning agency and more like a life-coaching centre. In some ways, I thought, maybe that's what it was. I'd made a shelf for Cleo's pink Taylor Maid brand products which ran around the high shelves, and she'd bought two vintage wall decorations in the shape of stars, which refracted rainbows of light around the reception area. Trailing pothos and tradescantia hung from hooks in the beams, and hidden away in the back was her arsenal of equipment, potions, scrubbers, jumpsuits and tins of biscuits.

There was just one thing left to go in the window. My final job as a Taylor Maid.

'Oi!'

I turned round. Jim was standing by the van, pointing at the open doors. 'Are you going to stand there admiring the shop, or are you going to give me a hand?'

'You don't have to keep chivvying me along,' I reminded him. 'Neither of us work here any more.'

'Old habits,' he said as he slid the doll's house slowly out of the back so I could take one end. Very, very carefully we carried it up the steps and into the shop, positioning it on the sturdy table I'd bought to display it, centre stage, in the shop window.

I opened up the front doors so passers-by could enjoy the domestic scene within. The red tape Cleo had stuck down the middle was still there, separating her order from my chaos, although at the moment, the rooms were stark and empty, only the painted floral carpets there to break up the magnolia.

'Cleo!' I shouted through to the back of the shop. 'We're ready for you!'

Cleo appeared, looking frustrated. 'Jim, I can't make that stupid coffee machine work. It resents me for moving it. Can you have a look? I *need* a coffee before we open up.'

He raised his eyebrows at me. 'Did I put my overalls on?' he asked me mildly.

We were both in our flight wear (me, harems and T-shirt; Jim, chinos and a polo shirt, and, if I let him, a straw hat); this was our last stop before a week's intensive Greek cookery course, a choice designed to shove us both out of our comfort zones.

'Please?' Cleo flapped her hand at him, and he dutifully went to see what he could do.

I passed her an ancient Tupperware box. 'Go for it.'
'My side?'
'No.' I smiled. 'You do my side, I'll do yours.'

Epilogue

She prised off the lid and looked for a moment at the miniature wooden beds, tables, chairs, grandfather clocks, ladles, plastic aspidistras, cots, hatstands, plates and tiny dogs. She took a deep breath.

'I've already started,' I pointed out. I'd set up one bedroom. Metal-framed bed, wardrobe, dressing table, towel rail. I had to concentrate to get the clothes basket exactly level with the dressing table. What else? Cheval mirror. I shoved it in and immediately took it out and lined it up with the bed. Then I put a dog basket with a tiny corgi in the corner. 'There. Like the finest hotel bedroom.'

'What do I do?' wailed Cleo. 'I can't make it messy.'

'Yes, you can.' I pressed my lips together, concentrating on matching the right bathroom set. Avocado bath, avocado sink ... where was the avocado loo? It was actually easier to do it neatly, I realised. You didn't have to think.

Meanwhile Cleo was struggling to create a chaotic sitting room.

'Try putting the bath in there,' I suggested. 'I always thought that was funny as a kid. Who knew people would be putting baths in bedrooms and calling it luxury hotel living by the time we were grown-ups, eh?'

Cleo grunted and tried ramming an ironing board into the attic.

The idea, as we'd discussed it, was that the doll's house in the shop window would showcase the practical magic a Taylor Maid service could offer your house: two red-jump-suited house doctors could turn your home from *this* chaotic nightmare of a shambles on one side of the red line, to *this* soothing haven of tranquillity and order on the other.

I couldn't believe I'd finished my tidy side before Cleo even had a bedroom done. What a turnaround.

'That's me,' I said, putting the lid back on the box and placing it neatly under the table. 'All done. You can fiddle with the rest to your heart's content. I have a holiday to go on.'

Cleo abandoned the miniature television set in the bath and held out her arms. 'Thank you for everything,' she said, hugging me. 'Not just here. Everywhere. All the time.' Her hug intensified.

I waited for Cleo to say something – 'I'm pregnant' or 'I've won the Lottery' or 'we're moving to the Isle of Wight' – but nothing came. Just the hug. Then I realised that when a hug can be so eloquent, you don't need words. It was a hug that said 'don't speak, stinker'.

I hugged her back, and sent a thank you up in the ether that this particular combination of DNA and genes and whatever else human souls were made of had ended up being my sister. I couldn't imagine a better one.

'We have to go,' said Jim, behind us. 'Phones are working, Wi-Fi's working, coffee's on. We're leaving you to it.'

'Have a wonderful holiday,' she chirped, waving as Jim headed out to his car. Then she dropped her voice, and added, 'I always said you two would either make or break each other.'

What did she mean by that?

'Did you …?' I dropped my voice to a whisper. '*Set us up?*'

'Not as such. But Jim was so uptight, you have no idea. Insisting on working on his own, driving everyone mad with his standards. I was running out of people to pair him with. But I'm happy to say you worked your miracle and between you …' She did an annoying chef's kiss gesture.

Epilogue

'Stop doing that,' I said. 'It's very two years ago.'

'Whatever,' said Cleo, and the phone ringing saved us both from a light pre-holiday squabble.

In the car, Jim was checking the satnav and arranging the cold drinks in the back seat cooler.

'Robyn, I've been thinking,' he said when I got in. 'You know that aspidistra? It's still alive, right?'

'Astrid? Yes, she is.'

'And that rubber plant Cleo and Elliot gave you as a moving-in present to Pear Tree Cottage, that's still going?'

'Yes. I mean, it's lost a leaf or two but I've checked and that's normal.'

I no longer got quite so panicky about my plants. The lady in the plant shop had given me some life-changing advice when I'd gone in to buy another monstera.

'If a plant's not happy in your house, give it to a friend whose house might suit it better,' she'd told me. 'Life's too short to feel sad looking at wilting plants. It might be happier somewhere else. And if it's dead, throw it out.'

I left with two monsteras and the sense that this advice might apply to more than just plants.

Jim gazed at me, as if he was taking a long run up to a big question, and I wondered where this was going.

Jim and I had discussed him moving in when his tenancy agreement ran out in a few months (he'd decided against Singapore. A job had come up in Birmingham). I was enjoying pottering in the cottage on my own; it made the anticipation even sweeter, counting down the days until he arrived like a sort of super-tidy Father Christmas.

'Well, I was thinking, maybe it's time …' He paused. 'Do you think you might be ready to keep that dog alive now? I'll help, obviously. Just something to look into, maybe we could take a trip up to the rescue when—'

But I was already stopping his words with a kiss, running my hand around his strong shoulders and pulling him closer, so my whole soul sank into the smell of his polo shirt and the warmth of his skin and the taste of his lips. So what if Cleo had set us up? The thought of never having met Jim otherwise made me quite anxious.

'Let's go!' I said, breaking away. 'Before Cleo finds us another job to do.'

He checked his mirrors, signalled and started to pull out; Cleo was rapping on the window and pointing triumphantly at the doll's house with her perfect red nail.

'OK, so she's got her messy side done,' I said, peering to see what she was pointing at. 'Oh, look!'

Mum and Kirsty's two dolls, Cleo and Suzi, had been returned to their home and were right there in the thick of the action. I'd assumed Cleo would have Cleo demurely hoovering the tidy sitting room while Suzi was upside down in the bath.

But Cleo was swinging from the chandeliers (safe on a cotton harness), and Suzi was sliding down the bannisters, little legs flying (carefully secured with a pipe cleaner). Both of them were having a wild old time.

Two sisters, having fun together, and not caring too much about the mess.

Cleo blew me a kiss and waved.

I blew her a kiss back.

ACKNOWLEDGEMENTS

This book was such a lot of fun to write, even if it hasn't noticeably improved the quality of my own cleaning. I do have a Brownie Housekeeping badge (*can* they revoke them? Asking for a friend). I'm very grateful, as always, for everyone who helped make *Irresponsible Adult* better in a hundred different ways, beginning with my amazing agent, Lizzy Kremer, who understands characters before I do. She is magnificent. If Longhampton has a visionary mayor/president, it is LK. Her capable cabinet colleagues would of course be Maddalena Cavaciuti, Orli Vogt-Vincent, Margaux Vialleron, Kaynat Begum, Alice Lowe and Georgie Smith. Thank you, DHA, all of you.

I'm very lucky to be published by a dream team at Hodder: my editor extraordinaire, Jo Dickinson, whose observations, notes and enthusiasm were inspirational from the very start; Sofia Hericson, who magicked up the perfect front cover Robyn from a Zoom call; patient, kind and super-efficient Olivia Robertshaw; Alainna Hadjigeorgiou, Olivia French, Charlea Charlton, Catherine Worsley and Claudette Morris, who took *Irresponsible Adult* from Word file to bookshelf. A big thank you, especially, to Kimberley Atkins whose brilliant creative input (and top tips about estate agents) made every idea sparkle brighter.

Writing can be an unsociable job, involving strange hours and stranger conversations, usually with yourself.

I'm grateful to my friends Chris Manby and Alex Potter for engaging in cheerfully forensic explorations of characters' tragic backstories – explorations probably still triggering nightmares for the unwitting eavesdroppers at the next table in Peter Jones café; to my husband Scott for enduring one-sided 'discussions' about story arcs while trapped in the car, and my long-suffering dogs for listening to actual dialogue rehearsed aloud on walks. I am sorry your owner is known as the confused woman who thinks she's being interviewed for a podcast in the middle of an orchard.

Never has a 'no characters are based on real people' disclaimer been more urgently required than for this book. Thank you to my sister Alex, for being strong, loyal, practical, hilarious, and a fantastic pal. And thanks to the various anony-friends I spoke to off the record about cleaning, selling houses or child acting; all mistakes are mine, and, dear reader, I genuinely am truly sorry I can't share some of the juicier stories – like the one about the holiday cottage and the mysterious fire.

And finally, a big thank you to you! To everyone who has emailed, written, DM'd or got in touch some other way to share their thoughts: it is easily the best thing about writing a book, and it always, always makes my day. ☺